Praise for Javier Marías's

The Infatuations

"The unspoken romance at the heart of Marías's work is the recuperation of old-fashioned adventure within perfectly serious, cerebral contemporary fiction."
—*The Daily Beast*

"Great art often emerges from breaking, or at least tweaking, rules. A work that transcends its conventions can produce special results. Here's such a book. . . . *The Infatuations* takes you where very few novels do."
—*Paste* magazine

"A masterly novel. . . . The classical themes of love, death, and fate are explored with elegant intelligence by Marías in what is perhaps his best novel so far. . . . Extraordinary. . . . Marías has defined the ethos of our time."
—*The Guardian* (London)

"Marías has created a splendid tour de force of narrative voice. . . . A luminous performance." —*The Wichita Eagle*

JAVIER MARÍAS

The Infatuations

Javier Marías was born in Madrid in 1951. The recipient of
numerous prizes, including the International IMPAC Dublin
Literary Award and the Prix Femina Étranger, he has written
thirteen novels, three story collections, and nineteen works of
collected articles and essays. His books have been translated
into forty-three languages, in fifty-two countries, and have
sold more than seven million copies throughout the world.

www.javiermarias.es

INTERNATIONAL

The Infatuations

The Infatuations

A NOVEL

JAVIER MARÍAS

Vintage International
Vintage Books
A Division of Random House LLC
New York

FIRST VINTAGE INTERNATIONAL EDITION, APRIL 2014

Translation copyright © 2013 by Margaret Jull Costa

All rights reserved. Published in the United States by Vintage Books, a division
of Random House LLC, New York, and in Canada by Random House of Canada
Limited, Toronto, Penguin Random House companies. Originally published in Spain
as *Los enamorameintos* by Alfaguara, Santillana Ediciones Generals, S. L., Madrid, in
2011. Copyright © 2011 by Javier Marías. This translation originally published in the
United Kingdom by Hamish Hamilton, an imprint of Penguin Books Ltd., London,
and subsequently published in hardcover in the United States by Alfred A. Knopf,
a division of Random House LLC, in 2013.

Vintage is a registered trademark and Vintage International and colophon are
trademarks of Random House LLC.

This is a work of fiction. Names, characters, places, and incidents either are the
product of the author's imagination or are used fictitiously. Any resemblance to actual
persons, living or dead, events, or locales is entirely coincidental.

The Library of Congress has cataloged the Knopf edition as follows:
Marías, Javier.
[Enamoramientos]
The infatuations / By Javier Marías ; translated by Margaret Jull Costa. — First
American Edition.
pages cm.
I. Costa, Margaret Jull, translator. II. Title.
PQ6663.A721813E5313 2013   863'.64—dc23   2013016429

Vintage Trade Paperback ISBN: 978-0-307-95073-4
eBook ISBN: 978-0-307-96073-3

Book design by Iris Weinstein

www.vintagebooks.com

Printed in the United States of America
10 9 8 7 6 5

To Mercedes López-Ballesteros,
for visiting me and telling me stories

And to Carme López Mercader,
for continuing to laugh in my ear
and for listening to me

I

THE LAST TIME I saw Miguel Desvern or Deverne was also the last time that his wife, Luisa, saw him, which seemed strange, perhaps unfair, given that she was his wife, while I, on the other hand, was a person he had never met, a woman with whom he had never exchanged so much as a single word. I didn't even know his name, or only when it was too late, only when I saw a photo in the newspaper, showing him after he had been stabbed several times, with his shirt half off, and about to become a dead man, if he wasn't dead already in his own absent consciousness, a consciousness that never returned: his last thought must have been that the person stabbing him was doing so by mistake and for no reason, that is, senselessly, and what's more, not just once, but over and over, unremittingly, with the intention of erasing him from the world and expelling him from the earth without further delay, right there and then. But why do I say "too late," I wonder, too late for what? I have no idea, to be honest. It's just that when someone dies, we always think it's too late for anything, or indeed everything—certainly too late to go on waiting for him—and we write him off as another casualty. It's the same with those closest to us, although we find their deaths much harder to accept and we mourn them, and their image accompanies us in our mind both when we're out and about and when we're at home, even though for a long time we believe that we will never get accustomed to their absence. From the start, though, we know—from the moment they die—that we can no longer count on them, not even for the most petty thing, for a trivial phone call or a banal question ("Did I leave my car keys there?" "What time did the kids get out of school today?"), that we can count on them for nothing. And nothing means nothing. It's incomprehensible really, because it assumes a certainty, and being certain of anything goes against our nature: the certainty that someone will never come back, never speak again, never take another step—whether to come closer or to move further off—will never look at us or look away. I don't know how we bear it, or how we recover. I don't know how it is that we do gradually begin to forget, when time has passed and distanced us from them, for they, of course, have remained quite still.

But I had often seen him and heard him talk and laugh, almost every morning, in fact, over a period of a few years, and quite early in the morning too, although not so very early; indeed, I used to delay slightly getting into work just so as to be able to spend a little time with that couple, and not just with him, you understand, but with them both, it was the sight of them together that calmed and contented me before my working day began. They became almost obligatory. No, that's the wrong word for something that gives one pleasure and a sense of peace. Perhaps they became a superstition; but, no, that's not it either: it wasn't that I believed the day would go badly if I didn't share breakfast with them, at a distance, that is; it was just that, without my daily sighting of them, I began work feeling rather lower in spirits or less optimistic, as if they provided me with a vision of an orderly or, if you prefer, harmonious world, or perhaps a tiny fragment of the world visible only to a very few, as is the case with any fragment or any life, however public or exposed that life might be. I didn't like to shut myself away for hours in the office without first having seen and observed them, not on the sly, but discreetly, the last thing I would have wanted was to make them feel uncomfortable or to bother them in any way. And it would have been unforgivable and to my own detriment to frighten them off. It comforted me to breathe the same air and to be a part—albeit unnoticed—of their morning landscape, before they went their separate ways, probably until the next meal, which, on many days, would have been supper. The last day on which his wife and I saw him, they could not dine together. Or even have lunch. She waited twenty minutes for him at a restaurant table, puzzled but not overly concerned, until the phone rang and her world ended, and she never waited for him again.

IT WAS CLEAR to me from the very first day that they were married, he being nearly fifty and she slightly younger, not yet forty. The nicest thing about them was seeing how much they enjoyed each other's company. At an hour when almost no one is in the mood for anything, still less for fun and games, they talked non-stop, laughing and joking, as if they had only just met or met for the very first time, and not as if they had left the house together, dropped the kids off at school, having first got washed and dressed at the same time— perhaps in the same bathroom—and woken up in the same bed, nor as if the first thing they'd seen had been the inevitable face of their spouse, and so on and on, day after day, for a fair number of years, because they had children, a boy and a girl, who came with them on a couple of occasions, the girl must have been about eight and the boy about four, and the boy looked incredibly like his father.

The husband dressed with a slightly old-fashioned elegance, although he never seemed in any way ridiculous or anachronistic. I mean that he was always smartly dressed and well coordinated, with made-to-measure shirts, expensive, sober ties, a handkerchief in his top jacket pocket, cufflinks, polished black lace-up shoes—or else suede, although he only wore suede towards the end of spring, when he started wearing lighter-coloured suits—and his hands were carefully manicured. Despite all this, he didn't give the impression of being some vain executive or a dyed-in-the-wool rich kid. He seemed more like a man whose upbringing would not allow him to go out in the street dressed in any other way, not at least on a working day; such clothes seemed natural to him, as though his father had taught him that, after a certain age, this was the appropriate way to dress, regardless of any foolish and instantly outmoded fashions, and regardless, too, of the raggedy times in which we live, and that he need not be affected by these in the least. He dressed so traditionally that I never once detected a single eccentric detail; he wasn't interested in trying to look different, although he did stand out a little in the context of the café where I always saw him and even perhaps in the context of our rather scruffy city. This naturalness was matched by his undoubtedly cordial, cheery nature, almost hail-fellow-well-met, you might say (although he addressed the waiters formally as *usted* and treated them with a kindness that never toppled over into cloying familiarity): his frequent outbursts of laughter were somewhat loud, it's true, but never irritatingly so. He laughed easily and with gusto, but he always did so sincerely and sympathetically, never in a flattering, sycophantic manner, but responding to things that genuinely amused him, as many things did, for he was a generous man, ready to see the funny side of the situation and to applaud other people's jokes, at least the verbal variety. Perhaps it was his wife who mainly made him laugh, for there are people who can make us laugh even when they don't intend to, largely because their very presence pleases us, and so it's easy enough to set us off, simply seeing them and being in their company and hearing them is all it takes, even if they're not saying anything very extraordinary or are even deliberately spouting nonsense, which we nevertheless find funny. They seemed to fulfil that role for each other; and although they were clearly married, I never caught one of them putting on an artificial or studiedly soppy expression, like some couples who have lived together for years and make a point of showing how much in love they still are, as if that somehow increased their value or embellished them. No, it was more as if they were determined to get on together and make a good impression on each other with a view to possible courtship; or as if they had been so drawn to each other before they were married or lived together that, in any circumstance, they would have spontaneously chosen each other—not out of conjugal duty or convenience or habit or even loyalty—as companion or partner, friend, conversationalist or accomplice, in the knowledge that, whatever happened, whatever transpired, whatever there was to tell or to hear, it would always be less interesting or amusing with someone else. Without her in his case, without him in her case. There was a camaraderie between them and, above all, a certainty.

THERE WAS SOMETHING very pleasant about Miguel Desvern or Deverne's face, it exuded a kind of manly warmth, which made him seem very attractive from a distance and led me to imagine that he would be irresistible in person. I doubtless noticed him before I did Luisa, or else it was because of him that I also noticed her, since although I often saw the wife without the husband—he would leave the café first and she nearly always stayed on for a few minutes longer, sometimes alone, smoking a cigarette, sometimes with a few work colleagues or mothers from school or friends, who on some mornings joined them there at the last moment, when he was already just about to leave—I never saw the husband without his wife beside him. I have no image of him alone, he only existed with her (that was one of the reasons why I didn't at first recognize him in the newspaper, because Luisa wasn't there). But I soon became interested in them both, if "interested" is the right word.

Desvern had short, thick, very dark hair, with, at his temples, just a few grey hairs, which seemed curlier than the rest (if he had let his sideburns grow, they might have sprouted incongruously into kiss-curls). The expression in his eyes was bright, calm and cheerful, and there was a glimmer of ingenuousness or childishness in them whenever he was listening to someone else, the expression of a man who is, generally speaking, amused by life, or who is simply not prepared to go through life without enjoying its million and one funny sides, even in the midst of difficulties and misfortunes. True, he had probably known very few of these compared with what is most men's common lot, and that would have helped him to preserve those trusting, smiling eyes. They were grey and seemed to look at everything as if everything were a novelty, even the insignificant things they saw repeated every day, that café at the top of Príncipe de Vergara and its waiters, my silent face. He had a cleft chin, which reminded me of a film starring Robert Mitchum or Cary Grant or Kirk Douglas, I can't remember who it was now, and in which an actress places one finger on the actor's dimpled chin and asks how he manages to shave in there. Every morning, it made me feel like getting up from my table, going over to Deverne and asking him the same question and, in turn, gently prodding his chin with my thumb or forefinger. He was always very well shaven, dimple included.

They took far less notice of me, infinitely less, than I did of them. They would order their breakfast at the bar and, once served, take it over to a table by the large window that gave on to the street, while I took a seat at a table towards the back. In spring and summer, we would all sit outside, and the waiters would pass our orders through a window that opened out next to the bar, and this gave rise to various comings and goings and, therefore, to more visual contact, because there was no other form of contact. Both Desvern and Luisa occasionally glanced at me, merely out of curiosity, but never for very long or for any reason other than curiosity. He never looked at me in an insinuating, castigating or arrogant manner, that would have been a disappointment, and she never showed any sign of suspicion, superiority or disdain, which I would have found most upsetting. Because I liked both of them, you see, the two of them together. I didn't regard them with envy, not at all, but with a feeling of relief that in the real world there could exist what I believed to be a perfect couple. Indeed, they seemed even more perfect in that Luisa's sartorial appearance was in complete contrast to that of Deverne, as regards style and choice of clothes. At the side of such a smartly turned-out man, one would have expected to see a woman who shared the same characteristics: classically elegant, although not perhaps predictably so, but wearing a skirt and high heels most of the time, with clothes by Céline, for example, and earrings and bracelets that were striking, but always in good taste. In fact, she alternated between a rather sporty look and one that I'm not sure whether to describe as casual or indifferent, certainly nothing elaborate anyway. She was as tall as him, olive-skinned, with shoulder-length, dark, almost black hair, and very little make-up. When she wore trousers—usually jeans—she accompanied them with a conventional jacket and boots or flat shoes; when she wore a skirt, her shoes were low-heeled and plain, very like the shoes many women wore in the 1950s, and in summer, she put on skimpy sandals that revealed delicate feet, small for a woman of her height. I never saw her wearing any jewellery and, as for handbags, she only ever used the sort you sling over your shoulder. She was clearly as pleasant and cheerful as he was, although her laugh wasn't quite as loud; but she laughed just as easily and possibly even more warmly than he did, revealing splendid teeth that gave her a somewhat childlike look, or perhaps it was simply the way her cheeks grew rounder when she smiled—she had doubtless laughed in exactly the same unguarded way ever since she was four years old. It was as if they had got into the habit of taking a break together before going off to their respective jobs, once the morning bustle was over—inevitable in families with small children—a moment to themselves, so as not to have to part in the middle of all that rush without sharing a little animated conversation. I used to wonder what they talked about or told each other—how could they possibly have so much to say, given that they went to bed and got up together and would presumably keep each other informed of their thoughts and activities—I only ever caught fragments of their conversation, or just the odd word or two. On one occasion, I heard him call her "princess."

You could say that I wished them all the best in the world, as if they were characters in a novel or a film for whom one is rooting right from the start, knowing that something bad is going to happen to them, that at some point, things will go horribly wrong, otherwise there would be no novel or film. In real life, though, there was no reason why that should be the case, and I expected to continue seeing them every morning exactly as they were, without ever sensing between them a unilateral or mutual coolness, or that they had nothing to say and were impatient to be rid of each other, a look of reciprocal irritation or indifference on their faces. They were the brief, modest spectacle that lifted my mood before I went to work at the publishing house to wrestle with my megalomaniac boss and his horrible authors. If Luisa and Desvern did not appear for a few days, I would miss them and face my day's work with a heavier heart. In a way, without realizing it or intending to, I felt indebted to them, they helped me get through the day and allowed me to fantasize about their life, which I imagined to be unblemished, so much so that I was glad not to be able to confirm this view or find out more, and thus risk breaking the temporary spell (my own life was full of blemishes, and the truth is that I didn't give the couple another thought until the following morning, while I sat on the bus cursing because I'd had to get up so early, which is something I loathe). I would have liked to give them something similar in exchange, but how could I? They didn't need me or, perhaps, anyone: I was almost invisible, erased by their contentment. A couple of times when he left, having first, as usual, kissed Luisa on the lips—she never remained seated for that kiss, but stood up to reciprocate it—he would give me a slight nod, almost a bow, having first looked up and half-raised one hand to say goodbye to the waiters, as if I were just another waiter, a female one. His observant wife made a similar gesture when I left—always after him and before her—on the same two occasions when her husband had been courteous enough to do so. But when I tried to return that gesture with my own even slighter nod, both he and she had looked away and didn't even see me. They were so quick, or so prudent.

DURING THE TIME when I used to see them, I didn't know who they were or what they did, although they were clearly people with money. Not immensely rich, perhaps, but comfortably off. I mean that if they had belonged in the former category, they would not have taken their children to school themselves, as I was sure they did before enjoying that brief pause in the café; perhaps their kids went to a local school such as Colegio Estilo, which was very close, although there are several others in the area, in refurbished houses, or *hotelitos* as they used to be called, in the swish El Viso district; indeed, I myself went to an infants' school in Calle Oquendo, not far from there; nor would they have had breakfast almost daily in that local café or gone off to their respective jobs at about nine o'clock, he slightly before and she slightly after, as the waiters confirmed to me when I asked about them, as did a work colleague with whom I discussed the macabre event later on, and who, despite knowing no more about them than I did, had managed to glean a few facts; I suppose people who like to gossip and think the worst always have ways of finding out whatever they want, especially if it's something negative or there's some tragedy involved, even if it has nothing to do with them.

One morning towards the end of June, neither of them appeared at the café, not that there was anything unusual about that, for it did occasionally happen, and I assumed that they must have gone away somewhere or were too busy to share that brief pause in the day which they both clearly enjoyed so much. Then I was away for most of a week, dispatched by my boss to some stupid book fair abroad, mainly to press the flesh on his behalf and generally play the fool. When I returned, they still did not appear, not once, and that worried me, more for my own sake than for theirs, because I was suddenly deprived of my morning fillip. "How easy it is for a person simply to vanish into thin air," I thought. "Someone only has to move jobs or house and you'll never know anything more about them, never see them again. All it takes is a change in work schedule. How fragile they are, these connections with people one knows only by sight." This made me wonder if, after spending so long endowing them with such joyful significance, I shouldn't perhaps have tried to exchange a few words with them, not with the intention of bothering them or spoiling their moment of togetherness nor, of course, with the idea of establishing some kind of social relationship outside of the café, that wasn't what I wanted at all; but merely to show them how much I liked and appreciated them, so as to be able to say hello to them from that point on, and to feel obliged to say goodbye to them if, one day, I were to leave the publishing house and thus cease to frequent that particular area, and to make them feel slightly obliged to do the same if they were the ones to move on or to change their habits, just as a local shopkeeper would forewarn us if he were going to close or sell his business, just as we would warn everyone if we were about to move house. To, at least, be aware that we are about to cease to see people we've grown accustomed to seeing every day, even if only at a distance or in some purely utilitarian way, barely noticing their face. Yes, that's what one usually does.

So, in the end, I asked the waiters. They told me that, as far as they knew, the couple had already gone on holiday. This sounded to me more like supposition than fact. It was still a little early to go away, but there are people who prefer not to spend July in Madrid, when the heat is at its worst, or perhaps Luisa and Deverne could allow themselves the luxury of spending the whole two months on vacation, they certainly looked wealthy enough and free enough too (perhaps they were self-employed). While I regretted having to wait until September for my little morning stimulant, I was reassured to know that they would be back and hadn't disappeared from the face of my earth for ever.

During that time, I remember happening upon a newspaper headline about a Madrid businessman who had been stabbed to death, and recall that I rapidly turned the page without reading the whole item, precisely because of the accompanying photo, which showed a man lying on the ground in the middle of the street, in the street itself, without a jacket or tie or shirt, or with his shirt unbuttoned and the tails hanging out, while the ambulance men were trying to revive or save him, and with a pool of blood all around, his white shirt drenched and stained, or so I thought from that one quick glance. Given the angle from which the photo had been taken, you couldn't see the man's face clearly and, besides, I didn't stop to look properly, I hate the current mania in the press for not sparing the reader or viewer even the most gruesome of images, as if the verbal description were not enough—or perhaps the ones who want those images are the readers and viewers, who must, by and large, be disturbed individuals; why else insist on being shown something you already know or have been told about—and with not the slightest consideration for the person who has been so cruelly mistreated and who can no longer defend or protect himself from the kind of prying gaze to which he would never willingly have submitted when fully conscious, just as he would not have appeared before perfect strangers or indeed acquaintances in dressing gown and pyjamas, considering himself, quite rightly, to be unpresentable. Photographing a dead or dying man, especially one who has died a violent death, seems to me an abuse showing a gross lack of respect for someone who has just become a victim or a corpse—if he can still be seen, that means he's not quite dead or does not belong entirely in the past, in which case, he should be left to die properly and to make his exit from time with no unwanted witnesses and no audience—and I'm not prepared to be a part of this new custom being imposed on us, I don't want to look at what they urge or almost oblige us to look at, and to add my curious, horrified eyes to the hundreds of thousands of others whose minds will be thinking as they watch, with a kind of repressed fascination and, no doubt, relief: "The person I can see before me isn't me, it's someone else. It's not me because I can see his face and it's not mine. I can read his name in the papers and it's not mine either, it's not the same, not my name. It happened to someone else, but whatever could he have done, what kind of trouble must he have been in, what debts must he have incurred, what terrible damage must he have caused for someone to want to stab him to death like that? I never get involved in anything and I don't make enemies either, I keep myself to myself. Or rather I do get involved and I do cause my own kind of damage, but no one has yet caught me. Fortunately, the dead man they're showing us here is someone else and not me, so I'm safer than I was yesterday, yesterday I escaped. This poor devil, on the other hand, didn't." At no point did it occur to me to associate the item of news, which I merely skim-read, with the pleasant, cheerful man whom I watched every day having his breakfast, and who, quite unawares, along with his wife, had the infinite kindness to raise my spirits.

FOR A FEW DAYS after I got back from my trip, I still somehow expected to see the couple, even though I knew they wouldn't come. I now arrived punctually at the office (I ate my breakfast at the café and left immediately, with no reason to linger), but I did so reluctantly, half-heartedly, it's surprising how much our routines resent change, even when those changes are for the best, which this was not. I found it harder to face my various jobs, to have to watch my boss preening himself and to be on the receiving end of the unbelievably tedious calls or visits from writers, which, for some reason, had become one of my designated tasks, perhaps because I tended to take more interest in them than did my colleagues, who openly avoided them, especially, on the one hand, the more conceited and demanding among them and, on the other, the more tedious and disoriented variety, those who lived alone, the complete disaster areas, the inappropriately flirtatious, the ones who used any excuse to phone us up as a way of starting their day and letting someone know that they still existed. Writers are, for the most part, strange individuals. They get up in exactly the same state of mind as when they went to bed, thinking about their imaginary things, which, despite being purely imaginary, take up most of their time. Those who earn their living from literature and related activities and who, therefore, have no proper job—and there are quite a few of them, because, contrary to what most people say, there's money to be made in this business, although mainly by the publishers and the distributors—rarely leave their houses and so all they have to do is go back to their computer or their typewriter—a few madmen still continue to use these, which means that their typewritten texts, once delivered, have to be scanned—with an incomprehensible degree of self-discipline: you have to be slightly abnormal to sit down and work on something without being told to. And so I was neither in the mood nor feeling sufficiently patient to give my almost daily advice on what to wear to a novelist called Cortezo, who would call me up on the flimsiest excuse and then say: "While I've got you on the phone," and ask my advice on the collection of hideous old tat he was wearing or thinking of wearing, and which he would then describe to me:

"Do you think a pair of argyle socks would go with these fine-pinstripe trousers and a pair of brown tasselled moccasins?"

I refrained from saying that I had a horror of argyle socks, fine-pinstripe trousers and brown tasselled moccasins, because that would have worried him no end and the conversation would have gone on and on.

"What colour are the argyle socks?" I asked.

"Brown and orange, but I've got them in red and blue and in green and beige too. What do you reckon?"

"Brown and blue would be best, isn't that what you said you've got on?" I replied.

"No, I haven't got that particular combination. Do you think I should go out and buy a pair?"

I felt the tiniest bit sorry for him, although it irritated me intensely that he should ask me these things as if I were his widow-to-be or his mother, and the guy was so vain about his writing, which the critics loved, but which I found just plain silly. Anyway, I didn't want to send him off into the city in search of yet more ignominious socks, which, besides, would not solve his problem.

"No, it's not worth it, Cortezo. Why don't you cut the blue diamonds from one pair of socks and the brown ones from another and stitch them together? You can make a 'patchwork,' as we say in Spanish now. A patchwork work of art."

He took a while to realize that I was joking.

"But I wouldn't know how to do that, María, I can't even sew on a button, and I have to be at my appointment in an hour and a half. Ah, I get it, you're pulling my leg."

"Me?! Not at all. But you'd be better off with some plain socks, navy blue if you've got any, and in that case, black shoes would go best." I did usually help him out in the end, insofar as I could.

Now that I was in a far less sanguine mood, however, I would rather irritably fob him off with some vaguely ill-intentioned "advice." If he told me that he was going to a cocktail party at the French Embassy wearing a dark grey suit, I would unhesitatingly recommend a pair of Nile-green socks, assuring him that these were all the rage and that everyone there would be amazed, which wasn't so very far from the truth.

I found it equally hard to be nice to another novelist, who signed himself Garay Fontina—just that, two surnames and no first name, which he may have thought was original and enigmatic, but in fact made him sound like a football referee—and who considered that the publishing house had a duty to solve every and any possible problem or difficulty, even if it had nothing to do with his books. He would ask us to go to his house to pick up an overcoat and take it to the dry-cleaner's, or else send him an IT person or some painters or find him accommodation in Trincomalee or in Batticaloa and make all the arrangements for what was a purely private trip, a holiday with his tyrannical wife, who occasionally phoned or turned up in person at the office and who didn't ask, but ordered. My boss held Garay Fontina in high esteem and did his best to please him—through us—not so much because Garay Fontina sold lots of books as because he had led my boss to believe that he was frequently invited to Stockholm—I happened to know that he always went there at his own expense in order to plot alone in the void and breathe the air—and that he was in line for the Nobel Prize, even though no one had publicly put his name forward, in Spain or anywhere else. Not even in his home town, as so often happens. In front of my boss and his subordinates, however, he would present it as a fait accompli, and we would blush to hear him say such things as: "My Nordic spies tell me that I'm a dead cert for this year or the next" or "I've memorized the speech I'm going to give to Carl Gustaf at the ceremony—in Swedish! He'll be flabbergasted, it will be the most extraordinary thing he's ever heard, and in his own language too, a language no one ever learns." "And what's in the speech?" my boss would ask with anticipatory glee. "You'll read it in the world's press the next day," Garay Fontina would tell him proudly. "Every newspaper will carry it, and they'll all have to translate it from Swedish, even the Spanish newspapers, isn't that funny?" (I thought it enviable to have such confidence in a goal, even though both goal and confidence were fictitious.) I tried to be as diplomatic as possible with him, I didn't want to risk losing my job, but I found this increasingly hard now, when, for example, he would ring me up early in the morning with his overblown desires.

"María," he said to me one morning over the phone, "I need you to get me a couple of grams of cocaine for a scene in my new book. Have someone come over to my house as soon as possible, or, at any rate, before it gets dark. I want to see what colour cocaine is in daylight, so that I don't get it wrong."

"But, Señor Garay . . ."

"I've told you before, my dear, it's Garay Fontina. Just plain Garay could be anyone, be it in the Basque Country, in Mexico or in Argentina. It could even be the name of a footballer." He insisted on this so much that I became convinced he had made up that second surname (I looked in the Madrid telephone directory one day and there was no Fontina, only a certain Laurence Fontinoy, an even more improbable name, like a character out of *Wuthering Heights*), or perhaps he had made up both surnames and was really called Gómez Gómez or García García or some other such repetitive name that would have offended his sensibilities. If it was a pseudonym, he was doubtless unaware when he chose it that Fontina is a type of Italian cheese, made either from goat's or cow's milk, I'm not sure, and which is produced, I believe, in Val d'Aosta, and which apparently melts easily. But then again there are some peanuts called Borges, and I doubt Borges would have been greatly bothered by that.

"Sorry, Señor Garay Fontina, I was merely trying to keep things short. But listen," I had to say this, even though it was far from being the most important thing I had to say, "don't worry about the colour. I can assure you that cocaine is white, both in daylight and under artificial lighting, almost everyone knows that. It's always coming up in films, didn't you ever go to any Tarantino films? Or that other one starring Al Pacino where there's a shot of the stuff in little piles?"

"That much I know, dear María," he retorted, rather stung. "I do live on this grubby planet of ours, you know, even though it may not seem so when I'm in full creative flow. But please don't undersell yourself, you who not only make books, like your colleague Beatriz and so many others, but read them too, and show excellent judgement if I may say so." He used to come out with such comments occasionally, I imagine so as to win me over; I had never actually given my opinion on any of his books, that wasn't what I was paid to do. "I'm just worried about not choosing the right adjectives. Can you tell me, for example, is it milky white or more calcareous? And what about the texture? Is it like chalk dust or sugar? Like salt or flour or talcum powder? Come on, tell me."

Given the susceptibility of the Nobel Laureate-to-be, I found myself embroiled in an absurd and dangerous conversation. And it was entirely my fault.

"It's like cocaine, Señor Garay Fontina. There's no point in describing it these days, because even if someone hasn't tried it, they will have seen it. Apart from old people, of course, but they're sure to have seen it on television thousands of times."

"Are you telling me how I should write, María? Whether I should or should not use adjectives? What I should describe and what is superfluous? Are you trying to give lessons to Garay Fontina?"

"No, Señor Fontina . . ." I was incapable of calling him by his two surnames every time, it took too long, was hardly a sonorous combination of words and, more to the point, I simply didn't like it. Oddly, he seemed less put out if I omitted the Garay.

"I have my reasons for asking you for those two grams of cocaine today. Probably because tonight the book is going to need them, and you want there to be a new book and you want it mistake-free, don't you? All you have to do is get me the cocaine and send it to me, not argue with me. Or must I speak personally to Eugeni?"

Here I took a risk by digging my heels in, and came out with a Catalan turn of phrase. I picked them up from my boss, who was Catalan by birth and full of Catalanisms, despite having lived in Madrid all his life. If Garay's request reached his ears, he was capable of sending us all out into the street to pick up drugs (in dodgy areas and places where taxi drivers refuse to go) just to please the author. He took his most conceited author far too seriously; it never ceases to amaze me how these vain people manage to persuade so many others of their worth; it's one of the world's great enigmas.

"*¿Que nos toma por camellos?*" I said. "What do you take us for, Señor Fontina? Drug-pushers? I don't know if you realize it, but you're asking us to break the law. As I'm sure you're aware, you can't buy cocaine at the local tobacconist's nor in your local bar. And what are you going to do with two whole grams? Do you have any idea how much two grams of cocaine is, how many lines of coke you could get out of that? You might overdose, and imagine what a loss that would be! To your wife and to literature. You might have a stroke. You could become an addict and be unable to think of anything else, not even writing, a mere piece of human flotsam unable to travel, because you can't cross frontiers if you have drugs on you. You could kiss goodbye to the ceremony in Sweden and to that impertinent speech of yours to Carl Gustaf."

Garay Fontina remained silent for a moment, as if weighing up whether or not he had overstepped the mark with his request. But I think he was more concerned by the dreadful prospect of never treading the red carpets of Stockholm.

"No, not drug-pushers," he said at last. "You would just have to buy it, not sell it."

I took advantage of his hesitation to clarify in passing an important detail of the operation he was proposing:

"Ah, but what about us handing it over to you? We would give you the two grams and you, presumably, would give us money. What's that if not drug-pushing? A policeman would certainly think so." This was a somewhat sore point, because Garay Fontina did not always reimburse us for the cost of the dry-cleaning or the painters' wages or the hotel reservations in Batticaloa, or, at best, took a long while to cough up, and my boss would get embarrassed and nervous whenever the time came to demand payment. The last thing we needed was to start financing the vices he was writing about in his new and unfinished novel for which he had not even been given a contract yet.

This, I saw, gave him further pause for thought. Perhaps, unaccustomed as he was, he hadn't stopped to think of the expense. Like so many writers, he was a mean, spineless little scrounger. He ran up large debts in the hotels he stayed at when he went to give lectures here, there and everywhere, or, rather, very occasionally and usually in some provincial town. He would demand that he be given a suite and that any extras should be paid for. It was rumoured that he took his sheets and his dirty washing on these trips, not because he was eccentric or obsessive, but so that he could have them washed at the hotel, even the socks—about which he did not consult me. This can't have been true—travelling with all that extra weight in your luggage would have been a terrible hassle—but how else could one explain the huge laundry bill (about one thousand two hundred euros, so it was said) that the organizers of such an event were left to pay?

"Do you happen to know how much cocaine sells for nowadays, María?"

I didn't know with any exactitude, but I thought it was about sixty euros a gram. I deliberately opted for a higher price in order to frighten and dissuade him. I was beginning to think I might succeed, or at least avoid the awful prospect of having to go and buy him some cocaine in who knows what dens of iniquity or godforsaken places.

"I've an idea it's about eighty euros a gram."

"Good heavens!" He thought for a moment. I imagined he was making miserly calculations. "Yes, you may be right. Perhaps one gram would be enough, or even half. Can you buy half a gram?"

"I have no idea, Señor Garay Fontina. I never use the stuff. But probably not." It was best not to let him think there was a cheap alternative. "Just as you can't buy half a bottle of cologne, I suppose. Or half a pear." As soon as I said this, I realized how absurd these comparisons were. "Or half a tube of toothpaste." That seemed more sensible. However, I still needed to put him off the idea entirely, or else persuade him to buy the drugs himself, without forcing us into crime or giving him money up front. With him, you couldn't rule out the possibility that he might do a runner, and the company really wasn't in a position to throw money around like that. "If you don't mind my asking, do you want it so that you can get stoned or do you simply want to look at it and touch it?"

"I'm not sure yet. That depends on what my book asks of me tonight."

It seemed to me ridiculous that a book would ask anything day or night, especially when the book wasn't yet written and the person being asked was the writer himself. I assumed he was being poetic and let the remark pass without comment.

"You see, if it's only the latter and all you want to do is describe cocaine . . . Now how can I put this? As a writer, you aspire to being universal, and you are, of course, which is why you attract readers of all ages. If you start explaining what cocaine is and what its effects are, your younger readers might think that you're a drugs novice and that you've only just cottoned on, and then they might take the mickey. Because describing cocaine nowadays would be a bit like describing a traffic light. Let's see, what adjectives would you use? Green, amber, red? Static, erect, imperturbable, metallic? People would laugh."

"Do you mean a traffic light in the street?" he asked, alarmed.

"The very same." What else could "traffic light" possibly mean, at least in ordinary, everyday language?

He fell silent for a moment.

"Take the mickey, eh? Only just have cottoned on," he repeated. I saw that my use of those expressions had been a good move, they had made their mark.

"But only as regards that part of the book, I'm sure, Señor Fontina."

The thought that some young readers might take the mickey out of anything he had written was obviously unbearable to him.

"All right, let me think about it. Another day won't make any difference. I'll tell you tomorrow what I've decided."

I knew he would do nothing of the sort, that he would abandon any further idiotic experiments and investigations and would never again refer to that telephone conversation. He always made out that he was anti-conventional and trans-contemporary, but deep down he was just like Zola or some other such writer: he did his best actually to live what he imagined, with the result that his books sounded affected and contrived.

When I hung up, I was surprised at my success in denying Garay Fontina one of his many requests, all by myself, without consulting my boss. I put this down to being more bad-tempered and more fed up than usual, to no longer enjoying breakfast with the perfect couple and thus no longer being infected by their optimism. Losing them did at least have that one advantage: it made me less tolerant of weaknesses, vanities and stupidities.

THAT WAS the only advantage, which was, of course, worth nothing. The waiters were wrong, and when they found out they were wrong they didn't bother telling me. Desvern would never come back, nor, therefore, would the cheerful couple, who had, as such, also been erased from the world. My colleague Beatriz—who also occasionally breakfasted at the café and with whom I had discussed that extraordinary pair—was the first to mention the incident to me, doubtless assuming that I would know, that I would have found out on my own account, either from the newspapers or from the waiters, and assuming, too, that we would have already talked about it, completely forgetting that I had been away during the days immediately after the murder. We were having a quick cup of coffee outside the café, when she suddenly paused, aimlessly stirring her coffee with her spoon, and said softly, looking over at the other tables, all of which were full:

"How dreadful to have such a thing happen to you, I mean what happened to your favourite couple. To begin a day like any other with not the faintest idea that someone is going to take your life, and in the most brutal manner. Because, in a way, her life has been taken from her too. At least that's how it will be for a long time, years probably, if you ever do recover from something like that, which I doubt. Such a stupid death, so unlucky, one of those deaths where you could spend your whole life thinking: 'Why did it have to happen to him, why me, when there are millions of other people in the city?' I don't know. I mean, I don't really love Saverio any more, but if something like that happened to him, I'm not sure I could go on. It wouldn't be the sense of loss so much as the feeling that I had somehow been marked out, as if someone had set my course for me and that there was no way of changing it, do you know what I mean?" Beatriz was married to a cocky, parasitical Italian guy she could barely stand, but whom she put up with because of the kids, and also because she had a lover who filled her days with his salacious phone calls and the prospect of the occasional sporadic encounter, not that there were many of those, since both of them were married with children. And one of our authors filled her nocturnal imaginings, although not, it should be said, stout Cortezo or Garay Fontina, who was repulsive both physically and personally.

"What *are* you talking about?"

And then she told me or, rather, started to tell me, astonished by my evident confusion and exclamations of ignorance, because it was getting late and her position at the publishing house was even more precarious than mine and she didn't want to run any risks, as it was, Garay Fontina had taken against her and frequently complained about her to Eugeni.

"Didn't you read about it in the newspapers? There was even a photo of the poor man, all bloody and lying on the ground. I can't remember the exact date, but if you look on the Internet, you're sure to find it. His name was Deverne, apparently he was a member of the film distribution family, you know, 'Deverne Films presents,' you'll have seen it thousands of times at the cinema. You'll find everything you need to know there. It was just horrible. Such terrible bad luck. Enough to make you despair. I don't think I'd ever get over it if I was his wife. She must be out of her mind with grief." That was when I found out his name or, if you like, his stage name.

That night, I typed in "Deverne Murder" on my computer and

the item came up at once, drawn from the local news sections of two or three Madrid papers. His real surname was Desvern, and it occurred to me that perhaps his family had changed it at some point for business purposes, to make it easier to pronounce for speakers of Castilian and possibly so that Catalan speakers would not immediately associate them with the town of Sant Just Desvern, a place I happened to know because several Barcelona publishing houses have their warehouses there. And perhaps also to give the appearance of being a French film distributor, because when the company was founded—in the 1960s or even earlier—everyone would still have been familiar with Jules Verne, and everything French was considered chic, not like now with that President who looks like Louis de Funès with hair. I learned, too, that the Deverne family used to own several large cinemas in the centre of Madrid and that, perhaps because such cinemas have been gradually disappearing, to be replaced by shopping malls, the company had diversified and now specialized in property development, not just in Madrid, but elsewhere too. So Miguel Desvern must have been even richer than I thought. I found it even more incomprehensible that he should have breakfasted nearly every morning in a café that was well within my more modest means. The incident had occurred on the last day that I saw him there, which is how I knew that his wife and I had said goodbye to him at the same time, she with her lips and I with my eyes only. In a further cruelly ironic touch, it was his birthday; he had thus died a year older than he had been the day before, at fifty.

The versions in the press differed in some details (it doubtless depended on which neighbours or passers-by the reporters had spoken to), but they all agreed on the main facts. Deverne had parked his car, as, it seems, he always did, in a side street off Paseo de la Castellana at around two in the afternoon—he was probably going to meet Luisa for lunch at the restaurant—quite close to their house and even closer to a small car park belonging to the Technical College for Industrial Engineers. When he got out, he was accosted by a homeless guy who used to park cars in the area in exchange for tips from drivers—what we call a *gorrilla*—and who had then started berating Desvern, making incoherent, outrageous accusations. According to one witness—although none of them really understood what the man was talking about—he accused Deverne of having got his daughters involved in some international prostitution ring. According to others, he gave vent to a stream of unintelligible invective, of which they could make out only two phrases: "You're trying to take my inheritance away from me!" and "You're stealing the bread from my children's mouths!" Desvern tried to shake the man off and reason with him for a few seconds, telling him that he had nothing to do with his daughters, whom he didn't even know, and that he had clearly mistaken him for someone else. However, the *gorrilla*, Luis Felipe Vázquez Canella according to the reports, thirty-nine years old, very tall and heavily bearded, had grown even angrier and continued to hurl abuse at Desvern and heap him with incomprehensible curses. The porter of one house had heard him screaming hysterically: "You're going to die today and, by tomorrow, your wife will have forgotten you!" Another newspaper reported a still more wounding version: "You're going to die today and, by tomorrow, your wife will have found another man!" Deverne had made a dismissive gesture as if giving up on the fellow, and was about to set off towards Paseo de la Castellana, abandoning any further attempt to calm the man down, but then the *gorrilla*, as if he had decided to wait no longer for his curse to take effect, but to become, instead, its artificer, had produced a butterfly knife with a seven-centimetre blade and launched himself on Deverne from behind, stabbing him repeatedly, in the chest and side according to one newspaper, in the back and abdomen according to another, in the back, the chest and the side of the chest according to a third. The reports also disagreed on the number of stab wounds: nine, ten and sixteen, but the reporter who gave that last figure—and who was possibly the most reliable because he mentioned "autopsy results"—added that "every blow struck a vital organ" and that "according to the pathologist who carried out the autopsy, five proved fatal."

Desvern had initially tried to get away from the man and escape, but the blows had been so fast and furious and brutal—and, apparently, so accurate—that there had been no way he could evade them and he soon collapsed and fell to the ground. Only then did the murderer stop. A security guard at a nearby company "saw what was happening and managed to detain the man until the police arrived, saying: 'You're not leaving here until the police arrive!' " There was no explanation as to how, with mere words, he had managed to immobilize an armed man, who was completely out of control and who had just spilled a great deal of blood—perhaps he did so at gunpoint, but none of the articles mentioned a gun or that he had got a gun out and pointed it at the assailant—because various sources stated that the *gorrilla* was still holding the knife when the police arrived, and that they had been the ones who ordered him to drop it. The man then threw it down on the ground, was handcuffed and taken to the local police station. "According to Madrid's chief of police"—these or similar words appeared in all the newspapers—"the alleged murderer was brought before a court, but refused to make a statement."

Luis Felipe Vázquez Canella had been living for some time in the area in an abandoned car, and here again the testimony of neighbours differed, as always happens when one asks or tells a story to more than one person. For some, he was a very calm, polite individual who never caused any trouble: he spent his time earning a little money by looking for parking spaces and guiding drivers to them with the usual imperious, obliging gestures that go with the job—his services were sometimes unnecessary or unwanted, but that is how all *gorrillas* work. He would arrive at about midday, leave his two blue rucksacks at the foot of a tree, and set about his intermittent task. Other residents, however, said that they had become fed up with "his violent outbursts and evident insanity," and had often tried to get him thrown out of his static mobile home and have him removed from the neighbourhood, but without success. Although Vázquez Canella had no previous police record, Deverne's chauffeur had been the victim of one of his outbursts only a month before. The beggar had addressed him very rudely and, taking advantage of the fact that the chauffeur had his window wound down, had punched him in the face. The police were duly informed and arrested him briefly for assault, but, in the end, the chauffeur, although "injured," had taken pity on the man and decided not to make a formal complaint. And on the eve of Desvern's death, victim and executioner had had their first argument. The *gorrilla* had made his usual wild allegations. According to one of the more talkative concierges in the street where the stabbing took place, "He talked about his daughters and about his money, saying that 'they' wanted to take his money away from him." Another version described how: "The victim explained to him that he had got the wrong person and that he had nothing to do with his affairs. The bewildered beggar then wandered off, muttering to himself." Somewhat embellishing the narrative and taking a few liberties with the people actually involved, it added: "Miguel could never have imagined that, twenty-four hours later, Luis Felipe's delusions would cost him his life. The script written for him had begun to take shape a month earlier"—this was a reference to the incident with the chauffeur, who some neighbours saw as the real object of the beggar's rage:

"Who knows, perhaps he had it in for the chauffeur," one of them was reported to have said, "and got him mixed up with his boss." It was suggested that the *gorrilla* had been in a foul mood for a month or more, because, with the installation of parking meters in the area, he could no longer earn any money with his already sporadic work. One of the newspapers mentioned in passing a disconcerting fact that none of the others had picked up: "The alleged murderer refused to make a statement, and so we have been unable to confirm whether or not he and his victim were related by marriage, as some people in the neighbourhood believed."

An ambulance had sped to the scene of the crime. The ambulance men had given Desvern first aid, but because he was so gravely injured, all they could do was "stabilize" him and drive him immediately to the Hospital de La Luz—or, according to a couple of newspapers, to the Hospital de La Princesa; they couldn't even agree on that—where he was rushed into the operating room with cardiac arrest and in a critical condition. He hovered on the brink of life and death for five hours, during which time he never recovered consciousness; he finally "succumbed late that evening, with the doctors unable to do anything more to save him."

All this information was published over a period of two days, the two days following the murder. Then the item vanished from the press completely, as tends to happen with all news nowadays: people don't want to know why something happened, only what happened, and to know that the world is full of reckless acts, of dangers, threats and bad luck that only brush past us, but touch and kill our careless fellow human beings, or perhaps they were simply not among the chosen. We live quite happily with a thousand unresolved mysteries that occupy our minds for ten minutes in the morning and are then forgotten without leaving so much as a tremor of grief, not a trace. We don't want to go too deeply into anything or linger too long over any event or story, we need to have our attention shifted from one thing to another, to be given a constantly renewed supply of other people's misfortunes, as if, after each one, we thought: "How dreadful. But what's next? What other horrors have we avoided? We need to feel that we, by contrast, are survivors, immortals, so feed us some new atrocities, we've worn out yesterday's already."

Oddly enough, during those two days, little was said about the man who had died, only that he was the son of one of the founders of the well-known film distributors and that he worked for the family firm, which was now almost an empire that had been growing for decades and constantly adding to its many ramifications, currently even including low-cost airlines. In the days that followed, there was no sign of any obituary for Deverne anywhere, no memoir or evocation written by a friend or colleague or comrade, no biographical sketch that spoke of his character and his personal achievements, and that was strange. Any wealthy businessman, especially if he has links with the cinema, and even if he isn't famous, has contacts in the press or friends with contacts, and it wouldn't be difficult to persuade one of those contacts to place a heartfelt note of homage and praise in some newspaper, as if that might compensate the dead person in some way for being dead or as if the lack of an obituary were an added insult (so often we only find out that someone has existed once they have ceased to do so, in fact, *because* they have ceased to exist).

And so the only available photo was the one snapped by some quick-witted reporter while Deverne was lying on the ground, before he was taken away, when he was still receiving treatment there in the street. Fortunately, it was hard to see the image on the Internet—a very small, rather bad reproduction—because that seemed to me a truly vile thing to do to a man like him, who, in life, had always been so cheerful, so impeccable. I barely looked at it, I didn't want to, and I had already thrown away the newspaper where I had first glimpsed the photo in its larger version without realizing who it was and not wishing to spend time over it. Had I known then that he was not a complete stranger, but a person I used to see every day with a sense of pleasure and almost gratitude, the temptation to look would have been too hard to resist, but then I would have averted my gaze, feeling even more indignant and horrified than I had when I failed to recognize him. Not only do you get killed in the street in the cruellest way possible and completely out of the blue, without so much as an inkling that such a thing could happen, but also, precisely because it did happen in the street—"in a public place" as people reverentially and stupidly say—it is deemed permissible to exhibit to the world the humiliating havoc wrought on you. In the smaller photo on the Internet, I would barely have recognized him, and then only because the text assured me that the dead or soon-to-be-dead man was Desvern. He, at any rate, would have been horrified to see or know himself to have been thus exposed, without a jacket or tie or even a shirt, or with his shirt open—you couldn't quite tell, and where would his cufflinks have gone if his shirt had been removed?—full of tubes and surrounded by ambulance staff manhandling him, with his wounds on display, unconscious and lying sprawled in the middle of the street in a pool of blood, watched by passers-by and drivers alike. His wife would have been equally horrified by this image, if she had seen it, although she would probably have had neither the time nor the desire to read the newspapers the following day. While you weep for and watch over and bury the dead, all uncomprehending, and when you have children to tell as well, you're in no fit state for anything else, the rest does not exist. But she might have seen it afterwards, perhaps prompted by the same curiosity I felt a week later, and have gone on to the Internet to find out what other people had known at the time, not just close friends and family, but strangers like me. What effect would that have had on her? Her more distant friends would have found out via the press, from that local Madrid newspaper or from a death notice, one or even several must have appeared in various papers, as usually happens when someone wealthy dies. That photo, above all else that photo—as well as the manner of his death, foul and absurd and, how can I put it, tinged with misfortune—was what allowed Beatriz to refer to him as "the poor man." No one would ever have called him that while he was alive, not even one minute before he got out of his car in that charming, peaceful part of town, next to the small garden surrounding the college, where there are trees and a drinks kiosk with a few tables and chairs, and where I've often sat with my young nephews. No, not even a second before Vázquez Canella opened his butterfly knife; apparently, you have to be quite skilled to open one of those double-handled things, which are, I believe, not available to buy and may even be banned. And now, there were no two ways about it, he would be that for ever: poor, unfortunate Miguel Deverne. Poor man.

"YES, IT WAS his birthday, can you believe that? The world normally allows its characters to enter and leave the stage in too disorderly a fashion for someone actually to be born and to die on the same date, with a gap of fifty years, exactly fifty years, in between. It doesn't make any sense, precisely because it seems to. It could so easily not have happened like that. It could have been any other day or no day. Better if it had never happened at all."

Several months passed before I saw Luisa Alday again, and a few more before I knew her name, that name, and before she spoke those words and many more. I didn't know then if she talked continually about what had happened to her, with anyone prepared to listen, or if she had found in me a person with whom she felt comfortable opening up her heart, a stranger who would not report what she heard to any of her close friends or family and whose incipient friendship could be interrupted at any moment without explanation or consequences, and who was also compassionate, loyal and curious and whose face was both new to her and vaguely familiar and associated with happier times unclouded by sorrow, although I had always thought that she had barely noticed my presence, even less so than her husband.

Luisa reappeared towards the tail-end of summer, late into September, and she arrived at the usual time, accompanied by two women friends or work colleagues; the tables were still set out on the pavement and I watched her arrive and sit or, rather, drop on to a chair; I saw how one of her friends grabbed her forearm with mechanical solicitude, as if fearing that Luisa might lose her balance and taking her friend's fragility for granted. Luisa looked terribly thin and not at all well, and had the kind of profound pallor that blurs all the features, as though not only her skin had lost its lustre and its colour, but also her hair, brows, lashes, eyes, teeth and lips, all dull and diffuse. She seemed to be there on temporary loan, I mean on loan to life. She no longer talked vivaciously as she used to with her husband, but with a false naturalness that betrayed a sense of obligation and indifference. It occurred to me that she might be on medication. They had sat down quite close to me, with only an empty table between us, which meant that I could hear scraps of their conversation, mostly what her friends said, rather than her, for she spoke only in muted tones. They were consulting or questioning her about the details of a memorial service, doubtless Desvern's, although I couldn't tell whether this would be a service held to commemorate the three-month anniversary of his death (which would, I calculated, be around that time) or if it was the first such service, which had not been held after the usual one- or two-week interval, as is still sometimes the custom, at least in Madrid. Perhaps she hadn't felt strong enough so soon after the incident, or the gruesome circumstances had made such a service inadvisable—people can never resist poking their nose into such public ceremonies, or spreading rumours—and so, assuming the family liked to keep to the traditional way of doing things, it was still pending. Or perhaps some protective figure—a brother, for example, or her parents or a woman friend—had whisked her away from Madrid after the funeral, so that she could become accustomed to her husband's absence from a distance, without the usual familiar, domestic scenes that only underlined his absence or made it all the more poignant: a pointless postponement of the horror awaiting her. The most I

heard her say was: "Yes, that's fine" or "If you say so, you're thinking more clearly than me" or "Make sure the priest keeps it short,
Miguel wasn't too keen on priests, they made him a bit nervous"
or "No, not Schubert, he's too obsessed with death, and we've had
quite enough of that."

I noticed that the two waiters at the café, after a moment's discussion behind the bar, went over to her table together, stiffly rather
than solemnly, and although they spoke shyly and very quietly, I
heard them offer their brief condolences: "We just wanted to say
how very sad we were to hear about your husband, he was always
very kind to us," said one. And the other contributed the usual old,
vacuous phrase: "Please accept our deepest sympathy. A real tragedy." She thanked them with her lacklustre smile and that was all,
and it seemed perfectly understandable to me that she should prefer
not to go into detail or to comment or to prolong the conversation.
When I got up, I felt an impulse to follow their example, but did
not dare to further interrupt her desultory conversation with her
friends. Besides, time was getting on, and I didn't want to arrive late
at work, now that I had mended my ways and arrived punctually at
my post every day.

Another month passed before I saw her again, and although the
leaves were falling and the days were growing cooler, there were
still those who preferred to breakfast al fresco—speedy breakfasts
eaten by people in a hurry, people who would subsequently spend
many hours shut up in an office and who didn't linger long enough
at the café to get cold; most, like me, ate in sleepy silence—and so
the tables were still outside on the pavement. This time, Luisa Alday
arrived with her two children and ordered them each an ice cream.
I imagined—basing myself on a remote childhood memory—that
she had taken them to the doctors for a blood test without letting
them have any breakfast beforehand and was giving them a treat to

make up for both the jab and for having had to go hungry, a treat that included allowing them to miss the first hour of school. The little girl was very attentive to her brother, who was about four years younger than her, and I got the impression that she was also, in her fashion, looking after her mother, as if they occasionally swapped roles, or, if they didn't perhaps go quite that far, as if they both occasionally competed for the role of mother, in the few areas where such competition was possible. I mean that, while the little girl was eating her ice cream from a glass, wielding her spoon with child-like meticulousness, she was also making sure that Luisa did not let her coffee go cold and urging her to drink it. She kept one eye on her mother all the time, watching her every gesture and expression, and if she noticed that her mother was becoming too abstracted and sunk in her own thoughts, she would immediately speak to her, make some remark or ask a question or perhaps tell her something, as if to prevent her mother from becoming entirely lost, as if it made her sad to see her mother plunging back into memory. When a car drew up and double-parked outside the café, very faintly sounding its horn, and the children sprang to their feet, grabbed their satchels, quickly kissed their mother and walked, hand in hand, towards the car, knowing that it had come to pick them up, I had the feeling then that the daughter was more concerned about leaving Luisa than the other way around (she it was who fleetingly stroked her mother's cheek as if counselling her to be good and not to get into any trouble, or wishing to leave her some small tactile consolation until they saw each other again). The car had probably come to pick them up and take them to school. I looked to see who was driving, and could not help a sudden quickening of the pulse, because although I know nothing about cars, which all look the same to me, this one I recognized instantly: it was the same car Deverne used to drive when he went off to work, leaving his wife to stay on for a while in the café either alone or with a friend. It was doubtless the same car he had driven and parked next to the college, the car he should never have got out of on that day, his birthday. There was a man at the wheel, and at first I thought it must be the chauffeur with whom Deverne occasionally alternated as driver and who could have replaced him on that fateful day, could have died instead of him, and who was perhaps the person the *gorrilla* actually wanted to kill, the intended murder victim, and who had, therefore, narrowly escaped death— by pure chance, who knows, perhaps he had a doctor's appointment that day. If he was the chauffeur, he wasn't wearing a uniform. I couldn't quite see him, half-concealed as he was by the other cars parked alongside the pavement; nevertheless, I thought he looked rather attractive. He didn't resemble Miguel Desvern, but they had certain characteristics in common or were at least not complete opposites; it was easy to see how a mistake could be made, especially by someone mentally disturbed. From her table, Luisa waved good-bye, or waved hello and goodbye, from the moment he arrived until he left. Yes, she waved three or four times, slightly absurdly, while the car was parked. She repeated the gesture with an absorbed look in her eyes, eyes that saw perhaps only a ghost. Or was she only waving goodbye to her children? I didn't see if the driver waved back or not.

THAT WAS WHEN I decided to go over to her. The children had left in what had been their father's car, and she was alone, with no one for company, no work colleague or fellow mother from school or friend. She was using the long, sticky spoon that her son had left in his glass to absent-mindedly stir what remained of his ice cream, as if she were intent on instantly reducing it to liquid, thus accelerating its inevitable fate. "How many small eternities will she experience in which she will struggle to make time move on," I thought, "if such a thing is possible, which I doubt. You wait for time to pass during the temporary or indefinite absence of the other—of husband, of lover—as well as during an absence which is not yet definitive, but that bears all the marks of being so, as our instinct keeps whispering to us, and to whose voice we say: 'Be quiet, be quiet, keep silent, I don't yet want to hear you, I'm still not strong enough, I'm not ready.' When you have been abandoned, you can fantasize about a return, you can imagine that the abandoner will suddenly see the light and come back to share your pillow, even if you know he has already replaced you and is involved with another woman, with another story, and that he will only remember you if that new relationship suddenly turns sour, or if you insist and make your presence felt against his will and try to pester him or win him round or force him to feel sorry for you or take your revenge by giving him a sense that he'll never be entirely free of you and that you don't intend to be a slowly fading memory but an immovable shadow that will stalk and haunt him for ever; making his life impossible and, ultimately, making him hate you. On the other hand, you cannot fantasize about a dead man, unless you have lost your mind, and there are those who choose to do that, even if only temporarily, those who consent to do so while they manage to convince themselves that what happened really happened, the improbable and the impossible, the thing that did not even have a place in the calculation of probabilities by which we live in order to get up each morning without a sinister, leaden cloud urging us to close our eyes again, thinking: 'What's the point if we're all doomed anyway? It's all pointless. Whatever we do, we'll only be waiting, like dead men on leave, as someone once said.' I don't believe, though, that Luisa has lost her mind, but that's just a feeling, I don't know her. And if she hasn't, then what is she waiting for, how does she spend the hours, the days, the weeks and now months, to what purpose does she drive time forwards or flee from it and withdraw, and how, at this very moment, is she managing to push it away from her? She doesn't know that I am about to come over and speak to her, as the waiters did the last time I saw her here, not that I've ever seen her anywhere else. She doesn't know that I'm going to lend her a hand and erase a couple of minutes for her with my conventional words of commiseration, perhaps three or four minutes at most if she says anything beyond 'Thank you.' She'll still be left with hundreds more until sleep comes to her aid and clouds her ever-counting consciousness, because it's her consciousness that is always counting: one, two, three and four; five, six and seven and eight and so on ceaselessly and indefinitely until she falls asleep."

"Forgive the intrusion," I said, standing by her table; she did not get up at once. "You don't know me, but my name's María Dolz. I've been having breakfast here at the same time as you and your husband for years now. And I just wanted to say how terribly sad I am about what happened, what he went through and what you must have been going through ever since. I read about it in the news-paper, somewhat belatedly, after not seeing you for several morn-ings. I only ever knew you by sight, but you obviously got on so well and I always thought you made such a lovely couple. I can't tell you how sorry I am."

I realized that with my penultimate sentence, I had killed her off as well, by using the past tense to refer to them both and not just to her late husband. I tried to think of some way to remedy this, but couldn't come up with anything that wasn't either clumsy or unnecessarily complicated. I imagined, though, that she would have understood what I meant, that I had enjoyed seeing the two of them as a couple, and as such they no longer existed. Then I thought that perhaps I had highlighted something she was trying to hold in sus-pense or confine to some kind of limbo, because it would be impos-sible for her to forget or deny it to herself: that they were not two people any more and that she was no longer part of a couple. I was about to add: "That's all I wanted to say, I won't delay you any fur-ther," then turn and leave, when Luisa Alday stood up, smiling—it was a broad smile that she made no attempt to repress, she was inca-pable of deceit or malice, she could even be ingenuous—and placed one hand affectionately on my shoulder and said:

"Yes, of course, we know *you* by sight as well." She unhesitat-ingly addressed me as *tú* despite my more formal approach, well, we were the same age more or less, or she was possibly just a couple of years older; she spoke in the plural and in the present tense, as if she had not yet become used to being singular or perhaps considered herself to have already crossed over to the other side, to be as dead as her husband and therefore an inhabitant of the same dimension or territory: as if she hadn't yet separated from him and saw no reason to give up that "we" to which she had been accustomed for nearly a decade and which she wasn't going to abandon after a mere three months. However, she did then go on to use the imperfect tense, perhaps because the verb demanded it: "We used to call you the Prudent Young Woman. You see, we even gave you a name. Thank you so much for your kind words. Won't you sit down?" And she indicated one of the chairs that had been occupied by her children, still keeping her hand on my shoulder, and now I had a sense that I was a support for her or a handle to hold on to. I was sure that, had I moved even slightly closer, she would, quite naturally, have embraced me. She looked fragile, like a hesitant novice ghost, who is not yet fully convinced that she is one.

I looked at my watch and saw that it was late. I wanted to ask her about that nickname, I felt surprised and slightly flattered. They had noticed me, had spoken about me and given me a name. I smiled unwittingly, we both smiled with a kind of tentative happiness, that of two people recognizing each other in the very saddest of circumstances.

"The Prudent Young Woman," I repeated.

"Yes, that's how we see you." She returned again to the present tense, as if Deverne were at home and still alive or as if she could separate herself from him only in some respects. "You don't mind, I hope. Please, sit down."

"Why should I mind? I had my own private name for you too." I was still using the formal *usted*, not because I didn't want to address her as *tú*, but because, having included him in that plural "you," I didn't dare address her husband in such familiar terms, just as one cannot refer to a stranger who has died by his first name. At least one shouldn't, but nowadays no one worries about such niceties, everyone is overfamiliar. "I'm so sorry, I can't stop now, I have to go to work." I glanced at my watch again, either mechanically or simply to corroborate that I was in a hurry, because I knew perfectly well what time it was.

"Of course. If you like, we can meet later on. Come to our house.

What time do you leave work? What do you do, by the way? And what was the name that you gave us?" She still had her hand on my shoulder, she wasn't demanding, but rather pleading. A superficial plea, born of the moment. If I declined, come the evening, she would probably have forgotten all about our encounter.

I didn't answer her penultimate question—there wasn't time—still less her last one, because telling her that I had thought of them as the Perfect Couple could only have added to her pain and sorrow, after all, she was about to be left alone again, as soon as I left. But I said, yes, I would drop by on my way home from work, if that suited her, at around half past six or seven. I asked for her address and she told me, it was quite near by. I said goodbye and briefly placed my hand on hers, the hand resting on my shoulder, and I took the opportunity to squeeze that hand gently before removing it, again very gently, and she seemed grateful for that contact. I was just about to cross the road, when I realized I had forgotten something and had to go back.

"How silly of me to forget," I said. "I don't know your name."

And it was only then that I found out, for her name had not appeared in any newspaper, and I hadn't seen any of the death notices.

"Luisa Alday," she answered. "Luisa Desvern," she added, correcting herself. In Spain, a woman doesn't lose her maiden name when she gets married, and I wondered if she had decided to call herself that now as an act of loyalty or homage. "No, Luisa Alday," she said, correcting herself again. That's probably how she had always thought of herself. "It's a good job you remembered, because Miguel's name doesn't appear on the door, only mine." She paused for a moment, then added: "He did that as a precautionary measure, because his name has so many links with business. Much good it did him."

"THE STRANGEST THING is that it's changed the way I think," she said to me that same evening or, rather, when night had already fallen in her living room. Luisa was on the sofa and I was seated in a nearby armchair, I had accepted her offer of a glass of port, which had been her choice of drink; she took frequent small sips and kept pouring herself a little more and was, if I'm not mistaken, already on her third glass; she had a naturally elegant way of crossing her legs, right leg over left, then left over right, she was wearing a skirt that day, and shiny, black, low-vamp shoes with small but very dainty heels, which made her look rather like an American college girl; in contrast, the soles of her shoes were almost white, as if she hadn't yet worn them out in the street; her children or one of them would occasionally come in to tell her something or to ask a question or settle an argument, they were watching television in the next room, which was like an extension of the living room, with no separating door; Luisa had explained to me that there was another TV in the little girl's bedroom, but that she preferred to have the children close by, where she could hear them, in case anything happened or they quarrelled, as well as for the company, and so she obliged them to stay near her, if not in sight at least within earshot; they didn't disturb her concentration because she couldn't concentrate on anything anyway, and had given up hope of ever doing so again, whether reading a book or watching a film all the way through or preparing a class in anything more than a haphazard fashion or in the taxi on her way to the university, and she could listen to music only now and again, short pieces or songs or a single movement from a sonata, anything longer simply wearied and irritated her; she also followed the occasional TV series, because the episodes were usually short, and she bought them on DVD now so that she could rewind if she lost track of the plot, she found it so hard to pay attention, her mind wandering off to other places, or, rather, always to the same one, to Miguel, to the last time she had seen him alive, which was also the last time I had seen him, to the peaceful little garden next to the college off Paseo de la Castellana, along with the man who had stabbed and stabbed and stabbed him with one of those apparently illegal butterfly knives. "I don't know, it's as though I had a different mind entirely, I'm continually thinking things that would never have occurred to me before," she said with genuine bewilderment, her eyes very wide, as she scratched one knee with the tips of her fingers as if she had an itch, although it was probably just her general state of unease. "It's as though I've become a different person since then, or a different sort of person, with an unfamiliar, alien mentality, someone given to making strange connections and being frightened by them. I hear a siren from an ambulance or a police car or a fire engine, and I wonder who's dying or being burned or perhaps choking to death, and then I'm assailed by the dreadful idea of all the people who would have heard the siren on the police car that arrived to arrest the *gorrilla* or of the ambulance that went to help Miguel in the street and take him to hospital, they would have listened to it distractedly or even irritably, thinking, 'Why do they have to make such a racket?'— you know the kind of thing, it's what we all say—'Why so loud, it can't be that urgent.' We almost never ask ourselves what very real misfortune they're rushing to, it's just another familiar city sound, a sound with no specific content, a mere nuisance, empty of meaning. Before, when there weren't so many of them and they didn't make so much noise, we never suspected the drivers of turning on their sirens for no reason, just so that they could drive faster and make the other cars get out of the way, people used to stand on their balcony to see what was going on and even assumed that there would be a report in the next day's newspaper. No one rushes out on to their balcony now, we all just wait for the siren to go away and remove from our auditory field the ill or injured or wounded or perhaps dying person, so that they'll stop bothering us and stop setting our nerves on edge. I don't actually stand on the balcony either, but during the weeks immediately following Miguel's death, I couldn't resist rushing over there or going to the window and trying to spot the police car or ambulance and follow it with my eyes for as long as I could, but you can't usually see them from the house, only hear them, and so, after a while, I gave up, and yet still, every time I hear a siren, I stop what I'm doing and look up and listen until it's gone; I listen to it as if it were someone moaning or pleading with me, as if each siren were saying: 'Please, I'm a gravely wounded man, fighting for my life, and it's not my fault, I haven't done anything to make someone stab me like this, I just got out of my car as I have on many other days and suddenly felt a sharp pain in my back, then another and another and another in other parts of my body, I don't even know how many, and then I realized that I was bleeding profusely and was going to die even though I wasn't ready to and even though I'd done nothing to deserve it. Let me through, I beg you, you can't be in anywhere near as much of a hurry as me, and if there is a chance I can be saved, I have to get to the hospital quickly. Today's my birthday, and my wife has no idea what's happened, she's sitting in a restaurant waiting to celebrate, she's probably bought me a gift, a surprise, don't let her find me dead.' "

Luisa stopped and took another sip of port, it was a mechanical gesture really, because there was only a tiny drop left in her glass.

Her eyes no longer had an absent look, rather, they were very bright and alert, as if her imaginings, far from distracting her, had given her a momentary burst of energy, made her feel more part of the real world, even if that real world existed only in the past. I hardly knew her, but my feeling was that she found her present life so bewildering that she felt much more vulnerable and powerless now than when she placed herself back in the past, as she had done just now, even in that most painful and final of moments. Her brown, almond-shaped eyes looked lovely lit up like that; she had one eye visibly larger than the other, but that didn't spoil her looks in the least, her eyes were filled with a new intensity and vitality when she put herself in the shoes of the dying Desvern. Even in the midst of her suffering, she was still almost pretty, especially when she was happy, as she had been on the mornings when I used to see her at the café.

"But he couldn't possibly have thought any of that, if what they said in the newspapers was right," I pointed out. I didn't know what else to say or perhaps there was no need to say anything, but it seemed wrong to stay silent.

"No, of course he couldn't," she said quickly and slightly defiantly. "He couldn't have thought it while they were taking him to the hospital, because he was unconscious by then and never regained consciousness. Perhaps he thought something like that before, though, while he was being stabbed. I can't stop imagining that moment, those seconds, from the time the attack began until he stopped trying to defend himself and became unaware of anything, until he lost consciousness and felt nothing, neither despair nor pain nor . . ." She fumbled briefly for what else he might have felt before he collapsed, half-dead. "Or farewell. I had never thought anyone else's thoughts before, never wondered what another person might be thinking, not even him, it's not my style, I lack imagination, I don't have that kind of mind. And yet now I do it almost all the time. Like I say, it's changed my way of thinking, and it's as if I don't recognize myself any more; or, rather, it seems to me sometimes that I never knew myself in my previous life, and that Miguel didn't know me either: he couldn't have, it would have been beyond him, isn't that strange? If the real me is this woman constantly making all these connections and associations, things that a few months ago would have seemed to me completely disparate and unrelated; if I am the person I've been since his death, that means that for him I was always someone else, and had he lived, I would have continued to be the person I'm not, indefinitely. Do you understand what I mean?" she added, realizing that what she was saying was pretty abstruse.

It was almost like a mental tongue-twister to me, but I did more or less understand. I thought: "This woman is in a very bad way indeed, and who can blame her? Her grief must be immense, and she must spend all day and all night going over and over what happened, imagining her husband's final conscious moments, wondering what he could have been thinking, when he would probably have had quite enough to do trying to avoid the first knife-thrusts and get away, get free, he probably never gave her so much as a thought, he would have been focused entirely on what he foresaw might be his death and on doing all he could to avoid it, and if anything else crossed his mind it would have been merely his sense of infinite astonishment, incredulity and incomprehension, what's going on here, how is this possible, what is this man doing and why is he stabbing me, why has he chosen me out of millions and who has he mistaken me for, doesn't he realize that I am not the cause of his ills, and how ridiculous, how awful, how stupid to die like this, because of someone else's mistake or obsession, to die violently and at the hands of a stranger or of someone so secondary in my life that I had barely noticed him until forced to by his intemperance and his disruptive behaviour, by the fact that he increasingly made himself a nuisance and one day even attacked Pablo, to die at the hands of a man who is of even less importance to me than the pharmacist on the corner or the waiter at the café where I have breakfast, someone purely anecdotal, insignificant, as if I suddenly found myself being attacked by the Prudent Young Woman who is also there at the café every morning and with whom I have never exchanged a word, people who are merely vague extras or marginal presences, who inhabit a corner or lurk in the obscure background of the painting and whom we don't even miss if they disappear, or whose absence we don't notice, this can't be happening because it's just too absurd, a stroke of inconceivably bad luck, I won't even have a chance to tell someone about it, which is the one thing that very slightly makes up for the worst misfortunes, you never know what or who will don the disguise or shape of your unique and individual death, which is always unique even if you depart this world at the same time as many others in some massive catastrophe, but there are usually some warning signs, an inherited disease, an epidemic, a car accident, a plane crash, some bodily organ wearing out, a terrorist attack, a landslide, a derailment, a heart attack, a fire, a violent raid on your house at night, or straying into a dangerous area as soon as you've arrived in an, as yet, unexplored city, I've found myself in just such places on my travels, especially when I was younger and travelled a lot and took more risks, something could easily have happened to me through my own imprudence or ignorance in Caracas and Buenos Aires, and in Mexico, in New York and in Moscow and in Hamburg and even in Madrid itself, but not right here, yes, perhaps in one of Madrid's more troubled, downtrodden, darker streets, but not in this bright, quiet, well-heeled area which is more or less my home patch, and which I know like the back of my hand, not while getting out of my car as I have on so many other occasions, why today and not yesterday or tomorrow, why today and why me, it could easily have happened to someone else, even to Pablo, who had already had a far more serious altercation with this man, if only he had made a formal complaint to the police when the brute punched him, I was the one who advised him to drop the matter, what a fool, I felt sorry for this man whose name I don't even know, but that would have got rid of him, and now that I think of it, I had my warning yesterday, when he shouted at me, and I just shrugged it off and put it out of my mind, I should have been afraid and have acted more cautiously and not entered his territory again for several days or at least until I had ceased to be a target, I shouldn't have put myself within range of this furious madman who has got it into his head to stick his knife into me again and again, and the knife is sure to be filthy, although that's hardly important now, it won't be an infection that carries me off, the point plunging into my body and the blade turning inside are killing me far more quickly, he's so close to me and he stinks, he can't have washed in ages, he doesn't have anywhere to wash, always stuck in his abandoned car, I don't want to die with that stench in my nostrils, but we don't get a choice, why does that have to be the last thing to surround me before I say goodbye, that and the now overwhelming smell of the blood, a metallic smell from childhood, which is when one tends to bleed most, it's my blood, it can't be anyone else's, not this madman's blood, I haven't wounded him, he's very strong and very overwrought and there's no way I could have fought him off, I have no knife to stick in him, whereas he has opened and pierced my skin, my flesh, and my life is flowing out through those wounds, I'm slowly bleeding to death, so many wounds, there's nothing I can do, so many, he's done for me." And then I, too, thought: "But he couldn't have thought any of that. Or perhaps he could, in very concentrated form."

"I'M IN NO POSITION to give advice to anyone," I said to Luisa, ending my prolonged silence, "but it seems to me that you really shouldn't think so much about what went through his head during those moments. After all, they were very brief moments and, in the context of his whole life, almost non-existent; perhaps he didn't have time to think anything. It doesn't make sense that, for you, on the other hand, they should have lasted all these months and will perhaps last still longer, what do you gain from that? What does he gain? Nothing. However often you go over and over it in your head, there's no way you could have accompanied him during those moments or died with him or taken his place or saved him. You weren't there, you knew nothing about it, and however hard you try, you can't change that."—I realized that I was the one who had spent most time over those borrowed thoughts, albeit incited or infected by her; it's very risky imagining yourself into someone else's mind, it's sometimes hard to leave, I suppose that's why so few people do it and why almost everyone avoids it, preferring to say: "That's not happening to me, I'm not having to live through what he's living through, and why on earth should I take on his sufferings? He's the one having a rough time of it, so to each his own."—"Whatever the truth of the matter, it's over, it no longer is and no longer counts. He's no longer thinking those thoughts and it's no longer happening."

Luisa refilled her glass—they were very small glasses—and put her hands to her cheeks, a gesture that was part thoughtful, part pained. She had long, strong hands, adorned only by her wedding ring. With her elbows resting on her thighs, she seemed to shrink or diminish. She spoke as if to herself, as though thinking out loud.

"Yes, that's what most people believe. That what has ceased to happen is not as bad as what is happening, and that we should find relief in that cessation. That what has happened should hurt us less than what is happening, or that things are somehow more bearable when they're over, however horrible they might have been. But that's like believing that it's less serious for someone to be dead than dying, which doesn't really make much sense, does it? The most painful and irremediable thing is that the person has died; and the fact that the death is over and done with doesn't mean that the person didn't experience it. How can one possibly not think about it, if that was the last thing the dead person shared with us, with those of us who are still alive? What came after that moment is beyond our grasp, but, on the other hand, when it took place, we were all still here, in the same dimension, him and us, breathing the same air. We shared the same time and the same world. Am I making any sense?" She paused and lit a cigarette, her first; the pack of cigarettes had been beside her since the start of our conversation, but she hadn't lit one until then, as though she had lost the habit of smoking, perhaps she had given up for a while and had now gone back to it or maybe only half-heartedly: she bought them, but tried to avoid them. "Besides, nothing ends entirely, I mean, think of dreams; the dead appear in them alive and sometimes the living die in them. I often dream about that final moment, and then I really am present, I really am there, I really do know what he's feeling, I'm in the car with him and we both get out, and I warn him because I know what's going to happen and even then he can't escape. Well, that's what dreams are like, simultaneously confusing and precise. I shake them off as soon as I wake up, and in a matter of minutes they're gone, I forget the details; but I immediately realize that the fact remains, the fact that it's true, that it happened, that Miguel is dead and was killed in a very similar way to what happened in my dream, however quickly the dream vanished." She stopped and stubbed out her half-smoked cigarette, as if she found it odd to be holding it between her fingers. "Do you know what one of the worst things is? Not being able to get angry or to blame anyone. Not being able to hate anyone even though Miguel suffered a violent death, even though he was murdered in the street. It's not as if he'd been murdered for a reason, because someone was after him and knew who he was, because someone saw him as an obstacle and wanted revenge or whatever, or at least intended to rob him. If he'd been a victim of ETA, I could join with the families of other victims and together we could hate the terrorists or even hate all Basques, and the more you can share hatred, share it out, the better, don't you agree? The more the merrier. I remember that when I was very young, a boyfriend of mine left me for a girl from the Canary Islands. I not only hated her, I hated all Canary Islanders. Ridiculous, I know, an obsession, if you like. If they showed a match on TV in which Tenerife or Las Palmas were playing, I would hope they would lose regardless of who their opponents were, not that I particularly care about football and even if I wasn't the one watching it, but my father and my brother. If there was one of those idiotic beauty contests on, I would always hope that the girls from the Canaries didn't win, and would throw a tantrum if they did, which was often the case, because they tend to be very pretty." And she laughed gaily at herself, she couldn't help it. If something amused her, it amused her, even in the midst of her grief. "I even vowed never to read Galdós again; however much of a denizen of Madrid he became, he was still born in the Canaries, and so I imposed a complete ban on him, which lasted for

ages." And she laughed again, and her laughter was so contagious
that I laughed too at such an inquisitorial idea. "Such reactions are
childish and irrational, I know, but they help momentarily by vary-
ing your mood. Anyway, I'm not young any more and I don't even
have the option of spending part of the day feeling furious, instead
of feeling sad all the time."

"What about the man who killed Miguel?" I asked. "Can't you
hate him or hate all down-and-outs?"

"No," she said, without a moment's hesitation, as if she had
already considered the question. "I don't want to know anything
more about the man, I understand he refused to make a statement,
and that, from the start, he opted to remain silent, but it's obvious
that he made a mistake and is not right in the head. Apparently, two
of his daughters are prostitutes, and he decided that Miguel and
Pablo, the chauffeur, were in some way responsible for that. How
stupid. He killed Miguel just as he might have killed Pablo or anyone else from the area whom he happened to have a grudge against.
I suppose *he* needed enemies too, someone to blame for his misfortune. It's what everyone does: the working classes, the middle
and upper classes and the socially mobile: we just can't accept that
sometimes things happen for which no one is to blame, or that there
is such a thing as bad luck, or that people go off the rails, lose their
way, and bring unhappiness and ruin upon themselves."—"You
yourself have shaped your own fate," I thought, quoting Cervantes,
whose words, it's true, are no longer heeded.—"No, I can't get
angry with the person who killed him like that for no reason, with
the person who, if you like, chose him entirely by chance; that's the
worst thing; with someone who's mad, mentally unhinged, someone
who felt no animus against him personally and didn't even know his
name, who simply saw him as the embodiment of his misfortune or
the cause of his own painful situation. Well, I've no idea what he

saw, of course, I'm not inside his head and I don't want to be. Sometimes my brother tries to talk to me about it, as does the lawyer, or Javier, one of Miguel's best friends, but I stop them and tell them that I don't want to hear their more or less hypothetical explanations or their half-baked theories, because what happened was so serious that the reason why it happened really doesn't matter to me, especially when the reason is utterly incomprehensible and exists only inside that sick, crazed mind into which I prefer not to venture." Luisa spoke well, using a wide vocabulary, words like "animus" and "venture" that crop up rarely in general conversation; after all, she was, as she had told me, a university lecturer in English, and, as a language teacher, she would, inevitably, have to read and translate a lot. "To exaggerate slightly, that man has the same value to me as a bit of plaster cornice that breaks off and falls on your head just as you're walking by underneath; you could so easily not have passed by at that particular moment; a minute earlier and you would have known nothing about it. Or like a stray bullet from a hunting party, fired by some inexperienced hunter or by a fool; you could so easily not have gone into the countryside that day. Or like an earthquake you get caught up in while on a trip abroad; you could so easily not have gone to that place. No, hating him serves no purpose, it doesn't console or give me strength, I take no comfort from waiting for him to be sentenced or hoping that he rots in prison. Not that I feel sorry for him either, of course; I can't. He's a matter of complete indifference to me, because nothing and no one will bring Miguel back. I imagine he'll be sent to some psychiatric hospital, if such things still exist, I don't know what they do now with the mentally ill who commit violent crimes. I suppose they put them out of circulation because they constitute a danger to society and so as to prevent them committing a similar crime again. But I don't seek his punishment, that would be as stupid as the kind of thing armies used to do—in more naive times—arresting and even executing a horse that had thrown an officer and brought about his death. Nor can I take it out on beggars and homeless people in general, although I do feel afraid of them now. When I see one, I tend to move away or cross the road, a perfectly justifiable reflex action that will stay with me for ever. But that's different. What I can't do is actively devote myself to hating them, as I could hate a group of rival businessmen, say, who had hired a hit man to kill him, apparently that's becoming increasingly common, even in Spain, flying in a murderer from another country, a Colombian, a Serbian, a Mexican, to get rid of an overly successful competitor who's cramping their style, in other words, a simple business arrangement. They bring in a hit man, he does his job, they pay him and he leaves, all in the space of one or two days, and the police never find these killers, they're discreet and professional, entirely neutral, leaving no trace, and by the time the body is found, they're already at the airport or on the return flight home. There's rarely any way of proving anything, still less who hired the killer, who instigated the murder or gave the order. If something like that had happened, I couldn't even hate that abstract hit man very much, he just drew the short straw, and it could have been someone else, whoever happened to be free at the time; he wouldn't have known Miguel or had anything against him personally. But I could hate the instigators, that would give me the chance to suspect people right, left and centre, a competitor or someone who felt resentful or hard done by, because every businessman creates victims either accidentally or deliberately, even among close colleagues, as I read again the other day in Covarrubias." Luisa saw my look of vague incomprehension. "Don't you know it? *Tesoro de la lengua castellana o española*. It was the first Spanish dictionary, written in 1611 by Sebastián de Covarrubias." She got to her feet, picked up a fat green book from a nearby table, and began leafing through it. "I had to look up the word '*envidia*' to compare it with the English definition of 'envy,' and this is how the entry ends." And she read out loud to me. "'Unfortunately, this poison is often engendered in the breasts of those who are and who we believe to be our closest friends, in whom we trust; they are far more dangerous than our declared enemies.' And that's obviously a very old idea, because look what it goes on to say: 'This is a commonplace, written about by many; but since it is not my intention to dig over ground others have already dug, I have nothing to add.'" And then she closed the book and sat down again, with the book on her lap; I noticed that various pages were marked by bits of paper. "My mind would have something else to occupy it then, rather than just grief and longing. Because I miss him all the time, you see. I miss him when I wake up and when I go to bed and when I dream and throughout the whole of the intervening day, it's as if I carried him with me all the time, as if he were part of my body." She looked at her arms, as though her husband's head were resting on them. "People say: 'Concentrate on the good memories and not on the final one, think about how much you loved each other, think about all the wonderful times you enjoyed that others never have.' They mean well, but they don't understand that all my memories are now soiled by that sad and bloody ending. Each time I recall something good, that final image rises up before me, the image of his cruel, stupid, gratuitous death, which could so easily have been avoided. Yes, that's what I find hardest to bear, the sheer stupidity of it and the lack of someone to blame. And so every good memory grows murky and turns bad. I don't really have any good memories left. They all seem false to me. They've all been contaminated."

SHE FELL SILENT and looked over at the adjoining room where the children were. The television was on in the background, so it seemed that everything was fine. From what I'd seen of them, they were well-brought-up kids, far more so than children usually are nowadays. Curiously, I didn't find it surprising or embarrassing that Luisa should speak to me so openly, as if I were a friend. Perhaps she couldn't talk about anything else, and in the intervening months since Deverne's death, she had exhausted all those closest to her with her shock and her anxieties, or she felt awkward about going on and on at them, always harping on about the same thing, and was taking advantage of the novelty of my presence there to vent her feelings. Perhaps it didn't matter who I was, it was enough that I was there, an as yet unused interlocutor, with whom she could start afresh. That's another of the problems when one suffers a misfortune: the effects on the victim far outlast the patience of those prepared to listen and accompany her, unconditional support never lasts very long once it has become tinged with monotony. And so, sooner or later, the grieving person is left alone when she has still not finished grieving or when she's no longer allowed to talk about what remains her only world, because other people find that world of grief unbearable, repellent. She understands that for them sadness has a social expiry date, that no one is capable of contemplating another's sorrow, that such a spectacle is tolerable only for a brief period, for as long as the shock and pain last and there is still some role for those who are there watching, who then feel necessary, salvatory, useful. But on discovering that nothing changes and that the affected person neither progresses nor emerges from her grief, they feel humiliated and superfluous, they find it almost offensive and stand aside: "Aren't I enough for you? Why can't you climb out of that pit with me by your side? Why are you still grieving when time has passed and I've been here all the while to console and distract you? If you can't climb out, then sink or disappear." And the grieving person does just that, she retreats, removes herself, hides. Perhaps Luisa clung to me that afternoon because with me she could be what she still was, with no need for subterfuge: the inconsolable widow, to use the usual phrase. Obsessed, boring, grief-stricken.

I looked across at the children's room, indicating it with a lift of my head.

"They must be a great help to you in the circumstances," I said. "I imagine having to look after them must give you a reason to get up every morning, to be strong and put on a brave face. Knowing that they depend on you entirely, even more than before. They're doubtless a burden, but a lifeline too, a reason to start each day. Or perhaps not," I added, when I saw her face grow still darker and her larger eye contract, so that it was the same size as the smaller one.

"No, it's quite the opposite," she replied, taking a deep breath, as if she had to muster all her serenity in order to say what she then went on to say: "I would give anything for them not to be here now, not to have them. Don't misunderstand me: it's not that I suddenly regret having had them, their existence is vital to me and they're what I love most, more even than Miguel probably, or, rather, I realize that their loss would have been far worse, the loss of either of them, it would have killed me. But I just can't cope with them at the moment, they weigh too much on me. I wish I could put them in parentheses or into hibernation, I don't know, send them to sleep and not wake them up until further notice. I'd like them to leave me in peace and not ask or demand anything of me, not keep tugging at me and hanging on me, poor loves. I need to be alone, without responsibilities, and not to have to make a superhuman effort of which I feel incapable, not to have to worry if they've eaten or are well wrapped up or if they've got a cold or a fever. I'd like to stay in bed all day or do what I like without having to concern myself about anything except me, and just get better gradually, with no interruptions and no obligations. If, that is, I ever do get better, I hope I do, although I don't see how. It's just that I feel so debilitated that the last thing I need is to have by my side two even weaker people, who can't cope on their own and who have even less of an understanding of what happened than I do. More than that, I feel so sad for them, so unalterably, constantly sad for them, and that feeling goes beyond the present circumstances. The circumstances simply accentuate that feeling, but it's always been there."

"What do you mean, 'constantly'? What do you mean, 'beyond the present circumstances'? What do you mean by 'always'?"

"Do you not have any children?" she asked. I shook my head. "Children bring a lot of joy and all the other things people say they bring, but you can't help but feel permanently sad for them too, and I don't think that changes even when they're older, although rather fewer people mention that. You see your children's bewilderment when they're confronted by certain situations, and that makes you sad. You see their willingness to help, when they want to contribute and do their bit and they can't, and that makes you sad too. Their seriousness makes you sad, as do their silly jokes and their transparent lies, their expectations and their minor disappointments, their innocence, their incomprehension, their very logical questions, and even their occasional bad idea. It makes you sad to think how much they have to learn, and about the long, long road that lies ahead and which no one can travel for them, even though we've spent centuries doing it and can't understand why everyone who's born has to start all over from the beginning. What sense does it make that each person should have to experience more or less the same griefs and make more or less the same discoveries, and so on for eternity? And of course something completely out of the ordinary has happened to them, something that needn't have happened, a great, unforeseeable misfortune. It isn't normal in our society for one's father to be killed, and the sadness they feel is an added sadness for me. I'm not the only one who has suffered a loss, if only I was. It's up to me to explain it to them, and I haven't got an explanation. It's quite beyond my capabilities. I can't tell them that the man hated their father or that he was his enemy, and if I tell them that he was mad, mad enough to kill their father, they can't really understand that either, well, Carolina can sort of grasp it, but not Nicolás."

"So what have you told them? How are they coping?"

"Well, I told them a slightly modified version of the truth. I wasn't sure whether I should say anything to Nicolás, with him being so young, but people said it would be worse if he heard it from his school friends. Because it came out in the press, everyone who knows us found out straight away, and you can imagine what four-year-olds might make of it, their versions could be even more gruesome and outrageous than reality. So I told them that the man was very angry because someone had taken his daughters away, and that he got muddled up and attacked their papa instead of the person who had stolen his daughters. Then, of course, they asked me *who* had stolen the daughters and I said I didn't know, and that the man obviously didn't know either, which was why he was so angry and in need of someone he could take it out on. That he couldn't really tell people apart and was suspicious of everyone, which was why he hit Pablo one day, believing that he was the one to blame. It's odd, they grasped that at once, that he should get angry because someone had stolen his daughters, and even now they sometimes ask me if there's any news of them or if they've been found, as if it were an ongoing story, I suppose they think the daughters were children like them. I said it was simply a case of bad luck. That it was like an accident, like when a car hits a pedestrian or a builder falls off the building he's working on. That their father wasn't to blame and that he hadn't harmed anyone. Nicolás asked me if he was ever coming back. And I said no, that he'd gone very far away, like when he used to go on trips only much further, so far away that he couldn't return, but from where he was he could still see them and still care for them. It also occurred to me to tell them, so that it wasn't quite so sudden and definitive, that I could speak to him now and then, and that if they wanted anything from him, anything important, they should tell me and I would pass it on. I don't think Carolina believed that bit, because she never gives me any message for him, but Nicolás does and sometimes asks me to tell his father something, some silly little thing that's happened at school but which looms very large for him, and the following day, he asks me if I told his father and what he said, or if he was pleased to know that he'd started playing football. And I tell him that I haven't had a chance to speak to him just yet, that he'll have to wait, that it's not always easy to make contact, then I let a few days pass, and if he remembers and asks again, then I invent an answer. I'll let more and more time pass until he stops asking and forgets about it, and he will in the end. He'll mostly think he's remembering what his sister and I tell him. Carolina is more of a worry. She hardly mentions it at all, she's more serious and more silent than she used to be, and when, for example, I tell Nicolás that their father laughed when I told him what he'd said or that he told me to tell Nicolás to kick the ball and not the other boys, she looks at me with the same sadness I feel for them, as if my lies saddened her, and so there are moments when we feel sad for each other, I feel sad for them and they for me, well, Carolina does anyway. They see that I'm sad, they see me in a state they've never seen me in before, even though, believe me, I try very hard not to cry and to make sure when I'm with them that they don't notice how sad I am. But I'm sure they do. I've only cried once in their presence." I remembered the impression the little girl had made on me when I saw the three of them that morning at the café: how attentive she was to her mother, almost watching over her, insofar as that was possible; and the way she had briefly stroked her mother's cheek when she said goodbye. "And they're afraid for me," added Luisa, with a sigh, pouring herself another glass. She hadn't drunk anything for a while, she had slowed down, perhaps she was one of those people who know when to stop or who are even moderate in their excesses, who skirt round dangers and never fall into them, even when they feel they have nothing to lose and are beyond caring. She was clearly in desperate straits, but I couldn't imagine her in a state of wild abandon: getting hopelessly drunk or hooked on drugs or neglecting her children or missing work or (later on) going with one man after another in order to forget the person who really mattered to her; it was as if she possessed a last resort of common sense, or a sense of duty or serenity or self-preservation or pragmatism, I wasn't quite sure which. And then I saw it very clearly: "She'll get over this," I thought, "she'll recover sooner than she thinks, everything she's been through during these months will seem quite unreal, and she'll get married again, perhaps to someone as perfect as Desvern, or someone with whom she will, at least, make a similarly perfect or almost perfect couple."—"They've discovered that people die, that even the people who seemed most indestructible, their parents, die. It's not just a bad dream, because Carolina has reached the age of having nightmares, you see: she dreamed once that I was dying or that her father was dying, and that was before all this happened. She called to us from her bedroom in the middle of the night, she was really frightened, and we had to convince her that we wouldn't die, that such a thing was impossible. She's seen now that we were wrong or were perhaps lying to her; that she was right to be afraid, that what she saw in her dreams has come to pass. She hasn't ever reproached me with this directly, but the day after Miguel was buried and there was clearly no going back and the only thing to do was to continue living without him, she said to me twice, as if what she was saying were unimpeachable: 'You see? You see?' And I asked her uncomprehendingly: 'What is it I should see, sweetheart?' I was still too dazed to understand. Then she retreated and has continued to do so ever since: 'Oh, nothing,' she said, 'just that Papa won't be at home with us any more, don't you see?' All my strength went from me, and I sat down on the edge of the bed, we were in my bedroom. 'Of course I see that, my love,' I said and burst into tears. She hadn't seen me cry before and she felt sorry for me, and she still does now. She came over to me and started drying my tears with her dress. As for Nicolás, he's discovered death too soon, without even being able to dream about it or fear it, when he still had no awareness of death, I'm not sure he even knows quite what it is, although he's starting to realize that it means people cease to exist, that you won't ever see them again. And given that their father has died and disappeared from one day to the next, or, worse, that their father has been killed and ceased to exist suddenly and without warning, that he proved fragile enough to be felled by some wretch's first blow, they're bound to think that the same thing could happen to me some day, because they see me as being the weaker of the two. Yes, they're afraid for me, afraid that something bad might happen to me and that I'll leave them all alone, they look at me apprehensively, as if I were more vulnerable and at risk than they are. It's an instinctive reaction in Nicolás, but in Carolina it's more conscious. I notice that she's always looking around when we're out in the street and immediately goes on the alert whenever she spots a stranger or, rather, a strange man. She's happier when I'm accompanied by some of my female friends. She's all right now, because I'm at home and with you, she's stopped finding pretexts to keep coming in here and checking on me or bothering me. She's only just met you, but she trusts you, you're a woman, and she doesn't see you as a danger. On the contrary, she sees you as a shield, a defence. That worries me a little, that she should become afraid of men, be on her guard and feel nervous in their company, the ones she doesn't know, of course. I hope it will pass, she can't go through life in fear of half the human race."

"Do they know how exactly their father died?" I hesitated, unsure whether to bring it up again. "About the knife, I mean."

"No, I've never gone into detail, I just told them that he'd been attacked by that man, but never explained how. But Carolina must know, I'm sure she's read about it in some newspaper and that her friends will have talked about it, well, they're bound to be shocked. She must have found the idea so horrifying that she's never asked me or referred to it. It's as if we had a tacit agreement not to discuss it, not to think about it, to erase that element from Miguel's death (the key element, the one that caused his death), so that it can remain an isolated, neutral fact. Besides, that's what everyone does with their dead. We try to forget the how and keep only the image of the person when alive or, possibly, when dead, but we avoid thinking about the frontier, the crossing, the actual process of dying, the cause. They're alive one moment and dead the next, and in between there is nothing, as if they passed without transition or reason from one state to the other. But I can't not think about it, not yet, and that's what stops me living or prevents me from beginning to recover, always assuming one can recover from something like this."—"You will, you will," I thought again, "and much sooner than you think. And that's what I wish for you, poor Luisa, with all my heart."—"I can do it with Carolina, because that's what's best for her and that's all I want. When I'm alone, though, I find it impossible, especially around this time of evening, when it's neither day nor night. I think of that knife going in, what Miguel must have felt, and whether he had time to think anything, if he realized that he was dying. Then I despair and I feel positively ill. And that's not just a manner of speaking: I really do feel ill. My whole body hurts."

THE DOORBELL RANG and even though I had no idea who it was, I knew that our conversation and my visit were over. Luisa had asked nothing about me, she hadn't even gone back to the questions she had asked at the café that morning, what I did and what nickname I had given to her and Deverne when I used to watch them during our shared breakfasts. She wasn't yet ready to be curious about others, she was in no state to take an interest in anyone or to probe other people's lives, her own life was all-consuming and took all her energy and concentration, and doubtless all her imagination too. I was merely an ear into which she could pour her unhappiness and her persistent thoughts, a virgin but interchangeable ear, or perhaps not entirely interchangeable: as with her little girl, I obviously inspired both her confidence and her familiarity, and she would not perhaps have confided in just anyone in quite the same way. After all, I had often seen her husband and could, therefore, put a name to her loss, I knew the absence that was the cause of her desolation, the figure that had disappeared from her field of vision, day after day after day and so on monotonously and irremediably until the end. In a way, I belonged to the "before" and was capable of missing the departed in my own way, even though they had always ignored me, and Desvern would now be obliged to do so for all eternity, I had arrived too late for him and would never be more than the Prudent Young Woman whom he had barely noticed and then only glancingly. "And yet," I thought with some surprise, "I'm only here because of his death. If he hadn't died, I wouldn't be in his house, because, after all, this was his house, he lived here, and this was his living room and I am perhaps sitting where he used to sit; he left here on the last morning I saw him alive, which was also the last morning his wife saw him alive." It was clear that she liked me and could tell that I was on her side, that I felt sympathetic to and saddened by her loss; she might think vaguely that, in other circumstances, we could have been friends. But now she was inside a bubble, talkative but basically isolated and indifferent to everything outside her, and that bubble would take a long time to burst. Only then would she be able to see me properly, only then would I cease to be the Prudent Young Woman from the café. If I had asked her what my name was, she would probably not have remembered, or perhaps only my first name, but not my surname. I didn't even know if we would meet again, if there would be another occasion: when I left there, I would be lost in a mist.

She didn't wait for one of the servants to answer, because there was at least one maid, who had answered when I arrived. She got up and went over to the door and picked up the entryphone. I heard her say "Hello" and then "Hi. I'll open the door for you." It was obviously someone she knew well, someone she was expecting or who dropped by every day at about that time, because there wasn't a hint of surprise or excitement in her voice, he could even have been the boy from the grocer's delivering some shopping. She waited with the door open for the person to cross the small stretch of garden that separated the street door from the house itself; she lived in a detached house, there are various such developments in central parts of Madrid, not just in El Viso, but behind Paseo de la Castellana and in Fuente del Berro and other places, miraculously hidden away from the appalling traffic and the perpetual generalized chaos. I realized then that she hadn't actually talked to me about Deverne either. She hadn't spoken about him at all or described his character or his manner, she hadn't said how much she missed a particular trait of his or something they used to do together, or how dreadful it was that he was no longer alive, adding, for example, particularly someone who had enjoyed life so much, which had been my impression of him. I realized that I knew no more about that man than when I had arrived. It was as if his anomalous death had darkened or erased everything else, which happens sometimes: the way a person's life ends can be so unexpected or so painful, so striking or so premature or so tragic—occasionally even picturesque or ridiculous or sinister—that it becomes impossible to speak of that person without him being instantly swallowed up or contaminated by that ending, without the dramatic manner of his death blackening the whole of his previous existence and, even more unfairly, stealing that existence from him. The spectacular death so dominates the person who died that it becomes very difficult to recall him without that ultimate annihilating fact immediately hovering over one's recollection, or even to remember how he was during the long years when no one suspected that the heavy curtain would fall on him so abruptly. Everything is seen in the light of that denouement, or rather the light of that denouement is so blindingly bright that it prevents us recovering what went before and being able to smile at the reminiscence or fantasy; you could say that those who die such a death die more deeply, more completely, or perhaps they die twice over, in reality and in the memory of others, because their memory is forever lost in the glare of that stupid culminating event, is soured and distorted and also perhaps poisoned.

It might also be that Luisa was still in the phase of extreme egotism, that is, capable of seeing only her own misfortune and not so much Desvern's, despite the concern she expressed for his final moments, which he must have known were his last. The world belongs so much to the living and so little to the dead—although it may well be that they all remain on earth and are, doubtless, far more numerous—that the former tend to think that the death of a loved one is something that has happened more to them than to the deceased, who is, after all, the person who has died. He is the one who has had to say goodbye, almost always against his will, he is the one who has lost everything that was to come (the person, for example, in the case of Deverne, who will not see his children grow up or change), who has had to renounce his desire to know and his curiosity, who left plans unfulfilled and words unspoken, thinking that there would always be time later on, he is the one who will not be there; if he was an artist, he is the one who will be unable to finish a book or a film or a painting or a composition, or if he was only the recipient of those, the one who won't be able to finish reading the first or seeing the second or listening to the fourth. You only have to glance around the room of the person who has vanished to comprehend how much was interrupted and left hanging, how much becomes, in that instant, unusable and useless; yes, the novel with the page turned down, which will remain unread, but also the medicines that have suddenly become utterly superfluous and that will soon have to be thrown away, or the special pillow or mattress on which head and body will no longer lie; the glass of water from which he will never take another sip, and the forbidden pack of cigarettes of which only three are left, and the sweets someone bought for him and which no one will dare to finish, as if doing so were an act of theft or profanation; the glasses that will be of no use to anyone and the expectant clothes that will stay hanging in his wardrobe for days or years, until someone gathers enough courage to remove them; the plants that the disappeared person lovingly cared for and watered, and which no one will perhaps want to take on, and the person's soft fingerprints still there in the skin cream applied each night;

someone will doubtless want to inherit and take away the telescope with which the departed used to amuse himself watching the storks nesting on a distant tower, but what they will use it for, who knows, and the window through which he gazed during a pause in his work will be left sightless, with no one to look through it; the diary in which he noted down his appointments and his daily tasks will not move on to the next page, and the last day will lack the final annotation that used to mean: "I've done what I had to do today." All those speaking objects have been left dumb and meaningless, as if a blanket had been thrown over them to silence and soothe them, making them think that night has come, or as if they, too, regretted the loss of their owner and had withdrawn instantaneously, strangely aware that they had become redundant, futile, and were thinking: "What will we do here now? We'll be taken away. We have no master now. All that awaits us is exile or the rubbish bin. Our mission is over." Perhaps that is how Desvern's things had felt months before. Luisa, though, was not a thing. Luisa, therefore, would not have thought that.

I HAD ASSUMED she meant "you" in the singular, but two people arrived. I heard the voice of the first person, the one she had said hello to, announcing the second person, who was obviously not expected: "Hi, I've brought Professor Rico with me so as not to leave him hanging around out there in the street. He's kicking his heels until supper. The restaurant's somewhere near here and there isn't time for him to go back to his hotel first. You don't mind, do you?" And then he introduced them: "Professor Francisco Rico, Luisa Alday." "Of course I don't mind, it's an honour," I heard Luisa say. "I have another visitor with me, but come in, come in. Would you like a drink?"

I knew Professor Rico's face well, he often appears on television and in the press, with his wide, expressive mouth, immaculate bald head, which he carries off with great aplomb, his rather large glasses, his casual elegance—slightly English, slightly Italian—his disdainful way of speaking and his half-indolent, half-scathing manner, which is perhaps a way of concealing the underlying melancholia evident in his eyes, as if, already feeling himself to be a man of the past, he hates having to deal with his contemporaries, most of whom are ignorant, trivial individuals, and, at the same time, feels a twinge of anticipatory regret that, one day, he will be obliged to cease dealing with them—dealing with them must also, in a way, be a relief—when his sense that he is a man of the past finally becomes a reality. The first thing he did was to refute what his companion had said:

"Now look here, Díaz-Varela, I am never to be found 'hanging around,' as you put it, even when I find myself out in the street without knowing what to do—quite a frequent occurrence as it happens. I often sally forth in Sant Cugat, where I live," and he directed this explanation, with an accompanying oblique glance, at Luisa and at me, to whom he had not yet been introduced, "and I suddenly realize that I have no idea why I came out. Or I go into Barcelona and, once there, I can't for the life of me remember the reason for my trip. Then I stand still for a while—I don't wander around or pace up and down—until I can recall the purpose of my visit. Anyway, even on those occasions, I could not be said to be 'hanging around,' indeed, I am one of the few people capable of standing in the street motionless and bewildered without actually giving that impression. Rather, the impression I give is of being very focused, let's say, on the verge of making some crucial discovery or of putting the finishing touches in my head to a complicated sonnet. If some acquaintance spots me in these circumstances, he would never venture to say so much as a 'Hello,' even though I'm standing alone, stock-still in the middle of the pavement (I never lean against the wall, that would look as if I'd been stood up), for fear of interrupting some demanding line of reasoning or a moment of deep meditation. Nor am I ever at risk of being mugged, because my stern, absorbed appearance dissuades all malefactors. They can tell I am a man whose intellectual faculties are on full alert and fully functioning (or 'working flat out,' to use a more colloquial expression), and they wouldn't dare pick a fight with me. They can see that it would prove dangerous to them, that I would react with a rare violence and speed. I rest my case."

Luisa couldn't help but laugh, and nor, I believe, could I. The fact that she could switch so rapidly from being immersed in the anxious thoughts she had been telling me about to being amused by someone she had only just met made me think again that she had an enormous capacity for enjoyment and—how can I put it—for being ordinarily and momentarily happy. Some people are like that, not many, it's true, people who grow impatient and bored with unhappiness and in whom it rarely lasts very long, even though, for a while, it could be said to have taken a terrible toll on them. From what I had seen of him, Desvern must have been the same, and it occurred to me that had Luisa been the one to die and he the one to survive, it was likely that he would have had a similar reaction to his wife's now. ("If he were still alive and a widower, I would not be here," I thought.) Yes, there are people who cannot bear misfortune. Not because they're frivolous or empty-headed. They're not, of course, immune to grief, and they doubtless experience grief as intensely as anyone else. But they're designed to shake it off more quickly and without too much difficulty, as if they were simply incompatible with such states of mind. It's in their nature to be light-hearted and cheerful and they see no particular prestige in suffering, unlike most of the rest of boring humanity, and our own nature always catches up with us, because almost nothing can break or distort it. Maybe Luisa was a simple mechanism: she cried when something made her cry and laughed when something made her laugh, and one emotion could follow seamlessly on from the other, she was simply responding to a stimulus. Not that simplicity is necessarily at odds with intelligence. I knew she was intelligent. Her lack of malice and her ready laughter did not diminish that fact in the slightest, for these are things that depend not on intelligence, but on character, which belongs in another category and another sphere.

Professor Rico was wearing a charming Nazi-green jacket and an ivory-coloured shirt; his nonchalantly knotted tie was a brighter, more luminous green—melon-green perhaps. He was extremely well coordinated without, however, seeming to have put much thought into that excellent combination of colours, apart from the clover-green handkerchief protruding from his breast pocket, which was, perhaps, a green too far.

"But I thought you were mugged once, Professor, here in Madrid," protested the man called Díaz-Varela. "It was years ago now, but I remember it well. In the Gran Vía, it was, after you'd drawn some money from a cashpoint, isn't that right?"

The Professor did not care to be reminded of this. He took out a cigarette and lit it, as if doing so without first asking permission were as normal today as it was forty years ago. Luisa immediately handed him an ashtray, which he took with his other hand. Then, with both hands occupied, he spread his arms wide and said, like an orator exasperated by lies or stupidity:

"That was completely different. Not the same thing at all."

"Why? You were in the street and the malefactor certainly didn't show you much respect."

The Professor made a condescending gesture with the hand holding the cigarette, which he then dropped. He looked at it where it lay on the floor with a mixture of displeasure and curiosity, as if it were a live cockroach that had nothing to do with him, and he was waiting for someone else to pick it up or stamp on it or kick it out of sight. When none of us gave any sign of bending down, he again produced his pack of cigarettes and took out another. It didn't seem to bother him that the fallen cigarette might burn the wooden floor; he must have been one of those men who doesn't really notice such things and leaves it to others to sort out any awkwardnesses or imperfections. This is not because they are thoughtless or because they consider themselves too high and mighty, it's simply that their brains don't register these practicalities or the world around them. Luisa's children had looked up when they heard the doorbell and had now sneaked into the living room to observe the visitors. It was the boy who ran to pick up the cigarette, but his mother, pre-empting him, picked it up and stubbed it out in the ashtray she had been using before, for her equally unfinished cigarettes. Rico lit his second cigarette and gave his reply. Neither he nor Díaz-Varela seemed prepared to interrupt their discussion, and having them there was like being at the theatre, as if two actors had strolled on to the stage talking and ignoring the audience, as was their professional duty.

"First: I had my back to the street, in the undignified position forced on one by all cashpoints, namely, with my face to the wall, and so my normally dissuasive gaze was invisible to the mugger. Second: I was busy tapping in my answers to all those tedious questions they ask you. Third: when asked in what language I wished to communicate with the machine, I had answered 'Italian' (a habit born of my many visits to Italy, where I spend half my life) and I was distracted by all the crass spelling and grammatical errors appearing on the screen, the thing had obviously been programmed by some fraud with very dodgy Italian. Fourth: I had been on the go all day with various people and had had no option but to have a few drinks here and there in different places; I am not my usual alert self when tired and a little tipsy—well, who is? Fifth: I was late for an appointment which was already very late in the day and I was feeling disoriented and harassed and worried that the person waiting impatiently for me would give up and leave the place where we had agreed to meet (I'd already had a hard job persuading her to prolong her night in order that we might see each other alone), only that we might converse, you understand. Sixth: for all the above reasons, the first indication that I was about to be mugged came when I noticed, with my money in my hand, but not yet in my pocket, the point of a knife being pressed against my lumbar region, it even penetrated a little: when, at the end of the night, I got undressed in the hotel, there was a tiny spot of blood here. Just here."—And lifting up the tails of his jacket, he quickly touched some point immediately above his belt, so quickly that I doubt if any of those present could have said precisely where.—"You have to have experienced that slight pricking, there or in any other vital zone—aware that your attacker would only have to press a little harder for that point to enter the flesh unopposed—to know you have no alternative but to give them whatever it is they want, and all the fellow said was: 'Give us your money.' Oddly enough, you feel an unbearable tingling in your groin, which then spreads throughout the body. But the origin of that sensation is not in the part of your body under threat, but here. Just here."—And he indicated the two sides of his groin with his two middle fingers.—"Not, you will notice, in the balls, but in the groin, which is quite a different matter, although people sometimes get confused and describe some frightening event as being 'ball-shrivelling' or say 'my heart leapt into my mouth or throat' "—and he touched his throat with index finger and thumb—"but that's only because the sensation spreads outwards and upwards from the groin. Anyway, as everyone has known since the weak wheel of the world first began to turn, given the nature of such an ambush or treacherous attack, there is no preventive action to be taken or, indeed, defence. I rest my case. Or would you like me to continue my enumeration? I can easily keep going at least as far as ten."—When Díaz-Varela did not respond, Rico assumed he had won the argument by sheer force of logic and, looking around him for the first time, he noticed me, the children and Luisa too, in a way, even though she had already been introduced to him. I think he really hadn't properly taken us in before, otherwise he would, I think, have refrained from using the word "balls," mainly because of the children.—"Now who have we here?" he asked without the slightest hint of embarrassment.

I noticed that Díaz-Varela had suddenly gone very silent and serious, and for precisely the same reason that Luisa had taken three steps towards the sofa and sat down on it before even inviting the two men to do so, as if her legs had given way beneath her and she could no longer remain standing. She had gone from the spontaneous laughter of a moment before to an expression of grief, her gaze clouded and her skin pale. Yes, she must have been a very simple mechanism. She raised her hand to her forehead and lowered her eyes, and I feared that she might cry. There was no reason why Professor Rico should have known that her life had been destroyed by a knife that had stabbed and stabbed, perhaps his friend hadn't told him—although that was strange, because one tends to recount other people's misfortunes almost without thinking—or if Díaz-Varela had told him, he had quite forgotten about it: he had a (considerable) reputation for retaining information only about the remote past, on which he was a world authority, and for listening to accounts of more recent events politely, but with scant attention. Any crime, any event dating from the Middle Ages or the Golden Age was of far more importance to him than what had happened the day before yesterday.

Looking concerned, Díaz-Varela went over to Luisa, took her hands in his and said softly:

"It's all right, it's all right, don't worry. I'm so sorry. It hadn't occurred to me where this nonsense might lead." And I thought I sensed in him an impulse to stroke her cheek, as one would when consoling a child for whom one would give one's very life; in the end, though, he repressed that impulse.

If his murmured comment was audible to me, it was equally so to the Professor.

"Whatever's wrong? What did I say? It wasn't the word 'balls,' was it? Well, you are a thin-skinned lot. I could have used something far worse; after all, 'balls' is a euphemism. Vulgar and graphic and overused, I agree, but a euphemism nonetheless."

"What does 'thin-skinned' mean? What are 'balls'?" asked the little boy, who had noticed the Professor's gesture of pointing towards his groin. Fortunately, everyone ignored him and his question went unanswered.

Luisa recovered at once and realized that she hadn't yet introduced me. She could not, in fact, remember my surname, because although she gave the full names of the two men ("Professor Francisco Rico, Javier Díaz-Varela"), she gave only my first name, as she did with the children, and then added my nickname by way of compensation ("This is my new friend María; Miguel knew her as the Prudent Young Woman when we used to have breakfast most mornings in the same café, but today is the first time we've actually spoken"). I thought it only right that I should make up for her faulty memory ("María Dolz," I added). Javier must have been the person she had mentioned earlier, referring to him as "one of Miguel's best friends." He was, at any rate, the man I had seen that morning at the wheel of what had once been Deverne's car, the man who had picked up the children from the café, presumably to take them to school, a little later than usual. He was not, therefore, the chauffeur, as I had thought. Perhaps Luisa had felt obliged to dispense with a chauffeur; when someone is widowed, their first step is always to try to reduce expenses, it's like a reflex reaction of vulnerability and retreat, even if they've inherited a fortune. I did not, of course, know the state of her finances, although I imagined she was quite well off, but she might still have felt her situation to be precarious even if it wasn't, the whole world seems to totter after the death of someone important to us, nothing seems solid or firm, and the person most closely affected tends to wonder: "What's the point of this and why bother with that, what's the point of money or a business and all its complications, why a house and a library, why go out to work and make plans, why have children, why anything? Nothing lasts long enough because everything ends and, once it's over, it was never enough, even if it lasted a hundred years. I only had Miguel with me for a few years, so why should anything he left behind, anything that survives him, last any longer. Not even the money or the house or me or the children. We are all merely in abeyance and under threat." And there is also an impulse towards death: "I want to be where he is, and the only place where we could coincide is the past, in that place of not being but of having been. He is past, whereas I am still present. If I were also past, at least I would be the same as him in that respect, which would be something, and I would be in no position to miss him or remember him. I would be on the same level as him or in the same dimension, in the same time, and we would not be left alone in this precarious world in which everything familiar is being taken away from us. Nothing more can be taken away from us if we are not here. Nothing more can die on us if we are already dead."

HE WAS A very calm fellow, Javier Díaz-Varela, virile and hand-some. Even though he was clean-shaven, there was still a hint of beard, a slight bluish shadow, especially on his square chin, like that of a comic-book hero (depending on the angle and on the light, he had or didn't have a cleft chin). A little chest hair was visible above his shirt, which he wore with the top button undone, because, unlike Desvern, he wasn't wearing a tie, Desvern always used to wear one, but his friend was slightly younger. He had delicate features, almond eyes with a vaguely myopic or abstracted expression, rather long lashes and a full, fleshy, shapely mouth, so much so that his lips looked like those of a woman transplanted on to a man's face, it was very difficult not to notice them, I mean, not to keep staring at them, they were like a magnet for the eyes, both when speaking and when silent. It made you feel like kissing them or touching them or using your finger to trace their outline—which looked as if it had been drawn with a fine pencil—and then, with your fingertip, pressing the fleshy part, at once firm and soft. He was discreet too, allowing Professor Rico to hold forth at will without attempting to compete with him or outshine him (not that this would have been possible). He also had a sense of humour, because he knew how to play along with the Professor and act to some extent as his straight man, allow-ing him to show off before these strangers or semi-strangers, for it was clear at once that the Professor was a flirtatious man, the sort who sets his theoretical cap at a woman in almost any circumstance.

By "theoretical" I mean that his flirtatiousness lacked any real intention and was not seriously aimed at seducing anyone (certainly not
me or Luisa), he wished merely to arouse the flirtee's curiosity or, if
possible, to dazzle her, even if he was never going to see the dazzled
party again. Díaz-Varela was amused by his friend's puerile exhi-
bitionism and allowed or even encouraged him to expatiate, as if
he were unafraid of any competition or else had a definite, long-
awaited goal of his own, which he did not doubt for a moment he
would attain sooner or later, overcoming all eventualities or threats.

I didn't stay long, well, I had no part to play at that meeting,
which was improvised as far as Rico was concerned and probably customary as regards Díaz-Varela, who gave the impression
of being a habitual, almost continuous presence in that house or in
that life, that of Luisa the widow. It was the second time he had
appeared in one day, as far as I knew, and that must have been the
case almost every day, because when he arrived with Rico, the children had greeted him with a naturalness bordering on indifference,
as if they took for granted his evening visit (his "dropping by").
Of course, they had already seen him that morning, and the three
had made a brief journey together in the car. He seemed to be more
involved in Luisa's life than anyone else, more than her own family, because I knew she had at least one brother, she had mentioned
him in the same sentence as Javier and the lawyer. And it seemed
to me that this was how Luisa saw him, as an additional or adopted
brother, someone who comes and goes, enters and leaves, someone
who helps out with the children or with any other unforeseen event,
on whom you can count for almost anything and without asking first
and who you automatically go to for advice, who keeps you company without your even noticing, neither him nor his company, who
offers his help spontaneously and for free, someone who doesn't
need to phone before coming round, and who slowly, imperceptibly,

ends up sharing the whole territory and making himself indispensable. Someone whom one barely notices is there, but who would be missed immeasurably if he were to withdraw or disappear. That could happen with Díaz-Varela at any moment, because he wasn't a devoted, unconditional brother who is never going to leave for good, but a friend of her dead husband, and friendship is not transferable. Although it can sometimes be usurped. Perhaps he was one of those bosom pals of whom, in a moment of weakness or dark foreboding, one asks a favour or from whom one exacts a promise:

"If anything bad were to happen to me and I was no longer here," Deverne might have said one day, "I'm counting on you to take care of Luisa and the kids."

"What do you mean? What are you talking about? Why do you say that? You're not ill, are you?" Díaz-Varela would have replied, anxious and taken aback.

"No, I don't foresee any problems, nothing imminent or even impending, nothing concrete, my health's fine. But for those of us who think about death and pause to observe the effect it has on the living, we can't help but ask ourselves sometimes what will happen after our own death, how will it leave the people to whom we matter, how far will it affect them. I don't mean the financial side of things, that's more or less sorted out, but everything else. I imagine that the children will have a rough time of it for a while, and that Carolina's memory of me will last for the rest of her life, growing ever vaguer and more diffuse, which means that she might begin to idealize me, because we can do what we like with the vague and the diffuse and manipulate it at will, transforming it into a lost paradise, into a golden age when everything was in its proper place and no one lacked for anything. But she's too young really not to be able to let go of that eventually and to get on with her life and nurture other kinds of hopes, the hopes appropriate to each age as she reaches it.

She'll be a perfectly normal girl, with just an occasional trace of melancholy. She'll tend to take refuge in my memory whenever she experiences an upset or things turn out badly, but that's what we all do to a greater or lesser extent, seeking refuge in what once existed, but no longer does. Nevertheless, it would help her to have some living person who could take my place, insofar as that's possible, someone she could talk to. Having a father-figure close by, someone she saw often and was used to. And I can't think of anyone who could fulfil the role of substitute father better than you. I worry less about Nicolás; he's very young and is sure to forget me. But it would still be useful if you could be around to sort out his problems, because he's the kind of boy who'll attract quite a few problems. It's Luisa who will feel most lost and vulnerable. Obviously, she might marry again, but I don't think that's very likely, nor, of course, that she would remarry in haste, and the older she gets, the more difficult remarriage will become. I imagine that once she has got over her initial despair and grief, both of which last a long time, she probably couldn't be bothered with the whole process, you know, meeting someone new, giving him a potted version of her life story, allowing herself to be courted or accepting someone's advances, being encouraging and interested, showing herself in the best possible light, explaining herself and listening to the other person explaining himself, overcoming any residual distrust, getting used to someone else and having that other person get used to her, overlooking any little things she might dislike. She would find all that really tedious, well, who wouldn't? It's a tiring business, and there's inevitably something repetitious and stale about the whole process, I know I wouldn't want to go through all that at my age. It might not seem so, but it takes a lot of hard work before you can finally settle down again with someone. I find it difficult to imagine her feeling the slightest curiosity or interest, because she's not by nature restless or discontented. If she were, after some time had passed following my death, she might start to see some advantage or compensation in that loss. Without thinking of it as such, of course, but she would. Bringing one story to an end and starting over again, if you have to, isn't in the long run such a bad thing. Even if you were happy with what has just ended. I've known inconsolable widows and widowers who, for a long time, thought they would never get back on their feet again. And yet, later, once they've recovered and found another partner, they have a sense that he or she is the real one, the best one, and they're secretly glad that their former partner disappeared, leaving the field clear for this new relationship they've built. That is the awful power of the present, which crushes the past more easily as the past recedes, and falsifies it too without the past getting a chance to speak, protest, contradict or refute anything. Not to mention the husbands or wives who daren't or don't know how to leave their partner or who feel that they couldn't possibly inflict such pain on them: they secretly want the other person to die, preferring their death to having to confront the problem and find some sensible solution. It's absurd, but that's how it is: it's not that they don't wish them ill and are eager to preserve them from all ills by dint of their personal sacrifice and enforced silence (because in order to be rid of them, they *do* wish them ill—the worst and most irreversible of all ills) it's just that they aren't prepared to be the cause of those ills, they don't want to feel responsible for someone else's unhappiness, not even for the unhappiness of the person whose mere existence by their side is a torment to them, the tie that binds and which they could cut if they were brave. But, since they are not brave, they fantasize or dream about something as radical as another person's death. 'It would be an easy solution and an enormous relief,' they think, 'and I would have nothing to do with it, I wouldn't have to cause him any pain or sadness, he wouldn't have to suffer because of me, it could be an accident, a devastating illness, a misfortune in which I would play no part; on the contrary, in the eyes of the world and in my own eyes too, I would be the victim, both victim and beneficiary. And I would be free.' But Luisa isn't like that. She is fully installed and settled in our marriage and can conceive of no other life than the one she has chosen to live. She only wants more of the same, with no changes. One identical day after another, with nothing added or subtracted. So much so that what crosses my mind would never cross hers, that is, our possible death, mine or hers, that simply isn't on her horizon, there's no room for it. I feel the same about her death, I can hardly bear to think of it and barely consider it as a possibility. But I do consider my own death sometimes, now and then, well, we each have to struggle with our own vulnerability, not with that of other people, however much we love them. I don't know quite how to put it, but there are times when I can very easily imagine the world without me. So if something were to happen to me one day, Javier, something final, you must be there as a back-up. I know that's a very pragmatic, rather undignified word, but it's the right one. Don't misunderstand me, don't be alarmed. I'm not, of course, asking you to marry her or anything. You have your bachelor lifestyle and your many women, which you wouldn't give up for the world, still less to do a posthumous favour for a friend who can no longer call you to account or reproach you, who will be safely silent in the unprotesting past. But, please, stay close to her if ever I'm not here. Don't withdraw because of my absence, on the contrary: keep her company, offer her support and conversation and consolation, go and spend a little time with her every day and call her as often as you can even if there's no need to, but so that it becomes a natural part of her day-to-day life. Be a kind of unhusbandly husband, an extension of me. I don't think Luisa could cope without some daily contact like that, without someone to share her thoughts with and talk to about her day, without a replacement for what she has with me now, at least in some respects. She's known you for ages, and she wouldn't feel as inhibited as she would with a stranger. You could even entertain her by telling her about your adventures and allow her to experience vicariously what it will seem to her impossible ever to experience again on her own account. I know it's a lot to ask, and you wouldn't get much out of it, it would be more of a burden really, but Luisa could, in turn, be a partial replacement for me, she could be an extension of me, as far as you're concerned, I mean. Our loved ones are always extensions of us in a way, and they recognize each other and come together through the dead person, as if their past contact with him made them members of a brotherhood or a caste. That way you wouldn't lose me completely, a little of me would be preserved in her. You're always surrounded by your various women, but you don't have that many male friends. You would miss me, you know. And, for example, she and I share the same sense of humour. And you and I have been joking around with each other on a daily basis for years now."

Díaz-Varela would probably have laughed, perhaps to take the edge off his friend's ominous tone, but also because this extravagant, unexpected request made him laugh despite himself.

"You're asking me to replace you if you die," he would have said, halfway between a statement and a question. "For me to become Luisa's non-husband and a sort of live-out dad. Why think of such things, I mean, why think that you could leave their lives at any moment, if, as you say, you're in good health and there's no real reason to believe that anything bad might happen to you? Are you sure you're all right? No diseases? You're not mixed up in some mess I know nothing about, are you? You haven't run up a lot of unpayable debts or debts that can't be paid off in cash? No one has threatened you, have they? You're not thinking of skipping off, are you, doing a runner?"

"No, really, I'm not hiding anything from you. It's exactly as I said, that sometimes I start thinking about what the world would be like without me and I feel afraid. For the kids and for Luisa, not for anyone else, I can assure you, I don't think I'm that important. I just want to be sure that you would be there to take care of them, at least initially. So that they would have someone as similar to me as possible to support them. Whether you like it or not, whether you know it or not, you are the person who most resembles me. Even if only because we've known each other such a long time."

Díaz-Varela would have thought for a moment, then given a half-sincere, certainly not wholly sincere, answer:

"But do you realize what you would be getting me into? Do you realize how difficult it would be to become a non-husband without subsequently going on to become a real husband? In the kind of situation you described, it would be all too easy for the widow and the bachelor to believe that they mean rather more to each other, and who can blame them? Put someone in another person's daily life, make him feel responsible and protective and with a duty to make himself indispensable to that other person, and you can imagine how things will end up. Always assuming they're both reasonably attractive and there isn't a vast age difference between them. It will come as no surprise to you if I say that Luisa is very attractive, and I can't complain about my own success with the ladies. I don't think I'll ever marry, that's not it, but if you were to die and I started going to your house on a daily basis, I find it very hard to believe that what should never have happened while you were alive wouldn't happen once you were dead. Would you want to die knowing that? More than that, you would be encouraging it, procuring it, propelling us into it."

Desvern would have remained silent for a few seconds, thinking, as if he had not considered that scenario before formulating his request. Then he would have given a rather paternalistic laugh and said:

"You are incorrigibly vain and incorrigibly optimistic. That's why you would make such a good handle to hold on to, such a good support. I don't think what you describe would happen at all. Precisely because you're too familiar a figure, like a cousin whom it would be impossible to see in any other way, with any other eyes," here he would have hesitated for a moment or pretended to, "any other eyes than mine, that is. Her view of you comes from me, it's inherited, tainted. You're an old friend of her husband, a friend of whom she has often heard me speak, as you can imagine, with a mixture of affection and mockery. Before Luisa met you, I had already told her what you were like, I had painted a picture of you for her. She has always seen you in that light and with those features, and there's no changing them now, she had a complete portrait of you before you were even introduced. And I can't deny that your entanglements and, how can I put it, your smugness, often made us laugh. I'm afraid you're not someone she could take seriously. I'm sure you don't mind me saying that. That's one of your virtues, and it's what you've always strived for, isn't it, not to be taken too seriously. You're not going to deny that, are you?"

Díaz-Varela would doubtless have felt slightly put out, but would have disguised the fact. No one likes to be told that he or she stands no chance with someone, even if that person is of no interest and has never been seen as a potential conquest. Many seductions have taken place, or at least begun, out of nothing more than pique or defiance, because of a bet or to prove someone wrong. Any genuine interest comes later. And it often does, provoked by the manoeuvring and the effort involved. But it's not there at the beginning, certainly not before the dissuasive arguments or the challenge. Perhaps, at that moment, Díaz-Varela wanted Deverne to die so that he could prove to him that Luisa could take him seriously when there were no mediators, no go-betweens. Although, of course, how can you prove something to a dead man? How can you gain their acknowledgement, their recognition that they were wrong? They never tell us we were right when we need them to, and all you can think is: "If he or she were to come back today . . ." But they never do. He would prove it to Luisa, in whom, according to Desvern, he, the husband, would carry on or continue to live for a while longer. Perhaps it would be like that, perhaps he was right. Until he swept him away. Until he erased his memory and all other traces and supplanted him entirely.

"No, I don't deny it, and of course I don't mind. But our views of people change a lot, especially if the person who painted the original portrait can no longer go on retouching it and the portrait is left in the hands of the portrayed. The latter can correct and redraw every line, one by one, and leave the original artist looking like a liar. Or just plain wrong, or like a bad artist, superficial and lacking in perception. 'They gave me an entirely false impression of him,' someone looking at the picture might think. 'This man isn't as he was described to me at all, he has substance, passion, integrity and maturity.' It happens every day, Miguel, all the time. People start out seeing one thing and end up seeing quite the opposite. They start out loving and end up hating, or shifting from indifference to adoration. We can never be sure of what is going to be vital to us and who we will consider to be important. Our convictions are transient and fragile, even the ones we believe to be the strongest. It's the same with our feelings. We shouldn't trust ourselves."

Deverne would have sensed a touch of wounded pride and ignored it.

"Even so," he would have said, "even if I don't think it's possible, what does it matter if it does happen afterwards, after my death? I'll know nothing about it. But I would have died convinced of the impossibility of such a bond between you and her, it's what you think will happen that counts, because what you see and experience

in your final moment is the end of the story, the end of your personal story. You know that everything will carry on without you,
that nothing stops because you have disappeared. But that 'afterwards' doesn't concern you. What matters is that you stop, because
then everything stops, the world is frozen in that moment when the
person whose life is ending finally ends, even though we know that
this isn't true in actual fact. But that 'actual fact' doesn't matter.
It's the one moment when there is no future, in which the present
seems to us unchangeable and eternal, because we won't witness
any more events or any more changes. There have been people who
have tried to bring forward the publication of a book so that their
father would see it in print and die thinking that their son was an
accomplished writer; what did it matter if, after that, the son never
wrote another line? There have been desperate attempts to bring
about a momentary reconciliation between two people so that the
person dying would believe that they had made their peace and
everything was sorted and settled; what did it matter if, two days
after the death, the hostile parties had a blazing row? What mattered
was what existed immediately before that death. There have been
people who have pretended to forgive a dying man so that he can die
in peace or more happily; what did it matter if, the following morning, his forgiver hoped privately to see him rot in hell? There have
been those who have lied their socks off at the deathbed of a wife
or husband and convinced them that they had never been unfaithful
and had loved them unwaveringly and constantly; what did it matter
if, a month later, they had moved in with their lover of many years?
The only definitive truth is what the person about to die sees and
believes immediately before his or her departure, because nothing
exists after that. There is a great chasm between what Mussolini,
executed by his enemies, believed and what Franco, on his deathbed, believed, the latter surrounded by his loved ones and adored by

his compatriots, whatever those hypocrites may say now. My father once told me that Franco kept a photograph in his office of Mussolini strung up like a pig in the petrol station in Milan where they took his corpse and that of his lover, Clara Petacci, to be put on display and publicly mocked, and that whenever visitors expressed shock and bewilderment on seeing the photograph, Franco would say: 'Yes, take a good look: that's never going to happen to me.' And he was right, he made sure that it didn't. He doubtless died happy—if such a thing is possible—believing that everything would continue as he had ordained. Many people console themselves for this great injustice or for their rage with the thought: 'If he were to come back today . . .' or 'Given the way things have turned out, he must be spinning in his grave,' forgetting that no one ever comes back or spins in his grave or knows what happens once he has expired. It's like thinking that someone who has not yet been born should care about what's going on in the world. To someone who does not yet exist everything is, inevitably, a matter of complete indifference, just as it is for someone who has died. Both are nothing, neither possesses any consciousness, the former cannot even sense what its life will be and the latter cannot recall it, as if he or she had never had a life. They are on the same plane, that is, they neither exist nor know anything, however hard that is for us to accept. What does it matter to me what happens once I am gone? All that counts is what I can believe and foresee now. I believe that, in my absence, it would be better for my children if you were around. I foresee that Luisa would recover sooner and suffer a little less if you were on hand as a friend. I can't fathom other people's conjectures, even yours or Luisa's, I can only know my own, and I can't imagine you two in any other way. So I ask you again, if anything bad should happen to me, give me your word that you'll take care of them."

Díaz-Varela might still have disputed certain points with him.

"Yes, you're right in part, but not about one thing: not having been born is not the same as having died, because the person who dies always leaves some trace behind him and he knows that. He knows, too, that he'll know nothing about it, but that he will, nonetheless, leave his mark in the form of memories. He knows he'll be missed, as you yourself said, and that the people who knew him won't behave as if he had never existed. Some will feel guilty about him, some will wish they had treated him better while he was alive, some will mourn him and be unable to understand why he doesn't respond, some will be plunged into despair by his absence. No one has any difficulty recovering from the loss of someone who has not been born, with the exception, perhaps, of a mother who has undergone an abortion and finds it hard to abandon hope and wonders sometimes about the child who might have been. But in reality there is no loss of any kind, there is no void, there are no past events. On the other hand, no one who has lived and died disappears completely, not at least for a couple of generations: there is evidence of his actions and, when he dies, he'll be aware of that. He knows that he won't be able to see or ascertain anything of what happens thereafter and he knows that his story ends in that instant. You yourself are concerned about what will happen to your wife and children, you've taken care to put your affairs in order, you're aware of the gap you would leave and you're asking me to fill that gap, to be some kind of substitute for you if you're not here. None of that would concern someone who had never been born."

"Of course not," Desvern would have replied, "but I'm doing all of those things while I'm still alive, and a living person is not the same as a dead person, even though that isn't what we tend to think. When I'm dead, I won't even be a person, and won't be able to sort out or ask for anything, or be aware of or concerned about anything. In that respect a dead person is the same as someone who has never been born. I'm not talking about the others, those who survive us and think of us and who still exist in time, nor of myself now, of the me who has not yet departed. He still does things, of course, and, needless to say, thinks them; he plots, takes steps and decisions, tries to influence others, has desires, is vulnerable and can also inflict harm. I'm talking about myself dead, which you obviously find harder to imagine than I do. You shouldn't confuse us, the living me and the dead me. The former is asking you for something that the latter won't be able to question or remind you about or else check up on you to see whether or not you have carried out his wishes. What's so difficult, then, about giving me your word? There's nothing to prevent you from failing to keep it, it will cost you nothing."

Díaz-Varela would have put one hand to his forehead and sat looking at his friend oddly and slightly irritably, as if he had just emerged from a daydream or some drug-induced torpor. He was, at the least, emerging from an unexpected and inappropriately gloomy conversation.

"Fine, you have my word of honour, you can count on it," he would have said. "But please, no more of these macabre conversations, they give me the creeps. Let's go and have a drink and talk about something more cheerful."

"What rubbishy edition is this?" I heard Professor Rico muttering as he took a book off a shelf; he had been snooping around looking at the books, as if no one else were in the room. I saw that he was holding an edition of *Don Quixote* with the very tips of his fingers, as though the book made his skin crawl. "How can anyone possibly own this edition when they could have mine? It's full of a lot of intuitive nonsense, there's no method or science in it, it's not even original, he's just copied from other people. And to find it in the house of someone who is, as I understand it, a university teacher, well, that really takes the biscuit. But then that's Madrid University for you," he added, looking reprovingly at Luisa.

She burst out laughing. Even though she was the object of the reprimand, she obviously found his rudeness vastly amusing. Díaz-Varela laughed too, perhaps infected by her laughter or perhaps to flatter Rico into further excesses—he could hardly have been surprised by Rico's impertinence or by the liberties he took; he then tried to provoke him further, possibly to make Luisa laugh more and draw her out of her momentarily sombre mood. And yet he seemed perfectly spontaneous. He was utterly charming and he pretended very well, if he was pretending.

"You're not telling me that the editor of that edition isn't a respected authority," he said to Rico, "indeed, he's rather more respected than you are in some circles."

"Huh, respected by ignoramuses and eunuchs, of which this country is filled to bursting, and by literary and philosophical societies in Spain's lazier, lowlier provincial towns," retorted Professor Rico. He opened the book at random, cast a quick, disdainful eye over the page and stabbed at one particular line with his index finger. "I've seen one glaring error already." Then he closed the book as if there were no point in looking any further. "I'll write an article about it." He looked up with a triumphant air and smiled from ear to ear (an enormous smile made possible by his flexible mouth) and added: "Besides, the fellow's jealous of me."

II

I DIDN'T SEE Luisa Alday again for quite some time, and in the long between-time I began going out with a man I vaguely liked, and fell stupidly and secretly in love with another, with her adoring Díaz-Varela, whom I met shortly afterwards in the most unlikely of places, very close to where Deverne had died, in the reddish building that houses the Natural History Museum, which is right next to or, rather, part of the same complex as the technical college, with its gleaming glass-and-zinc cupola, about twenty-seven metres high and about twenty in diameter, erected around 1881, when these buildings were neither college nor museum, but the brand-new National Palace for the Arts and Industry, which was the site of an important exhibition that year; the area used to be known as the Altos del Hipódromo, the Hippodrome Heights, because of its various promontories and its proximity to a few horses whose ghostly exploits have become doubly or definitively so, since there can be no one alive who saw or remembers them. The Natural History Museum is rather a poor affair, especially compared with those one finds in England, but I used to take my young nieces and nephews there sometimes so that they could see and get to know the static animals in their glass display cases, and I then acquired a taste for going there on my own from time to time, mingling with—but invisible to—the groups of junior- and secondary-school students and their exasperated or patient teachers and with a few bewildered tourists with too much time on their hands, who probably learned of the museum's existence from some overly punctilious and exhaustive guide to the city: for apart from the large number of museum attendants, most of whom are Latin Americans now, these tend to be the only living beings in the place, which has the unreal, superfluous, fantastical air of all natural history museums.

I was studying a scale model of the vast gaping jaws of a crocodile—I always used to think how easily I would fit inside them and how lucky I was not to live in a place inhabited by such reptiles—when I heard someone say my name and was so taken aback that I spun round, feeling slightly alarmed: when you're in that half-empty museum, you have the almost absolute, comforting certainty that no one has the least idea where you are at that precise moment.

I recognized him at once, with his feminine lips and his falsely cleft chin, his calm smile and that expression, at once attentive and discreet. He asked me what I was doing there, and I replied: "I like to come here now and then. It's full of tame wild beasts you can get right up close to." And as soon as I said this, I thought that, actually, there were very few wild beasts there and that what I had said was just plain silly, and I realized, too, that I had merely been trying to make myself seem interesting, doubtless with dire results. "And it's a nice quiet place," I added lamely. I, in turn, asked him what was he doing there, and he answered: "I like to come here sometimes too," and I waited for him to add some silly comment of his own, but, alas, I waited in vain. Díaz-Varela had no desire to impress me. "I live quite near. When I go out for a walk, my feet occasionally lead me here." That bit about his feet leading him there seemed slightly literary and twee and gave me some hope. "I sit out on the terrace for a while and then I go home. Anyway, let me buy you a drink, unless you want to continue studying those crocodile teeth or visit one of the other rooms." Outside, on the hill, beneath the shade of the trees, opposite the college, there's a refreshment kiosk with tables and chairs.

"No," I said, "I know these teeth by heart. I was just considering going to see the absurd Adam and Eve they've got downstairs." He didn't react, he didn't say "Oh, right" or anything, as I would have expected from someone who was a regular visitor to the museum: in the basement, there's a vertical display case, not that big, made by an American or an English woman, Rosemary Something-or-other, which contains a highly eccentric representation of the Garden of Eden. All the animals surrounding the original couple are supposedly alive and either in motion or alert, monkeys, hares, turkeys, cranes, badgers, perhaps a toucan and even the snake, which is peering out with an all-too-human expression from among the vivid green leaves of the apple tree. By contrast, Adam and Eve, standing side by side, are mere skeletons, and the only way of telling them apart, to the uneducated eye at least, is that one of them is holding an apple in its right hand. I've probably read the explanatory notice at some point, but I don't think it provided me with a satisfactory explanation. If it was a matter of illustrating the differences between the bones of a man and those of a woman, then why make them into our first parents, as the Catholic faith used to call them, and place them in that particular setting; and if it was intended to show Paradise and its rather sparse fauna, then why the skeletons when all the other animals are complete with their flesh and their fur or feathers? It's one of the museum's most incongruous exhibits, and no visitor can fail to notice it, not because it's pretty, but because it makes no sense at all.

"It's María Dolz, isn't it? I'm right, aren't I, it is Dolz?" Díaz-Varela said once we had sat down on the terrace, as if keen to show off his retentive memory; after all, I alone had said my surname and then only hurriedly, slipping it in like an insert of no interest to any of the others present. I felt flattered by this gesture, but didn't feel I was being courted.

"You obviously have a good memory—and a good ear," I said, so as not to be impolite. "Yes, it's Dolz, not Dols or Dolç with a cedilla." And I drew a cedilla in the air. "How's Luisa?"

"Oh, haven't you seen her? I thought you had become friends."

"Well, yes, if you can be friends with someone for a day. I haven't seen her since that one time in her house. We did get on very well, it's true, and she spoke to me as if I were a friend, more out of need than anything, I think. But I haven't seen her since. How is she?" I asked again. "You must see her every day, I imagine."

He seemed slightly put out by my response and remained silent for a few seconds. It occurred to me that perhaps all he wanted was to pump me for information, in the belief that she and I kept in touch, and that his encounter with me had now lost its purpose almost before it had begun, or, even more ironically, that he would be the one to give me news and information about her.

"Not very good," he replied at last, "and I'm starting to get worried. I know it hasn't been that long, of course, but she just can't seem to pull herself together, she hasn't progressed a millimetre, she can't even raise her head, however fleetingly, and look about her and see how much she still has. Despite the death of her husband, she, nonetheless, has a lot going for her; I mean, at her age, she has a whole life ahead of her. Most widows get over their grief quite quickly, especially if they're fairly young and have children to look after. But it's not just the children, who soon cease to be children. If she were only able to imagine herself in a few years' time, or even a year, she would see then how the image of Miguel, which, at the moment, haunts her incessantly, will fade and shrink with each passing day, and how her new love will allow her to remember him occasionally and with surprising serenity, always with sorrow, yes, but with hardly any sense of unease. Because she *will* experience new love, and her first marriage will eventually seem almost like a dream, a dim, flickering memory. What seems like a tragic anomaly today will be perceived as an inevitable and even desirable normality, given that it will have happened. Right now it seems to her unbelievable that Miguel should no longer exist, but a time will come when it will seem incomprehensible that he could ever be restored to life, that he could ever exist, when merely imagining a miraculous reappearance, a resurrection, a return, will seem to her intolerable, because she will already have assigned him a place in time, both him and his character frozen for ever, and she will not allow that fixed and finished portrait to be exposed once more to the changes that afflict everything that is still alive and therefore unpredictable. We tend to hope that, of the people and habits we cherish, no one will die and none will end, not realizing that the only thing that maintains those habits intact is their sudden withdrawal, with no possible alteration or evolution, before they can abandon us or we abandon them. Anything that lasts goes bad and putrefies, it bores us, turns against us, saturates and wearies us. How many people who once seemed vital to us are left by the wayside, how many relationships wear thin, become diluted for no apparent reason or certainly none of any weight. The only people who do not fail or let us down are those who are snatched from us, the only ones we don't drop are those who abruptly disappear and so have no time to cause us pain or disappointment. When that happens, we despair momentarily, because we believe we could have continued with them for much longer, with no foreseeable expiry date. That's a mistake, albeit understandable. Continuity changes everything, and something we thought wonderful yesterday would have become a torment tomorrow. Our reaction to the death of someone close to us is similar to Macbeth's reaction to the news that his wife, the Queen, has died. 'She should have died hereafter,' he replies rather enigmatically, meaning: 'She should have died at some point in the future, later on.' Or he could have meant, less ambiguously and more plainly: 'She should have waited a little longer, she should have held on'; what he means is 'not at this precise moment, but at the chosen moment.' And what would be the chosen moment? The moment never seems quite right, we always think that whatever pleases or brings us joy, whatever solaces or succours us, whatever drives us through the days, could have lasted a little longer, a year, a few months, a few weeks, a few hours, we always feel it is too soon for things or people to end, we never feel there is a right moment, one in which we ourselves would say: 'Fine, that's enough. That's all over with and a good thing too. Anything that happens from now on will be worse, a deterioration, a diminution, a blot.' We never dare to go so far as to say: 'That time is past, even if it was our time,' which is why the ending of things does not lie in our hands, because if it did, everything would continue indefinitely, becoming grubby and contaminated, and no living creature would ever die."

He paused briefly to drink his beer, because talking always dries the throat, and, after an initial hesitation, he launched into his speech almost vehemently, as if seizing the opportunity to vent his feelings. He spoke fluently and eloquently, his English pronunciation was good and unaffected, what he said was interesting and his thoughts coherent, I wondered what he did for a living, but I couldn't ask him without interrupting what he was saying and I didn't want to do that. I was looking at his lips as he talked, staring at them, quite blatantly I fear, I was letting myself be lulled by his words and couldn't take my eyes off the place out of which those words had emerged, as if he were all kissable mouth, the source of all abundance, from which everything flows, what persuades and what seduces us, what changes and charms us, what sucks us in and what convinces us. In the Bible somewhere it says: "Out of the abundance of the heart the mouth speaketh." I was puzzled to find myself so attracted to that man, even fascinated, a man I barely knew, and even more puzzled when I recalled that for Luisa, on the other hand, he was almost invisible and inaudible, because she had seen and heard him so often. How could that be? We believe that whoever we fall in love with should be desired by everyone. I didn't want to say anything so as not to break the spell, but it occurred to me also that, if I said nothing, he might think I wasn't paying attention, when the fact is I hung on his every word, everything that came from those lips interested me. I must be brief, though, I thought, so as not to distract him too much.

"Yes, but how things end does lie in our hands if those hands are suicidal, not to mention murderous," I said. And I was on the point of adding: "Right here, right next door, your friend Desvern was cruelly cut down. It's strange us sitting here in this clean and peaceful place, as if nothing had happened. If we had been here on that other day, we might perhaps have saved him. Although if he hadn't died, we wouldn't be together anywhere. We wouldn't even have met."

I WAS ON the point of adding this, but I didn't, because, among other reasons, he suddenly cast a rapid glance—he had his back to the street, I was facing it—at the spot where the stabbing had taken place, and I wondered if he might perhaps be thinking the same as me or something similar, at least as regards the first part of my thought. He ran his fingers through his slightly receding hair, which he wore combed backwards, like a musician. Then with those same four fingers, he drummed with his nails—hard, neatly trimmed nails—against his glass.

"Those are the exceptions, the anomalies. Of course there are people who decide to end their own life, and they do, but they're the minority, which is why it seems so shocking, because their actions go completely counter to the longing to endure, which is shared by the vast majority of us and which makes us believe that there is always time and, when time does run out, makes us ask for a little more, just a little more. As for the murderous hands you mention, they can never be seen as *our* hands. They end a life much as an illness does, or an accident, I mean, they are external causes, even in those cases where the dead person has brought it upon himself, because of the disreputable life he has led or the risks he has taken or because he has himself killed and thus laid himself open to someone else's revenge. Not even the most bloodthirsty mafioso or the President of the United States, to give just two examples of individuals at permanent risk of assassination, and who know that it is a real possibility and live with that possibility every day, even they do not long for that threat, that latent torture, that unbearable anxiety to be over. They don't want anything that exists or anything they have to end, however horrible or burdensome that might be; they live from day to day in the hope that the following day will be there too, identical or very similar to every other day, if I exist today, they think, why shouldn't I continue to exist tomorrow, and tomorrow leads to the day after tomorrow and the day after tomorrow to the day after that. That is how we all live, the happy and the unhappy, the fortunate and the unfortunate, and if it was up to us, we would go on like that until the end of time."—It seemed to me that he had become slightly confused or was trying to confuse me. "Those murderous hands," I thought, "are not, of course, *ours* unless they do suddenly become our hands, and besides, they always belong to someone, who will call them 'my hands.' And regardless of who they belong to, it isn't true that those hands do not want any living being to die, because that is precisely what they do want, more than that, they can't wait for a chance to bring it about nor for time to do its work; they take it upon themselves to transform life into death. They don't want everything to continue uninterrupted, on the contrary, they feel a need to annihilate and destroy someone else's cherished habits. They would never say of their victim 'She should have died hereafter' but, rather, 'He should have died yesterday,' years ago, a long, long time ago; if he had never been born and never left any trace in the world, then we wouldn't have had to kill him. With one thrust of his knife, the *gorrilla* had destroyed his own habits and those of Deverne, along with those of Luisa and the children and the chauffeur, who was saved perhaps by a case of mistaken identity, by a whisker; as well as Díaz-Varela's habits and even mine in part. And those of other people I don't even know." But I didn't say any of this, I didn't want to take the floor, I didn't want to speak, I wanted him to carry on talking. I wanted to hear his voice and track his thoughts, and to keep watching his lips moving. So spellbound was I by them that I ran the risk of not taking in what he was saying. He took another sip of his drink and went on, first clearing his throat as if he were trying to focus his thoughts.—"What's amazing is that when these things happen, when these interruptions or deaths occur, more often than not, people eventually come to accept them. Don't misunderstand me. No one can ever find a death, still less a murder, acceptable. Deaths and murders will always be sources of regret, whenever they happen, but ultimately, life prevails over us, so much so that, in the long run, it's almost impossible for us to imagine ourselves without the sorrows life brings, to imagine, for example, that something that happened didn't happen. 'My father was killed during the Civil War,' someone might say bitterly, sadly or angrily. 'They came for him one night, dragged him from the house and bundled him into a car, I saw how he struggled and how they manhandled him. They dragged him along by the arms as if his legs were paralysed and could no longer bear his weight. They drove him to the outskirts of town, where they shot him in the back of the neck and threw his body in a ditch, so that the sight of his corpse would be a warning to others.' The person telling that story doubtless regrets and deplores it and might even spend his whole life seething with hatred for his father's assassins, a universal, abstract hatred if he doesn't know exactly who they were, their names, as was so often the case during the Civil War; in many instances, all they knew was that 'the other side' had done it. However, in large measure that horrible event constitutes the essence of that person, which he could never relinquish because that would be tantamount to denying himself, to erasing what he is and having nothing to replace it with. He is the son of a man who was cruelly murdered during the Civil War; he is a victim of Spanish violence, a tragic orphan; that fact shapes and defines and determines him. That is his story or the beginning of his story, his origin. In a sense, he cannot wish that it hadn't happened, because if it hadn't, he would be a different person, and he has no idea who that person would be. He can neither see nor imagine himself, he doesn't know how he would have turned out, and how he would have got on with that living father, if he would have hated or loved him or felt quite indifferent, and, above all, he cannot imagine himself without that background of grief and rancour that has always accompanied him. The force of events is so overwhelming that we all end up more or less accepting our story, what happened and what we did or failed to do, regardless of whether we believe or acknowledge it; in fact, it's something most of us refuse to acknowledge. The truth is that we almost all curse our fate at some point in our lives and yet almost no one admits that."

At this point, I could not help but interrupt:

"Luisa cannot possibly accept what has happened to her. No woman could accept that her husband had been stupidly and gratuitously stabbed to death, by mistake, for no reason, and when he had done nothing to provoke it. No one can accept that their life has been destroyed for ever."

Díaz-Varela sat looking at me intently, his cheek resting on one fist and his elbow resting on the table. I looked away, troubled by those eyes fixed on mine, by that gaze, which was neither transparent nor penetrating, but perhaps hazy and enveloping or merely indecipherable, and tempered at any rate by his myopia (he was probably wearing lenses), it was as if those almond eyes were saying to me: "Why don't you understand?" not impatiently, but regretfully.

"That's the mistake people make," he said after a few seconds, without looking away or changing his posture, as though, rather than speaking, he was waiting, "a childish mistake that many adults cling to until the day they die, as if throughout their entire existence they had failed to grasp how things work, as if they lacked all experience. The mistake of believing that the present is for ever, that what happens in each moment is definitive, when we should all know that as long as we still have a little time left, nothing is definitive. We have all experienced enough twists and turns, not just in terms of luck but as regards our state of mind. We gradually learn that what seems really important now will one day seem a mere fact, a neutral piece of information. We learn that there will come a time when we don't even give a thought to the person we once couldn't live without and over whom we spent sleepless nights, without whom life seemed impossible, on whose words and presence we depended day after day, and if we ever do, very occasionally, give that person a thought, it will merely be to shrug and think at most: 'I wonder what became of her?' without a flicker of concern or curiosity. What do we care now about what happened to our first girlfriend, when we used to long for her phone call or to be with her? What indeed do we care about our penultimate girlfriend, after a year without seeing her? What do we care about our friends from school or university and afterwards, even though whole swathes of our existence revolved around them and seemed as if they would never end? What do we care about those who break away, who leave, those who turn their backs on us and distance themselves, those whom we discard and who become invisible to us, mere names that we recall only when, by chance, their names happen to reach our ears, or, indeed, those who die and thus desert us? For example, my mother died twenty-five years ago, and although I feel obliged to be sad whenever I think of her, and do, in fact, feel sad, I'm incapable of reliving what I felt at the time, let alone of weeping as I did then. It has become just that, a fact: my mother died twenty-five years ago, and I have been without a mother ever since. It's simply a part of me, one of many facts that have shaped the person I am; I've been without a mother since I was a young man, that's all, or almost all, just as I'm single or as someone else might have been orphaned in childhood or an only child or the youngest of seven siblings or the descendant of a soldier or a doctor or a criminal, what does it matter, in the end, these are simply facts and not of any great importance, everything that happens to us or that precedes us could be summed up in a couple of lines in a story. Luisa's present life has been destroyed, but not her future life. Think how much time she has left in which to move forward, she isn't going to stay trapped in the moment, no one ever is, still less in the very worst of moments, from which we always emerge, unless we're sick in the head and feel justified by and even protected by our comfortable misery. The bad thing about terrible misfortunes, the kind that tear us apart and appear to be unendurable, is that those who suffer them believe or almost demand that the world should end right there, and yet the world pays no heed and carries on regardless and even tugs at the sleeve of the person who suffered the misfortune, I mean, it won't just let them depart this world the way a disgruntled spectator might leave the theatre, unless the unfortunate person kills him or herself. That does happen, I don't deny it. But very rarely, and it's far less frequent in our age than it was in any other. Luisa might shut herself away, withdraw for a while, be seen by no one apart from her family and myself, always assuming she doesn't weary of me and decide to do without me as well; but she won't kill herself, even if only because she has two children to look after and because it's not in her character. It will take the time it takes, but in the end, the pain and the despair will become less intense, the sense of shock will diminish and, above all, she will get used to the idea: 'I'm a widow,' she will think or 'I've been widowed.' That will be the fact, the piece of information, that she will tell people to whom she's introduced and who ask about her marital status, she'll probably choose not to explain how it happened, because it's too gruesome and wretched a tale to tell to a new acquaintance whom she barely knows, it would cast an immediate pall over any conversation. And that will be what others say about her, and what others say about us plays a part in defining us, however superficially and inexactly, after all, for most people, we are only superficial beings, a sketch, a few scrawled lines. 'She's a widow,' they'll say, 'she lost her husband in horrific circumstances that have never been fully explained, I'm not even sure what happened myself, I think he was attacked by a man in the street, whether by a madman or a hit man, I don't know, or perhaps it was a kidnap attempt that went badly wrong because he resisted with all his might and was killed on the spot for his pains; he was a wealthy man, so he had a lot to lose or perhaps he just instinctively put up a hard fight.' And when Luisa marries again, which will be in a couple of years from now at most, that fact, that piece of information, will have changed, while remaining the same as before, and she will no longer say of herself: 'I've been widowed' or 'I'm a widow,' because she won't be, and will say instead 'I lost my first husband, and he's moving further away from me all the time. It's such a long time since I saw him, whereas this other man is here by my side and is always by my side. I call him "husband" too, which is odd. But he has taken the other husband's place in my bed and by virtue of that juxtaposition is gradually blurring and erasing him. A little more each day, a little more each night.' "

THIS CONVERSATION CONTINUED on other occasions; in fact, the subject seemed to come up, or Díaz-Varela would himself bring it up, every time we met—which wasn't very often—I still can't bring myself to call Díaz-Varela "Javier" even though that was what I called him and how I thought of him on certain nights when I returned home late to my apartment after having spent a while in bed with him (one is only ever in someone else's bed for "a while," on loan, unless invited to spend the whole night there, and that never happened with him; indeed, he would invent absurd, unnecessary excuses to get rid of me, unnecessary because I've never stayed anywhere longer than I should have, unless asked). Before closing my eyes, I would stare out of the open window of my own bedroom and look across at the trees opposite, which, having no streetlamp to light them, are barely visible, but I would hear them stirring close by in the darkness, like a prelude to the storms that sometimes pass over Madrid, and I would say to myself: "What is the point of this, for me at least? He's not pretending, he's not deceiving me, he doesn't conceal his hopes from me or his motivation, which, although he may not know it, are all blindingly obvious: he's just waiting for her to emerge from her state of deep depression or enervation and begin to see him differently, not merely as the faithful friend her husband bequeathed to her. He has to be very careful, though, with the small steps he takes, which must, inevitably, be very small if he is not to look as if he were showing a lack of respect for her natural grief or even for the dead man's memory, and he must, at the same time, remain alert in case someone else slips in before him, which means that he cannot discount as rivals even the ugliest or stupidest or most casual or most boring or most languid of suitors, because any one of them could present an unforeseen danger. While he keeps watch over her, he sees me from time to time and possibly other women too (we tend to avoid asking each other questions), and maybe I'm doing the same as him in a way, trying to make myself indispensable without him noticing, making myself one of his habits, even if only a very sporadic habit, so that he will find me hard to replace when he does decide to abandon me. Some men make things very clear from the start without anyone needing to ask: 'I must warn you that there will never be anything more between us than there is already, and if you're hoping for more, then we'd better finish right now' or 'You're not the only one nor should you aim to be; if you're looking for exclusivity, this isn't the place' or, as was the case with Díaz-Varela: 'I'm in love with someone else who hasn't yet realized that she could be in love with me. That time will come, though, I just have to be constant and patient. There's nothing wrong, however, with you keeping me amused in the meantime, if you want to, but be quite clear, that's all we are to each other, temporary companionship and amusement and sex; at most, camaraderie and a little affection.' Not that Díaz-Varela has ever said those precise words to me, there's no need, because that is the unequivocal message that emerges from our encounters. On the other hand, those same men who issue warnings sometimes eat their words later on, and a lot of us women tend to be optimistic and conceited in a way, more profoundly so than many men, who, in the field of love, remain conceited only briefly and forget to be so after a while: we think men will change their mind or their beliefs, that they will gradually discover that they can't do without us, that we will be the exception in their lives or the visitors who end up staying, that they will eventually grow tired of those other invisible women whose existence we begin to doubt or whom we prefer to think do not exist, the more we see of the men and the more we love them despite ourselves; that we will be the chosen ones if only we have the necessary staying power to remain by their side, uncomplaining and uninsistent. When we don't arouse immediate passion, we believe that loyalty and our mere persistent presence will finally be rewarded and prove stronger and more durable than any momentary rapture or caprice. In such cases, we know that we will be hard-pressed to feel flattered even if our fondest hopes come true, but if they do, we will feel inwardly triumphant. There is, however, no certainty of this for as long as the struggle continues, and even the most justifiably confident of women, even those who, up until then, have been universally courted, can be badly let down by those men who refuse to surrender and issue them with arrogant warnings. I don't belong to the category of the confident, the truth is that I harbour no real hopes of triumphing, or, rather, the only hopes I allow myself revolve around Díaz-Varela's failure to win Luisa, and then, perhaps, with luck, he'll stay with me out of pure inertia, because even the most restless and diligent and scheming of men can grow lazy, especially after a frustration or a failure or a very long and pointless wait. I know that it wouldn't offend me to be a substitute, because we are all of us substitutes for someone, especially initially: Díaz-Varela would be a substitute for Luisa's dead husband; as far as I was concerned, my substitute for Díaz-Varela would be Leopoldo, whom I have not yet ruled out—just in case, I suppose—even though I only half-like him, and with whom I only started going out—how very opportune—just before I met Díaz-Varela in the Natural History Museum and heard him talk and talk while I ceaselessly watched his lips as I still do whenever we're together, only taking my eyes off them to look up at his clouded gaze; perhaps Luisa was a substitute for someone else when she met Deverne, who knows, perhaps for his first wife, although it was incomprehensible that anyone could wound or leave such a pleasant, cheerful man, and yet there he is, stabbed to death for no reason and now en route to oblivion. Yes, we are all poor imitations of people whom, generally speaking, we never met, people who never even approached or simply walked straight past the lives of those we now love, or who did perhaps stop, but grew weary after a time and disappeared without leaving so much as a trace, or only the dust from their fleeing feet, or who died, causing those we love a mortal wound that almost always heals in the end. We cannot pretend to be the first or the favourite, we are merely what is available, the leftovers, the leavings, the survivors, the remnants, the remaindered goods, and it is on this somewhat ignoble basis that the greatest loves are built and on which the best families are founded, and from which we all come, the product of chance and making do, of other people's rejections and timidities and failures, and yet we would give anything sometimes to stay by the side of the person we rescued from an attic or a clearance sale, or won in a game of cards or who picked us up from among the scraps; strange though it may seem, we manage to believe in these chance fallings in love, and many think they can see the hand of destiny in what is really nothing more than a village raffle at the fag-end of summer . . ." Then I would turn out the light on my bedside table and, after a few seconds, the trees being blown about by the wind would become slightly more visible and I could go to sleep watching, or perhaps merely sensing, the swaying of their leaves. "What is the point?" I would think. "The only point, in these silly, insurmountable circumstances, is to cling on to the smallest thing, the smallest handhold. Another day, another hour at his side, even if that hour takes ages to arrive; the vague promise of seeing him again even though many days, many empty days, must pass before that happens. We note down in our diary the dates when he phoned us or we saw him, we count the days that pass with no news from him, and stay awake into the small hours before giving the night up as definitively barren and lost, just in case, at the last moment, the phone should ring and he should whisper some nonsense or other that fills us with an entirely unjustified euphoria and a sense that life is kind and merciful. We interpret every inflection of his voice and every insignificant word, which we nevertheless repeat to ourselves and endow with stupid, promising meaning. We value any contact, however brief, even if it's only to receive some flimsy excuse or to be let down or to listen to a barely elaborated lie. 'At least, at some point, he thought of me,' we tell ourselves gratefully. 'He thinks of me when he's bored or if he's suffered some setback with Luisa, the person he really cares about, I may only be in second place, but that's better than nothing.' It occurs to us sometimes— but only sometimes—that all it needs is for the person occupying first place to fall, a feeling familiar to all younger brothers of kings and princes and even to more distant relatives and remote, isolated bastard children, who know that this is how one can pass from tenth place to ninth, from sixth to fifth and from fourth to third, and, at some point, all will have silently formulated the inexpressible desire: 'He should have died yesterday,' or the wish that appears in the minds of the boldest pretenders: 'There's still time for him to die tomorrow, which will be the yesterday of the day after tomorrow, assuming I'm alive then.' We don't care about humiliating ourselves to ourselves, after all, no one is going to judge us and there are no witnesses. When we get caught in the spider's web, we fantasize endlessly and, at the same time, make do with the tiniest crumb, with hearing him, smelling him, glimpsing him, sensing his presence, knowing that he is still on our horizon, from which he has not entirely vanished, and that we cannot yet see, in the distance, the dust from his fleeing feet."

WITH ME, DÍAZ-VARELA made no attempt to hide the impatience that he was obliged to conceal from Luisa, whenever, that is, we returned to his favourite topic of conversation, the one he could not have with her and the only one, it seemed to me, of any real importance to him, as if until that matter was settled, everything else was postponable and provisional, as if the effort invested in it were so huge that all other decisions had to remain in abeyance, waiting for some resolution, and as if his whole life depended on the failure or success of that stubborn hope of his, which had no definite completion date. Perhaps there was no indefinite completion date either: what would happen if Luisa failed to respond to his entreaties and advances, to his passion, if he gave voice to it, but chose, rather, to remain alone? When would he consider that it was time to abandon his long wait? I didn't want to find myself sliding imperceptibly into the same situation and so I continued to cultivate Leopoldo, whom I had decided to keep in the dark about Díaz-Varela. It was ridiculous enough that *my* steps depended, indirectly, on those taken or not taken by an inconsolable widow, and it would have been even more ridiculous to lengthen the chain still further and add to it the steps of a poor, unwitting man who didn't even know her: with a little bad luck and a few more lovers of the kind who allow themselves to be loved and neither reject nor reciprocate that love, the chain could have gone on for ever. A series of people lined up like dominoes, all waiting for the surrender of one entirely oblivious woman, to find out who would fall next to them.

At no point did it occur to Díaz-Varela that I might be upset by his statement of intent, although it is also true that he never presented himself as Luisa's salvation and destiny; he never said, "When she climbs out of the abyss and breathes again by my side, and smiles," still less, "When she marries again, marries me, that is." He never put himself forward as a candidate or included himself, but it was perfectly clear that he was the immovable man who waits; had he lived in another age, he would have been counting off the remaining days of the mourning period, then those of half-mourning and would have consulted the older women—who knew most about such matters—as to what would be an acceptable moment for him to remove his mask and make a play for her. That's the worst thing about losing our old codes of conduct, we don't know which is the right moment to act or what rules to follow, when it would be too soon or so late that we would have missed our turn. We have to be guided by ourselves and then it's very easy to make a blunder.

I don't know if it was simply that his desires coloured everything or if he deliberately sought out literary and historical texts that would support his arguments and come to his aid (perhaps he received guidance from Rico, that man of compendious knowledge, although, as I understand it, it is impossible to extract that disdainful scholar from the Renaissance and the Middle Ages, for it seems that nothing that has happened since 1650, including his own existence, merits his attention).

"I read a book recently, which, although I hadn't heard of it before, is, apparently, very famous," Díaz-Varela said, taking a French book down from the shelf and waving it before my eyes, as if he could speak more authoritatively with it in his hand and prove, moreover, that he had actually read it. "It's a novella by Balzac which agrees with me as regards Luisa, as regards what will happen to her in the fullness of time. It tells the story of one of Napoleon's colonels who was given up for dead at the Battle of Eylau. The battle took place between the 7th and 8th of February 1807 near the town of that name in East Prussia, and pitted the French and Russian armies against each other in Arctic conditions; they say that the battle was fought in what was possibly the most inclement weather ever, although I've no idea how they can know this, still less state it as a fact. This Colonel, Chabert by name, is in charge of a cavalry regiment and, during the fighting, receives a terrible blow to the skull from a sword. There is a moment in the novella when, in removing his hat in the presence of a lawyer, he accidentally removes the wig he is wearing too and reveals a monstrously long scar that begins at the nape of his neck and ends just above his right eye, can you imagine?"—and he demonstrated the line of the scar by running his index finger slowly over his head—"forming what Balzac described as 'a prominent seam,' adding that one's first thought on seeing the wound was: 'His intelligence must have escaped through that gash!' Marshal Murat, the same man who crushed the 2nd of May uprising in Madrid, promptly dispatches fifteen hundred horsemen to rescue him, but all of them, with Murat at the head, ride straight over him, over his prostrate body. He is assumed to be dead, despite the Emperor—who greatly admires him—sending two surgeons on to the battlefield to check that he is dead; those negligent men, however, knowing that his skull has been sliced open and that he has then been trampled on by two cavalry regiments, do not even bother to take his pulse and officially and hastily certify him as dead, and that death then appears in the French army's bulletins, where it is recorded in detail, thus becoming historical fact. He is thrown into a grave along with the other naked corpses, as was the custom: he had been a famous man while alive, but now he is just another corpse lying in a cold grave, and all corpses go to the same place. The Colonel tells his improbable but entirely convincing story to a Parisian lawyer, Derville, who he hopes will take on his case, he recounts how he recovered consciousness before being buried, thought, at first, that he was actually dead, then realized he was still alive, and with great difficulty and great luck managed to escape from that pyramid of ghosts, after having himself been one of them for who knows how many hours and having heard, or as he says, thought he could hear . . ."—and here Díaz-Varela opened the book and looked for a particular quotation, he must have underlined various sections, which is perhaps why he had picked up the book, so as to be able to read out the actual words to me—" 'groans from the world of the dead amongst whom I was lying,' adding 'there are nights when I think I still hear those stifled moans.' His wife is left a widow and, after a decent interval, she marries again, a certain Count Ferraud, by whom she has two children, her first marriage having been childless. She inherits a considerable fortune from her fallen hero, she recovers and carries on with her life, she is still young, after all, she has a fair stretch of road before her and that is the determining factor: the road that foreseeably lies ahead of us and how we want to travel that road once we have decided to remain in the world and not go chasing after ghosts, which exercise a powerful attraction when they are still recent, as if they wanted to drag us after them. Whether many people die around us, as happens during a war, or just one much-loved individual, we feel an initial temptation to join them, or at least to carry their weight and not let them go. Most people, though, do let go of them after a time, when they recognize that their own survival is at risk, that the dead are a great burden and prevent any possible advance, and even stop your breath, if you're too wrapped up in them, if you live too much in their dark shadow. Regrettably, they are as fixed as paintings, they don't move, they don't add anything, they don't speak and never respond, and drive us into a blind alley, into one corner of their painting, which, being finished, allows for no retouching. The novella doesn't describe the widow's grief, if she went through what Luisa is going through; it doesn't mention her pain or her grief, it doesn't show the character at all during the period when she would have received the fateful news, but only ten years later, in 1817, I believe, but given that she doesn't appear to be a heartless person or at least not someone who was heartless from the start—the fact is we don't know, because it's left unexplored—one assumes that she experienced all the usual stages of bereavement (shock, desolation, sadness, languor, apathy, anxiety, fear upon realizing that time is passing, and consequent recovery)."

Díaz-Varela broke off and took a sip of the whisky and ice he had poured himself. He hadn't sat down again after getting up to take the book off the shelf, I was lying on the sofa, we hadn't yet gone to his bed. That was what usually happened, we would sit down first and talk for at least an hour, and I was never sure whether there would be a second act or not, our behaviour gave no indication either way, it was that of two people who have things to tell each other or to talk about and who will not inevitably end up having sex together. I always had the feeling that it might or might not happen, and that the two possibilities were equally natural and neither could be taken for granted, as if each time were the first time and as if there had been no accumulation of experiences from whatever had happened previously in that regard—not even a sense of trust, not even a caress—and we would eternally have to start the same journey from the beginning. I was also sure that we would do whatever he wanted or rather proposed, because the fact is that he was always the one, with a word or gesture, who would propose moving to the bedroom, but only after we had talked, and in the face of my invincible timidity. I feared that one day, instead of making the gesture or saying the word that would invite me to join him in bed or to pull up my skirt, he would suddenly—or after a pause—bring the conversation and our meeting to a close as if we were two friends who had run out of things to say or had various errands to do and would send me out into the street with a kiss, I could never be certain that my visit would end up with our bodies entangling. I both liked and didn't like that strange uncertainty: on the one hand, it made me think that he enjoyed my company whatever the circumstances and didn't see me merely as an instrument for his sexual hygiene or relief; on the other hand, it infuriated me that he could hold off for so long, that he didn't feel an urgent need to pounce on me without further ado, as soon as he opened the door, in order to satisfy his desire; that he found it so easy to postpone that moment, or perhaps his desire was merely accumulating while I looked at him and listened. But that quibble can be put down to the dissatisfaction that predominates in us all and without which we cannot live, especially since, in the end, the thing I always feared wouldn't happen did happen, and I had no reason to complain.

"Go on, what happened next, in what way does that book prove you right?" I said. He definitely had the gift of the gab and I loved to listen to him, regardless of what he talked about and even if he was recounting an old Balzac story that I could easily read for myself, a story not invented by him, but doubtless interpreted in his own free and possibly distorted fashion. I found anything he said interesting or, worse, amusing (worse, because I was aware that one day I would have to stand aside). Now that I never go to his apartment, I recall those visits as forays into a secret territory, as a small adventure, perhaps more because of the first act of each encounter than the second, although, at the time, the very uncertainty of that second act made it seem even more desirable.

"The Colonel wants to recover his name, career, rank, dignity, fortune or part of it (he has spent years living in dire poverty) as well as the most complicated thing of all: his wife, who will be shown to be a bigamist if Chabert can prove that he really is Chabert and not an impostor or a lunatic. Perhaps Madame Ferraud really loved him and mourned his death when she was told of it, and felt that the world had fallen in on her; but his reappearance is surplus to requirements, his resurrection a real nuisance, a great problem, threatening catastrophe and ruin, and, paradoxically, it brings with it again the sense that the world is falling in on her: how can the return of the person whose disappearance first evoked those feelings evoke precisely the same feelings? We see quite clearly that, with the passing of time, what *has been* should continue to *have been*, to exist only in the past, as is always or almost always the case, that is how life is intended to be, so that there is no undoing what is done and no unhappening what has happened; the dead must stay where they are and nothing can be corrected. We can allow ourselves to miss them because we know they are safely gone: we lost someone and, knowing that he is never going to come back or reclaim the place he vacated, a place that, besides, has since been swiftly filled, we are free to long for his return with all our might. We can miss him safe in the knowledge that our proclaimed desires will never be granted and that there is no possible return, that he can no longer intervene in our existence or in mundane matters, that he can no longer intimidate or inhibit or even overshadow us, that he will never again be better than us. We sincerely regretted his departure, and when it happened, we truly wished he could have gone on living; a vast gap or even abyss opened up and we were tempted to hurl ourselves after him; that, at least, is what we felt momentarily. It's rare, though, for that initial temptation not to expire. Then the days and months and years pass and we adapt; we get used to that gap and don't even consider the possibility that the dead man will come back to fill it, because the dead don't do that, and we are safe from them, and, besides, that gap has been filled in and is no longer the same or has become purely fictitious. We remember those closest to us every day and still feel sad to think that we will not see them again or hear them or laugh with them or kiss those we used to kiss. But there is no death that is not also, in some way, a relief, that does not offer some advantage. Once it has occurred, of course; we do not desire anyone's death in advance, possibly not even that of our enemies. We mourn our father, for example, but we are left with a legacy, his house, his money and his worldly goods, which we would have to give back to him were he to return, which would put us in a very awkward position and cause us great distress. We might mourn a wife or a husband, but sometimes we discover, although this may take a while, that we live more happily and more comfortably without them or, if we are not too advanced in years, that we can begin anew, with the whole of humanity at our disposal, as it was when we were young; the possibility of choosing without making the old mistakes; the relief of not having to put up with certain annoying habits, because there is always something that annoys us about the person who is always there, at our side or in front or behind or ahead, because marriage surrounds and encircles. We mourn a great writer or a great artist when he or she dies, but there is a certain joy to be had from knowing that the world has become a little more vulgar and a little poorer, and that our own vulgarity and poverty will thus be better hidden or disguised; that he or she is no longer there to underline our own relative mediocrity; that talent in general has taken another step towards disappearing from the face of the earth or slipping further back into the past, from which it should never emerge, where it should remain imprisoned so as not to affront us except perhaps retrospectively, which is less wounding and more bearable. I am speaking of the majority, of course, not everyone. This glee is observable even in journalists, who come up with such headlines as 'The last genius of the piano dies' or 'Death of the last great cinema legend,' as if they were joyfully celebrating the fact that, finally, there are no more geniuses and never will be, that this latest demise frees us from the eternal nightmare of knowing that superior, very gifted people exist and that, much to our regret, we cannot help but admire them; that we are a step closer to banishing that curse or, at least, bringing it down a peg or two. Naturally, one mourns a friend, as I have mourned Miguel, but there is also the pleasant sense of having survived and of better prospects, of being present at a friend's death rather than your own, of being able to view his finished portrait and tell his story, to defend and console the people he has left behind. As your friends die, you feel more shrunken and more alone, but, at the same time, you count them off, 'One less, and another, I know what their lives were like up until the final instant, and I am the only one who can tell the tale. In my case, though, no one who really cares about me will see me die or be able to tell my whole story, and so, in a sense, I will remain forever unfinished, because, not having seen me fall, how can anyone be certain that I won't continue to live eternally?' "

HE HAD A marked tendency to discourse and expound and digress, as I have noticed to be the case with many of the writers I meet at the publishing house, as if it weren't enough for them to fill pages and pages with their thoughts and stories, which, with few exceptions, are either absurd, pretentious, gruesome or pathetic. But Díaz-Varela wasn't a writer, and I didn't mind his digressions, in fact, my response was exactly the same as it had been the second time I met him, in the café next to the museum, namely, that, while he continued to expatiate, I couldn't take my eyes off him and delighted in his grave, somehow inward-turned voice and the often arbitrary syntactic leaps he made, the whole effect seeming sometimes not to emanate from a human being, but from a musical instrument that does not transmit meanings, perhaps a piano played with great agility. On this occasion, however, I wanted to find out more about Colonel Chabert and Madame Ferraud, and, more especially, how, according to him, the novella proved him to be right about Luisa, although I could easily imagine his reasoning.

"Yes, but what happened to the Colonel?" I said, interrupting his flow, and I saw that he didn't mind my interruption, for he was aware of his own discursive tendencies and was perhaps glad when someone stopped him. "Was he accepted by the world of the living to which he wanted to return? Did his wife accept him? Did he manage to resume his existence?"

"What happened is the least of it. It's a novel, and once you've finished a novel, what happened in it is of little importance and soon forgotten. What matter are the possibilities and ideas that the novel's imaginary plot communicates to us and infuses us with, a plot that we recall far more vividly than real events and to which we pay far more attention. Besides, you can find out what happened to the Colonel on your own, it would do you good to read a few non-contemporary authors now and then. I can lend you the book, if you like, or don't you read French? There's a Spanish translation available, but it's not much good. And so few people know French these days."—He had studied at the Lycée; we had talked little about our respective histories, but that much he had told me.—"What's important here is that Chabert's reappearance is, of course, an absolute disaster for his wife, who has recovered and made another life in which there is no room for him, or only as a figure from the past, as he had once been, as an ever-fainter memory, well and truly dead, buried in a distant, unknown grave alongside others who fell in that Battle of Eylau, which, ten years on, almost no one remembers or wants to remember, because, among other things, the person who led that battle has been sent into lonely exile on St. Helena, and Louis XVIII now sits on the throne, and the first thing any new regime does is to forget and minimize and erase the previous regime, and to convert those who served it into putrefying nostalgics, who are left with nothing to do but slowly burn out and die. The Colonel realizes this from the very first moment and knows that his inexplicable survival is a curse for the Countess, who doesn't answer his first letters and has no wish to see him, for fear that she might recognize him, preferring to believe that he will turn out to be a madman or a fraud, or, if not, that he will simply give up eventually out of exhaustion, bitterness and desolation. Or that when he can no longer maintain his stubborn refusal to leave, he will return to the snowy fields and die again—once and for all. When they do finally meet and talk, the Colonel, who has had no reason to cease loving her during his long exile from earth, during which he suffered all the infinite hardships of being dead, asks her . . ." And here Díaz-Varela looked for another quote in the small book, although this one was so short that he must have known it by heart: " 'Are the dead quite wrong, then, to come back?' Or perhaps: 'Is it a mistake for the dead to return?' In French it says: *Les morts ont donc bien tort de revenir?*' "—And it seemed to me that his accent in French was as good as it was in English.—"The Countess's hypocritical answer is: 'No, no, Monsieur! Don't think me ungrateful,' and adds: 'It is no longer in my power to love you, but I know how much I owe you and I can still offer you the affection of a daughter.' And Balzac says that, after hearing the Colonel's sympathetic and generous response to these words"—and Díaz-Varela again read from the book (with his fleshy, kissable mouth)—" 'The Countess shot him a look of such intense gratitude that poor Chabert would gladly have returned to Eylau and climbed back into his grave.' Meaning that he wishes to cause her no further problems or anxieties or to intrude upon a world that is no longer his, to cease being her nightmare or ghost or torment, and to remove himself and disappear."

"And is that what he did? Did he just abandon the field and accept defeat? Did he return to his grave, did he retreat?" I asked, taking advantage of a pause.

"You'll find out when you read it for yourself. The great misfortune of remaining alive having once died and been assumed dead even according to the army records ('an historical fact'), doesn't affect only his wife, but him as well. You cannot pass from one state to the other, or, rather, of course, from the second to the first, and he is fully aware of being a corpse, an official and, to a large extent, real corpse, because he himself had thought he was dead and had heard the moans of his fellow corpses, which no living person could hear. When, at the beginning of the novel, he turns up at the lawyer's office, one of the clerks or messengers asks him his name. He answers: 'Chabert,' and the other man says: 'The Colonel who died at Eylau?' And the ghost, far from protesting or rebelling and growing angry and immediately contradicting him, merely nods and says meekly: 'The very same, sir.' And a little later, he makes this definition his own. When, at last, he manages to see the lawyer, Derville, and the latter asks him: 'To whom do I have the honour of speaking?' he responds: 'Colonel Chabert.' 'Which one?' insists the lawyer, and the answer is an absurdity, but absolutely true for all that: 'The one who died at Eylau.' Later, Balzac himself refers to Chabert in the same terms, albeit ironically: "Sir," said the dead man . . . ,' that's what he writes. The Colonel cannot escape from his vile condition as a man who did not die when he should have died or, indeed, when he did die, as Napoleon himself had regretfully ordered two doctors to verify. When he sets out his case to Derville, he says the following"—and Díaz-Varela searched through the pages to find the quotation—" 'To be frank, during that period, and even now sometimes, my name is distasteful to me. I would prefer not to be me. My sense of what should be mine by rights is killing me. If my illness had taken from me all memory of my past existence, I would have been happy.' That's what he says: 'My name is distasteful to me. I would prefer not to be me.' "—Díaz-Varela repeated the words to me, underlined them.—"The worst thing that can happen to anyone, worse than death itself, and the worst thing one can make others do, is to return from the place from which no one returns, to come back to life at the wrong time, when you are no longer expected, when it's too late and inappropriate, when the living have assumed you are over and done with and have continued or taken up their lives again, leaving no room for you at all. For the person who returns, there is no greater misfortune than to discover that he is surplus to requirements, that his presence isn't wanted, that he is disturbing the universe, that he constitutes a hindrance to his loved ones, who don't know what to do with him."

" 'The worst thing that can happen to anyone'? Oh, come on. You're talking as if the story were real, but things like that never happen, or only in fiction."

"Fiction has the ability to show us what we don't know and what doesn't happen," he retorted, "and in this case, it allows us to imagine the feelings of a dead man who finds himself obliged to come back, and shows us why the dead shouldn't come back. With the exception of mad people or the very old, everyone, sooner or later, tries to forget the dead. They avoid thinking about them, and when, for some reason or other, they can't avoid it, they grow sad and gloomy, they stop whatever they're doing, their eyes fill with tears, and they find themselves unable to go on until they have shaken off the dark thought or suppressed the memory. Believe me, in the long term, and in the medium term too, everyone ends up shaking off the dead, because that is their final fate, as they would doubtless agree, and, once they have tried and experienced their new condition, they wouldn't be prepared to come back anyway. No one who has departed this life and washed his hands of it, even if his death occurred against his will and much to his regret, as the victim, say, of a murder, no one would choose to be reinstated and thus resume the terrible fatigue of existing. Think about it, Colonel Chabert endured unspeakable suffering and saw what we all believe to be the worst of horrors, namely war; you would think that no one could give lessons in horror to someone who had taken part in pitiless battles fought in sub-zero temperatures, as happened in Eylau, and that was not his first battle, but the last; there, two armies of seventy-five thousand men confronted each other; we don't know exactly how many died, but they say there were at least forty thousand, and that they fought for fourteen hours or more to achieve very little: the French took possession of the field, a field that was nothing but a vast snowy waste piled with corpses, and although the Russian army was badly battered when it retreated, it was not destroyed. The French were so debilitated and exhausted and so stiff with cold, that it was four hours, when night had already fallen, before they realized that the enemy was silently slipping away. Not that they would have been in any condition to pursue them. It's said that the following morning, Marshal Ney rode round the battlefield and that his only comment reflected a mixture of horror, disgust and disapproval: 'What slaughter! And for what?' And yet, despite all this, it is not the soldier, it is not Chabert, but the lawyer, Derville, who has never seen a cavalry charge or a bayonet wound or the havoc caused by cannon fire, who has spent his life either in his chambers or in court, safe from physical violence, barely leaving Paris, he is the one who, at the end of the novel, is allowed to speak and enlighten us about the horrors he has seen during his entirely non-military career, not at war but at peace, not at the front line but in the rearguard. He says to his former clerk, Godeschal, who is about to take his first case as a lawyer: 'You know, my dear friend, there are three men in modern society who can never think well of the world: the Priest, the Doctor, and the Man of Law. They all wear black robes, worn perhaps in mourning for lost virtues and lost hopes. The unhappiest of these three is the lawyer.' He explains that when a man goes to a priest, he does so prompted by feelings of remorse and repentance, by beliefs that make him more interesting, which elevate him, and that, in a way, are a comfort to the soul of his intercessor. 'But we lawyers' "—and here Díaz-Varela read in Spanish from the final page of the book, presumably translating as he went, because he was hardly likely to have made a version beforehand—" 'we see the same wicked feelings repeated over and over, and nothing can correct them, our offices are sewers that can never be washed clean. I cannot begin to tell you the things I have seen in the exercise of my profession! I have seen a father left to die in a garret, without a penny to his name, abandoned by two daughters to whom he had given forty thousand pounds a year! I've seen wills burned; I've seen mothers rob their children, husbands rob their wives, wives kill their husbands or else use their husbands' love to drive them into madness or imbecility, in order that they might live contentedly with their lover. I have seen women administer lethal drops to a legitimate child born of the marriage bed in order to bring about its death and thus benefit a love-child. I can't tell you everything I've seen, because I have been privy to crimes against which justice is impotent. All the horrors that novelists think they invent are as nothing compared to the truth. You will come to know all these delightful things. I bequeath them to you. Meanwhile, I am going to live in the countryside with my wife. Paris disgusts me.' "

Díaz-Varela closed the slender volume and kept the brief silence appropriate to any ending. He didn't look at me, but remained with his eyes fixed on the cover, as if unable to decide whether to reopen the book and resume his reading. I couldn't resist asking about the Colonel again.

"And what happened to Chabert? Nothing good, I imagine, given such a pessimistic conclusion. But it offers a very partial view of things, as the character himself admits: the view of one of the three kinds of men who cannot think well of the world; the view, according to him, of the unhappiest of the three. Fortunately, there are plenty of other viewpoints, most of which are quite different from that of priests, doctors and lawyers."

But he didn't respond. In fact, my initial impression was that he hadn't even heard me.

"And that's how the story ends," he said. "Well, almost. Balzac has Godeschal give an entirely irrelevant response, which very nearly cancels out the force of that vision; but it's a minor defect. The novel was written in 1832, one hundred and eighty years ago, although, strangely enough, Balzac places the conversation between the veteran and the novice lawyer in 1840, that is, at a point in the future, a date when he couldn't even be sure he would still be alive, as if he knew, absolutely, that nothing would change, not just in the next eight years, but ever. If that was his intention, then he was quite right. It's not just that things are exactly the same now as they were when he was describing them—well, the same, if not worse, ask any lawyer. It's always been like that. Far more crimes go unpunished than punished, not to speak of those we know nothing about or that remain hidden, for there must inevitably be more hidden crimes than crimes that are known about and recorded. It's only natural really that Balzac should leave it to Derville rather than to Chabert to speak of the horrors of the world. After all, a soldier tends to play relatively fair, it's clear what he's there to do, he doesn't betray or deceive and he acts not just in obedience to orders, but out of necessity: it's either his life or that of the enemy who is equally intent on taking his or, rather, who finds himself in exactly the same dilemma. The soldier doesn't usually act on his own initiative, he doesn't harbour feelings of hatred or resentment or jealousy, he isn't motivated by long-held desires or personal ambition; the only motivating force is a vague, rhetorical, empty patriotism, for those soldiers, that is, who are moved by such feelings or allow themselves to be convinced: that happened in Napoleon's day, but not so much now, because that kind of man no longer exists, at least not in countries like ours with our armies of mercenaries. The carnage of wars is horrific, of course, but those who take part in them are only following orders, they don't plan the wars, the wars aren't even entirely planned by the generals or the politicians, who have an increasingly abstract and unreal vision of those bloodbaths and, needless to say, are never present, now less than ever; it's as if they were dispatching toy soldiers to the front or on a bombing mission, toys whose faces they never see, as though they were simply immersed in some video game. Crimes committed in ordinary life, however, send shudders down the spine, fill you with fear, not so much the crimes in themselves, which are less striking and more scattered, more spaced out, one here, another there; and because they only trickle into our consciousness, they cause less outrage and tend not to provoke waves of protest however incessantly they occur. No, it's what the crimes themselves mean that's frightening. They always involve an individual will and a personal motive, each crime is conceived and planned by a single mind, or a few minds if it's some kind of conspiracy; and given all the crimes that have been and still are being committed, those many different crimes, separated from each other by kilometres or years or centuries, could not, therefore, have been the product of mutual contagion; and that, in a sense, is more discouraging than a massive act of carnage ordered by a single man, a single mind, which we will always consider to be an unfortunate and inhuman exception: the kind of mind that declares an unjust, all-out war or sets in motion a cruel persecution or institutes a programme of extermination or unleashes a *jihad*. But however atrocious, that isn't the worst thing, or only in quantitative terms. The worst thing is that so many disparate individuals in every age and every country—each on his own account and at his own risk, each with his own thoughts and particular, untransferable aims—should all choose the same methods of robbery, deception, murder or betrayal against the friends, colleagues, brothers, sisters, parents, children, husbands, wives, or lovers of whom they now wish to dispose, and who were doubtless the very people whom they once loved most, for whom, at another time, they would have given their life or killed anyone who threatened them, indeed, it's possible that they would have confronted themselves had they been able to see themselves in the future as they prepare, without remorse or hesitation, to unleash upon their former loved one the fatal blow. That's what Derville was talking about: 'We see the same wicked feelings repeated over and over, and nothing can correct them, our offices are sewers that can never be washed clean. I cannot begin to tell you the things I have seen in the exercise of my profession . . .' "—This time, Díaz-Varela quoted from memory and stopped, perhaps because he couldn't remember any more, perhaps because there was no point in going on. He looked again at the cover, which featured a portrait, possibly by Géricault, of a hussar with a long, curled moustache and a helmet; and he added, as if finally tearing himself away from that abstracted gaze and emerging from a daydream: "Apparently, it's a very famous novel, although I'd never heard of it before. They've even made three films of it, imagine that."

WHEN SOMEONE IS in love, or, more precisely, when a woman is in love and in the early stages of an affair, when it still has all the allure of the new and surprising, she is usually capable of taking an interest in anything that the object of her love is interested in or speaks about. She's not just pretending as a way of pleasing him or winning him over or establishing a fragile stronghold, although there is an element of that, she really does pay attention and allow herself to be genuinely caught up in what he feels and transmits, be it enthusiasm, aversion, sympathy, fear, anxiety or even obsession. Not to mention accompanying him in his improvised lucubrations, which are what most bind and attract her because she is there at their birth and pushes them out into the world and watches them stretch and waver and stumble. She develops a sudden passion for things to which she had never before given a moment's thought, she acquires unexpected dislikes, picks up on details that had previously passed her by unnoticed and that her senses would have continued to ignore until the end of her days, she focuses her energies on matters that affect her only vicariously or because she is under some sort of spell or influence, as if she had decided to live out her life on screen or on stage or inside a novel, in an alien fictional world that absorbs and amuses her more than her real life, which she puts temporarily on hold or relegates to second place, and takes a brief rest from it (there is nothing more tempting than to surrender yourself to someone else, even if only in your imagination, and to make his problems your own and to submerge yourself in his existence, which, because it is not yours, seems easier to bear). I'm possibly going too far in putting it like that, but initially we women do place ourselves at the service or at the disposal of the person we happen to love, and mostly we do this innocently, that is, not knowing that there will come a day, if we ever feel solid and established enough, when he will look at us with disappointment and perplexity as it dawns on him that, in fact, we care nothing for what once excited us, that we are bored by what he tells us, even though he hasn't changed his topics of conversation, which are no less interesting than they used to be. It just means that we will have stopped struggling to maintain that initial enthusiasm and passion, but not that we were pretending or were being false from the very start. With Leopoldo there was never any crux moment, because I never felt the same wilful, ingenuous, unconditional love for him that I felt for Díaz-Varela, into whom I threw myself body and soul—albeit prudently and discreetly, so that he would barely notice—despite knowing beforehand that he could never reciprocate my love, that he, in turn, was at Luisa's service and had, inevitably, been waiting a long time for his opportunity.

I borrowed the Balzac novella (yes, I do know French) because he had read it to me and talked to me about it, and how could I not be interested in something that had interested him, given that I was still in that early phase of falling in love when everything about him was a revelation. I did so out of curiosity too: I wanted to know what had happened to the Colonel, although I assumed he had not met with a happy end, that he had failed to recover wife, fortune or dignity, that he might perhaps have ended up yearning for his condition as corpse. I had never read anything by Balzac, he was another famous writer who, like so many others, I hadn't so much as glanced at, because, paradoxical though it may seem, working in a publishing house prevents you from reading almost any of the truly great literature that has been written, the literature that time has sanctioned and miraculously authorized to endure beyond that briefest of moments, which grows ever briefer. I was also intrigued to know why Díaz-Varela had found it so fascinating and spent so much time over it, why it had led him into those thoughts, why he was using it as evidence that the dead are fine where they are and should never come back, even if their death was untimely and unjust, stupid, gratuitous and unfortunate, like that of Desvern, and even if there was no risk of them ever reappearing. It was as if he feared that, were his friend to be resurrected, were such a thing possible, he wanted to convince me or convince himself that any resurrection would be inopportune, a mistake, and even bad for both the living and for the dead man, as Balzac ironically dubbed the surviving and ghostly Chabert, and that it would even cause everyone unnecessary suffering, always assuming that the truly dead can still suffer. I also had the impression that Díaz-Varela was keen to endorse and accept the lawyer Derville's pessimistic vision, his gloomy ideas about the infinite capacity of normal individuals (like you and me) for covetousness and crime, for placing their own miserly interests before any consideration of pity, affection or even fear. It was as if he wanted to find verification for this in a novel—not in a chronicle or in the annals or in a history book—and to find there persuasive arguments to prove that this was simply how humankind always was and had been, that there was no escaping this and that one should expect only the basest of deeds, betrayals and cruelties, the broken promises and deceptions that have sprung up and been committed in every time and place with no need for examples or models to imitate, although most such crimes remain secret, covered up, and were performed surreptitiously and never came to light, not even after a hundred years had passed, when no one can be bothered to find out what happened all that time ago. And although he hadn't said as much, it was easy to deduce that he didn't even believe that there were many exceptions, apart, perhaps, from a few unusually innocent beings, but, rather, that any seeming exceptions could usually be attributed to a lack of imagination or boldness or possibly the physical inability to carry out a robbery or a crime, or were the product of our own ignorance, our lack of knowledge as to what people had done or planned or ordered to be done and had very successfully concealed.

When I reached the end of the novel and the words spoken by Derville, of which Díaz-Varela had improvised a translation in Spanish, I noticed that he had made a mistake or had perhaps misunderstood, either unwittingly or, possibly, on purpose, to prove his point; perhaps he had chosen or opted to read something into the text that wasn't there, so that his mistaken interpretation, whether deliberate or not, would reinforce what he was trying to endorse or emphasize, that is, the ruthlessness of men or, in this case, women. He had translated it thus: "I have seen women administer lethal drops to a legitimate child born of the marriage bed in order to bring about its death and thus benefit a love-child." When I heard that sentence, my blood froze, because it seems unimaginable that a mother could make such distinctions between her children, especially when those distinctions depended solely on who the father was, that she should have loved one and detested or only tolerated the other, still less that she could be capable of causing the death of the first-born in order to benefit her favourite child, by giving the former some sort of poisoned bait, perhaps in the shape of curative drops for a cough, thus taking advantage of the child's blind faith in the person who had brought him into the world and who had fed and cared for and tended him throughout his whole existence. But that isn't what the original said, it didn't say: *"J'ai vu des femmes donnant à l'enfant d'un premier lit des gouttes qui devaient amener sa mort . . .* ," but *"des goûts,* "which doesn't mean "drops" but "tastes," although you couldn't translate it like that, because it would be ambiguous, to say the least, and lead to confusion. Díaz-Varela's French was doubtless better than mine, he had, after all, studied at the Lycée, but I was tempted to think that a more accurate translation of what Balzac had written would be something like this: "I have seen women instil in a legitimate child born of the marriage bed certain tastes" (or perhaps "inclinations") "that would bring about its death and thus benefit a love-child." The meaning still wasn't very clear even in that interpretation, nor was it easy to imagine what exactly Derville meant. To give or instil in a child tastes or inclinations that would bring about his death? Drink or opium or gambling or a tendency to criminal behaviour perhaps? A taste for luxury that he would be unable to give up and that would lead him to commit crimes in order to satisfy that taste? A morbid lust that would expose him to diseases or propel him into rape? A character so weak and fearful that the slightest setback would drive him to suicide? It was obscure and almost enigmatic. Whatever the true interpretation, what a long time it would take to produce that desired and carefully planned death, what a very slow process and what a large investment of time. And the mother's level of perversity would be far greater than if she had simply given her child a few murderous drops disguised as something else, and which perhaps only an inquisitive, stubborn doctor would be able to detect. There is a difference between preparing someone for their early ruin and death and killing them outright, and we tend to believe that the latter is the graver and more reprehensible of the two, because we have a horror of violence and find direct intervention more shocking, or maybe it's because there is then no room for doubts or excuses, the person carrying out or committing the act has no hiding place, and cannot say it was a mistake or an accident or a miscalculation or an error. A mother who had ruined her son's life, who had intentionally spoiled or perverted her child, could always say, when faced by the unfortunate consequences: "That wasn't what I intended at all. How stupid of me, how could I possibly have imagined that things would turn out this way? I did everything out of excessive love and with the best of intentions. I may have kept him wrapped in cotton wool for so long that I made a coward of him, I may have given in to his every whim and so twisted his mind that he turned into a despot, but my one thought was always his happiness. How blind I have been and how unthinkingly pernicious!" And she could even come to believe this herself, whereas she couldn't possibly think or tell herself such things if her child had died at her hands, because of something she had done and at an hour she herself had determined. Actually causing someone's death is a very different matter, says the person not holding the weapon (and we, unwittingly, accept his reasoning), from, say, preparing the ground for it and waiting for it to come about or to happen of its own accord; as is desiring and ordering someone's death, for the desire and the order sometimes become confused and can prove indistinguishable for those accustomed to having their desires satisfied as soon as they have been expressed or even implied, or to having their desires carried out as soon as they have been conceived. That is why the most powerful and most cunning of people never dirty their own hands or even their tongue, because that way they still have the option of saying, when they are at their smuggest, or when most troubled and wearied by their conscience: "I didn't actually do it. Was I there, was I holding the gun, the spoon, the knife that finished him off? I wasn't even there when he died."

IT WAS ONE NIGHT, after I came back from Díaz-Varela's apartment feeling cheerful and in a good mood, that I began not to suspect so much as to wonder, and lying in bed looking out at my dark, agitated trees, I found myself wishing or, rather, fantasizing about the possibility that Luisa might die and thus leave the field open for me with Díaz-Varela, since she was doing nothing to occupy that field herself. He and I got on well, what he had to say interested me or at least it cost me no great effort to take an interest, and it was clear that he found my company pleasant and amusing, both in bed and out of it, and it is the latter that counts, or, while the former may be necessary, it's still not enough without the latter, and I enjoyed both those advantages. In my vainer moments, I would think that, but for his long-held fixation, his cerebral passion—I didn't dare to call it his long-held plan, because that would have implied suspicion, which I did not yet feel—he would not only have been perfectly content with me, I would also gradually have made myself indispensable to him. I sometimes had the feeling that he couldn't let himself go with me, couldn't entirely give himself, because he had decided in his head, a long time ago, that Luisa was the chosen one, and she had remained so with all the conviction that hopelessness brings with it, since there was not the remotest chance of his dream coming true, given that she was the wife of his best friend whom they both loved very much. Perhaps he had also made her the ideal excuse for never fully committing himself, instead jumping from one woman to another and letting none of those relationships become either very important or very lasting, because, as he lay awake with some woman in his arms, he was always looking out of the corner of his eye or over her shoulder (or should I say, over our shoulder, since I must include myself among the women thus embraced). When you want something for a long time, it's very difficult to stop wanting it, I mean, to admit or to realize that you no longer desire it or that you would prefer something else. Waiting feeds and fosters that desire, waiting is accumulative as regards the thing awaited, it solidifies desire and turns it to stone, and then we resist acknowledging that we have wasted years expecting a signal, which, when it finally comes, no longer tempts us, or else we simply can't be bothered to answer a belated call that we no longer trust, perhaps because it doesn't now suit us to move. One grows accustomed to waiting for an opportunity that never comes, feeling deep down rather calm and safe and passive, unable quite to believe that it never will present itself.

But, alas, at the same time, no one entirely gives up on that hope, and that itch keeps us awake or prevents us from fully submerging ourselves in sleep. After all, the most unlikely things do happen, and that is something everyone feels, even those who know nothing of history or what happened in the previous world, or even what is happening in this world, which advances at the same hesitant pace as they do. Who hasn't been witness to some unlikely event, which we often don't even notice until someone points it out to us and puts it into words: the school dunce is made a minister and the layabout turns banker; the coarsest, ugliest boy in class enjoys a wild success with the best-looking women; while the most simple-minded student becomes a venerated writer and a candidate for the Nobel Prize, as may well be the case with Garay Fontina, for, who knows, perhaps the day will yet come when he gets that call from Stock-

holm; the most tedious and ordinary of fans manages to get close
to her idol and ends up marrying him; the corrupt, thieving jour-
nalist passes himself off as a moralist and a champion of honesty;
the most distant and pusillanimous of heirs, the very last on the list
and the most disastrous, ascends to the throne; the most annoying, stuck-up, scornful woman is adored by the masses whom she
crushes and humiliates from her leader's podium and who should,
by rights, loathe her; the greatest imbecile and the greatest rogue
gain a landslide victory from a population mesmerized by baseness
or perhaps driven by a suicidal desire to be deceived; the murderous
politician, when the tables turn, is liberated and acclaimed as a hero
and a patriot by the crowd who had, until then, concealed their own
criminal tendencies; and an out-and-out yokel is appointed ambas-
sador or President of the Republic or made prince consort if love
is involved, and love tends always to be idiotic and foolish. We are
all waiting or looking out for that golden opportunity, sometimes
it depends solely on how much effort you invest in getting what
you wish for, how much enthusiasm and patience you put into each
objective, however megalomaniac and preposterous that might be.
How could I help nurturing the idea that Díaz-Varela would one day
be mine, either because he finally saw the light or because it didn't
work out with Luisa even though the opportunity had now arisen
and he could doubtless count on his dead friend Deverne having
given him permission, or even a commission, to take on the task?
How could I help thinking that my turn would come, when even
the ancient spectre of Colonel Chabert had believed for a moment
that he would be able to rejoin the narrow world of the living and
recover his fortune and the affections, even if only filial, of the terrified wife who felt so threatened by his resurrection? How could such
thoughts not occur to me on certain hopeful, overexcited nights or
on nights when I was feeling slightly emotionally tipsy, given that

we are surrounded by people with zero talent who succeed in convincing their contemporaries that their talent is, in fact, boundless, or by fools and flatterers who successfully pretend, for half or more than half their lives, to be extremely intelligent and who are listened to as if they were oracles; when there are people with no gift at all for what they do and yet who, nonetheless, enjoy a brilliant career that is greeted by universal applause, at least until they depart this world and are plunged into instant oblivion; when there are uncouth boors who dictate what the polite classes should wear, and to whom the polite classes, for some mysterious reason, listen with rapt attention; when there are unpleasant, twisted, malicious men and women who rouse passions wherever they go; and when there is no shortage of lovers with grotesque pretensions seemingly doomed to defeat and mockery, who, however, triumph in the end against all the odds and against all reason. Anything is possible, anything can happen, and most of us know this, which is why few give up on their great task, though they may rest or momentarily lose sight of it, those, that is, who have set themselves a great task, and there are never so many that they risk swamping the world with their endless vigour and determination.

Sometimes, though, all it takes is for a person to pour his energies into becoming something or into reaching a particular goal for him eventually to become that thing or reach that goal, even though, objectively speaking, everything is against him, and even though he wasn't born for that or hasn't received a call from God to follow that path, as people used to say, and this phenomenon is most apparent in conquests and in confrontations: someone may look as if he's on a hiding to nothing with his enmity for or hatred of someone else, he may lack the power or the means to eliminate the other man, like a hare attacking a lion, and yet that person will often emerge victorious thanks to sheer tenacity and lack of scruples, by dint of

stratagems and spleen and concentration, because his sole objective
in life is to harm his enemy, to bleed him dry and undermine him
and then finish him off, woe betide anyone who acquires an enemy
with those characteristics, however weak and needy he may seem;
if you don't have the time or the will to direct the same passionate
loathing at him and to respond with equal intensity, you will end up
succumbing, because you can't afford to be distracted when fighting
a war, regardless of whether that war is open or hidden or secret,
nor to underestimate your stubborn opponent, even if you believe
him to be innocuous and incapable of harming you or inflicting so
much as a scratch: the reality is that anyone can destroy us, just as
anyone can conquer us, and that is our essential fragility. If someone sets out to destroy us, then it's very difficult to avoid destruc-
tion, unless we drop everything and focus entirely on that struggle.
The first requisite, however, is knowing that such a struggle exists,
for we often don't notice, the enemies most likely to succeed being
of the crafty, silent, treacherous kind, who resemble one of those
undeclared wars or a war in which the attacker remains invisible or
disguises himself as an ally or a neutral force, I, for example, could
launch an offensive against Luisa behind her back, one so oblique
that she wouldn't be aware of it because she wouldn't even know
that an enemy was stalking her. We might, entirely unwittingly and
unintentionally, become an obstacle to someone, we might, quite
unintentionally, be standing in the way or blocking someone else's
upward path, and that means no one is safe, we are all capable of
becoming the object of someone's hatred or of their violent ambi-
tions, even the most wretched and inoffensive of us. Poor Luisa was
both those things, but no one ever completely gives up hope and
I was no different from anyone else. I knew what to expect from
Díaz-Varela and I never deceived myself in that regard, and yet I
still couldn't help hoping for a stroke of luck or for some strange

transformation to take place, for him to realize one day that he couldn't live without me, or that he needed us both. That night, I saw that the only real and possible stroke of luck would be for Luisa to die, and that once the possibility of achieving his objective, his goal, his long-desired trophy, had disappeared, Díaz-Varela would have no option but to see me clearly at last and to seek refuge in me. We should never feel offended when someone makes do with our company for lack of a better companion.

IF, WHEN ALONE at night in my bedroom, I was capable of desiring or fantasizing about the death of Luisa, who had never harmed me and whom I had nothing against, who inspired my sympathy and pity and even a degree of affection, would the same thoughts not have occurred to Díaz-Varela, I wondered, and with far more reason, regarding his friend Desvern. We never, in principle, desire the death of those who are so close to us that they almost constitute our life, but sometimes we surprise ourselves by wondering what would happen if one of them disappeared. On occasions, that thought is provoked by fear and horror, by our excessive love for them and our panic at the idea of losing them: "What would I do without him, without her? What would become of me? I couldn't carry on living, I would want to go with him." The mere idea makes us dizzy, and we usually drive the thought away at once, with a shudder and a saving sense of unreality, as when we shake off a persistent nightmare that doesn't entirely end when we wake up. But on other occasions, the daydream is murky and impure. We never dare to desire anyone's death, still less that of someone close to us, but we know intuitively that if a certain person were to have an accident or become ill towards the end of his life, it would in some way improve the universe or, which comes to the same thing, our own personal situation. "If he or she did not exist," we might think, "how different everything would be, what a weight would be lifted from me, there would be an end to penury and to my unbearable feeling of unease,

I would no longer have to live in his shadow." "Luisa is the only impediment," I would think sometimes, "all that stands between me and Díaz-Varela is his obsession with her. If he were to lose her, if he were to be deprived of his mission, his goal . . ." At the time, I didn't force myself to refer to him only by his surname, he was still "Javier" and that name was adored as being something always beyond my grasp. Yes, if even I found myself drifting into that kind of thinking, how could the same idea not have occurred to him as long as Deverne remained an obstacle? A part of Díaz-Varela must have longed every day for his bosom pal to die, to vanish, and that same part, or an even larger part perhaps, would have rejoiced at the news of his unexpected death by stabbing, a death with which he would have had nothing to do. "How unfortunate and how lucky," he would perhaps have thought when he found out. "How regrettable, how wonderful, what a terrible tragedy that Miguel should have been there at that precise moment, when the man launched into his homicidal attack; it could have happened to anyone, including me, and Miguel could have been somewhere else, why did it have to happen to him, how fortunate that he has been got rid of and thus left the field clear, a field I thought occupied for ever, and I did nothing to make it happen, not even by omission, negligence or by some chance act that one will curse retrospectively, perhaps because I didn't keep him by my side for longer and didn't stop him going to that place, although that would only have been possible had I seen him on that day, but I didn't see or speak to him, I was going to call him later on to wish him a happy birthday, what a misfortune, what a blessing, what a stroke of luck and how dreadful, what a loss and what a gain. And I have no reason to reproach myself."

I never woke up in his apartment, I never spent the night by his side or knew the joy of his face being the first thing I saw in the morning; but there was one occasion, or more than one, when I happened to fall asleep in his bed in the late evening or when it was getting dark, a brief but profound sleep after the satisfying exhaustion I experienced in that bed—whether it was equally satisfying for him I have no idea, one never knows if what another person tells you is true, you can only be sure of what comes from yourself, and even then. On that occasion—the last—I was vaguely aware of a doorbell ringing, I opened my eyes slightly, just for a moment, and saw him by my side, already completely dressed (he always got dressed at once, as if he wouldn't allow himself even a minute of the weary, contented indolence that follows any amorous encounter); he was reading by the light of the bedside lamp, sitting as still as a photo, resting his back against the pillow, not watching me or taking any notice of me at all, and so I remained asleep. The doorbell rang again, more than once, longer and more insistently each time, but I didn't stir or sit up, certain that it was nothing to do with me. I didn't move or open my eyes again, even though I noticed, at the third or fourth ring, that Díaz-Varela was quickly and silently slipping sideways off the bed. It could only be something concerning him, not me, because no one knew I was there (there, in that bed, of all the possible places in the world). My consciousness, however, began to stir, albeit still without fully waking me from sleep. I had dozed off on the bedspread, half-naked or as undressed as he had decided I should be, and I noticed now that he had thrown a blanket over me so that I didn't catch cold or perhaps so that he wouldn't have to continue seeing my body, so that what he had just done with me would be less glaringly obvious, because he always remained completely unchanged after our amorous excesses, he behaved as if they hadn't even happened, however noisy and flamboyant they might have been, he was exactly the same before and afterwards. I instinctively pulled the blanket up around me and that gesture drew me further into wakefulness, although I still kept my eyes closed, half-awake, vaguely listening out for him now that he had left the room and me.

The person must have been downstairs in the street, because I didn't hear the apartment door open, just Díaz-Varela's muffled voice answering the entryphone, I didn't understand the words, only the tone, half-surprised and half-irritated, then resigned and reluctantly acquiescent, like someone unwillingly agreeing to something he finds really annoying or that he doesn't want to get involved in. After a few seconds—or possibly a couple of minutes—the voice of the new arrival sounded louder and clearer, an angry male voice, Díaz-Varela had waited with the front door open so that his visitor wouldn't have to ring that bell too, or perhaps he was hoping to deal with him right there and then, without even inviting him in.

"Fancy having your mobile turned off," the man said reproachfully. "That's why I've had to come traipsing all the way over here."

"Keep your voice down. Like I said, I'm not alone. I've got a bird with me, she's sleeping now, but you wouldn't want her to wake up and hear us. Besides, she knows the wife. Anyway, do you really expect me to have my mobile on all the time just in case you need to call me? Besides, why *would* you call me, we haven't spoken in ages. This had better be important. Wait a moment."

That was enough to jerk me completely awake. All it takes is for someone not to want us to hear something for us to do all we can to find out what that something is, not realizing that sometimes people conceal things from us for our own good, so as not to disappoint or involve us, so that life doesn't seem as bad as it usually does. Díaz-Varela had tried to lower his voice when he answered, but had failed because he was feeling irritated or perhaps apprehensive, and I heard his words quite clearly. His final words, "Wait a moment," made me think that he was going to come into the bedroom to check that I was still asleep, and so I lay very still and with my eyes tight shut, even though I was now completely awake. And that was what happened, I heard him come in and take four or five steps until he was level with my head on the pillow, from where he studied me for a few seconds, like someone carrying out an examination; the steps he took were cautious, but quite normal, as if he were alone in the room. When he left, however, his steps were far more wary; it seemed to me that, having made sure I was still sleeping deeply, he didn't want to risk waking me. I heard him close the door very gently and, once outside, give the handle a tug just to be quite certain that there wasn't the slightest crack through which his conversation might sneak in. The bedroom was next to the living room. There was no click, however, which meant the door was not properly closed. "A bird," I thought, half-amused, half-wounded; not "a friend," not "a date," certainly not "a girlfriend." I was possibly not yet the first or the second and would never be the third, not even in the broadest, vaguest sense of that all-purpose word. He could have just said "a woman." Or perhaps his companion was one of that large band of men with whom you can only use a particular vocabulary, their own, rather than the vocabulary you would normally use, the sort of man for whom you have to adapt your language so that they don't feel alarmed or uncomfortable or inadequate. I didn't take it personally at all, for most of the "blokes" of this world, I would be just that, "a bird."

Half-clothed as I was (I had kept my skirt on throughout), I immediately leapt off the bed, crept over to the door and put my ear to it. That way I caught only a murmur and the occasional word, for both men were too agitated to be able to keep their voices permanently lowered, however much they wanted to and however hard they tried. I decided to widen the crack that Díaz-Varela's gentle tug from the outside had failed to eliminate; fortunately, no tell-tale creak betrayed me; and if they did become aware of my indiscreet presence, I could always say that I had heard voices and wanted to confirm that there was, indeed, a visitor, in which case I would have stayed in the bedroom, thus saving Díaz-Varela the bother of having to introduce me or explain my presence. Not that our sporadic encounters were clandestine, at least there had been no agreement between us to that effect, but I sensed that he probably hadn't told anyone else about them, perhaps because I hadn't either. Or maybe it was because we would both have doubtless concealed them from the same person, Luisa, although why I should do that, I have no idea, apart from a vague, incongruous respect for the plans that he was silently hatching, and for the idea that, if he succeeded in his plans, he and Luisa might one day become husband and wife. The minimal crack that barely deserved the name (the wood was slightly swollen, which was why the door didn't quite close) allowed me to distinguish who was speaking when and, sometimes, to hear entire sentences, at others only fragments or almost nothing, depending on whether the men succeeded in talking in whispers, as was their intention. Contrary to their intention, however, their voices would immediately rise a notch, for they were clearly excited about something, if not somewhat alarmed or even frightened. If Díaz-Varela were to find me spying on them later (he might come and look in on me again, just in case), the more time passed, the more awkward it would be for me, although I could always say, by way of an excuse, that I had assumed he had closed the door simply in order not to wake me and not because he was talking to his visitor about some secret matter. He wouldn't believe me, of course, but I would keep my cool, at least on the surface, unless he confronted me sharply or furiously, regardless of the consequences, and accused me of lying. And he would be right, too, because the truth is, I knew from the beginning that his conversation was not for my ears, not just for reasons of discretion, but because, as he had said, I knew "the wife," and he used the Spanish word "*mujer*" in the sense not of "woman" but of "wife," in this case, someone else's wife, and for the moment, that someone could only be Desvern.

"ALL RIGHT, WHAT'S UP, what's so damn urgent?" I heard Díaz-Varela say, and I heard the response from the other man, who had a resonant voice and very clear, correct diction, not one of those cold Madrid accents—people say that we *madrileños* separate and emphasize every syllable, and yet I've never heard anyone from my city speak like that, well, only in antiquated films and plays, or as a joke—but he barely elided his words, and so each was easily distinguishable when he wasn't speaking in the whisper to which he aspired and of which his speech or tone of voice seemed incapable.

"Apparently the guy's started to blab. He's not as silent as he was."

"Who? Canella?" I heard Díaz-Varela's question very clearly too, and I heard that name as someone might hear a terrifying curse—I remembered that name, I had read it on the Internet, in fact, I remembered the man's whole name, Luis Felipe Vázquez Canella, as if it were a catchy title or a line of poetry—or as someone might hear sentence being pronounced on herself or on the person she most loves, telling herself that this is simply impossible, that this can't be happening, she can't be hearing what she's hearing and what's happened can't have happened, as when our lover announces in that universal phrase, which is the same in all languages, "We need to talk, María," even addressing us by our name, which he barely uses otherwise, not even when his flattering mouth is breathing hard against our neck, and then goes on to condemn us: "I don't know what's wrong with me at the moment, I can't understand it myself" or "I've met someone else" or "You may have noticed that I've been a bit strange and distant lately," all of which are preludes to misfortune. Or like someone hearing the doctor utter the name of an illness that has nothing to do with us, an illness that afflicts other people but not us, and yet, ridiculous though it may seem, this time, he's saying that we have that illness, how can that be, there must be some mistake or else he didn't say what I think he said, that sort of thing doesn't happen to me, it just doesn't, I've never been unlucky like that, and I'm not going to start being unlucky now.

I was startled too, filled by a momentary panic, and I almost stood back from the door so as not to hear any more, so that I could then persuade myself later on that I'd misheard or hadn't actually heard anything. But once we've started, we always go on listening, the words fall or float out on to the air and no one can stop them. I wished they would just lower their voices, so that it wasn't up to me to listen or not, I wished their talk would become muffled or entirely indistinct, and then I could have my doubts, and not have to trust my own ears.

"Of course, who do you think?" retorted the other man slightly scornfully and impatiently, as if now that he had given the alarm, he had the upper hand, the bearer of news always does, until he blurts out what he has to tell and hands it over and is left with nothing, and the person listening no longer needs him. The bearer's dominant position is short-lived and lasts only for as long as he can still announce that he knows something, but has as yet said nothing.

"And what's he saying? Not that he can say much. I mean, what can he say? What can the wretch say? What does it matter what a madman says?" Díaz-Varela kept nervously repeating the same thing over and over, to himself really, as if he were trying to exorcize a curse.

The visitor gabbled his response—he could hold it in no longer—and in doing so, his voice rose and fell erratically. I caught only fragments of his response, but of these quite a few.

". . . talking about the calls he got, the voice telling him things," he said; ". . . about the man in leather, meaning me," he said. "It's no joke . . . it's hardly a serious matter . . . but I'm going to have to mothball them, which is a shame because I really like them, I've been wearing them for years now . . . They didn't find a mobile phone on him, I took care of that . . . so they'll think it's all in his imagination . . . They're not going to believe him, I mean, the man's a nutter . . . The danger would be if it was to occur to someone . . . not spontaneously, but with a bit of nudging . . . It's unlikely, because if there's one thing the world isn't short of, it's lazy sods . . . It's been a while now . . . It's what we expected, the fact that he refused to speak initially was a real bonus, it's just that things now are as we thought they would be from the start . . . We had relaxed a bit, that's all . . . At the time, in the heat of the moment . . . worse, but more credible . . . Anyway, I wanted you to know straight away, because it's a change, and not a minor one either, although it doesn't affect us at the moment and I don't think it will . . . But I thought it best you should know."

"No, you're right, Ruibérriz, it isn't a minor change," I heard Díaz-Varela say, and I heard that unusual surname clearly, Díaz-Varela being too upset to moderate his voice, incapable now of whispering. "He may be a nutter, but he's saying that someone persuaded him, in person and via telephone calls, or else put the idea in his head. He's sharing out the blame, or broadening it, and you're the next link and I'm right behind you, damn it. What if they show him a photo of you and he picks you out. You've got a record, haven't you? You're on their files, aren't you? And, as you yourself say, you've been wearing those leather coats all your life, that's how people recognize you, that and your T-shirts in summer, which, by the way, you're far too old for. At first, you told me that you wouldn't go, that you wouldn't be seen, that if he needed a bit of a push, you'd send a third party to feed him a little more poison and show him a face he could trust. You said there would always be at least two steps between you and him, not one, that the third party wouldn't even know of my existence. Now it turns out there's only you between me and him, and he could easily identify you. You've got a record, haven't you? Go on, tell me the truth, this is no time to pull punches, I'd rather know where I stand."

There was a silence, perhaps that man Ruibérriz was wondering whether or not to tell the truth, as Díaz-Varela had asked him to, and if he was, that meant he did have a record and his photo would be on file. I was afraid that the pause might have been sparked by some noise I had made without realizing it, my foot on a creaking floorboard perhaps, I didn't think so, but fear will not allow us to discount anything, not even something that doesn't exist. I imagined the two of them standing motionless, holding their breath for a moment, suspiciously pricking up their ears, looking out of the corner of their eye at the bedroom, making a gesture with one hand, a gesture meaning "Hang on, she's woken up." And suddenly I felt afraid of them, those two men frightened me; I tried to believe that Javier on his own wouldn't frighten me: I had just been to bed with him, I had embraced and kissed him with all the love I dared show him, that is, with a great deal of repressed, disguised love, I let it show in tiny details that he probably wouldn't even notice, the last thing I wanted was to frighten him, to scare him off prematurely, to drive him away—although that time would come, I was sure of it. Now I noticed that any feelings of repressed love had vanished— love, in any of its forms, is incompatible with fear; or else those feelings were deferred until a better moment, that of denial and forgetting, but I knew that neither of those things was possible. And so I stepped away from the door in case he should come back into the room to see if I was still asleep, and to check that I had not been an ear-witness to their conversation. I lay down on the bed, adopted what I thought was a convincing posture and waited, I couldn't hear anything now, I missed Ruibérriz's reply, which he must have given sooner or later. I stayed there for one minute, two, then three, but no one came, nothing happened, and so I screwed up my courage and got off the bed, went over to the false crack in the door, still half-undressed as he had left me, still with my skirt on. The temptation to listen is irresistible, even if we realize that it will do us no good. Especially when the process of knowing has already begun.

The voices were less audible now, just a murmur, as if they had calmed down after the initial shock. Perhaps before that, they had both been standing up and now had sat down for a moment; people talk more quietly when they're sitting down.

"So what do you think we should do?" I heard Díaz-Varela say at last. He wanted to bring the discussion to a close.

"We don't have to do anything," answered Ruibérriz, raising his voice, perhaps because he was giving the orders now and felt, momentarily, in charge again. It sounded to me like he was summing up, he would leave soon, perhaps he had already picked up his coat and draped it over his arm, always assuming he had taken it off, for his was an untimely, lightning visit, Díaz-Varela probably hadn't even offered him a glass of water. "This information doesn't point to anyone, it doesn't concern us, neither you nor I has anything to do with it, any interference from me would be counter-productive. Just forget you know about it. Nothing is going to change, nothing has changed. If there's any other news, I'll find out, but there's no reason why there should be. They'll probably make a note of his claim, file it away and do nothing. How are they going to investigate what he says if there's no trace of that mobile phone, if it doesn't exist? Canella never even knew the number, apparently he's given them four or five different numbers, he's not sure what it was, which is perfectly normal, since they're all invented or dreamed up by him. He was given the phone but never told the number, that's what we agreed and that's what happened. So what's new? The guy claims he heard voices talking about his daughters and telling him who was to blame. Like lots of other nutcases. There's nothing so very odd about him hearing those voices through a mobile phone rather than in his head or coming down from the sky, they'll just assume he's a loony showing off. Even losers, even madmen, know about the latest trends, and these days, anyone who doesn't have a mobile phone is an idiot. Just let it go. Don't get too alarmed about it, because that's not going to help either."

"And what about the man in the leather coat? You yourself were alarmed about that, Ruibérriz. That's why you came running to tell me. Now you're saying there's no need to worry. So which is it to be?"

"To be honest, it did freak me out a bit. There we were, happily convinced that he wouldn't make a statement or say a word. It caught me by surprise, I just wasn't expecting it. But telling you about it now has made me realize that it'll be fine. And if he did get a couple of visits from a man in a leather coat, so what? Practically speaking, it's tantamount to him saying he's been visited by the Virgin of Fatima. Like I said, I'm only wanted in Mexico, and the warrant there has probably lapsed by now, not that I'm planning to fly over and check: a youthful misdemeanour, it happened years ago. And I didn't wear these leather coats then." Ruibérriz knew he was in the wrong, that he should never have allowed himself to be seen by the *gorrilla*. Perhaps that was why he was trying to play down the importance of the news he himself had brought.

"Well, you'd better get rid of the coats you've got, starting with that one. Burn it or shred it. We don't want some smart-arse linking you with what happened. You may not have a record here, but you're still known to a few cops. Let's just hope the murder squad doesn't swap information with other crime squads, although that seems unlikely, no one in Spain seems to swap information with anyone else. Each department keeps pretty much to itself, so I'd be surprised if they did." Díaz-Varela was trying to be optimistic now and to reassure himself. They sounded like normal people, as much the bumbling amateur as I would have been, people who are unaccustomed to crime or not fully convinced that they've committed, or from what I could gather, commissioned one.

I wanted to see that man Ruibérriz, who must have been about to leave; I wanted to see his face and see that famous leather coat before he destroyed it. I decided to leave the bedroom and was on the verge of getting dressed. But if I did that, Díaz-Varela might suspect that I'd been aware for a while that there was someone else in the apartment and had perhaps been listening or spying, at least during the few seconds it would have taken me to pull on the rest of my clothes. If, on the other hand, I burst into the living room as I was, I would give the impression that I had just woken up and had no idea that anyone else was there. I would have heard nothing, convinced that he and I were, as usual, still alone, with no witness to our occasional evening conjunctions. I was simply going to look for him, having discovered that he had left the bed while I was sleeping. It would be best if I presented myself in that state of half-undress, with no show of caution and making a normal amount of noise, like an innocent unaware of anything.

THE FACT IS, though, that far from being half-dressed, I was half- or almost-naked, and "the rest of my clothes" meant everything apart from my skirt, because that was all I was wearing, Díaz-Varela preferring to see me with it pulled up or preferring to pull it up himself during our labours, but for reasons of pleasure or comfort, he always removed my other garments; well, sometimes, he suggested I put my shoes back on once I'd taken off my tights, but only if I was wearing heels, a lot of men cling faithfully to certain classic images, and I can understand that—I have my own such images—and I've nothing against it, after all, it costs me nothing to please them and I even feel rather flattered to be conforming to a fantasy that has a certain prestige, and which has, rather commendably, endured now for a few generations. And so that near-complete lack of clothing—my skirt came to just above my knee when it was in its proper place and unwrinkled, but now it was crumpled and twisted and seemed far briefer—stopped me in my tracks and made me hesitate and wonder how I would behave if I genuinely thought I was alone in the apartment with Díaz-Varela, would I sashay forth from the bedroom with my breasts bare or would I cover them up? If you're going to appear in front of someone else, you have to be very confident that your breasts haven't grown slack, that they don't give you away by swaying and bouncing too much (I've never understood how nudists of a certain age can be so relaxed about this); having a man see them in repose or from close to and in the heat of battle, so to speak, is quite a different matter from him seeing them full on and at a distance and with them bobbing about uncontrollably. I failed to reach a conclusion, because modesty immediately got the better of me. The prospect of revealing myself like that to a complete stranger seemed completely unacceptable, especially when the stranger in question was a shady character with no scruples. Although, as I was discovering, Díaz-Varela lacked scruples too, possibly to an even greater extent, but he was nonetheless someone who knew those parts of my body that were visible, and not just that, he was someone whom I still loved, for what I felt was a mixture of utter incredulity and basic, unreflecting repugnance; I was incapable of taking in—let alone analysing—what I believed I now knew, and I say "believed" because I felt sure that I must have misheard, that this was some kind of misunderstanding, that I had entirely misinterpreted the conversation, that there was some explanation that would allow me to think later on: "How could I possibly have thought such a thing, how foolish and unfair I have been." And at the same time, I realized that I had, inevitably, already internalized and incorporated the facts that emerged from that conversation, that they were engraved on my brain until I received the denial I could not ask for without possibly exposing myself to grave danger. I had to pretend to have heard nothing, not just in order to avoid seeming, in his eyes, to be a spy and a busybody—insofar as I cared how he viewed me, which I still did, because no change is ever immediate and instantaneous, not even one brought about by a horrendous discovery—but because it was advisable and even, quite literally, vital. I felt afraid too, for myself, well, a little afraid, I couldn't be very afraid, as I gauged the dimensions of what had happened and what it meant, it wasn't easy to move from post-coital placidity or torpor to fearing the person with whom I had achieved that state. There was something improbable and unreal about the whole situation, like a dark, defamatory dream that weighs unbearably on our soul, I was incapable of suddenly seeing Díaz-Varela as a murderer who, having once crossed that line, having once transgressed, might well reoffend. He wasn't really a murderer, I tried to think later on: he hadn't held the knife or stabbed anyone, he had never even spoken to that homicidal *gorrilla*, Vázquez Canella, he hadn't ordered him to do anything, he'd had no contact with him, indeed, from what I could gather, they had never exchanged a single word. Perhaps the plot hadn't even been his idea, he might have told his troubles to Ruibérriz, who had then planned it all himself—eager to please, a fool, a hothead—and come to him when the deed was done, like someone turning up with an unexpected present: "See how I have smoothed the way for you, see how I have cleared the field, now it is all within your grasp." Even that man Ruibérriz had not been the actual executioner, he hadn't held the weapon or given precise instructions to anyone: he had, at least initially and as I understood it, been a third party, and had merely poisoned the crazed mind of the beggar, trusting in the latter's eventual violent reaction or response, which might or might not happen; if it was a premeditated crime, much had been left strangely to chance. To what extent had they been sure that he would act, to what extent were they responsible? Unless they had given him instructions or orders and put pressure on him and provided him with that butterfly knife with its seven-centimetre blade, every centimetre of which enters the flesh; after all, given that, in theory, such knives are banned, it can't be easy to buy one nor would it be affordable to someone who exists solely on tips and sleeps in a clapped-out car. They had obviously given him a mobile phone so that they could phone him, not so that he could make any calls himself—perhaps he had no one to phone, his daughters' whereabouts were unknown or they may deliberately have kept their distance, avoiding their angry, puritanical, unhinged father like the plague—but to persuade him, like someone whispering in his ear, people forget that what is said to us on the phone comes not from far away, but from very near, which is why what we are told over the phone is so much more persuasive than the same words spoken by someone face to face, for such an interlocutor will not, or only in very rare cases, brush our ear with his lips. Generally speaking, this argument doesn't work at all, on the contrary, it's merely an aggravating factor, but it helped momentarily to reassure me and make me feel less threatened, not in principle and not then, not in Díaz-Varela's apartment, in his bedroom, in his bed: he had not actually stained his hands with blood, with the blood of his best friend, that man I had become so fond of, at a distance and over the years, when we breakfasted in the same café.

Then there was this other man, whose face I wanted to see, who was the reason I was prepared to emerge from the bedroom half-naked, before he left and I lost sight of him for ever. He might prove to be the far more dangerous of the two and might not be at all amused to see me or for me to preserve an image of him for ever afterwards; with him I might really be exposing myself to danger and might read in his eyes the following words: "I won't forget your face; I can easily find out your name and where you live." He might be tempted to get rid of me.

But I had to hurry, I could hesitate no longer, and so I put on my bra and my shoes—I had taken these off again, rubbing the heels against the bottom end of the bed, where they had fallen to the floor just before I fell asleep. The bra was enough, I might have put it on anyway, even if there hadn't been an intruder, aware that it would be more flattering once I was standing up and in movement: even to Díaz-Varela, who had just seen me with nothing on. It was a size smaller than I normally wear, a very old trick which always works on romantic dates, it gives a bit of uplift to your breasts, makes them look fuller, not that I've ever had any problems with mine, so far anyway. It's a small enticement and never fails, when you go on a date with a preconceived idea of what that date will involve, along with other less predictable things. The bra might even make me look more striking—well, more attractive perhaps—in the stranger's eyes, but it also helped me feel more protected, less embarrassed.

I prepared to open the door, I had already put my shoes on, not worrying if the heels made a noise on the wooden floor, it was a way of warning them, if they were listening acutely enough and not too absorbed in their own problems. I had to watch my expression, which should be one of complete surprise when I saw that man Ruibérriz, but I hadn't yet decided what my initial response should be, I would probably turn on my heel in alarm and rush back into the bedroom and not reappear until I had put on the slightly, or sufficiently, low-cut V-neck sweater I had chosen to wear that day. And I would probably cover my bust with my hands, or would that seem overly modest? It's never easy to put yourself in a non-existent situation, I can't understand how so many people spend their whole life pretending, because it's impossible to keep every factor in mind, down to the last, unreal detail, when there are no details and they have all been made up.

I TOOK A deep breath and opened the door, ready to play my part, and I knew then that I was already blushing, even before Ruibérriz had entered my field of vision, because I knew he was about to see me in a bra and tight skirt and I found it embarrassing to appear like that before a stranger who had already made the worst possible impression on me. Perhaps all that heat came, in part, from what I had just overheard, from the mixture of indignation and horror that my encircling sense of incredulity did nothing to diminish; I was, at any rate, extremely upset and troubled, filled by confused feelings and thoughts.

The two men were standing up and both of them immediately glanced round, they obviously hadn't heard me putting on my shoes or anything. In Díaz-Varela's eyes I noted an immediate coldness or mistrust, censure and even severity. In Ruibérriz's I saw only surprise and a flicker of male appreciation, which is easy enough to spot and which he doubtless made no effort to conceal, for some men's eyes are very quick to make such evaluations, a reflex action they can't avoid, they're even capable of ogling the bare thighs of a woman who has been involved in a car accident and is still lying, all bloody, on the road, or of staring at the hint of cleavage revealed by the woman who crouches down to help them if they happen to be the injured party, it's beyond their will to control or perhaps it has nothing to do with will at all, it's a way of being in the world that will last until the day they die, and before closing their eyes for ever, their gaze will linger appreciatively on the nurse's knee, even if she's wearing lumpy white tights.

Instinctively, and feeling genuinely embarrassed, I covered myself with my hands, but what I didn't do was turn on my heel and disappear at once, because I felt that I should say something, give voice to my embarrassment and shock. This proved less spontaneous.

"Oh, I'm sorry," I said to Díaz-Varela, "I didn't know anyone was here. Forgive me, I'll go and put something on."

"It's all right, I was just leaving," said Ruibérriz, holding out his hand to me.

"Ruibérriz, a friend," Díaz-Varela said, introducing me in stark, awkward fashion: "This is María." Like Luisa, he failed to give my surname, but he possibly did so consciously, to provide me with a minimum of protection.

"Ruibérriz de Torres," added the introducee, "delighted to meet you." He was clearly keen to highlight that "de" with its hypothetically noble connotations, and continued to hold out his hand.

"Pleased to meet you," I said, rapidly shaking his hand—his eyes flew straight to the one breast left momentarily uncovered—then hurried back into the bedroom, leaving the door open to make it clear that I intended rejoining them, the visitor would hardly leave without saying goodbye to someone he could still see. I picked up my sweater, put it on—aware that his gaze was fixed on my figure, as I stood, sideways on to him, to get dressed—and then returned to the living room. Ruibérriz de Torres was wearing a scarf around his neck—a mere adornment, he had not perhaps removed it all the time he had been there—and draped over his shoulders was the famous leather coat, which hung about him like a cape, in vaguely theatrical, carnivalesque fashion. It was long and black, like the coats worn by members of the SS or perhaps by the Gestapo in films about the

Nazis, he was the kind of man who preferred the quick and easy route to attracting attention, even at the risk of causing revulsion, and now, if he did as Díaz-Varela said, he would have to renounce his overcoat. My first thought was: "How could Díaz-Varela have placed his trust in someone who was so visibly a rogue?" It was written all over his face and physique, his mannerisms and his manner, a single glance was all it took to detect his essential self. He was over fifty, and yet everything about him oozed youthfulness: his attractive hair combed back so that it formed a wave on either side of his slightly broad, bulbous, but entirely orthodox forehead, with streaks or blocks of grey hair, the colour of quicksilver, that failed to make him look any more respectable because they looked artificial, as if he'd had highlights put in; his athletic trunk, slightly convex as tends to be the case with those who try, at all costs, to avoid acquiring a belly and so take pains to cultivate their pectorals instead; his broad smile that revealed flashing teeth; his upper lip that folded back to reveal its moist inside, thus emphasizing his overwhelmingly salacious nature. He had a straight, pointed nose with a very prominent central bone, indeed, he looked more like a citizen of Rome than of Madrid and reminded me of that actor, Vittorio Gassman, not in his noble old age, but when he used to play crooks. Yes, it was obvious to anyone that he was an amiable fraud. He folded his arms so that each hand rested on the opposite biceps muscle—he tensed them briefly, a purely reflex action—as if he were stroking or measuring them, as if he wanted to draw attention to them even though they were now covered by his overcoat, a sterile gesture. I could easily imagine him in a T-shirt, and even wearing high boots, a cheap imitation of a frustrated polo player who had never been allowed on a horse. Yes, it was strange that Díaz-Varela should have chosen him as his accomplice in such a secret and delicate enterprise, an enterprise that soils all those involved: that of causing someone's death, one "who should have died hereafter," perhaps tomorrow or if not tomorrow then the day after, but not now. Therein lies the problem, because we all die, and in the end, it makes little difference—deep down—if you cause someone's turn to come earlier than expected by murdering them, the problem lies in when, but who knows which is the right or appropriate time, what does "hereafter" or "at some point from now on" mean, when "now" is, by its very nature, always changing, what does "at another time" mean if there is only one continuous, indivisible time that is eternally snapping at our heels, impatient and aimless, stumbling on as if powerless to stop and as if time itself were ignorant of its purpose. And why do things happen when they happen, why this date and not the previous day or the next, what is so special or decisive about this moment, what marks it out and who chooses it, and how can anyone say what Macbeth went on to say—I had looked it up after Díaz-Varela had quoted the lines to me—because what he goes on to say is this: "There would have been a time for such a word," that is, for the fact or phrase that he has just heard from the lips of his attendant Seyton, the bringer of relief or of misfortune: "The queen, my lord, is dead." As is so often the case, Shakespeare's editors are unable to agree on the meaning of Macbeth's famously ambiguous and mysterious lines. What did he mean by "hereafter"? "She could have died at a more appropriate time"? "She could have chosen a better moment, because this doesn't suit me at all"? Perhaps "a more opportune, peaceful time, when she could have been properly honoured, when I could have stopped and mourned as I should the loss of the woman who shared so much with me, ambition and murder, hope and power and fear"? Macbeth has a moment, that's all, before he launches into his ten most famous lines, into the extraordinary soliloquy that so many people round the world have learned by heart and which begins: "Tomorrow, and tomorrow, and

tomorrow . . ." And when he has finished—although who knows if
he has finished speaking or if he would have added something more
had he not been interrupted—the messenger arrives demanding his
attention, for he brings Macbeth the terrible and supernatural news
that Birnam Wood is on the move and advancing on the high hill of
Dunsinane, where he is encamped, and this means that he will be
defeated. And if he is defeated, he will be killed, and once he is dead,
they will cut off his head and display it like a trophy, sightless and
separated from the body that still supports it now, while he is speaking. "She should have died later on, when I wasn't alive to hear the
news, or to see or to dream anything; when I was no longer in time
and incapable, therefore, of understanding."

CONTRARY TO HOW I had felt when I was listening to them without seeing them, when Ruibérriz de Torres's face was still unknown to me, I did not feel afraid of the two men during the brief time I spent in their company, even though the new arrival's features and manners were hardly reassuring. Everything about him revealed him to be an utter rogue, and yet he was not in the least sinister; he was doubtless capable of a thousand minor despicable deeds, which might lead him to commit worse things from time to time, as if drawn briefly into a neighbouring country, rather as one might make a short incursion into alien territory, an experience that would horrify him if repeated on a daily basis. The two men were clearly not on friendly or harmonious terms, and it seemed to me that far from making them a potentially murderous duo, the presence of one neutralized the dangerousness of the other, and neither of them, I felt, would dare to reveal his suspicions or interrogate me or do anything to me with a witness present, even if that witness was their accomplice in planning a murder. It was as if they had come together purely by chance and only temporarily for that one act, they were certainly not a permanent partnership nor did they have any longer-term plans, as though they had joined forces exclusively to carry out that one now completed enterprise and to face any likely consequences, an alliance of convenience, possibly unwished for by both parties, and in which Ruibérriz had become involved perhaps to earn a little money or to pay off debts, and Díaz-Varela because he knew no other—more crooked—crook, and so had no alternative but to entrust himself to a wide boy. "Besides, why *would* you call me, we haven't spoken in ages. This had better be important," the former had said to the latter when the latter had told him off for not having his mobile phone switched on. They weren't usually in contact, the intimacy that allowed them to reproach each other came solely from their shared secret or shared guilt, if they felt any guilt, although I didn't have that impression at all, they had sounded completely devoid of scruples. People feel bound to each other when they commit a crime together, when they conspire or plot, even more so when they put a plan into action. And that does breed a kind of instant overfamiliarity, because the plotters have taken off their masks and can no longer pretend to their fellows that they are not what they are nor that they would never do what they have, in fact, done. They are bound together by that mutual knowledge, rather as clandestine lovers are and even those lovers who are not clandestine and have no need to be, but who opt for discretion, those who believe that their private lives are not the business of the rest of the world, and that there is no reason to tell the world about every kiss and every embrace, as was the case with Díaz-Varela and me, for we kept silent about our affair, indeed, that man Ruibérriz was the first to know anything about it. Every criminal knows what his accomplice is capable of and knows that his accomplice knows exactly the same about him. Every lover knows that the other person has a weak point and that in her presence he can no longer pretend that he doesn't find her physically alluring, that he finds her repulsive or is indifferent to her, he can no longer pretend that he scorns or rejects her, not at least in the field of carnal relations, a deeply prosaic field in which, much to women's regret, most men tend to get stuck for far too long—until they get used to us and grow sentimental. Indeed, we're lucky if our encounters with them have a slightly humorous edge, which is often a first step towards softening even the surliest of men.

If we are irritated by the overfamiliarity of, say, a stranger or an acquaintance after he has spent a brief time in our bed—or we in his bed, it makes no difference—how much more galling must it be between partners in crime, a relationship that must engender a complete lack of respect, especially if the malefactors in question are mere amateurs, ordinary individuals who, just a few days before they had conceived their own vile deeds and doubtless after they had carried them out as well, would have been horrified to hear an account of those deeds as committed by others. The kind of person who, after bringing about a murder or even ordering it, will still think smugly: "I'm not a murderer, I certainly don't consider myself to be one. It's just that things happen and occasionally one has to intervene at a certain point, it makes no difference if it's half-way through, at the end or at the beginning, you can't have one without the other. There are always many factors involved and one factor alone cannot be the cause. Ruibérriz could have refused, as could the man he dispatched to poison the *gorrilla*'s mind. The *gorrilla* could have failed to answer the calls to the mobile phone he had in his possession for a time, we gave it to him, we made the calls and managed to convince him that Miguel was the person responsible for prostituting his daughters; he could have ignored those malicious lies or chosen the wrong person to attack and instead stabbed the chauffeur sixteen times, five times fatally—after all, only a few days before, the man had punched the chauffeur. Miguel might have chosen not to drive the car on his birthday and then nothing would have happened, not on that day or perhaps on any other, the necessary elements might never have come together . . . The tramp might not have had a knife, the one I ordered to be bought for him, it opens so quickly . . . What responsibility do I bear for that cluster of coincidences, any plans one draws up are only ever attempts and experiments, cards to be turned over one by one, and, more often than not, the card you want doesn't appear, doesn't match. The only thing you can be found guilty of is picking up a weapon and actually using it yourself. Everything else is pure contingency, things that one imagines—a bishop in chess making a diagonal move, a knight jumping over another piece—things that one desires, fears, instigates, ideas that one toys with and fantasizes about, and which, sometimes, actually happen. And if they do, they happen even if you don't want them to or don't happen even if you yearn for them to happen, at any rate, little depends on us, no intrigue, however carefully woven, is safe from a thread coming loose. It's like firing an arrow up into the sky in the middle of a field: the normal thing, once the arrow begins its descent, is for the arrow to fall straight to earth, without deviating, without striking or wounding anyone. Or only, perhaps, the archer."

I noticed this complete lack of mutual respect in the way Díaz-Varela addressed Ruibérriz, even ordering him to leave (after my brief exchange with Ruibérriz, he said bluntly: "Right, you've taken up quite enough of my time and I can't neglect my visitor any longer. So clear off, will you, Ruibérriz, scram!" He must have paid him money or was perhaps still paying him for his services as intermediary, for organizing the murder and keeping abreast of the consequences), and in the way that Ruibérriz ran his eyes over me from the very first moment right up until he left: for he maintained his initial appreciative gaze, understandable when I made my surprise appearance, even after he had realized that this wasn't the first time I had been there in that bedroom, that's something one always senses immediately; when he saw that my presence was neither the result of a chance encounter nor a trial run, that I wasn't a woman who has gone up to a man's apartment for the evening—an inaugural evening, shall we say, which often ends up being a one-off—just as she might have gone up to the apartment of some other man she fancied, but that I was, how can I put it, "taken" by his friend, at least for the time being, which, as it turned out, was almost the case. Not that this bothered him: he didn't for a moment moderate his appraising masculine gaze or his salacious, flirtatious, gummy smile, as if unexpectedly seeing a woman in bra and skirt and making her acquaintance was, for him, an investment for the near future and brought with it the hope of meeting me again very soon, alone and in another place, or even asking for my phone number later on from the person who had been obliged, against his will, to introduce us.

"I'm really sorry about that," I said, when I returned to the living room, this time wearing my sweater. "I wouldn't have appeared in that state if I'd known we weren't alone." I understood that I needed to emphasize this in order to dispel any suspicions. Díaz-Varela was still regarding me seriously, almost reprovingly or harshly; not so Ruibérriz.

"There's absolutely no need to apologize," he said with old-fashioned gallantry. "Your attire could not have been more striking. Sadly all too fleeting."

Díaz-Varela scowled, he was distinctly unamused by everything that had happened: the arrival of his accomplice and the news he had brought with him, my irruption on to the scene and the fact that Ruibérriz and I now knew each other, plus the possibility that I might have heard them through the door, when he thought I was safely asleep; he was doubtless equally displeased by the way Ruibérriz had gazed so covetously at my bra and skirt, or at the little they concealed, and by his subsequent compliments, even though these had been couched in the politest of terms. I felt a childish and, after what I had just discovered, incongruous pleasure—it lasted only an instant—in imagining that Díaz-Varela could feel something resembling or, rather, reminiscent of jealousy in my regard. He was visibly put out and even more so when we were left alone, once Ruibérriz had departed, his coat draped over his shoulders, as he walked slowly towards the lift, as if he were very pleased with his own image and wanted to give me time to admire him from behind: he was clearly an optimist, of the kind who doesn't believe that he'll ever get old. Before entering the lift, he turned to us, for we were watching him from the front door like a married couple, and he bade farewell by raising a hand to one eyebrow for a second, then raising it slightly higher in a gesture that mimicked doffing a hat. The problem he had brought with him seemed to have vanished, he was obviously a frivolous man whose anxieties were easily displaced by whatever cheering moment the present might bring him. It occurred to me that he would not do as his friend had asked and destroy his leather coat; he was too pleased with the way he looked in it.

"Who's he?" I asked Díaz-Varela, trying to use an indifferent, casual tone of voice. "What does he do? He's the first friend of yours I've met, and you seem an unlikely pair. He strikes me as a bit of an oddball."

"He's Ruibérriz," he replied tartly, as if that were an entirely new fact or a defining piece of information. Then he realized that he had been rather sharp with me and hadn't told me anything. He remained silent for a few moments, as if weighing up how much he could say without compromising himself. "You met Rico on one occasion," he said. "Anyway, as for Ruibérriz, he does all kinds of things and nothing in particular. He's not a friend, I only know him superficially, although I've known him for a while now. He has various vague business deals going on, none of which make him very much money, which is why he has his fingers in all kinds of different pies. If he wins the heart of some wealthy woman, he lives off her for a while until she gets fed up with him. Otherwise, he writes television scripts and speeches for ministers, company directors, bankers or whoever, and does some ghostwriting too. He carries out research for punctilious historical novelists: what did people wear in the nineteenth century or in the 1930s, what was the transportation system like, what weapons did they use, what were shaving brushes or hairpins made of, when was such and such a building put up or a certain film first shown, the kind of superfluous stuff that bores readers, but which writers think will impress. He trawls newspaper archives and provides whatever information people ask him for. He's picked up quite a lot along the way. I think, as a young man, he published a couple of novels, but they didn't sell. I don't know. He does favours here and there, and he probably lives off that more than anything else, off his contacts: he's a useful man in his uselessness, or vice versa." He stopped, hesitated as to whether or not it would be imprudent to add what he was about to say, then decided there was no reason why it would be imprudent or thought perhaps that it would be worse to give the impression that he didn't want to complete an apparently innocuous portrait. "He's currently part-owner of a restaurant or two, but they're doing very badly, his businesses never last, he opens them and closes them. The odd thing is that, after a while, once he's recovered, he always manages to start another."

"And what did he want? He just turned up without warning, didn't he?"

I immediately regretted asking so many questions.

"Why do you want to know? What's it got to do with you?"

He said this angrily, almost violently. I felt sure that, suddenly, he no longer trusted me, but saw me as a nuisance, maybe a threat, a possibly awkward witness, he had raised his guard, it was odd, just a short while before I had been a pleasant, inoffensive person, certainly not a cause for concern, probably quite the opposite, a most agreeable distraction while he waited for time to pass and to heal and for his expectations to be fulfilled, or for time to do the work he could not do, that of persuading, laying siege to, seducing, even making Luisa fall in love with him; I was merely someone who wanted no more than she already had and who asked of him nothing he was not prepared to give. Now he was gripped by a fear, a doubt. He couldn't ask me if I had heard their conversation: if I hadn't, he would be drawing my attention to whatever he and Ruibérriz might have been talking about while I was asleep, even though that was no concern of mine and of no great interest to me, I was just passing through, after all; if I had heard their conversation, I would obviously tell him that I hadn't, and he still wouldn't know the truth. It was inevitable, then, that I would be a potential problem from then on, or worse still, a nuisance, a hindrance.

Then I felt slightly afraid again, afraid of him, on his own, with no one there to restrain him. Removing me might be his only way of ensuring that his secret was safe, they say that once you've committed a crime it's not so very hard to commit another, that once you've crossed that line, there's no turning back, that the quantitative aspect becomes secondary given the magnitude of the leap taken, the qualitative leap that makes you forever a murderer until the very last day of your existence and in the memories of those who survive you, that is, if they know what happened or find out later on, when you are no longer there to obfuscate or deny. A thief can give back the thing he stole, a slanderer can acknowledge his calumny and put it right and wipe clean the good name of the person he accused, even a traitor can sometimes make amends for his treachery before it's too late. The trouble with murder is that it's always too late and you cannot restore to the world the person you killed, that is irreversible and there's no possible means of reparation, and saving other lives in the future, however many they might be, would never make up for the one life you took. And if, as they say, there is no forgiveness, then, whenever necessary, you must continue along the road taken. The important thing becomes not so much to avoid staining yourself, given that you carry in your breast an ineradicable stain, but to make sure that no one knows, that no one finds out, that what you did has no consequences and doesn't destroy you, because, then, adding another stain is not so very grave, it gets mixed up with the first or is absorbed, the two join together and become one, and you get used to the idea that killing is part of your life, that this is your fate as it has been for so many others throughout history. You tell yourself that there's nothing new about your situation, that innumerable other people have had the same experience and learned to live with it without too much difficulty and without going under, and have even managed intermittently to forget about it, for a brief moment each day in the day-to-day life that sustains and carries us along. No one can spend every hour regretting some concrete act or being fully conscious of what he did once, long ago, or twice or seven times, there are always going to be carefree, sorrow-free moments, and the very worst of murderers will enjoy them probably no less than an entirely innocent person. And he will continue to live and cease thinking of murder as a monstrous exception or a tragic mistake, but, rather, as another resource that life offers the boldest and toughest, the most resolute and most resistant. He doesn't feel in the least isolated, but part of a large, abundant, ancient band, a kind of lineage that helps him to feel less ill-favoured or anomalous and to understand himself and justify his actions: as if he had inherited those actions, or as if he had won them in a raffle at a fair from which no one is exempt, which means that he didn't wholly commit those acts, or not at least alone.

"OH, NO REASON," I said quickly, in the most surprised—surprised ostensibly at his defensive reaction—and innocent tone that my throat could manage. That throat was afraid now, his hands could encircle it at any moment and it would be easy for them to squeeze and squeeze, my throat is quite slender and would offer not the least resistance, my hands wouldn't be strong enough to push his away, to prise open his fingers, my legs would buckle, I would fall to the floor, he would throw himself on top of me as he had on other occasions, I would feel the weight of his body and his heat—or perhaps his cold—I would have no voice with which to persuade or implore. But as soon as I gave in to that fear, I realized that it was a false fear: Díaz-Varela would never take it upon himself to expel someone from the earth, he had not done so with his friend Deverne. Unless, of course, he was desperate and felt under imminent threat, unless he thought I would go straight to Luisa and tell her what I had discovered by a combination of chance and my own indiscretion. The trouble is, you can never rule out anything about anyone, and so that same slightly artificial fear came and went. "I was just asking for asking's sake."—And I even had the courage or lack of prudence to add: "And because if that Ruibérriz fellow does do favours, maybe I can do you the odd favour too. I doubt it, but if I can help you in anyway, here I am."

He looked at me hard for a few seconds that seemed to me very long, as if he were weighing me up, trying to decipher me, the way you look at people who don't know they're being looked at, and as if I weren't there but on a TV screen and he could observe me at his leisure, unconcerned about how I would react to such an insistent, penetrating gaze, his expression was now anything but dreamy and myopic, as it usually was, instead it was piercing and intimidating. I stood firm (we were, after all, lovers, who had contemplated each other in silence and with barely a shred of modesty), I held his gaze and even returned his scrutiny, wearing what I hoped was an expression of puzzlement and incomprehension. Until I could stand it no longer and I lowered my gaze to his lips, the lips I had grown so used to gazing at ever since the day I first met him, regardless of whether he was talking or silent, the lips of which I never tired and which had never inspired fear in me, only attraction. They were my momentary refuge, and there was nothing odd about my resting my gaze on his lips, I did that so frequently it was normal, and there was no reason why it should reinforce his suspicions, I raised one finger and touched his lips, gently traced their outline with the tip of my finger, a long caress, I thought it might calm him, fill him with a sense of confidence and security, a wordless way of saying to him: "Nothing has changed, I'm still here, I still love you. Not that I'm telling you anything you don't know already, you realized that a long time ago and you allow yourself to be loved by me, it's nice to feel loved by someone who isn't going to ask anything of you. I'll withdraw whenever you decide that enough is enough, when you open the front door and watch me walk over to the lift, knowing that I won't be back. When Luisa's grief finally runs its course and your love is reciprocated, I will stand aside without a murmur, I know I'm a purely temporary feature in your life, another day and another, then no more. But don't worry yourself now, it's all right, I didn't hear anything, I didn't find out anything you would want to hide or keep to yourself, and if I did, it doesn't matter, you're safe with me, I'm not going to betray you, I'm not even sure I heard what I heard, or, rather, I don't believe what I heard, I'm sure there must be some mistake, an explanation or even—who knows—a justification. Perhaps Desvern harmed you in some way, perhaps he had already tried to kill you, again through a third party, by sheer cunning, and then it was either you or him, perhaps you had no alternative, there wasn't room in the world for both of you, and that makes it almost like self-defence. There's no reason for you to fear me, I love you, I'm on your side, I'm not going to judge you. Besides, don't forget, this is all pure imagination on your part, I don't know anything."

I didn't actually think all this and certainly not as clearly, but that is what I tried to transmit to him through that fingertip lingering on his lips, and he let me stroke his lips, all the while fixing me with his eyes, trying to detect any signals that contradicted those I was intently giving out, for it was clear that he still didn't trust me. That lack of trust would be difficult if not impossible to rectify, it would never go away entirely, it would diminish or increase, shrink or expand, but it would always be there.

"He didn't come to do me a favour," he answered. "This time, he came to ask a favour of me, that's why he had to see me so urgently. Thanks for your offer, though."

I knew this wasn't true, they were both in the same tight spot, and it would be difficult for one to extricate the other, the most they could do was reassure each other and await events, trusting that nothing else would happen, that the tramp's words would fall on deaf ears and that no one would bother to investigate further. Yes, that's what they had done, calmed each other down and banished any feelings of panic.

"My pleasure."

Then he placed one hand on my shoulder, and it felt like a heavy weight, as if a great lump of meat had fallen on me. Díaz-Varela was not particularly big or strong, although he was reasonably tall, but nearly all men, or most, can dredge up strength from somewhere, at least they seem by comparison much stronger than us women, we are so easily frightened, all it takes is a single threatening or angry or immoderate gesture, the way they grab our wrist or embrace us too roughly or push us back violently on to the bed. I was glad that my shoulder was covered by my sweater, because that weight on my bare skin would, I thought, have made me shudder, it wasn't something he usually did. He squeezed my shoulder slightly, without hurting me, as if he were going to offer me a piece of advice or confide in me, I imagined how that one hand would feel around my throat, just one, let alone two. I feared that, with a rapid movement, he might transfer his hand to my throat, he must have sensed my alarm, my tension, because he maintained that pressure on my shoulder or, as it seemed to me, increased it, he wanted to frighten me, to subjugate me, his right hand on my left shoulder, as if he were a father or a teacher and I were a child, a pupil—I felt very small, and that was doubtless his intention, to make me answer him honestly or, if not honestly, anxiously.

"So you didn't hear anything he said? You were asleep when he arrived, weren't you? I came in to check before talking to him and you seemed to be deep asleep, you were asleep, weren't you? What he had to tell me was very private, and he wouldn't want anyone else to know about it. Even though you're a complete stranger. There are some things one would feel ashamed to have anyone hear, it was hard enough for him to tell me, even though that's why he came, and so he had no choice but to tell me if he wanted me to do him the favour he was asking. So you really didn't hear anything? What woke you up then?"

So he had decided to ask me straight out, pointlessly, or perhaps not: he could work out or deduce whether or not I was lying by the way I answered, or so he thought. But that's all it would be, a deduction, an imagination, a supposition, a conviction; it's extraordinary how, after so many centuries of ceaseless talking, we still don't know when people are telling us the truth. "Yes," they say, and that could always mean "No." "No," they say, and that could always mean "Yes." Not even science or all the infinite technological advances we have made can help us to know one way or the other, not with any certainty. And nevertheless, he could not resist asking me directly, what use was it to him if I answered "Yes" or "No"? What use to Deverne had been the professions of affection over the years by one of his best friends, if not the best friend? The last thing you imagine is that your friend is going to kill you, even if from a distance and without being there to witness it, without intervening or soiling so much as a finger, in such a way that he can occasionally think afterwards, in his happy or exultant days: "I didn't really do it, it was nothing to do with me."

"No, don't worry, I didn't hear anything. I slept really deeply, but not for long. Besides, you had closed the door, so I wouldn't have been able to hear you anyway."

The hand on my shoulder continued to squeeze, slightly harder I thought, almost imperceptibly so, as if, without my noticing, he wanted to drive me very slowly down into the floor. Or perhaps he wasn't squeezing and it was just that, as the weight and pressure continued, so the feeling of oppression intensified. I gently lifted my shoulder, delicately, timidly, not brusquely at all, as though to indicate to him that I would prefer my shoulder to be free of that lump of meat, there was something vaguely humiliating about that unaccustomed contact: "Feel my strength," it seemed to be saying. Or "Imagine what I might be capable of." He ignored that slight movement—perhaps it was too slight—and returning to his last question, which I had not yet answered, asked again:

"What woke you up then? If you thought I was the only person here, why did you put your bra on before coming out? You must have heard the sound of our voices, which means that you must have heard some of what we said."

I had to keep calm and continue denying that I had heard anything. The more suspicious he was, the firmer I had to be in my denials. But I had to deny it without a hint of vehemence or emphasis. What did I care about some deal he was doing with a guy I'd never even heard him mention before, that was my main weapon if I was to convince him or at least fend off his certainty for a while longer; why would I spy on him, what did I care what happened outside that bedroom or indeed inside it when I wasn't there, surely he must know that our relationship wasn't only transient, it was confined to and circumscribed by those occasional meetings in his apartment, in one or two of its rooms, what did any of the rest matter to me, his comings and goings, his past, his friendships, his plans, his entourage, his whole life, I wasn't part of that, nor would I be "hereafter," henceforth or later on, our days were numbered and that final number was never far away. And yet, although this was all true in essence, it wasn't absolutely true: I had felt curious, I had woken up when I heard a key word—perhaps "bird" or "know" or "wife" or probably the combination of all three—I had got up from the bed, pressed my ear to the door, opened it a tiny crack so that I could hear better, I had felt glad when he and Ruibérriz had proved incapable of moderating their voices, of keeping to a whisper, overcome by their own agitation. I started wondering why I had done that, and immediately began to regret it: why did I have to know what I now knew, why did I do it, why was it no longer possible for me to put my arms about his waist and draw him to me, it would have been so easy to remove his hand from my shoulder with that one movement, which would have seemed utterly natural and simple a few minutes before; why could I not force him to embrace me without further delay or hesitation, there were his beloved lips, which, as usual, I wanted to kiss, only I didn't dare to now, or else there was something about them that simultaneously repelled and attracted me, or the thing that repelled me lay not in his lips—poor, innocent lips—but in him. I still loved him and yet was afraid of him, I still loved him and yet my knowledge of what he had done disgusted me, not him, but that knowledge.

"You do ask some strange questions," I said breezily. "How should I know what woke me up, a bad dream, lying in an awkward position, knowing that I could be spending my time with you, I don't know, what does it matter? And why should I care what that man told you, I didn't even know he was here. And the reason I put my bra on was because it's not the same being seen lying down and close to or in short bursts as being seen standing up and walking around the house like a model for Victoria's Secret, except, of course, that they're always wearing lingerie. Do I have to explain everything to you?"

"What do you mean?"

He seemed genuinely bewildered and uncomprehending, and this—this shift in interest, this distraction—gave me a slight, momentary advantage, soon, I thought, he would stop asking me devious questions and then I could leave, I needed to shake off that hand and get out of there. Although my former self, which was still hanging around—it hadn't yet been substituted or replaced, or cancelled or exiled, that couldn't possibly happen so very quickly—was in no hurry to leave: each time I left, I never knew when I would return or if I ever would.

"You men are so dense sometimes," I said firmly, for some such clichéd comment seemed to me advisable in order to change the subject and guide the conversation into more vulgar territory, which also tends to be safer and more conducive to confidences and a lowering of guards.—"There are certain parts of the female anatomy that we women deem to be past it by the time we're twenty-five or thirty, let alone ten years later. We compare ourselves with ourselves as we were, remembering each year that passes. And that's why we prefer not to expose those areas in too unseemly or full-frontal a manner. Well, that's my view, but there are plenty of women who don't give a damn, the beaches are packed with brutal, catastrophic displays of flesh, among them women who've had a couple of those rock-hard implants put in, thinking that they will solve the problem. Frankly, they set my teeth on edge." I laughed briefly at my choice of phrase, and added another: "They really give me the creeps."

"I see," he said and he laughed briefly too, which was a good sign. "I wouldn't say that any parts of your anatomy were past it, they look pretty good to me."

"He's feeling calmer," I thought, "less worried and suspicious, because after the fright he's had, he needs to feel that. But later on, when he's alone, he'll convince himself again that I know what I shouldn't know, what no one but Ruibérriz should know. He'll ponder my attitude, remember my premature blush as I came out of the bedroom and my subsequent feigned ignorance, he'll think that after all that passionate sex, the normal thing would be for me not to care how I look, bra or no bra, sex does, after all, relax you and make you drop your defences; he'll cease to believe the explanation that he finds acceptable now because of its surprise value and because it would never have occurred to him that some women could be so perennially self-conscious about their appearance, about what they cover up and what they reveal, even how loudly they pant or moan, that they never entirely lose their modesty, even when very aroused. He'll turn it over in his mind again and won't know quite what to do, whether to distance me slowly and naturally or abruptly sever all contact or carry on as if nothing had happened in order to keep a close eye on me, to control me, to make a daily calculation as to how likely I am to betray him, that's a very stressful situation to be in, ceaselessly having to interpret someone, someone who has us in their power and who could destroy us or blackmail us, no one can stand such anxiety for very long, and so we try to remedy it as best we can, by lying, intimidating, deceiving, bribing, coming to some arrangement, removing the person, the latter being both the most certain route in the long run—the most definitive—and the most dangerous in the moment, as well as the most difficult both now and later, and, in a sense, the most enduring, for you are linked to the dead person forever after, and liable to have him or her appear to you alive in your dreams, so that it seems as if you didn't do the deed, and then you feel a great sense of relief because you didn't kill her or else feel so horrified or threatened that you plan to do it all over again; you run the risk that the dead person will haunt your pillow every night with her smiling or frowning face, her eyes wide open, eyes that were closed either centuries ago or only the day before yesterday, that she will whisper curses or pleas in that unmistakable voice that no one else hears any more, and the task will seem to you never-ending and exhausting, an endless undertaking, not knowing what each morning will bring. But all those things will come later, when Díaz-Varela goes over in his mind what happened or what he fears might have happened. He might find some excuse to send me to Ruibérriz so that he can sound me out, pump me for information, rather, I hope, than to do anything more alarming, and leave it to that intermediary to blur or weaken the link, because I'm not going to be able to live in peace from now on either. But that moment is not now, and time will tell, I need to make the most of the fact that I've distracted him from his fears and made him laugh, and get out of here as quickly as possible."

"Thanks for the compliment, you're not usually so lavish with them," I said. And with no physical effort, but with considerable mental effort, I leaned towards him and gently kissed him on the lips with my closed, dry lips—I was thirsty—and rather as my finger had before, my mouth caressed his, that's how it was I think. That's all.

Then he raised his hand and liberated my shoulder and removed that odious weight, and with that same hand that had almost caused me pain—that, at least, is how it was beginning to feel—he stroked my cheek, again as if I were a child and he had the power to punish or reward me, as he chose, with a single gesture. I very nearly reared back from that caress, there was a difference now between me touching him and him touching me, fortunately, though, I restrained myself and allowed him to caress my cheek. And when I left his apartment a few minutes later, I wondered, as I always did, if I would ever go back there. Except that this time, I did not think this with only mingled hope and desire, but with a mixture of feelings, perhaps repugnance or fear, or was it, rather, desolation?

III

IN ALL UNEQUAL relationships, those lacking a name or explicit recognition, there is usually one person who takes the initiative, who phones to suggest meeting up, while the other person has just two possibilities or ways of reaching the same goal of not fading away or vanishing, even though he or she believes that, whatever happens, this is sure to be his or her final fate. One way is simply to wait and do nothing, trusting that eventually the other person will miss you, that your silence and absence will become unexpectedly unbearable or even worrying, because we all very quickly grow accustomed to what is given to us or what is there. The second way is to try, subtly, to infiltrate the daily life of that other person, to persist without insisting, to make a space for yourself, to phone, not in order to suggest getting together—that is still forbidden—but to ask a question, some advice or a favour, to let him know what has been going on in your life—the most efficient and most drastic way of involving someone else—or offering information; being present, acting as a reminder to him of your existence, humming and buzzing away in the distance, creating a habit that imperceptibly, almost stealthily, installs itself in his life, until one day the other person, missing your, by now, customary phone call, feels almost affronted—or experiences something bordering on abandonment—and, overcome by impatience, invents some absurd excuse, awkwardly picks up the phone and finds himself dialling your number.

I did not belong to that bold and enterprising band, but to the silent kind, who, while prouder and more subtle, are also more exposed to being promptly erased or forgotten, and after that evening, I was glad to run that risk, to be, as usual, subordinate to the requests and suggestions of the person whom I still thought of as Javier, but who was already on the way to becoming a hard-to-remember double-barrelled name; and I was glad, too, not to have to call or seek him out, in the knowledge that failing to do so would not seem suspicious or incriminating. My not getting in touch with him would not mean that I wanted to avoid him, nor that I was disappointed in him—a rank understatement—nor that I was afraid of him, nor that I wanted to have no more to do with him after learning that he had plotted to have his best friend stabbed to death without even being sure that his plotting would achieve its end, for he was still left with the easier or perhaps more arduous task, one never knows, of making Luisa fall in love with him (the most insignificant or the most substantial part of the task). The fact that I gave no signs of life would not signify that I knew anything about the plot or anything new about him, my silence would not betray me, everything was as it always had been during our brief relationship, only if, in some vague way, he missed me or thought of me and summoned me to his bedroom, only then would I have to consider how I should behave and what to do. Making someone fall in love with you is insignificant, waiting for it to happen, on the other hand, is a thing of substance.

When Díaz-Varela had spoken to me about Colonel Chabert, I had immediately identified the Colonel with Desvern: the dead man who ought to remain dead because his death has been reported and itemized and set down in the annals and thus become historical fact, and whose new and incomprehensible life is a tiresome addendum, an intrusion into the lives of others; the person who comes back to disturb a universe which, knowing nothing about what really happened and unable to rectify matters, has carried on without him. The fact that Luisa could not immediately shake off Deverne, that she continued in her inert and routine way to be subject to him and his still recent memory—recent for the widow but remote for the person who had long been anticipating his departure—must have seemed to Díaz-Varela rather like being haunted by a ghost, as annoying a phantasm as Chabert, except that the latter had returned in the flesh, complete with scars, when he had already been forgotten and when his return was a nuisance even to time itself, which had to go against its nature and try to retrace its steps and correct the past, whereas Desvern had not entirely departed, at least not in spirit, he was still hanging around and did so with the connivance of his wife, who was still immersed in the slow process of getting over his abandonment or desertion of her; she was even trying to hold on to him for a little longer, knowing that, unlikely though it might seem, a day would come when his face would fade or become frozen in one of the many photos that she insisted on looking at again and again, sometimes with a foolish smile on her face and sometimes sobbing, but always alone, always in secret.

And yet now it seemed to me that it was Díaz-Varela who was more like Chabert. The latter had suffered countless sorrows and hardships, while the former had inflicted them; the latter had been the victim of a war, of negligence, of bureaucracy and incomprehension, while the former was a self-appointed executioner, who had gravely disturbed the universe with his cruelty, his possibly sterile egotism and his extraordinary frivolity. But both had to wait for a gesture, a kind of miracle, a word of encouragement, an invitation, Chabert for the near-impossibility that his wife would fall in love with him again and Díaz-Varela for the improbability that Luisa would fall in love with him or at least seek consolation in his company. There was something similar about the hope and patience shared by both men, although in the old soldier, those feelings were dominated by scepticism and incredulity, and those of my temporary lover by optimism and excitement or, perhaps, by necessity. Both men were like ghosts pulling faces and making signs and even occasionally gesturing, innocently, wildly, in the hope that they would be seen, recognized and perhaps summoned, longing to hear at last the words: "Yes, of course, I recognize you now, it's you," although in the case of Chabert this meant only the letter confirming his existence that was being denied to him and in Díaz-Varela's case: "I want to be by your side, come closer and stay here with me, fill this empty space, come to me and embrace me." And both must have thought something similar, something that gave them strength and sustained them in their waiting and kept them from giving up: "I can't have gone through everything I've gone through, being killed by a sword blow to the skull and by the galloping hooves of infinite horses, and then emerging from among a great pile of corpses after that long and futile battle that transformed forty thousand men like me into cadavers, of which I should have been one, just another corpse; I can't have gone through that whole difficult recovery process, enough to be able to stand on my own two feet and walk, to have wandered Europe like the poorest of beggars and with no one to believe my story, obliged instead to persuade every imbecile I met that I am still me, that I am not dead, even though my death has been formally recorded; and that I should arrive here, where I once had wife, house, rank and fortune, here where I used to live, and to have the person I most loved and who inherited my wealth not even to admit that I exist, to pretend she doesn't recognize me and call me an impostor. What sense would it make to survive my reiterated death, to emerge from the grave in which I had resigned myself to living, naked and with no distinguishing emblems or badges, made equal with all my fallen equals, officers and privates, compatriots and perhaps enemies, what sense would it make if what awaited me at the end of my journey was to have my existence denied, to be stripped of my identity, my memory and everything that happened to me after my death, the whole superfluity of my ill fortune, my ordeal, the enormous effort of survival, of what seemed so much like fate . . ." That is what Colonel Chabert must have thought as he came and went in Paris, while he begged to be received and seen by the lawyer Derville and by Madame Ferraud, who, in the light of his resurrection, was not his widow, but his wife, and, thus, alas for her, became again the equally buried, forgotten and loathed Madame Chabert.

And Díaz-Varela, in turn, must have thought: "I can't have done what I've done or what I conspired to do and set in train, after pondering it long and hard and being consumed by doubt, I can't have brought about a death, that of my best friend, pretending I was leaving it all slightly to chance, that it might or might not happen, might or might not come to pass, or perhaps I wasn't pretending and that's how it really was; perhaps I did devise an imperfect plan full of loose ends precisely so that I could still face myself and be able to tell myself that I had, after all, allowed for numerous loopholes and escape routes, that I hadn't made a cast-iron plan, hadn't sent in a hit man or issued anyone with the order: 'Kill him'; I can't have involved two—or perhaps three—other people, Ruibérriz, the assistant who made the phone calls and the beggar who listened to them, in order to distance myself as much as possible from the actual execution, from the events when they happened, if they did happen, because there was no guarantee as to how the *gorrilla* would react, he might have ignored the calls or simply hurled insults at Miguel or punched him as he did the chauffeur when he confused the two men, my attempt to sow discord might have fallen on barren ground from the start and had no effect whatsoever, but it did have

an effect, so what does that mean; no, my wishes can't, against all
probability, have come true and, in doing so, have lost any resemblance they might have had to a gamble or a wager and become,
instead, a tragedy and, most probably, murder by instigation which
has, in turn, made me, indirectly, the instigator, since it was my idea
and my decision to begin the process, to throw the loaded dice, to
tamper with the wheel and then set it turning, I was the one who
said: 'Get him a mobile phone and pour poison in his ear and thus
reach both the insane and the sane parts of his mind; buy him a
knife to tempt him, to have him stroke it and open and close it, only
someone in possession of a weapon is likely to think of using it';
no, I can't have done all that and left myself with an ineradicable
stain only for it all to come to nothing and for my intention to fail.
What would be the point of having impregnated myself like this,
with this murder, this conspiracy, this horror, of carrying the deceit
and the betrayal within my breast for ever, of never being able to
shake them off or forget them except in moments of unconscious-
ness or of a strange feeling of plenitude that I have not myself, as
yet, experienced, I don't know, what would be the point of having
established a link that will reappear in my dreams and that I will
never be able to break, what would be the point of all this vileness,
if I fail to reach my one goal, if what awaits me at the end of this
journey is a No or indifference or pity, or only the old affection she
always felt for me and which would merely keep me in my place,
or, worse still, if what awaits me is accusation, discovery, disdain,
her back turned on me and her icy voice saying, as if from inside a
helmet: 'Get out of my sight and never let me see you again'? As if
she were a Queen condemning her most fervent and adoring subject
to eternal exile. And that could happen now, that could easily happen if this woman, María, did hear what she shouldn't have heard
and decides to go and tell her, because even if I denied it, the tiniest

doubt would be enough for all my hopes to vanish, to cease to exist. I know I have nothing to fear from Ruibérriz, which is why I asked him to take charge of the operation, I've known him for a long time and he would never blab, not even if the beggar were to identify him and the police tracked him down, and he was questioned or arrested, not even under great pressure, because of the possible consequences to himself and because he's trustworthy. The others, Canella and the one who phoned him, the one who several times a day reminded him of his prostitute daughters and forced him to imagine them hard at work in mortifying detail, the one who fed his obsession and accused Miguel, they have never seen me or heard my name or my voice, so as far as they're concerned, I don't exist, only Ruibérriz exists with his T-shirts and his leather coats and his salacious smile. But I don't really know anything about María, I can see that she's falling or has fallen in love with me, far too quickly for that falling in love to be anything more than a generous impulse, one from which she can still walk away any time she wants, out of weariness or pique or common sense or disappointment, she doesn't appear to feel that second emotion nor seems likely to, she has accepted that there will be nothing more than there already is and she knows that one day I will stop seeing her and erase her from my life because Luisa will, finally, have summoned me, that isn't in any way certain, of course, but it could happen, more than that, sooner or later, it should happen. Unless María has a strong, stupid sense of justice, and her disappointment at discovering that I am a criminal overcomes all other considerations, in which case it would not be enough for her to renounce me and separate from me, she would also want to separate me from my love. And then, if Luisa knew, or if the idea even entered her head, that would be that, what point would there be then, if, having followed the foulest of paths, there was no hope, not even the remotest, most unreal of hopes, the kind that helps us to live? Perhaps even waiting would be forbidden to me, not just hope, but mere waiting, the last refuge of the poorest wretch, of the sick and the decrepit and the doomed and the dying, who wait for night to come and then for day and night to come again, just for that change in the light, which will at least tell them where they are, whether they are awake or sleeping. Even animals wait. The refuge of every being on earth, except me . . ."

THE DAYS PASSED with no news from Díaz-Varela, one, two, three and four, and that was entirely normal. Five, six, seven and eight, and that was normal too. Nine, ten, eleven and twelve, and that wasn't quite so normal, but nor was it so very strange either, sometimes he was away and sometimes I was too, we didn't tend to issue any advance warning of our movements and certainly didn't bother to say goodbye, we never reached that degree of intimacy nor was our relationship important enough for us to feel it either necessary or prudent to keep each other informed of any absences from Madrid. In the past, whenever he had taken that long or longer to call or get in touch, I would think sadly—but always philosophically or perhaps resignedly—that it was time for me to leave the stage, that the brief space I had allotted myself in his life had indeed been very brief; I assumed he had grown tired of me or that, true to his usual mode of behaviour, he had chosen a new playmate (I never thought I was more than that, even though I would like to have been more) for the duration of his—as I saw it—immemorial waiting, or, rather, his lying in wait; or that Luisa's acceptance of his new role was happening more quickly than expected and that there was now no room for me nor, presumably, for anyone else; or that he was devoting all his time and attention to her, to taking the children to school and helping her as much as he could, keeping her company and being there if she needed him. "That's it, he's gone, he's dumped me, it's over," I would think. "It was so short-lived that I'll just merge in with all the others and he'll find it hard to remember who I was. I will be indistinguishable, I will be a before, a blank page, the opposite of a 'hereafter,' relegated to the category of the no longer important. It doesn't matter, it's fine, I knew how it would be from the start, it's fine." If on the twelfth or fifteenth day the phone rang and I heard his voice, I couldn't help giving a little inner leap of joy and saying to myself: "So it's not quite over yet, I'll see him at least one more time." And during those periods of involuntary waiting on my part and absolute silence on his, each time the bell rang or my mobile phone told me that I'd missed a call or that someone had left a text message, I would think optimistically that it would be from him.

Now the same thing was happening, except that this time I felt only apprehension. I would glance at the tiny screen in alarm, hoping not to see his name and number and—this was the strange, disquieting thing—also hoping that I would. I didn't want to have anything more to do with him or risk another of our usual encounters, during which I had no idea how I would react or how I should behave. Were we to meet face to face, he would be more likely to notice any evasiveness or reluctance on my part than if we only talked on the phone and, of course, more likely to do so if we talked than if we didn't. But not answering or returning his call would have had the same effect, given that I had never neglected to do so before. If I agreed to go to his apartment and he proposed having sex, as he usually did in that tacit way of his, which allowed him to act as if what was happening wasn't happening or wasn't worthy of recognition, and I gave some excuse and declined, that could make him suspicious. If he phoned to make a date with me and I put him off, that would give him food for thought too, because I had, as far as possible, always gone along with his suggestions. I considered it a blessing and a boon that he had remained silent since that last evening, that he hadn't sought me out, that I was free from his wheedlings and his trick questions and his attempts to sniff out the truth, free from having to meet him again and not knowing what to do or how to behave with him, from feeling that mixture of fear and repulsion, doubtless mingled with attraction and infatuation, because those two things cannot be eliminated suddenly or at will, but tend to take a while to disappear, like a period of convalescence or like the sickness itself; indignation doesn't really help, it soon loses its impetus, you can't maintain that same level of virulence, or else it comes and goes, and when it goes it leaves no trace, it isn't cumulative, it does no real damage, and when it dies down it's forgotten, like intense cold once it abates or like fever or grief. The time it takes for feelings to change is slow and infuriatingly gradual. You settle into those feelings and it becomes very difficult to prise yourself out of them, you get into the habit of thinking about someone—and of desiring them too—in a particular, fixed way, and it's hard to give that up from one day to the next, or even over a period of months and years, that's how long the feelings can last. And if what you feel is disappointment, then you fight it at first, however ridiculous that might seem, you try to minimize, deny, bury it. I would think sometimes that perhaps I didn't hear what I heard, or the feeble idea would resurface in my mind that it must all be a mistake, a misunderstanding, that there must even be some acceptable reason why Díaz-Varela had arranged for Desvern to die—but how could that ever be acceptable—I realized that, during this waiting period, I avoided even thinking the word "murder." And so while I considered it fortunate that Díaz-Varela didn't phone me and thus allowed me to compose myself and catch my breath, the fact that he didn't get in touch also worried me and made me suffer. Maybe it seemed impossible—an insipid, maladroit ending—that everything should just dissolve once I had discovered his secret and, after a brief interrogation, aroused his suspicions, and that there should then be nothing. It was as if the play had ended too early, as if everything were left up in the air, unresolved, floating, lingering in its lack of resolution, like an unpleasant smell in a lift. My thoughts were confused, I both wanted and didn't want to hear from him, my dreams were contradictory too and, when I spent a sleepless night, I hardly noticed, aware only that my head was crammed with thoughts and that I was miserably incapable of emptying it.

As I lay unable to sleep, I wondered if I should speak to Luisa, who no longer had breakfast in the same café as me, she must have given up the habit so as not to increase her grief or else to help her forget more easily, or perhaps she went there later, when I had already gone to work (maybe it was her husband who had had to get up early and she had only gone with him in order to postpone their parting). I wondered if it wasn't my duty to warn her, to let her know who he was, that friend of hers, that possibly unnoticed suitor, her constant protector; but I lacked any proof, and she might think me mad or spiteful, vengeful and unhinged, it's awkward going to anyone with such a sinister, murky tale, the more bizarre and complex the story, the harder it is to believe; this, in part, is what those who commit atrocities rely on, that the sheer magnitude of the atrocity will make it hard for people to credit. But it wasn't so much that as something far stranger, because it's so rare: the majority of people would be glad to tell, most take delight in pointing the finger in secret, in accusing and denouncing, in grassing on friends, neighbours, superiors and bosses, to the police, to the authorities, uncovering and revealing those guilty of something or other, even if only in their imaginations; in destroying the lives of those other people if they can, or at least making things awkward for them, doing their best to create outcasts, rejects, discards, leaving casualties all around and excluding them from their society, as if it were a comfort to be able to say after each victim or each piece of silver: "He's been broken off, detached from the bunch, he has fallen, and I have not." Among these people there are a few—we grow fewer by the day— who feel, on the contrary, an indescribable aversion to taking on the role of betrayer. And we take that antipathy so far that it is not always easy for us to overcome it even when we should—for our own good or for that of others. There is something repugnant to us about dialling a number and saying, without giving our name: "I've seen a terrorist the police are after, his photo has been in the newspapers and he's just gone through that door." Well, we would probably do so in a case like that, but more with an eye to averting crimes than to meting out punishments for past crimes, because no one can put those right and there are so many unpunished crimes in the world; indeed, they cover an area so vast, so ancient, so broad and wide that, up to a point, what do we care if a millimetre more is added to it? It sounds strange and even wrong, and yet it can happen: those of us who feel that aversion would sometimes prefer to act unjustly and for someone to go unpunished than see ourselves as betrayers, we can't bear it—when all's said and done, justice simply isn't our thing, it's not our job; and that role is still more odious when it's a matter of unmasking someone we have loved or, even worse, someone who, however inexplicable this might seem, we have not entirely ceased to love—despite the horror and the nausea afflicting our conscience or our consciousness, which, nonetheless, grows less troubled with each day that passes and is gone. And then we think something that we can't quite put into words, managing only an incoherent, reiterative, almost feverish murmur, something like: "Yes, what he did is very grave, very grave, but he is still him, still him." During that time of waiting or of unspoken farewell, I just couldn't see Díaz-Varela as a future danger to anyone else, not even to me, although I had felt a momentary fear and still did intermittently in his absence, in retrospect or in anticipation. Perhaps I was being overly optimistic, but I didn't think he would be capable of doing the same thing again. I still saw him as an amateur, an accidental transgressor, as an essentially ordinary man, who had done one anomalous thing.

ON THE FOURTEENTH DAY, he phoned my mobile when I was in a meeting with Eugeni and a semi-young author recommended to us by Garay Fontina as a reward for the adulation bestowed on him by the former in his blog and in a specialized literary review of which he was editor, "specialized" meaning pretentious and marginal. I left the office for a moment and told Díaz-Varela that I would call him back later; he, however, seemed not to believe me and kept me on the phone for a moment longer.

"It won't take a minute," he said. "How about getting together this evening? I've been away for a few days and it would be good to see you. If you like, come over to my apartment when you finish work."

"I might have to stay late this evening, things are absolutely crazy here," I said, inventing an excuse on the spur of the moment; I wanted to think about it or at least give myself time to get used to the idea of seeing him again. I still didn't know what I wanted, his simultaneously expected and unexpected voice brought me both alarm and relief, but what immediately prevailed was my pleasure at feeling wanted, at knowing that he had not yet shelved me, washed his hands of me or allowed me silently to disappear, it was not yet time for me to fade into the background. "Look, I'll let you know later, and depending on how things go, I'll either drop by or phone to say I won't be able to make it."

Then he said my name, something he didn't usually do.

"No, María. Come and see me." And then he paused as if he really wanted what he had said to sound imperative, which it had. When I didn't immediately say anything in response, he added something to mitigate that impression. "It isn't just that I want to see you, María." He had used my name twice now, which was unheard of, a bad sign. "I need to discuss an urgent matter with you. It doesn't matter if it's late, I'm not going anywhere. I'll wait in for you anyway. If not, I'll come and fetch you from work," he concluded firmly.

I didn't often say his name either, and I did so this time only because he had said mine and so as not to be caught on the back foot, hearing your own name often makes you feel uneasy, as if you were about to receive a warning or as if it were the prelude to some mishap or to a farewell.

"We haven't seen each other in days, Javier, can it really be so urgent that it can't wait a day or two longer? I mean, if it turns out that I can't make this evening."

I was playing hard to get, but nevertheless hoping that he wouldn't give up, that he wouldn't be satisfied with a "we'll see" or a "perhaps." I found his impatience flattering, even though I could sense that this was not a merely carnal impatience. Indeed, it was likely that there wasn't an ounce of carnality in it, but had to do only with his haste to bring something verbally to a close: because once it becomes clear that things cannot simply drift on, that they are not going to dissolve of their own accord or quietly die or come to a peaceful conclusion, then, generally speaking, it becomes very difficult, almost impossible, to wait; one feels a need to say the words, to come out with them immediately, to tell the other person and then vanish, so that she knows where she stands and won't continue living in a fool's paradise, so that she won't still think that she matters to us when she doesn't, that she occupies a place in our thoughts and our heart when she has, in fact, been replaced; so that we can erase her from our existence without delay. I didn't care. I didn't care if Díaz-Varela was summoning me simply in order to get rid of me, to say goodbye, I hadn't seen him for fourteen days and had feared that I might never see him again and that was all that mattered to me: if he saw me again, it might be harder for him to keep to his decision, I could try, I could give him an inkling of what the future would be like without me, persuade him by my presence to reverse his decision. I thought this and realized at once how idiotic it was: such moments are unpleasant, when we don't even feel ashamed to realize how idiotic we are, but abandon ourselves to our idiocy anyway, fully aware of what we are doing and knowing that soon we will be saying to ourselves: "I knew it, I was sure of it. How stupid can you get?" And that reaction, which came to me as surely as iron to magnet, was even more inconsistent and idiotic, given that I had already half-decided to break off with him if he ever got back in touch. He had arranged to have his best friend murdered and that was too much for my awakened conscience. Now, however, I discovered that it wasn't too much, at least not yet, or that my conscience had grown murky or else simply fell asleep if I let my attention wander for an instant, and that made me think precisely those words: "God, I'm stupid!"

Díaz-Varela was, at any rate, not used to me putting any obstacles in the way when he suggested that we meet, apart from my work, that is, and there are few tasks that cannot be left until the following day, at least in the world of publishing. Leopoldo was never an obstacle for as long as that relationship lasted, he was in the same position as I was vis-à-vis Díaz-Varela, or perhaps in an even worse position, because I had to make a real effort to enjoy being with him, whereas it never felt to me that Díaz-Varela had to make such an effort of will when he was with me, although that may have been a mere illusion on my part, for who ever really knows what anyone else feels. With Leopoldo, I was the one who decided when we could and couldn't see each other and for how long; for him, I was always a woman absorbed in an inexhaustible string of activities about which I didn't even talk to him, he must have imagined my small, unhurried world as being a barely sustainable maelstrom, so rarely did I make time for him, so burdened with work did I seem. He lasted for as long as Díaz-Varela did in my life: as often occurs when you have two relationships on the go at once, the one cannot survive without the other, however different or even opposed they might be. Lovers often end their adulterous affair when the married party divorces or is widowed, as if they were suddenly terrified of finding themselves face to face or didn't know how to continue without all the usual impediments, how to live or how to develop what had, until then, been a circumscribed love, comfortably condemned to not manifesting itself in public, possibly never even leaving one room; we often discover that what began purely by chance needs always to cleave to that way of being, with any attempt at change being experienced and rejected by both parties as an imposture or a falsification. Leopoldo never knew about Díaz-Varela, I never so much as mentioned his existence, why should I, it was none of his business. We parted on good terms, I didn't wound him deeply, and he still phones me from time to time, but we don't talk for long, we bore each other and after the first three sentences find we have nothing else to say. His was merely a brief hope cut short, a hope that was inevitably tenuous and somewhat sceptical, because an absence of enthusiasm is not something that can be easily concealed and is obvious even to the most optimistic of lovers. That, at least, is what I think, that I barely hurt him at all, that he never knew. Not that I'm going to bother finding out now, what does it matter, or, rather, what does it matter to me? Díaz-Varela certainly wouldn't take the trouble to find out how much harm he had done me or if he had wounded me: I had, after all, always been sceptical about our relationship, I couldn't even say that I ever had any hopes of him. With others I did, but not with him. If I learned one thing from him as a lover, it was not to take things too seriously and not to look back.

What he said next sounded like a demand barely disguised as a plea.

"Please, María, come and see me, it can't be that difficult. The question I have to ask could possibly wait a day or two more, but *I* can't wait, and you know what it's like with these subjective emergencies, they refuse to be postponed. It would be to your advantage too. Please, come and see me."

I hesitated a few seconds before replying, just so that it wouldn't seem quite as easy to him as it usually did; something horrible had happened last time I was there, although he didn't know that, or perhaps he did. I was in fact burning to see him, to put us to the test, to enjoy looking at his face and his lips again, even go to bed with him, with his former self, who was still there in the new Díaz-Varela, where else would he be? Finally, I said:

"All right, if you insist. I can't be sure what time, but I'll be there. And if you get tired of waiting, phone me and save me the trip. Anyway, I must go now."

I hung up, switched off my mobile, and returned to my pointless meeting. From then on, I was incapable of paying any attention to the semi-young author who had been recommended to us, and who clearly disapproved of me because that is precisely what he wanted, namely, an audience and lots of attention. I was quite sure of one thing, though: he wasn't going to be published by us, certainly not if I had anything to do with it.

IN THE EVENT, I had more than enough time and it wasn't late at all when I set off for Díaz-Varela's apartment. So much so, in fact, that I was able to pause along the way to conjecture and hesitate, to take several turns about the block and put off the moment of arrival. I even went into Embassy, that archaic place where ladies and diplomats take afternoon tea, I sat down at a table, ordered a drink and waited. I wasn't waiting for a specific time—I was merely aware that the longer I delayed things, the more nervous he would get—but waiting, rather, for the minutes to pass and for me to pluck up enough resolve or for my impatience to become sufficiently condensed to make me stand up and take one step and then another and another, until I found myself at his front door agitatedly ringing the bell. But, having decided to meet him and knowing that it was in my power to see him again, neither the necessary determination nor the impatience came. "In a while," I thought, "there's no hurry, I'll wait a little longer. He'll stay there in his apartment, he's not going to run away or leave. May every second seem long to him, may he count them one by one, may he read a few pages of a book without taking anything in, aimlessly turn the TV on and then off again, grow exasperated, prepare or memorize what he's going to say to me, may he go out on to the landing every time he hears the lift and be disappointed when it stops before it reaches his floor or goes straight past. What can he possibly want to discuss with me? Those are the words he used, vacuous, meaningless words, a kind of stock phrase which usually conceals something else, the trap one lays for a person so that he or she feels important and, at the same time, curious." And after a few more minutes, I thought: "Why did I agree? Why didn't I say No, why don't I run away from him and hide, or, rather, why don't I simply report him? Why, even knowing what I know, did I agree to see him, to listen to him if he wants to explain himself, and probably go to bed with him if he suggests doing so with the merest gesture or caress, or even with that prosaic, male tilt of the head in the direction of the bedroom, not even bothering with any flattering, intervening words, being as lazy with his tongue as so many men are." I recalled a quote from *The Three Musketeers* that my father knew by heart in French and which he occasionally recited for no apparent reason, almost like a pet phrase he trotted out to fill a silence, he probably liked the rhythm, the sound and the concision, or perhaps it had impressed him as a boy, the first time he read it (like Díaz-Varela he had studied at a French lycée, San Luis de los Franceses, if I remember rightly). Athos is talking about himself in the third person, that is, he's telling d'Artagnan his story as if it were that of an old aristocratic friend, who had got married at twenty-five to an innocent, intoxicatingly beautiful young girl of sixteen, "*belle comme les amours,*" so says Athos, who, at the time, was not a musketeer, but the Count de la Fère. While they are out hunting, his very young, angelic wife—whom he had married despite knowing almost nothing about her and without bothering to find out where she came from, never imagining that she had a past to conceal—has an accident, falls from her horse and faints. Rushing to her aid, Athos notices that her dress is constricting her breathing and, to help her breathe more easily, he takes out his dagger and cuts open her dress, thus leaving her shoulder bare. And it is then that he sees the fleur-de-lys with which executioners branded prostitutes or female thieves or perhaps criminals in general, I'm not sure. "The angel was a devil," declares Athos, adding the somewhat contradictory statement: "The poor girl had been a thief." D'Artagnan asks him what the Count did, to which his friend replies with succinct coldness (and this was the quotation that my father used to repeat and which I remembered): *"Le Comte était un grand seigneur, il avait sur les terres droit de justice basse et haute: il acheva de déchirer les habits de la Comtesse, il lui lia les mains derrière le dos et la pendit à un arbre."* "The Count was a great lord, he had the right on his estates to mete out justice both high and low; he tore the rest of the Countess's dress to shreds, tied her hands behind her back and hanged her from a tree." And that, without a moment's hesitation, without listening to reason or seeking extenuating circumstances, without batting an eyelid, without pity or regret for her youth, that is what the young Athos did to the girl with whom he had fallen so deeply in love that, in his desire to treat her honestly, he had made her his wife, when, as he acknowledges, he could easily have seduced her or taken her by force if he liked; he was, after all, the great lord, and, besides, who would have come to the aid of a stranger, a girl about whom nothing was known except that her true or false name was Anne de Breuil? But no: "the fool, the simpleton, the imbecile" had to marry her, Athos says reproachfully of his former self, the Count de le Fère, as upright as he was fierce, who, as soon as he discovered the deception, the infamy, the indelible stain, abandoned all questions and conflicting feelings, all hesitations and postponements and compassion—he did not stop loving her, though, because he still continued to love her, or at least never fully recovered—and without giving the Countess an opportunity to explain or defend herself, to deny or to persuade, to beg for mercy or to bewitch him again, not even "to die hereafter," as perhaps even the most wretched creature on earth deserves, "he tied her hands behind her back and hanged her from a tree," without wavering for a moment. D'Artagnan is horrified and cries out: "Good heavens, Athos, a murder!" To which Athos replies mysteriously, or, rather, enigmatically: "Yes, a murder, nothing more," and then calls for more wine and ham, considering the story at an end. What remains mysterious or even enigmatic are those two words "nothing more," *"pas davantage"* in French. Athos doesn't refute d'Artagnan's cry of outrage, he doesn't justify himself or contradict him, saying: "No, it was simply an execution" or "It was an act of justice"; he doesn't even attempt to make the precipitate, ruthless and presumably solitary hanging of the wife he loved more comprehensible, for doubtless only he and she were there in the middle of a wood, a spur-of-the-moment decision with no witnesses, with no one to advise or help him, no one to whom he could appeal; nor did he say anything along the lines of: "He was blind with rage and couldn't restrain himself; he needed to take his revenge; he regretted it for the rest of his life." He admits that it was a murder, yes, but nothing more than that, not something more execrable, as if murder were not the worst conceivable thing or else so common and everyday that it need provoke no feelings of scandal or surprise, which is basically the view of the lawyer Derville, who took on the case of old Colonel Chabert, the living dead man who should have stayed dead, for Derville, like all lawyers, saw "the same wicked feelings repeated over and over," feelings that nothing could correct and which transformed his offices into "sewers that can never be washed clean"; murder is something that happens, an act of which anyone is capable and that has been happening since the dawn of time and will continue to do so until, after the last day, no dawn comes, nor is there any time in which to accommodate more murders; murder is something banal and anodyne and commonplace, purely temporal; the world's newspapers and televisions are full of murders, so why such hysteria, such horror, such outrage? Yes, a murder. Nothing more.

"Why can't I be like Athos or like the Count de la Fère, as he was initially and then ceased to be?" I wondered as I sat in the Embassy tea rooms, wrapped in the continuous buzz coming from ladies talking very fast and from the occasional idle diplomat. "Why can't I see things with that same clarity and act accordingly, and go to the police or to Luisa and tell them what I know, enough for them to revisit the crime and investigate and track down Ruibérriz de Torres, that would be a start? Why aren't I capable of tying the hands of the man I love behind his back and simply hanging him from a tree, if I know that he has committed an odious crime, as old as the Bible and for an utterly despicable motive too and carried out in a cowardly manner, making use of intermediaries to protect him and hide his face, making use of a poor, crazed wretch, a witless beggar who could not defend himself and would always be at his mercy? No, it isn't up to me to act with such ruthless rigour because I do not have the right to mete out justice high and low, and, besides, the dead man cannot speak, whereas the living can, he can explain himself, persuade and argue, and is even capable of kissing me and making love to me, while the former can neither see nor hear, but lies rotting in the grave and cannot answer or influence or threaten, nor give me the slightest pleasure; nor can he call me to account or feel disappointment or look at me accusingly with an expression of infinite sadness and immense grief, he cannot even brush my skin or breathe on me, there is nothing to be done with him."

I FINALLY PLUCKED UP enough resolve, or perhaps it was merely boredom or a desire to rid myself of the fear that assailed me now and then, or impatience to see the old me who continued to love and who had not yet entirely vanished and still prevailed over the sullied and the sombre, like the living image of a dead person, even one who had died a long time ago. I asked for the bill, paid and left and started walking in the direction I knew so well, towards the apartment I will never forget, even though I didn't visit it so very often and even though it no longer exists—not, at least, as far as I'm concerned, given that Díaz-Varela no longer lives there. I was still walking slowly, in no hurry to arrive, I walked as if I were out for a stroll, rather than heading for a particular place where someone had been waiting for me for quite a while now in order to discuss something, that is, to question me again or to tell or perhaps ask me something, or, possibly, to silence me. Another quotation from *The Three Musketeers* surfaced in my memory, one that my father did not quote, but which I knew in Spanish, for things that impress us as children endure like a fleur-de-lys engraved on our imagination: the marked woman who was hanged from a tree and began life as Anne de Breuil, who spent a brief period in a convent until she ran away, then, very fleetingly, became the Countess de la Fère, and was known later on as Charlotte, Lady Clarick, Lady de Winter, Baroness of Sheffield (as a child, I was amazed that anyone could change her name so often in a single lifetime), and who had become fixed in literature as plain "Milady," no, that marked woman had not died, just as Colonel Chabert had not died. But while Balzac explained in great detail the miracle of the Colonel's survival and how he had dragged himself out from beneath the pyramid of ghosts into which he had been thrown after the battle, Dumas, perhaps under pressure of deadlines and the constant demand for action, and, of course, freer or perhaps sloppier as a narrator, had not bothered to explain—at least as far as I could recall—how the devil that young woman had managed to escape death after that impassioned hanging dictated by rage and wounded honour disguised as a great lord's right to mete out justice high and low. (He also never explained how a husband could fail to have noticed the fatal fleur-de-lys while in the marital bed.) Making the most of her great beauty, her cunning and her lack of scruples—and, one imagines, her bitter resentment—she had become a powerful figure, who enjoyed the favour of Cardinal Richelieu no less, and had heaped up crimes without a flicker of remorse. During the novel, she commits a few more crimes, becoming possibly the most evil, venomous, ruthless female character in the history of literature, and, as such, has since been imitated ad nauseam. She and Athos meet in a chapter ironically entitled "A Conjugal Scene," and it takes her a few seconds to recognize, with a shudder, her former husband and executioner, whom she had assumed dead, just as he had assumed his beloved wife to be dead, and with rather more reason. "You have already crossed my path," says Athos, or words to that effect, "I thought I had crushed you, Madame, but either I am much mistaken or hell has resuscitated you." And he adds, in response to his own doubt: "Yes, hell has made you rich, hell has given you another name, hell has almost fashioned another face for you; but it has not erased the stains on your soul or the mark on your body." And shortly after that comes the quote I remembered as I walked towards Díaz-Varela for the last or next-to-last time: "You believed me dead, didn't you, just as I believed you to be dead. Our position is indeed a strange one; we have both lived up until now only because we believed each other to be dead, and because a memory is less troublesome than a living creature, although sometimes a memory can be a devouring thing."

If those words had stayed in my mind, or my mind had retrieved them, it was because, as we grow older, Athos's words ring ever truer: we can live with a feeling resembling peace or are, at least, capable of carrying on living when we believe that the person who caused us terrible pain or grief is dead and no longer exists on earth, when he is only a memory and not a living creature, no longer a real being who breathes and still walks the world with his poisoned steps, and whom we might meet again and see; someone, if we knew he had been found—if we knew he was still here—from whom we would fly at all costs, or have the even more mortifying experience of making him pay for his evil deeds. The death of the person who wounded us or made our life a living death—an exaggerated expression that has become something of a cliché—is not a complete cure nor does it enable us to forget, Athos himself carried his remote grief about with him beneath his disguise as a musketeer and his new personality, but it does appease us and allow us to live, breathing becomes easier when we are left only with a lingering remembrance and the feeling that we have settled our accounts with this the only world, however much the memory still hurts us whenever we summon it up or it resurfaces without being called. On the other hand, it can be unbearable knowing that we still share air and time with the person who broke our heart or deceived or betrayed us, with the person who ruined our life or opened our eyes too wide or too brutally; it can have a paralysing effect knowing that the same creature still exists and has not been struck down or hanged from a tree and could, therefore, reappear. That is another reason why the dead should not return, at least those whose departure brings us relief and allows us to carry on living, if you like, as ghosts, having buried our former self: so it was with Athos and Milady, with the Count de la Fère and Anne de Breuil, who could continue their lives thanks to their shared belief that the other was dead and, being incapable of breathing, could no longer make so much as a leaf tremble; as with Madame Ferraud, who started her new life unobstructed because, as far as she was concerned, her husband, Colonel Chabert, was only a memory and not even a devouring one.

"If only Javier had died," I found myself thinking that evening, while I took one step after another. "If only he were to die right now and didn't answer when I ring the bell because he's lying on the floor, forever motionless, unable to discuss anything with me and with me unable to speak to him. If he were dead, all my doubts and fears would be dispelled, I wouldn't have to hear his words or wonder what to do. Nor could I fall into the temptation of kissing him or going to bed with him, deluding myself with the idea that it would be the last time. I could keep silent for ever without worrying about Luisa, still less about justice, I could forget about Deverne, after all, I never actually knew him, or only by sight for several years, during the time it took me to eat my breakfast each morning. If the person who robbed him of his life loses his own life and thus also becomes a mere memory and if there's no one to accuse him, the consequences are less important and then what does it matter what happened. Why say or tell anything, indeed, why try to find out the truth, keeping silent is the far easier option, there's no need to trouble the world with stories of those who are already themselves corpses and therefore deserve a little pity, even if only because they have been stopped in their tracks, have ended and no longer exist. Our age is not one in which everything must be judged or at least known about; innumerable crimes go unresolved or unpunished because no one knows who committed them—so many that there are not enough pairs of eyes to look out for them—and it is rare to find anyone who can, with any credibility, be placed in the dock: terrorist attacks, the murders of women in Guatemala and in Ciudad Juárez, revenge killings among drug-traffickers, the indiscriminate slaughters that occur in Africa, the bombing of civilians by our aircraft with no pilot and therefore no face . . . Even more numerous are those that no one cares about and are never even investigated, it's seen as a hopeless task and their cases are filed away as soon as they happen; and there are still more that leave no trace, that remain unrecorded, undiscovered, and unknown. Such crimes have doubtless always existed and it may be that for many centuries the only crimes that were punished were those committed by servants, by the poor or the disinherited, whereas—with a few exceptions—those committed by the powerful and the rich, to speak in vague and superficial terms, went unpunished. But there was a simulacrum of justice, and, at least publicly, at least in theory, the authorities pretended to pursue all crimes and, on occasion, did actually pursue some, and any cases that were not cleared up were deemed to be 'pending,' however, it isn't like that now: there are too many cases that simply can't be cleared up or that people possibly don't want to clear up or else feel that it isn't worth the effort or the time or the risk. The days are long gone when accusations were uttered with extreme solemnity and sentences handed out with barely a tremor in the voice, as Athos did twice with his wife, Anne de Breuil, first as a young man and later when he was older: he was not alone the second time, but in the company of the other three musketeers, Porthos, d'Artagnan and Aramis, and Lord de Winter, to whom he delegated authority, and a masked man in a red cloak who turned out to be the executioner from Lille, the same man who ages before—in another life, on another person—had branded the shameful fleur-de-lys on Milady's shoulder. Each of them makes his accusation and all begin with a formula that is unimaginable today: 'Before God and before men I accuse this woman of having poisoned, of having murdered, of having caused to be assassinated, of having urged me to murder, of having afflicted someone with a strange disorder and brought about their death, of having committed sacrilege, of having stolen, of having corrupted, of having incited to crime . . .' 'Before God and before men.' No, ours is not a solemn age. And then Athos, perhaps pretending to delude himself, in order to believe, in vain, that this time he was not the one judging or condemning her, asks each of the other men, one by one, what sentence he is demanding for the woman. To which they answer one after the other: 'The penalty of death, the penalty of death, the penalty of death, the penalty of death.' Once the sentence had been heard, it was Athos who turned to her and, as master of ceremonies, said: 'Anne de Breuil, Countess de la Fère, Milady de Winter, your crimes have wearied men on earth and God in heaven. If you know a prayer, say it now, because you have been condemned and are going to die.' Anyone reading this scene as a child or in early youth will always remember it, can never forget it, nor what comes next: the executioner ties the hands and feet of the woman who is still *belle comme les amours,* picks her up and carries her to a boat, in which he crosses to the other side of the river. During the crossing, Milady manages to untie the rope binding her legs and, when they reach the other shore, she jumps out and begins to run, but immediately slips and falls to her knees. She must know she is lost then, because she doesn't even try to get up, but stays in that posture, her head bowed and her hands bound together, we're not told whether in front or behind, as they had been when, as a young girl, she was killed for the first time. The executioner of Lille raises his sword and lowers it, thus putting an end to the creature and transforming her for ever into a memory, whether a devouring one or not, it doesn't really matter. Then he removes his red cloak, spreads it on the ground, lays the body on it, throws in the head, ties the cloak by its four corners, loads the bundle on his shoulder and carries it back to the boat. Halfway across, where the river is deepest, he drops the body in. Her judges watch from the bank as the body disappears, they see how the waters open for a moment then close over it. But that was in a novel, as Javier pointed out to me when I asked what had happened to Chabert: 'What happened is the least of it. It's a novel, and once you've finished a novel, what happened in it is of little importance and soon forgotten. What matters are the possibilities and ideas that the novel's imaginary plot communicates to us and infuses us with, a plot that we recall far more vividly than real events and to which we pay far more attention.' That isn't true, or, rather, it's sometimes true, but one doesn't always forget what happened, not in a novel that almost everyone knew or knows, even those who have never read it, nor in reality when what happens is actually happening to us and is going to be our story, which could end one way or another with no novelist to decide and independent of anyone else . . ." "Yes, if only Javier had died and become merely a memory too," I thought again. "That would save me from my problems of conscience and from my fears, my doubts and temptations and from having to make a decision, from my feelings of love and from my need to talk. And from what awaits me now, the scene I'm walking towards, and which will perhaps bear some resemblance to a conjugal scene."

"SO WHAT'S ALL the urgency?" I said as soon as Díaz-Varela opened the door to me, I didn't even kiss him on the cheek, I just said hello as I went in, tried to avoid looking him in the eye, even preferring not to touch him. If I began by demanding an explanation, I might take the lead, so to speak, gain a certain advantage in managing the situation, whatever the situation was: he had arranged it, almost insisted on it, so how could I know? "I haven't got that much time, it's been a really exhausting day. Anyway, what it is you want to discuss?"

He was perfectly shaved and immaculately dressed, and didn't look at all as if he had been waiting at home for a long time, especially with no guarantee that his wait would not prove to be in vain—something which, without one realizing it, always has a deleterious effect on one's appearance—but, rather, as if he were about to go out. He must have been struggling with all that uncertainty and inaction by shaving over and over, combing his hair and then ruffling it up again, changing his shirt and trousers several times, putting his jacket on, then taking it off again, weighing up how he looked either with or without it, in the end, he had left it on as a warning to me perhaps that this encounter was not going to be like the others, that we would not necessarily end up in the bedroom, a move that we always pretended was unintentional. Anyway, he was wearing one more item of clothing than usual, although it's easy enough—even unnecessary—to remove anything. Now I did look up and meet his gaze, which was, as usual, dreamy and myopic, calmer than during my previous visit or, rather, during the final moments of that visit, when things took a strange turn, and he placed his hand on my shoulder and made me feel that he could destroy me simply by that slow, steady pressure. After all that time, he still seemed very attractive to me, because the more elemental part of me had missed him—we are capable of missing anything in our lives, even something that has not had time to take root, even something pernicious—and my gaze went immediately to the usual place, I couldn't help it. When that happens with someone, it's a real curse. Being incapable of looking away, you feel controlled, obedient, almost humiliated.

"Don't be in such a hurry. Rest for a moment, breathe, have a drink, take a seat. What I want to discuss can't be dispatched in a couple of sentences and while standing up. Come on, be patient, be generous. Have a seat."

I sat down on the sofa we usually occupied when we were in the living room. But I kept my jacket on and perched on the edge of the sofa, as if my presence there were nonetheless still provisional and a favour to him. He seemed calm and, at the same time, very focused, the way many actors are just before they go on stage, that is, they put on an artificial calm, which they need if they are not to run away and go back home and watch television. There appeared to be none of that morning's imperiousness and urgency, when he had phoned me at work and almost ordered me to come. He must have felt pleased and relieved that I was now there within his grasp, because in a way I had placed myself in his hands again, and not just in the figurative sense. But now I was free of that kind of fear, I had realized that he would never harm me, not with his own hands, not alone. But with someone else's hands and when he was not present, when the deed was done and there was no choice and he could say, like someone taken by surprise: "There would have been a time for such a word, she should have died hereafter"—yes, that was possible.

He went into the kitchen to get me a drink and poured one for himself. There was no sign of any other glasses, perhaps he had not allowed himself a single drop while he waited, so as to keep a clear head, maybe he had used the time to select and put in order what he was going to tell me, even memorizing part of it.

"Right, I'm sitting down now. What is it you want to say?"

He sat beside me, too close, although I wouldn't have thought that on any other day, it would have seemed perfectly normal or I might not even have noticed how much distance there was between us. I moved away a little, only a little, I didn't want to give the impression that I was rejecting him, besides I wasn't rejecting him physically, I realized that I still liked him to be close. He sipped his drink. He took out a cigarette, flicked his lighter on and off several times as if he were distracted or getting up the energy to do something, then, finally, lit the cigarette. He stroked his chin, which didn't have its usual bluish tinge, so carefully had he shaved this time. That was the preamble, and then he spoke to me, in a serious tone, but forcing himself to smile every now and then—as if he were telling himself to do so every few minutes or had programmed himself to smile and kept belatedly remembering to activate the programme.

"I know that you heard us, María, heard Ruibérriz and me. There's no point in you denying it or trying to convince me that you didn't, like the last time. It was an error on my part to talk like that with you in the apartment, while you were here, any woman who's interested in a man is always curious about anything to do with him: his friends, his business dealings, his tastes, it doesn't matter. Everything intrigues her, because she wants to know him better."—"He's been turning it over in his mind, just as I foresaw," I thought. "He'll have gone over every detail, every word, and reached that conclusion. At least he didn't say 'any woman in love with a man,' although that's what he meant and, as it happens, it's true. Or was true, I'm not sure, it can't be true now. But two weeks ago it was, so he's quite right really."—"It happened and there's no going back. I accept that, I'm not going to deceive myself; you heard what you shouldn't have heard, what neither you nor anyone else should have heard, but especially not you, otherwise we could have made a clean break from each other, without leaving a mark."—"He now bears the mark of his own fleur-de-lys," I thought.—"After hearing what you heard, you will have formed an idea, an image. Let's have a look at that idea, it's better than running away from it or pretending that it isn't in your mind, that it doesn't exist. You must be thinking the worst of me and I can't blame you, it must have sounded dreadful. Repellent. I'm grateful that, despite everything, you agreed to come here, it must have made you feel really uncomfortable having to see me again."

I tried to protest, but somewhat half-heartedly; I saw that he was determined to tackle the subject and leave me no way out, to speak clearly about that murder-by-delegation. He couldn't be absolutely sure that I knew, but he was nevertheless ready to make his confession or something similar. Or maybe he was going to put me in the picture, explain the circumstances, justify himself somehow or other, tell me what I would possibly prefer not to know. If I knew the details, that would make it even harder for me to ignore the facts or to take no action, as, in a way, and without exactly meaning to, I had successfully managed to do until that evening, although without ruling out a different future reaction, tomorrow might change me and bring with it an unrecognizable "I": I had stayed still and let the days pass, which is the best way to allow things in the real world to dissolve or break down, although they remain forever in our thoughts and in our knowledge, solid and putrid and stinking to high heaven. But that is bearable and we can live with it. Who doesn't carry something of that nature around with them?

"Javier, let's not talk about it. I've already told you that I didn't hear anything, and I'm really not as interested in you as you imagine . . ."

He stopped me with a wave of his hand ("Don't give me that," said the hand, "no pussyfooting around, please") and wouldn't let me continue speaking. He smiled slightly condescendingly, or perhaps it was self-irony, at finding himself in that entirely avoidable situation, because of his own carelessness.

"Don't go on. Don't take me for a fool. Although I was certainly very stupid. I should have taken Ruibérriz outside as soon as he turned up. Of course you heard us: when you came into the living room, you claimed that you didn't know anyone else was here, but you had put on your bra to cover yourself, at least minimally, in front of a stranger, not because it was cold or for some other round-about reason, and you were already blushing when you opened the bedroom door. You weren't embarrassed by what you found, you had embarrassed yourself beforehand with what you were going to do, namely reveal yourself in a state of near-undress to an undesirable individual you had never seen before; but you had heard him speak, and not about just anything, not about football or the weather."—"So he did notice what I feared he would notice," I thought fleetingly. "All my forward planning, my little schemes, my ingenuous precautions were in vain."—"The look of surprise on your face was quite convincing, but not entirely. The real give-away, though, was that, all of a sudden, you were afraid of me. I had left you there in bed, quiet and trusting, even affectionate and con-tented, I thought. You had fallen peacefully asleep and when you woke up and were once again alone with me, suddenly you were afraid. Did you really think I wouldn't notice? We always notice when we instil fear in someone. Perhaps women don't, or is it that you so rarely do instil fear that you're unfamiliar with the feeling, except with children, of course; you can terrorize them easily enough. I don't like it at all, although there are lots of men who love it and even seek it out, it gives them a sense of power, of being in command, a momentary, false sense of invulnerability. It makes me really uncomfortable having someone see me as a threat. A physical threat, I mean. You women have other ways of making us afraid. Your demands. Your obstinacy, which is often merely blindness. Your indignation, the kind of moral fury that grips you, sometimes for no reason at all. You must have been feeling that about me for two weeks now. I don't blame you either. That's perfectly understandable in your case, you had a reason to feel like that. And not an entirely mistaken reason either. Well, only half-mistaken."—He paused and raised a hand to his chin, which he stroked distractedly (for the first time, he looked away), as if he really were pondering or genuinely wondering what he would say next.—"What I don't understand is why you appeared, why you came out of the bedroom, why you exposed yourself to having what is now happening happen. If you had stayed still, if you had waited for me in bed, I would have assumed that you hadn't heard us, that you knew nothing, that everything was just as it had been before, in general and between you and me. Although I would probably have noticed your fear anyway, sooner or later, that day or today. Once a fear has been born, it's there and you can't hide it."

He paused, took another drink, lit another cigarette, got to his feet, walked around the room a couple of times and ended up standing behind me. When he first stood up, I was startled, I jumped, and he noticed, of course, and when he remained for a few seconds without moving, his hands near my head, I turned round at once, as if I didn't want to lose sight of him or to have him at my back. Then

he made a gesture with his open hand, as if to indicate an obvious truth ("You see?" said the hand. "You don't like not knowing
where I am. A few weeks ago it wouldn't have worried you in the
least if I had walked around you like this; you wouldn't even have
noticed"). The truth is, there was no reason for me to feel startled
or anxious, not really. Díaz-Varela was talking in a calm, civilized
manner, without getting angry or worked up, without even telling
me off or demanding an explanation for my indiscreet behaviour.
Perhaps that was the most striking thing, him talking to me about
a serious crime in that matter-of-fact way, about a murder committed indirectly by him or at his instigation, in a not yet remote, but
almost recent past, murder not being something that one usually
talks about calmly, at least it didn't use to be: when such a thing
was revealed or acknowledged, there were no cool explanations or
dissertations or conversations, no analysis, but horror and anger,
outrage, screams and vehement accusations, or people would grab
a rope and hang the self-confessed murderer from a tree, and he or
she, in turn, would try to flee and kill again if necessary. "What a
strange age we live in," I thought. "We allow people to talk about
anything and to be listened to, regardless of what they have done,
and not just in order to defend themselves, but as if the story of
their atrocities were itself of interest." And another thought came
to me that I myself found odd: "That is our essential fragility. But it
is not in my power to rebel against it, because I, too, belong to this
age, and I am a mere pawn."

AS DÍAZ-VARELA HAD SAID right at the start, there was no point in me continuing to deny all knowledge. He had already gone far enough ("It was an error on my part," "I should have taken Ruibérriz outside," "You had a not entirely mistaken reason to feel alarmed, well, a half-mistaken reason"), so far that I was left with no alternative but to ask him what the devil he was talking about, if, that is, I maintained my pose of innocence. Even if I insisted on pretending that this was all entirely new to me and that I had no idea what he was talking about, that wouldn't let me off the hook either: it was up to me to demand to be told the story and to hear it through to the end, from the beginning this time. It would be best to admit that I knew, thus avoiding having to repeat myself or possibly having to come up with some extravagant lie. The whole thing was going to be most unpleasant, but then it was a thoroughly unpleasant business. The less time he took to tell his story the better. Or perhaps it would turn out to be not a story but a disquisition. I wanted to leave, but didn't dare so much as try, I didn't even move.

"All right, I did hear you. But I didn't hear everything you said, not all the time. Enough though for me to feel afraid of you, what else would you expect? Anyway, now you know, you couldn't have been entirely sure before, but now you can. What are you going to do about it? Is that why you made me come here, to confirm your suspicions? You were pretty sure already, we could simply have let things run their course and not left any more 'marks,' to use your word. As you see, I haven't done anything yet, I haven't told anyone, not even Luisa. She, I imagine, would be the last to be told. It's often those who are most affected by something, those who are closest, who least want to know: children don't want to know what their parents did, just as parents don't want to know what their children have done . . . To impose a revelation on someone . . ." I paused, unsure as to how to end the sentence, and so I cut things short, simplified: "That's too great a responsibility. For someone like me."—"So I am the Prudent Young Woman after all," I thought. "That's how Desvern thought of me."—"You certainly have no reason to feel afraid of me. You should have allowed me to stand aside, to exit from your life silently and discreetly, more or less as I entered it and as I have remained, if I have remained. There was never any reason why we should see each other again. For me, each time was the last, I never assumed there would be a next time. It was always until further notice, until further orders from you, because you were always the instigator, the one who took the initiative. There's still time for you simply to let me go, I really don't know why I'm here at all, actually."

He took a few steps, moved away from his position at my back, but rather than sitting down again beside me, he remained standing, taking refuge this time behind an armchair opposite me. And the truth is I kept my eyes trained on him at all times. I watched his hands and watched his lips, both because they would speak and because that was what I always did, they were my magnet. Then he took off his jacket and, as usual, hung it over the back of the chair. Afterwards, he slowly rolled up his shirtsleeves and although that was normal too—he always had his sleeves rolled up when he was at home, indeed that was the only day I had ever seen him with his cuffs buttoned and then not for long—that gesture now put me even more on my guard, because it's so often a prelude to action, to some physical effort, and there was none in prospect. When he had finished rolling up his sleeves, he leaned on the back of the armchair, as if about to make a speech. For a few seconds, he stood observing me very intently in a manner I had seen before and yet the same thing happened as on that other occasion: I looked away, feeling troubled by those eyes fixed on mine, by that gaze, which was neither transparent nor penetrating, but perhaps hazy and enveloping or merely indecipherable, and tempered at any rate by his myopia (he was wearing lenses), it was as if those almond eyes were saying to me: "Why don't you understand?" not impatiently, but regretfully. And his posture was no different from what it had been on other evenings, when he had spoken to me about *Colonel Chabert* or about something else that had occurred to him or that he had noticed, and I would listen to whatever it was with pleasure. "On other late afternoons or evenings," I thought, "the twilight hour, which is doubtless the worst time for Luisa as it is for most people, the hardest time of day to bear, on those evenings when he and I would meet"—I realized at once that I was thinking in the past tense, as if we had already said goodbye and each already belonged to the other's day before yesterday; but I continued anyway: "On those evenings Javier didn't go to her house, didn't visit or distract her or keep her company or lend her a hand, he probably needed to have a rest sometimes—every ten or twelve days—from the persistent sadness of the woman he loved so constantly and for whom he waited with such inexhaustible patience; he would have needed to draw energy from somewhere, from me, from another close relationship, from someone else, so that he could carry that renewed energy back to her. Perhaps I had helped her a little in that way, indirectly, without intending to or imagining that I was, not that it bothered me. Who would he draw that energy from now, if I was no longer at his side? He'll have no problem replacing me, I'm sure of that." And as I thought this, I returned to the present tense.

"I don't want to leave any mark on you that has no reason to exist, that has no basis in reality, or has its basis only in what happened, but not in any possible motives or intentions, still less in the original conception, the starting point. Let's have a look at what you imagine to have happened, at the set of circumstances or story you have constructed for yourself: I ordered Miguel to be killed, making sure to keep myself at a safe distance. I drew up a plan that was not without risks (above all the risk that it might not work), but that left me beyond suspicion. I didn't go anywhere near the scene of the crime, I wasn't there, his death had nothing to do with me and it would be quite impossible to connect me with some barmy beggar with whom I had never exchanged so much as a single word. I left it to other people to find out what his problems were and to direct and manipulate his fragile mind. Miguel's death looked like a tragic accident, a piece of terrible bad luck. Why didn't I just get a hit man in? That would, apparently, have been far simpler and safer. Nowadays, they're flown in from all over the world, from Eastern Europe and South America, and they're not that expensive either: a return ticket, a few meals and three thousand euros or less, or possibly more, depending, but let's say three thousand if you don't want to hire a bodger or a greenhorn. They do their job and then leave, and by the time the police have begun their investigations, the killer has already checked in at the airport or is on the plane home. The snag is that there are no guarantees they won't do the same thing again, that they won't come back to Spain on another job or that they might like it here and stay. Some who have used their services have proved very careless, even giving a recommendation to a friend or colleague (very sotto voce needless to say), recommending either the killer himself or the intermediary who, very lazily, summons the same hit man back to Spain. Anyone who chooses that option is never entirely clean. The more frequently these hit men visit the country, the more likely they are to get caught, and the more likely they are to remember you or your frontman, and thus establish a link that cannot easily be broken, because there are people who can't bear to be left idle and can't resist taking on a little extra work. And if they get caught, they blab. Even those who are on the payroll of some mafia boss and live here permanently, and there are quite a few in Spain, presumably because there's plenty for them to do here. The code of silence isn't much respected any more, if at all. There's no sense of camaraderie, no sense of belonging: if one of them gets caught, tough, let him sort himself out, it was his fault for getting nabbed. He's expendable, and the organizations accept no responsibility, they've taken the necessary measures so that they don't get tarnished or tainted, and the hit men work more and more in the dark and only ever meet one person, if that: a voice at the other end of a telephone, with the photos of the victims being sent via a mobile. And so those who are arrested respond in kind. Nowadays, all anyone cares about is saving his own skin or getting his sentence reduced. They confess whatever they need to confess and that's that, the main thing being not to spend too long in prison. The more time they spend behind bars, trapped and easily locatable, the greater the risk that their own mafia boss will do them in, well, they're useless to him now, a dead weight, a liability. And since they have little to reveal about the mafia they work for, they try other ways of gaining brownie points: 'I did a job for a well-known businessman some years ago, or perhaps he was a politician or a banker. Yes, it's all coming back to me now. If I try very hard to remember, who knows what I might come up with?' More than one businessman has ended up in prison for that very reason. And the odd Valencian politician too, well, you know what showoffs they are, they don't even understand the meaning of the word 'discretion.'"

"How does Javier know all this?" I wondered as I listened to him.

And I recalled the one real conversation I'd had with Luisa, when she appeared to be *au fait* with these practices too, she had spoken about them and even used certain expressions very similar to those used by her suitor: "They bring in a hit man, he does his job, they pay him and he leaves, all in the space of one or two days, and the police never find these killers . . ." At the time, I assumed she must have read about it in the newspapers or heard Deverne talk about it, he was, after all, a businessman. But perhaps she had heard Díaz-Varela mention it. They disagreed, though, as to the efficacy of such a method, which he thought unworkable or too problematic, and he sounded far better informed than she. Luisa had added: "If something like that had happened, I couldn't even hate that abstract hit man very much . . . But I could hate the instigators, that would give me the chance to suspect people right, left and centre, a competitor or someone who felt resentful or hard done by, because every businessman creates victims either accidentally or deliberately, even among close colleagues, as I read again the other day in Covarrubias." Then she had picked up the fat green tome and read out part of the definition of "*envidia*"—or "envy"—written in 1611 no less, when both Shakespeare and Cervantes were still alive, four hundred years ago, and yet it was still valid, it's distressing to think that some things never change in essence, although it's also oddly comforting to know that something can still persist without moving a millimetre or changing a word: "Unfortunately, this poison is often engendered in the breasts of those who are and who we believe to be our closest friends . . ." Javier was recounting this case to me or confessing, but only as a hypothesis, and presumably in order to deny it; I assumed that he was describing what I imagined to have happened, the conclusion I had drawn after hearing him and Ruibérriz talking, so that he could immediately refute it. "Perhaps he's going to deceive me with the truth," I thought for the first but not the only time. "Perhaps he's telling me the truth now so that it will seem like a lie. An apparent or genuine lie."

"How do you know all this?"

"I found out. When you want to know something, there are always ways of finding out. You weigh up the pros and cons, then do some research." He gave a very quick response to my question and then fell silent. I thought he was about to add something else, for example, *how* he had found out. But he didn't. I had a sense that he was irritated by my interruption, that I had caused him momentarily to lose impetus, or, possibly, the thread of his argument. Perhaps he was more nervous than he seemed. He took a few steps around the room and sat down on the armchair on which he had hung his jacket and on which he had been leaning. He was still there before me, but now he was on the same level. He placed another cigarette between his lips, but without lighting it, and when he began talking again, it bobbed up and down. It didn't conceal his mouth, but, rather, emphasized it. "So using a hit man may, at first, seem like a good way of removing someone. Yet it turns out that there are always risks involved in contacting such people, however careful you are and even if you do so through a third party. Or a fourth or fifth party; in fact, the longer the chain, the more links it has, and the easier it is for one of those links to break, for something to go wrong. In a way, the best thing would be for the person inciting the murder to deal directly with the person carrying it out, with no need for intermediaries. But, of course, no paymaster, no businessman or politician would dare to reveal himself like that, thus laying himself open to blackmail. The fact is that there is no safe method, no appropriate way of ordering or asking for such a thing. Besides which, such an arrangement would inevitably arouse unnecessary suspicions. If it appeared that a man like Miguel had been the victim of some settling of scores or an arranged murder, the police would start looking in all directions, investigating rivals and competitors, then colleagues, anyone with whom he had done business or had dealings, employees who had been dismissed or taken early retirement, and lastly his wife and his friends. It's far more sensible, far cleaner, if a murder doesn't look like a murder, if the explanation for the tragedy appears so crystal-clear that there's no need to question anyone. Or only the person who did the killing."

DESPITE KNOWING THAT any further interruption might irritate him, I decided to intervene again. Or, rather, I didn't decide, my tongue simply got the better of me and I couldn't hold back.

"You mean the person who did the killing but who knows nothing, not even that it wasn't his decision, that someone else planted the idea in his head and incited him to murder. The person who very nearly killed the wrong man. I read about it in the press; how, shortly before, he had attacked the chauffeur and might easily have stabbed him, thus ruining your plans; I suppose you had to call him to order: 'Look, it's not him, it's the other guy who sometimes picks up the car; the man you hit isn't to blame, he's just a dogsbody.' The person who did the killing but can't explain himself or is too ashamed to tell the police, or, rather, the media and everyone else, that his daughters are prostitutes and so prefers to say nothing. The poor madman who refuses to make a statement and doesn't point the finger at anyone, until, that is, a couple of weeks ago, when he gave you the most almighty fright."

Díaz-Varela gave a faint smile, which was, how can I put it, cordial and pleasant. It wasn't cynical or paternalistic or mocking, it wasn't disagreeable, not even in that sombre context. It was as if he were merely acknowledging that my reaction was as he had expected, that everything was following the path he had foreseen. He flicked his lighter on and off a couple of times but still did not light his cigarette. I, on other hand, lit one of my own. He continued talking with his cigarette between his lips, it would end up getting stuck to one lip, probably his top lip, the one I liked to touch. He appeared unperturbed by my interruption.

"Yes, that was an unexpected stroke of luck, his adamant refusal to make a statement. I hadn't been counting on being so lucky. I had simply thought that, in his delirium, he would give a confused account of events, a garbled version, from which the police would glean only that he had been seized by some kind of angry fit, the product of a sick, absurd fixation and a few imaginary voices. After all, what could Miguel possibly have to do with a prostitution ring and the white-slave trade? But it was even better when he refused to say a word. That way there wasn't the slightest risk that he would involve third parties, however phantasmagorical; nor that he would mention strange calls to a mobile phone that either didn't exist or couldn't be found and that had never been registered in his name, a voice whispering in his ear, pointing the finger at Miguel, persuading him that Miguel was the cause of his daughters' misfortune. I understand that the police tracked the daughters down, but that they refused to go and see their father. Apparently, they'd had no contact with him for several years, had never got on with him, found him utterly impossible and had washed their hands of him; the beggar had, therefore, been alone in the world for some time. And while the girls did, it seems, work as prostitutes, they did so of their own free will, assuming, of course, that the will can remain intact in the face of necessity; let's just say that, given the various forms of slavery available to them, they chose prostitution and they're not doing too badly, they have no complaints. I understand that, although they're not high-ranking whores, only medium-ranking ones, they get by all right and are not, at least, at the bottom of the heap. Their father wanted nothing more to do with them, nor they with him; he had probably always been a very angry man. And doubtless, afterwards, in his solitude, in his increasingly unstable mental state, he remembered them as children rather than as young women, more as promises than disappointments, and convinced himself that they had been forced into prostitution. He didn't erase the fact, but perhaps he did expunge the reasons and the circumstances, replacing them with others that he found more acceptable, albeit more enraging, but then rage gives energy and life. I don't know, maybe he needed to keep those children safely stored away in his imagination, they would have been all he could salvage from the past, those two figures, the best memory from the best times. I don't know who or what he was before he became a beggar; why bother trying to find out; all such stories are sad ones, you only have to think about the person those men, or even worse, those women had once been, when they still had no inkling of the wretched future awaiting them, it's always painful to glimpse someone's oblivious past life. All I know is that he had been a widower for years, and perhaps that was the beginning of the slippery slope. There was no point looking into his background, I forbade Ruibérriz to tell me anything he happened to uncover, I already had a bad conscience about using Canella as a tool, but silenced my conscience with the idea that at least he would be better off wherever they put him, wherever he is now, than in the clapped-out old car he used to sleep in. He would be better looked after and better cared for, and, besides, he clearly was a danger to society. It's best for everyone that he's no longer living on the streets."—"He had a bad conscience?" I thought. "What a joke. In the middle of what he's telling me, and which I pretty much knew already, he's trying to present himself not as some heartless creature, but as a man with scruples. That's probably normal, I imagine most killers try to do the same thing, especially when they're found out; at least those who aren't hit men, those who kill once and never again, or so they hope, or else they think of it as

an exception, almost like a terrible accident in which they find themselves caught up against their will (like a parenthesis, in a way, after
which they can simply carry on): 'No, I didn't want it to happen. It
was a moment of blindness, of panic, the dead man forced me to do
it really. If he hadn't kept going on and on and taken things too far,
if he had been more understanding, if he hadn't kept pressuring me
or eclipsing me, if he had just disappeared . . . It really grieves me,
you know.' Yes, it must be unbearable knowing what you have done,
and you're bound, therefore, to lose yourself slightly. And yes, he's
right, it is painful to catch a glimpse of someone's oblivious past
life, for example that of poor Desvern, whose luck ran out on the
morning of his birthday, poor man, while he was having breakfast
with Luisa and I was enjoying watching them from a distance, as on
any other innocuous morning. Yes, what a joke," I thought again,
and noticed that I was blushing. But I remained silent, said nothing, kept my indignation to myself, the indignation he so feared in
women, and realized, just in time, that I had, at some point in his
speech (but when?), lost any notion that what Díaz-Varela was telling me was still a hypothesis, or a gloss on my deductions based on
what I had heard, and therefore, according to him, a fiction. His
narrative or retelling had started out that way, as a mere illustration
of my conjectures, a verbalization of my suspicions, and had, as far
as I was concerned, imperceptibly taken on an air or aura of truth, I
had started listening to it as if it were an out-and-out confession and
was true. There was still the possibility that it wasn't, according to
him, of course (I would never know more than what he told me, and
so I would never know anything for sure; yes, it's ridiculous, isn't
it, that after all these centuries of practice, after so many incredible
advances and inventions, we still have no way of knowing when
someone is lying; naturally, this both benefits and prejudices all of
us equally, and may be our one remaining redoubt of freedom). I

wondered why he had allowed that, why he had tried to give the ring of truth to something that would, inevitably, be denied later on. After his last words, I found it hard to wait for that probable, previously announced negation (he had begun by saying: "I don't want to leave any mark on you that has no reason to exist"); and yet that was what would happen, I couldn't leave now: I must hear the worst, keep waiting, be patient. These thoughts swept through my mind like a gust of wind, because he didn't stop speaking, but only paused for a second. "Anyway, his unexpected silence was like a blessing, like a confirmation that I had been right about my dangerous plan, and it was very dangerous, you know: that man Canella could have remained immune to my intrigues, or he could have become convinced that Miguel was to blame for his daughters' moral perdition, but then taken it no further, and there would have been no consequences whatsoever."

Once again, my tongue ran away with me, after I had reined it in only a moment before, a fat lot of good that had done me. I tried to make my words sound more like a reminder than an accusation or a reproach, although they were doubtless both those things (however, I didn't want to irritate him too much).

"But you were the ones who provided him with a knife, weren't you? And not just any knife, but one that was particularly dangerous and harmful, not to mention illegal. That had its consequences, didn't it?"

Díaz-Varela looked at me in surprise for a moment, and for the first time he seemed uncertain. He said nothing, perhaps he was rapidly trying to recall whether he had talked to Ruibérriz about the knife while I was spying on them. In the two weeks that had passed since then, he must have reconstructed every detail of what they had said on that occasion, he must have gauged precisely what and how much I had found out—doubtless with the collaboration of his friend, whom he would have informed of the mishap; suddenly I felt very troubled by the idea that Ruibérriz should know about my indiscretion, given the way he had looked at me—even though he was unaware then that I had only joined the conversation belatedly and, at times, had caught only fragments. He would have decided to imagine the worst and taken it for granted that I had heard everything, hence Javier's decision to phone me and neutralize me with the truth or with something that appeared to be the truth or a partial truth. And yet he hadn't noticed that they had mentioned the weapon, still less that they had bought it and given it to the *gorrilla*. I myself wasn't quite sure and thought perhaps that they hadn't, but I only became aware of this when I saw his puzzlement, the sudden wave of uncertainty that assailed him about his recollections and his meticulous recapitulations of what had been said. It was quite possible that I had deduced this fact and then taken it as real. He could no longer be sure, he must have asked himself quickly if I knew more than I should know, and how I knew. This gave me time to realize that, while I had used the second-person plural several times, to include Ruibérriz and his anonymous envoy (I had said: "But you were the ones who provided him with a knife, weren't you?"), he spoke always in the first-person singular (he had said: "I had been right about my dangerous plans"), as if he were taking sole responsibility for the crime, as if it were a matter for him alone, even though the manipulation of the actual killer had required the assistance of at least two accomplices, those who had done the work without him having to intervene personally or become involved. He had stayed well away from the dirt and gore, from the *gorrilla* and his stabbings, from the mobile phone and the asphalt, from the body of his best friend lying in a puddle of blood. He'd had no contact with any of that; and so when it came to telling someone about it, it was strange that he didn't take advantage of that non-participation, quite the contrary. That he didn't distribute the blame among the other participants, which is always a sure way of reducing one's own culpability, even though it's clear who pulled the strings and who wrote the plot and who gave the order. Conspirators have known this since time immemorial, as have spontaneous, leaderless mobs, urged on by anonymous instigators who do not stand out and to whom no one can put a name: there's nothing like sharing round the guilt if you want to emerge from a murky situation smelling of roses.

HIS UNCERTAINTY DID NOT last long and he soon regained his composure. Having scanned his memory and found no very clear evidence there, he must have thought that, basically, regardless of what I knew or didn't know, I was entirely dependent on him now, as one always is on the person doing the telling, for he is the one who decides where to begin and where to end, what to reveal and suggest and keep silent about, when to tell the truth and when to lie or whether to combine the two so that neither is recognizable, or whether to deceive with the truth, as I had initially suspected he was trying to do with me; no, it's not that difficult, you just have to present your story in such a way that it seems unbelievable or so hard to believe that your listener ends up rejecting it. Unlikely truths are useful and life is full of them, far more than the very worst of novels, no novel would ever dare give houseroom to the infinite number of chances and coincidences that can occur in a single lifetime, let alone all those that have already occurred and continue to occur. It's quite shameful the way reality imposes no limits on itself.

"Yes," he said, "that did have consequences, but might equally well not have had any, Canella was free to reject the knife or to take it and then throw it away or sell it. Or to hang on to it, but not use it. It was possible, too, that he might have lost it or had it stolen beforehand; among beggars, a knife is a prized possession, because every beggar feels under threat and defenceless. In short, providing someone with a motive and a weapon is absolutely no guarantee that he's going to use either of them. My plans were very dangerous even once they had been carried out. The man very nearly killed the wrong person. About a month before. Yes, of course, it was necessary to lecture him and badger him and generally clarify matters, a blunder like that was all we needed. Of course, that wouldn't have happened with a hit man, but as I said, they bring problems too, if not in the short term, then in the long term. I preferred to risk failure, for the plan to fail, rather than end up being found out."— He stopped, as if he regretted having spoken that last sentence, or, perhaps regretted having spoken it just then, maybe it wasn't the right moment; anyone telling a pre-prepared, pre-planned story usually decides beforehand what should come first and what should come later, and takes great pains not to violate or change that order. He took a sip of his drink, rolled up his already rolled-up sleeves with a familiar, mechanical gesture, then, finally, lit his cigarette. He smoked a very light German brand made by Reemtsma, a company whose owner was once kidnapped, and for whom the biggest ransom in the history of his country was paid—an enormous sum. He went on to write a book about the experience; I read the English translation at work and we considered publishing it in Spain, but, in the end, Eugeni judged it to be too depressing and turned it down. I imagine Díaz-Varela will still be smoking the same brand of cigarettes now unless he's given up, which I doubt, he isn't the kind of person to bow to social pressures, just like his friend Rico, who does and says whatever he wants wherever he is and doesn't care a fig for the consequences (I sometimes wonder if he knows what Díaz-Varela did, or if he even suspects: it's unlikely, I got the impression that he wasn't very interested in or even aware of what was near at hand and contemporary). Díaz-Varela seemed uncertain as to whether to continue along the same path. He did so, very briefly, perhaps so as not to draw attention to his feelings of regret with too brusque a change of direction.—"Strange though it may seem in a case of homicide, killing Miguel was much less important than not getting found out or caught. I mean that it wouldn't have been worth making sure that he died then, on that day or thereabouts, if, on the other hand, I ran the slightest risk of being exposed or coming under suspicion, even if that were to happen thirty years from now. I couldn't possibly allow that, and if there were the remotest possibility of that happening, it would have been better for him to remain alive and for me to abandon the plan and renounce his death for the time being. I should just say in passing that I did not choose the day; the *gorrilla* did that. Once my task was over, everything was in his hands. It would have been in extremely bad taste for me to choose Miguel's birthday of all days. That was pure chance, no one could possibly know when Canella would decide to do it or if he ever would. But I'll explain all that to you later. Let's go back to your idea, to your view of the situation; you'll have had plenty of time to take stock over the last two weeks."

I wanted to keep quiet and allow him to talk until he grew tired or had finished, but again I couldn't help myself, my mind had picked up on two or three things he had said, and they were buzzing too loudly inside my head for me to remain silent about them all. "Now he's talking about homicide rather than outright murder, how can that be if he isn't pretending any more?" I thought. "From the *gorrilla*'s point of view, it would be the former, and from Luisa's point of view too, and from that of the police and of any witnesses, and from that of the newspaper readers who came upon the news one morning and were horrified to see that such a crime was possible in what everyone considered to be one of Madrid's safest districts, and then they forgot all about it because the story was dropped and because, once their imaginations had been satisfied, that other man's misfortune made them feel that they themselves were out of danger:

'It didn't happen to me,' they said to themselves, 'and something like that is hardly going to happen twice.' But not from Javier's point of view, no, he sees it as a murder, he knows it makes no difference that there were defects in his plan or an element of chance, or that his calculations might not work out, he's too intelligent to be deceived by that. And why had he said 'then' and 'for the time being'?—'making sure that he died then' he had said and 'renounce his death for the time being'—as if he could have postponed it or left it for later on, that is, for 'hereafter,' in the certain knowledge that the time would come. He had also said: 'It would have been in extremely bad taste,' as if it wasn't in bad enough taste to have given orders for a friend to be killed." I was left with the last point, as always happens, even if it wasn't the most urgent one, although it was, perhaps, the most offensive.

"In extremely bad taste?" I repeated. "What are you saying, Javier? Do you really believe that changes the main issue in any way? You're telling me about a murder."—And I took the opportunity to give the act its proper name.—"Do you think that fixing on one date or another can actually add to or subtract from the seriousness of what happened? That it can add good taste or subtract a little bad taste? I don't understand you. Well, I don't really expect to understand any of this, I don't even know why I'm listening to you."—And now it was my turn to feel upset and to light a second cigarette and take a sip of my drink; I swallowed too quickly, before I had expelled the first mouthful of smoke, and almost choked.

"Of course you understand, María," he said hastily, "and that's why you're listening, to convince yourself, to check that you've got the story right. You've told it to yourself over and over, all day and all night for the last two weeks. You've realized that my desires override all other considerations, all restraints and all scruples. And all loyalties too. I have been absolutely clear for some time now that

I want to spend what remains of my life with Luisa. There is only one woman for me and that woman is Luisa and I know that you can't just trust to luck, to things happening of their own accord, you can't assume that all obstacles and barriers will suddenly fall away as if by magic. You have to set to work. The world is full of lazy people and pessimists who never achieve anything because they don't apply themselves, and then have the nerve to complain and feel frustrated and direct their resentment outwards: that's what most people are like, idle fools, who are defeated right from the start by the way they live their lives and by themselves. I've remained single all these years; yes, I've had some very enjoyable affairs, to distract me while I was waiting. Waiting, initially, for someone who had a weakness for me and I for her. Then . . . For me that's the only way of understanding a particular term that everyone here bandies about quite happily, but which clearly can't be quite that straightforward because it doesn't exist in many languages, only in Italian and Spanish, as far as I know, but then again, I don't know that many languages. Perhaps in German too, although I can't be sure: *el enamoramiento*—the state of falling or being in love, or perhaps infatuation. I'm referring to the noun, the concept; the adjective, the condition, are admittedly more familiar, at least in French, though not in English, but there are words that approximate that meaning . . . We find a lot of people funny, people who amuse and charm us and inspire affection and even tenderness, or who please us, captivate us, and can even make us momentarily mad, we enjoy their body and their company or both those things, as is the case for me with you and as I've experienced before with other women, on other occasions, although only a few. Some become essential to us, the force of habit is very strong and ends up replacing or even supplanting almost everything. It can supplant love, for example, but not that state of being in love, it's important to distinguish between the two things, they're easily confused, but they're not the same . . . It's very rare to have a weakness, a genuine weakness for someone, and for that someone to provoke in us that feeling of weakness. That's the determining factor, they break down our objectivity and disarm us in perpetuity, so that we cave in over every dispute, which is what happened with Colonel Chabert when confronted by his wife, when he saw her alone again, I told you about that novella, you read it. It happens with children, they say, and I can quite believe that, but it must be a different feeling, they're such vulnerable beings from the moment they're born, from the very first instant, and our weakness for them must have its roots in their absolute defencelessness, and, it would seem, that feeling continues . . . Generally speaking, though, people don't experience such feelings for another adult, nor do they hope to. They don't wait, they're impatient, prosaic, perhaps they don't even want to experience that feeling because it seems inconceivable, and so they get together with or get married to the first likely person they meet, which is not so very odd, in fact, it's always been the norm. Some people think that being in love or infatuated is a modern invention that appears only in novels. Be that as it may, it nevertheless exists, the invention, the word, and our capacity for such a feeling."—Díaz-Varela had left the odd phrase unfinished or hanging in the air, he had hesitated, been tempted to make digressions of his digressions, but stopped himself; he didn't want to speechify, despite his natural tendency to do so, but to tell me something. He had leaned forward and was sitting almost on the edge of the armchair now, his elbows on his knees and his hands together; his tone had grown vehement within the usually cold, expository, almost didactic limits he imposed on such speeches. And, as always happened when he spoke at length, I could not take my eyes off his face or his lips, which moved quickly as he uttered the words. Not that I wasn't interested in what he was saying, I had always been interested, all the more so now that he was confessing to me what he had done and why and how, or, rather, what he, quite rightly, believed that I believed. But even if I hadn't been interested, I would have continued listening to him indefinitely, listening and looking. He switched on another light, the lamp beside him (he sometimes sat reading in that armchair), because night had fallen and the one light that was on was not enough. I could see him better, I could see his rather long eyelashes and his somewhat dreamy expression, which was dreamy even then. His face showed no signs of anxiety or embarrassment at what he was telling me. He did not, for the moment, find it difficult. I had to remind myself how odious his overriding calm was in those circumstances, because the truth is I did not find him odious.—"You know that you would do anything for that person," he went on, "that you will help or support her no matter what, even if that involves undertaking some horrible enterprise (say, she wants someone bumping off, you'll assume she has her reasons and that there's no alternative), and that you will do whatever she asks of you. Such a person doesn't merely charm you, in the usual sense of the word, rather, you feel intensely drawn or bound to them, and that feeling is much stronger and longer-lasting. As we all know, such unconditionality has little to do with reason, or indeed with causes. It's really very odd, because the effect is huge and yet there are no real causes, at least not usually, or none that can be put into words. It seems to me that it's a lot to do with making a decision, but a decision that is entirely arbitrary . . . But that's another story."—Again he had been tempted into speechifying, and was forcing himself to resist. He was trying to get to the point, and my feeling was that, if he was still taking his time, he was not doing so unwillingly and unwittingly, but had an end in mind, perhaps he was trying to draw me in and gradually accustom me to the facts. Occasionally, I would stop and think: "We are talking about a murder, after all, not something ordinary, and yet here I am listening to him instead of hanging him from a tree." And I was immediately reminded of Athos's response to d'Artagnan's horrified reaction: "Yes, a murder, nothing more." And yet I thought this less and less.—"Almost no one can answer the questions that others ask about them, about anyone: 'Why did he fall in love with her? What did he see in her?' Especially when that person is deemed unbearable, which is not, I think, the case with Luisa; but then who am I to say, precisely for the reasons I've just set out. But not even you, María, to look no further, would be able to explain why you've been so attracted to me during the short time we've known each other, despite all my defects and despite knowing, from the start, that my real interest lay elsewhere, that I had a long-held, ineluctable objective, that you and I would go no further than we have done. You wouldn't be able to come up with an explanation, I mean, apart from mumbling a few vague, airy-fairy, highly subjective phrases, as arguable as they are unarguable, unarguable for you (how could anyone argue with you?), but highly arguable for other people."—"It's true, I wouldn't be able to explain," I thought. "Like a fool. What could I say, that I liked looking at him and kissing him, going to bed with him, that I enjoyed the anxiety of not knowing whether we would end up in bed or not, enjoyed listening to him. He's right, they're idiotic reasons that would convince no one, or would sound idiotic to someone who doesn't share our feelings or has never experienced anything similar. As Javier said, they aren't even reasons, they're probably more akin to a leap of faith than anything else; although perhaps they do constitute causes. And the effect is huge, he's right there. Irresistible." I must have blushed slightly, or perhaps even shifted uneasily on the sofa, out of discomfort and embarrassment. It bothered me that he should have spoken about me openly like that, that he should have referred to my feelings for him when I had always been so discreet and sparing in what I said, had never pestered him with pleas or declarations, or with subtle comments that invited some reciprocal expression of affection, I had never made him feel the least responsibility or obligation or need to respond, not once; nor had I harboured any hopes that the situation would change, or only in the solitude of my bedroom, looking out at the trees, far from him and in secret, like someone fantasizing to herself as sleep steals over her, but everyone has a right to do that, to imagine the impossible as wakefulness finally wanes, why not, and as the day closes. It troubled me that he should have included me in all that, he could have kept it to himself; he wouldn't have said it innocently, he had something in mind, he didn't just let it slip. Again I felt like getting up and going, and leaving that beloved, dreaded apartment for good, never to return; but now I knew that I would not leave until he had finished, until he had told me his whole truth or his whole lie, or his truth and his lie together, no, I would not leave just yet. Díaz-Varela noticed my flushed cheeks and my unease, or whatever it was, because he quickly added, like someone trying to pour oil on troubled waters: "Not that I'm suggesting you're in love with me or that you'd do absolutely anything for me, nor that you feel intensely drawn to me, not at all. I wouldn't be so presumptuous. I know that you're very far from having such feelings, that there's no comparison between what you feel for me after only a brief acquaintance and what I've felt for Luisa for years now. I know that I'm just a diversion, an amusement. As you are for me, unless I'm much mistaken, there's barely any difference. I only mention it as proof that even the most transient and trivial of infatuations lack any real cause, and that's even truer of feelings that go far deeper, infinitely deeper than that."

I REMAINED SILENT, for longer than I wished. I wasn't sure how to respond, and this time he had left a pause as if prompting me to say something. In just a few sentences, Díaz-Varela had dismissed and demeaned my feelings and revealed his, piercing me with a small, entirely unnecessary barb, for I already knew how he felt despite never having heard him speak so clearly on the subject, and certainly not in such wounding terms. However idiotic they might be, and all feelings are idiotic as soon as you describe or explain or simply give voice to them, he had deemed mine to be far inferior in quality to his feelings for another person, but how could he compare? What did he know about me, always so silent, so prudent? So meek and submissive, so lacking in aspiration, so little inclined to compete and fight, or, rather, not inclined at all. I was not, of course, capable of planning and commissioning a murder, but who knows what might have happened later on, had it festered away for years, our present relationship, or rather the relationship that had existed up until two weeks ago, when everything changed after that conversation with Ruibérriz, the conversation I had overheard. If I hadn't eavesdropped on them, Díaz-Varela could have continued to wait indefinitely for Luisa's slow recovery and her predicted falling in love and, meanwhile, not have replaced or discarded me, and I could have continued meeting him on the same terms. And then who wouldn't start wanting more, who wouldn't begin to grow impatient and disgruntled, and feel that with the passing of all those

259

identical months and years, with the mere accumulation of time, he or she had acquired certain rights as if something as insignificant and neutral as the passage of the days could be considered some kind of merit mark for the one traversing or perhaps enduring them and neither giving up nor giving in. The person who never expected anything ends up making demands, the person who was all devotion and modesty turns tyrant and iconoclast, the person who once begged for smiles or attention or kisses from her beloved plays hard to get and grows proud, and is miserly with her favours to that same beloved, who has succumbed to the drip-drip of time. The passing of time exacerbates and intensifies any storm, even though there wasn't the tiniest cloud on the horizon at the beginning. We cannot know what time will do to us with its fine, indistinguishable layers upon layers, we cannot know what it might make of us. It advances stealthily, day by day and hour by hour and step by poisoned step, never drawing attention to its surreptitious labours, so respectful and considerate that it never once gives us a sudden prod or a nasty fright. Each morning, it turns up with its soothing, invariable face and tells us exactly the opposite of what is actually happening: that everything is fine and nothing has changed, that everything is just as it was yesterday—the balance of power—that nothing has been gained and nothing lost, that our face is the same, as is our hair and our shape, that the person who hated us continues to hate us and the person who loved us continues to love us. And yet quite the opposite is true, but time conceals this from us with its treacherous minutes and its sly seconds, until a strange, unthinkable day arrives, when nothing is as it always was: when two daughters, their father's beneficiaries, leave him to die in a garret, without a penny to his name; when wills deemed unfavourable to the living are burned; when mothers rob their children and husbands their wives; when a wife, in order that she might live contentedly with her lover, kills her husband or else uses her husband's love to drive him into madness or imbecility; when a woman administers lethal drops to a legitimate child born of the marriage bed in order to benefit the bastard child she bore the man she now loves, although who knows how long that love will last; when a widow who inherited position and wealth from her soldier husband fallen at the battle of Eylau in the coldest of cold winters denies that she knows him and accuses him of being an impostor when, after many years and many hardships, he manages to return from the dead; when Luisa will beg Díaz-Varela, whom she took such a long time to see, will beg him, please, not to leave her, but to remain by her side, and when she will abjure her former love for Deverne, which will be dismissed as nothing and not to be compared with the love she now professes for this second, unfaithful husband, who is now threatening to leave her; when Díaz-Varela will implore me not to go, but to stay and share his pillow for ever, and will joke about the stubborn, ingenuous love he felt for Luisa for so very long and that led him to murder a friend, and will say to himself and to me: "How blind I was, why could I not see you, when there was still time"; a strange, unimaginable day, on which I will plan to murder Luisa, who stands between us and doesn't even know that there is an "us" and against whom I bear no grudge, and I might just see it through, because on that day, everything would be possible. Yes, it's all a matter of time, infuriating time, but our time is over, time, as far as we're concerned, has run out, time, which consolidates and prolongs even while, without our noticing, it is simultaneously rotting and ruining us and turning the tables on us. I will not see that day, because for me, as for Lady Macbeth, there is no "hereafter," fortunately or unfortunately, I am safe from that beneficent or harmful deferral.

"Who told you I'm not in love with you? What do you know? I've never talked to you about it. And you've never asked me."

"Oh, come on now, don't exaggerate," he replied, unsurprised. His last words were pure acting, he knew exactly how I felt or had felt up until two weeks before. I may well have felt the same then, but my feelings were stained or besmirched by things entirely incompatible with the state of being in love. He knew exactly how I felt, the loved one always does, if he's in his right mind and isn't himself in love, because in that case he won't be able to tell and will misinterpret the signs. But he wasn't in love, and didn't want me to love him, and, to be fair, had done little to encourage me.—"If you were in love with me," he added, "you wouldn't be so horrified by what you've discovered, nor would you have drawn your conclusions so quickly. You would be in suspense, waiting for me to provide some acceptable explanation. You would be thinking that perhaps, for some reason unknown to you, I had no alternative. And you would be prepared to accept that, you would be happy to deceive yourself."

I ignored these cunning comments, which were intended to lead me down a previously chosen path. I responded only to the first of them.

"Maybe I'm not exaggerating. As you well know, I may not be exaggerating at all. It's just that you don't want the responsibility, although I realize that isn't the right word to use: no one is responsible for someone else falling in love with them. Don't worry, I'm not making you responsible for some idiotic feelings that are entirely my concern. But you will, nevertheless, perceive them as a minor burden. If Luisa were aware of the intensity of your feelings for her (it may be that in her current self-absorbed state, she sees only the surface, your gallantry and affection for the widow of your best friend), let alone if she found out what those feelings had led to, then she would experience them as an unbearable burden. She might even kill herself, unable to carry that burden. That is one of the reasons I will say nothing to her. You don't need to worry on that score, I'm not that heartless."—I had not yet made a firm decision on the subject, my intentions kept wavering as I listened to him and grew angry or perhaps not angry ("I'll think about it later on, calmly and coolly, when I'm alone," I thought), but it was as well to reassure him so that I could leave there without feeling that a threat, either present or future, hung over me, although that feeling would never entirely disappear, I imagined, for as long as I lived. And I ventured to say teasingly, because teasing seemed like a good idea: "Of course, that would be the best way of getting rid of her, to do what you did to Desvern, although without soiling my hands quite as much."

Far from appreciating the humour of my remark—a very black humour it must be said—he became very serious and almost defensive. This time he really did roll up his sleeves still further, very energetically too, as if he were preparing to go into combat or about to attack me physically, he rolled them up above his biceps as if he were some exotic romantic lead from the 1950s, Ricardo Montalbán or Gilbert Roland, one of those attractive men now forgotten by almost everyone. He wasn't going into combat, of course, nor was he going to hit me, that wasn't in his nature. What I had said, I realized, had wounded him deeply and he was about to refute it.

"Don't forget, I didn't soil my hands. I took every care not to. You don't know what it means to really soil your hands. You don't know to what extent delegating distances you from the deed, you have no idea how helpful it is to have intermediaries. Why else, do you think, people do delegate, if they can, when confronted by any situation that's in any way uncomfortable or unpleasant. Why do you think lawyers are called in whenever there's a dispute or a divorce? It's not only to take advantage of their knowledge and skill. Why do you think actors and actresses and writers have agents, and bullfighters and boxers have managers? When, that is, boxing still existed. These modern-day puritans will end up doing away with everything. Why do you think businessmen hire frontmen, or why any criminal with enough money sends in the heavies or hires a hit man? It's not just because they, quite literally, don't want to soil their hands, nor out of cowardice, so as not to have to face the consequences or risk getting hurt. Most of those who turn to such people as a matter of course (unlike people like myself, for whom it's very much the exception) began by doing their own dirty work and may have been very good at it: they're accustomed to handing out beatings and even shooting people, and so it's unlikely they would emerge the worse for wear from any such encounter. Why do you think politicians send soldiers to the wars they declare, if, of course, they still go to the bother of declaring them? Of course, unlike criminals, they wouldn't be able to do the work of the soldiers, but it's more than that. In all these cases, mediation, keeping a distance from actual events and being privileged enough not to have to witness them, all provide scope for a high degree of autosuggestion. It seems incredible, but that's how it works, as I've found out for myself. You manage to convince yourself that you have nothing to do with what is happening on the ground, or in the head-on confrontation, even if you provoked or unleashed it and even if you paid for it to happen. The man suing for divorce ends up persuading himself that the mean, vicious demands he is making come not from him, but from his lawyer. Famous actors and writers, bullfighters and boxers apologize for the economic aspirations of their agents or the difficulties they create, as if their agents were not simply obeying orders and doing as they were told. When a politician sees on television or in the press the effects of the bombardments he initiated or learns of the atrocities his army is committing, he shakes his head in disapproval and disgust, he wonders how his generals can be so stupid, so inept, why they can't control their men when the fighting begins and they lose sight of them, but he never himself feels guilty about what is going on thousands of kilometres away, without him actually taking part or witnessing events: he has instantly forgotten that it was his decision, that he gave the order to advance. It's the same with the *capo* who unleashes his thugs: he reads or is told that they have overstepped the mark, that they didn't confine themselves, in accordance with his wishes, to bumping off a few people, but went on to cut off heads and balls, stuffing the latter in their victims' mouths; he shudders slightly when he imagines this and thinks what sadists his henchmen are, forgetting that he left them free to use their imaginations and their hands as they wished, saying: 'We want to terrify people, to teach them a lesson and spread panic.' "

Díaz-Varela stopped, as if this long enumeration had left him momentarily drained. He poured himself another drink and took a long, thirsty draught of it. He lit another cigarette. He sat for a while staring at the floor, absorbed in thought. For a few seconds, he looked the very image of the dejected, weary man, possibly full of remorse, even repentant. But none of this had been apparent up until then, either in this latest account or in his other digressions. On the contrary. "Why does he associate himself with such individuals?" I wondered. "Why does he summon them up for me, rather than shooing them away? What does he gain by showing me his actions in such a repellent light? You can always find some way of embellishing the most heinous crime, of finding some minimal justification for it, a not entirely sinister reason that at least allows one to understand it without feeling sick. 'That's how it works, as I've found out for myself,' he said, including himself in the list. I can see the connection with divorced men or bullfighters, but not with cynical politicians or professional criminals. It's as if, far from looking for palliatives, he wanted to drip-feed me with horror. Perhaps he's just setting me up so that I'll embrace any excuse, the excuses that he'll start offering me at any moment, they're sure to come along sooner or later, he can't possibly be owning up to me so frankly about his egotism and his baseness, his treachery, his lack of scruples, he hasn't even insisted overmuch on his love for Luisa, his passionate need for her, he hasn't stooped so low as to utter the ridiculous words that nonetheless touch and soften the listener, such as 'I can't live without her, you see. I just couldn't stand it any more, she's the air that I breathe, and I was suffocating with no hope of ever making her mine, whereas now I do have some hope. I didn't wish Miguel ill at all, on the contrary, he was my best friend, but he was, unfortunately, standing in the way of my one life, the only life I want, and if something or someone is stopping you from living, then he has to be removed.' People accept the excesses of those in love, not all excesses, of course, but there are occasions when it's enough to say that someone is or was very much in love to make all other reasons irrelevant. 'I loved her so much,' someone says, 'that I didn't know what I was doing,' and people nod sagely, as if he or she were talking about feelings familiar to everyone. 'She lived entirely for him and through him, he was the only man in the world as far as she was concerned, she would have sacrificed everything, nothing else mattered to her,' and this is taken as an excuse for all kinds of vile, ignoble acts and even as a reason to forgive. Why doesn't Javier lay more stress on his morbid obsession, saying that it could happen to anyone? Why doesn't he take refuge in that? He takes it for granted, but doesn't place much emphasis on it, he doesn't put it first, instead he associates himself with these cold, despicable characters. Yes, perhaps that's what it is: the more he shocks me and fills me with panic, and the more I feel the pull of vertigo, the more likely I will be to cling to any extenuating circumstance. And if that is what he intends, he would be quite right. I keep hoping for some such mitigating factor to appear, some explanation or extenuating circumstance that will lift a little of the weight off me. I can't cope with the facts as they stand and as I imagined them to be on that wretched day when I eavesdropped from behind that door. I was on the other side of the door then, and will never be there again, that much is certain. Even if Javier were to come to me and put his arms around me and caress me with fingertips and lips. Even if he were to whisper in my ear words he had never said before. Even if he were to say to me: 'How blind I've been, why could I not see you before, but there's still time.' Even if he were to lead me over to that door and beg me."

NOT THAT ANY of those things would happen. Not even if I were to blackmail him or threaten to tell someone or even if I were to beg him. He was still strangely distant, absorbed in his thoughts, still staring at the floor. I shook him out of his introspection rather than seizing the chance to escape, it was too late for that: after hearing what he had to say, I wished I had stuck to my sombre conjectures and to knowing nothing for certain; but now I wanted him to finish, to see if his story was less dreadful and less sad than it seemed.

"And what did you think? What did you manage to persuade yourself had happened? That you had nothing whatsoever to do with the murder of your best friend? That's rather hard to believe, isn't it? However heavily you rely on autosuggestion."

He looked up and rolled his sleeves down as far as his forearms again, as if he suddenly felt cold. But he didn't entirely emerge from the depression or exhaustion that seemed to have come over him. He spoke more slowly, less confidently and energetically, his eyes fixed on my face, and yet they still seemed slightly unfocused, as though he were looking at me from a long way off.

"I'm not sure," he said. "Yes, of course, deep down, you know the truth, how could you not, how could you possibly not know? You know that you've set a mechanism in motion, one that you have the power to stop, nothing is inevitable until it has happened and until the 'hereafter' that we all take for granted has ceased to exist for someone else. But, as I said before, that's the mysterious thing about delegating. I gave Ruibérriz a commission to carry out, and from that moment on, I felt that the whole business was somehow less mine, or was, at least, shared. Ruibérriz gave orders to someone else to get the *gorrilla* a mobile phone and then keep phoning him, they both called him in fact, taking it in turns, because two voices are more convincing than one, and together they set his brain buzzing; I don't even know quite how that third party manages to provide him with the mobile, I suppose he leaves it in the car the man was living in, so that it just appears there as if by magic, and presumably he does the same with the knife later on, so as not to be seen, it was impossible to anticipate how it would all turn out. At any rate, that other man, that third party, doesn't know my name or my face and I don't know his, and his anonymous intervention places me at a still further remove from it all, as I said, it's less mine, and my role in it all grows increasingly blurred, it's not entirely in my hands, but more and more dispersed. Once you activate something and pass it over to someone else, it's as if you let it go and got rid of it, I don't know if you can understand that, possibly not, you've never had to arrange and organize a death."—I picked up on the words "had to," what an absurd idea, he hadn't "had to" do anything, no one had forced him. And he had said "a death," using the most neutral term possible, not "a homicide" or "a murder" or "a crime."—"You get brief reports on how it's going and you supervise things, but you're not directly involved. Sure, a mistake happens, Canella attacks the wrong man and news of that reaches me, even Miguel mentions poor Pablo's misfortune, never suspecting that it could have had anything to do with the favour he'd asked of me, never connecting the two things, never imagining that I might be behind it, or if he did, he concealed the fact very well, that's something I'll never know."—I realized that I was getting lost (what favour? connecting what two things?

concealing what?), but he continued as if he had suddenly got a second wind and didn't give me a chance to interrupt.—"That idiot Ruibérriz doesn't trust the other man after that, and because I pay him well and he owes me various favours, he takes over and goes to see the *gorrilla* himself, just to make sure that Canella doesn't make the same mistake again and end up stabbing poor Pablo the chauffeur to death, thus ruining all our plans, he visits him cautiously, in secret, and it's true that there's never anyone hanging around in the street at night, but it means that the *gorrilla* sees him in that leather coat of his, I really hope he's thrown them all away by now. So, yes, I hear, for example, about that particular incident, but to me, it's just a story recounted to me in the safety of my own home, I don't move from here, I never go to that street, I don't soil myself in any way, and so I feel that none of what happens is wholly my responsibility or my work, they are simply remote events. Don't be so surprised, others go still further: there are those who order somebody's removal and don't even want to know about the actual process, the steps taken, the 'how.' They trust that in the end some minion will come and tell them that the person is dead. He was the victim of an accident, they say, or of medical negligence, or he threw himself off a balcony or was run over or he got mugged one night and, unfortunately, fought back and was killed by his attackers. And yet, strange though it may seem, the same person who ordered that death, without specifying how or when, can exclaim with relative sincerity or a certain degree of surprise: 'Oh dear God, how dreadful!' almost as if he'd had nothing to do with it and fate had conspired to carry out his desires. That's what I tried to do, to keep as far away from it all as possible, even though I had, in part, planned the 'how': Ruibérriz found out about the big drama in the beggar's life, the thing that really angered and affronted him, and whether he found this out by chance or not, I don't know, but, one day, he came to me with this story about how the guy's daughters had been forced or tricked into prostitution, Ruibérriz's into all kinds of things and has contacts in every social sphere, and so the plan was mine or, rather, ours. Nevertheless, I kept my distance, kept right out of it: there was Ruibérriz, along with that third party, his friend, and, above all, there was Canella, who would not only decide when to act, he could also decide to do nothing, so really it was completely out of my hands. So much is delegated, so much is left for others to do, so much is left to chance, there's so much distance between instigator and act, that it's easy enough to tell yourself, once it's happened: 'What have I got to do with that, with what some homeless nutter has done at an hour and in a street everyone assumes to be safe? He was obviously a public danger, a menace, he shouldn't have been on the loose, especially not after Pablo was attacked. It's all the fault of the authorities who refuse to take action, that and sheer bad luck, of which there's never any shortage in the world.'"

Díaz-Varela got up, took a turn about the room, then again came up behind me, put both hands on my shoulders and squeezed them gently, but not in the way he had gripped my shoulder two weeks before, when he and I were both standing up, that hand, then, had been intent on keeping me there, like a great slab of stone. I wasn't afraid this time, it felt like an affectionate gesture, and his tone of voice was different too. It had become tinged with a kind of sorrow or slight despair—slight because it was retrospective—in the face of something irremediable, and he had abandoned all cynicism, as if it had been pure artifice. He had started to mix up his tenses too, present and past and imperfect, as happens sometimes when someone relives a bad experience or is recounting a process from which he only *believes* he has emerged, but is not yet sure. His voice had gradually, not suddenly, taken on a truthful tone, and that made him more credible. But perhaps that was fake too. It's horrible not knowing, because what had gone before had also seemed true, and he had spoken in the same tone then, well, not the same perhaps, it had been different, but equally truthful. Now he had fallen silent and I could ask him about the incomprehensible references he had let slip. Or perhaps he hadn't let them slip at all, but had introduced them deliberately and was awaiting my reaction, knowing that I would pick up on them.

"You mentioned Deverne asking you a favour and about him possibly concealing something. What favour was that? What would he have to conceal? I don't understand."—And as I said that, I thought: "What the hell am I doing, how can I talk about all this so politely, how can I question him like this about the details of a murder? And why are we talking about it at all? It's hardly a proper topic of conversation, or only if it had happened many years ago, as with the story about Anne de Breuil who had been killed by Athos before he was Athos. Whereas Javier is still Javier, and hasn't had time to be transformed into someone else."

He again gently squeezed my shoulders, it was almost a caress. I had not turned round when I spoke, I didn't need to be able to see him now, that touch was neither unfamiliar nor worrying. I was filled by a sense of unreality, as if this were another day, a day prior to my eavesdropping, when I still knew nothing and there was no threat, no horror, only provisional pleasure and the resigned waiting of the unrequited lover, waiting to be either dismissed or driven from his side when it was Luisa's turn to be in love, or when she at least allowed him to fall asleep each night and wake each morning in her bed. It occurred to me now to think that this would not be long in coming. I hadn't seen her for ages, not even from a distance. Who knows how she would have evolved, if she had recovered from the blow, or to what extent Díaz-Varela had managed to inoculate her with his presence, if he had made himself indispensable to her in her solitary widow's life with children who sometimes weighed on her, when she wanted to shut herself away and cry and do nothing. Just as I had tried to become indispensable to him in his solitary bachelor's life, except that I had done so timidly and without conviction or determination, as if admitting defeat right from the start.

ON ANOTHER DAY, Díaz-Varela's hands might have slid from my shoulders down to my breasts, and not only would I have allowed him to do that, I would have mentally encouraged him: "Undo a couple of buttons and slip your hands under my jersey or my blouse," we think to ourselves, or even plead. "Come on, do it now, what are you waiting for?" And an impulse flashed through me to ask him, silently, of course, to do just that, such is the force of expectation, the irrational persistence of desire, which often makes us forget the circumstances and who is who, and erases the opinion we have of the person arousing our desire, and, at that moment, my predominant feeling was contempt. But he wouldn't give in to that plea today, he was even more aware than I was that this was not another day, but the one on which he had chosen to tell me about his conspiracy and his actions and then say goodbye to me for ever, because after that conversation, we could not continue to meet, that would be impossible, and we both knew that. And so he did not slowly slide his hands down, but quickly lifted them up like someone who has been told off for taking liberties or overstepping the bounds—although neither I nor my attitude had said anything— and he returned to his armchair, sat down in front of me again and fixed me with his hazy or indecipherable eyes that never entirely fixed on anything and with that same hint of sorrow or retrospective despair that had appeared in his voice shortly before and that would not leave him now, neither his tone of voice nor his gaze, as if he were saying to me once more, not impatiently but regretfully: "Why don't you understand?"

"Everything I've told you is true, as regards the facts," he said. "Except that I haven't told you the most important thing. That is something no one else knows, or only Ruibérriz, but he only half-knows, because fortunately he doesn't ask many questions now; he just listens, does as he's told, follows instructions and gets paid. He's learned. Life's difficulties have made him a man who is prepared to do all kinds of things in return for money, especially if the person paying him is an old friend, who isn't going to drop him in it or betray him or sacrifice him, he's even learned to be discreet. We really did do it like that, with no guarantee at all that our plan would work, it was almost like tossing a coin, but for the reasons I gave earlier, I didn't want to use a professional hit man. You drew your own conclusions and I don't blame you for that, well not entirely, I mean, I understand you in part: if you don't know the reason for something, you simply have to take things at face value. Nor am I going to deny that I love Luisa or that I intend to stay by her side, to be there if she needs me, if, one day, she finally does forget Miguel and take a few steps in my direction: I'll be waiting close by, so close that she doesn't have time for second thoughts or regrets as she takes those steps. I believe that will happen sooner or later, probably sooner, and she will recover, everyone does, because, as I said to you once before, people do, in the end, allow the dead to depart, however fond of them they were, when they realize that their own survival is at risk and that the dead are a great burden; and the worst the latter can do is to resist, to cling to the living and pursue them and stop them moving on, or even come back if they can, as Colonel Chabert did in that novel, souring his wife's life and causing her more pain than his death in that remote battle ever did."

"She caused him far more pain," I said, "by her denial of him and her cunning ploys to keep him dead, to deprive him of a legal existence and bury him alive for a second time. He had suffered greatly, what was his was his, and it wasn't his fault that he was still alive or that he still remembered who he was. In that passage you read out to me, the poor man even said: 'If my illness had taken from me all memory of my past existence, I would have been happy.'"

But Díaz-Varela was in no mood to discuss Balzac, he wanted to continue his story to the end. "What happened is the least of it," he had said when he spoke to me about *Colonel Chabert*. "It's a novel, and once you've finished a novel, what happened in it is of little importance and soon forgotten." Perhaps he thought the same applied to real events, to events in our own lives. That's probably true for the person experiencing them, but not for other people. Everything becomes a story and ends up drifting about in the same sphere, and then it's hard to differentiate between what really happened and what is pure invention. Everything becomes a narrative and sounds fictitious even if it's true. And so he went on as if I had said nothing.

"Yes, Luisa will emerge from her abyss, you can be sure of that. In fact, she's already beginning to, a little more with each day that passes, I can sense it and there's no going back once that process of farewell has begun, that second, final farewell, which is purely mental and pricks our conscience because it feels as if we were dismissing the dead person, which we are. There may be the occasional backward step, depending on how things go or on the occasional stroke of bad luck, but that's all. The dead only have the energy that the living give them, and if that energy is withdrawn . . . Luisa will free herself from Miguel, to a far greater degree than she can even imagine right now, and he knew that very well. More than that, he decided to make things easier for her, insofar as he could, and that was partly why he asked me that favour. Only partly. There was, of course, a weightier reason."

"What is this favour you keep talking about? What favour?" I couldn't help my impatience, I had the feeling that he wanted to draw me in through curiosity.

"I'm coming to that, because that's the cause of all this," he said. "Listen carefully. Months before his death, Miguel experienced a general feeling of lassitude, not significant or serious enough to merit seeing a doctor, he wasn't worried and was in good health. Soon afterwards, he noticed another trivial symptom, slightly blurred vision in one eye, but he thought it was a temporary thing and delayed visiting an ophthalmologist. When he did, when the blurred vision didn't clear up on its own, the ophthalmologist made a thorough examination and came up with a very gloomy diagnosis: a large intraocular melanoma, and sent him to a consultant for further tests. The consultant checked him over, gave him a CAT scan, a full-body MRI scan, as well as an extensive array of other tests. His diagnosis was even worse: generalized metastasis throughout the body, or as Miguel told me the doctor told him in his cold, aseptic jargon: 'a very advanced metastatic melanoma,' even though Miguel was almost asymptomatic at the time and had no other ailments."

"So," I thought, "Desvern couldn't have said to Javier, as I had once imagined he might: 'No, I don't foresee any problems, nothing imminent or even impending, nothing concrete, my health's fine,' quite the contrary. At least that's what Javier is saying now." That evening, I was still calling him Javier, although that would soon change, but at the time, I had not yet decided to think of him and refer to him by his surname alone, in order to distance myself from our past proximity or to at least allow myself that illusion.

"Right, and what does all this mean exactly, apart, obviously, from it being very bad news?" I asked, trying to give a note of scepticism or incredulity to my question: "Go on, go on, keep talking, but I'm not going to swallow this last-minute story of yours that easily, I have a pretty good idea where you're going with this." But at the same time, I was already intrigued by what he had started to tell me, regardless of whether it was true or not. Díaz-Varela often amused me and always interested me. And so I added, speaking now with genuine, credulous concern: "But can that happen, can you have such a serious illness with almost no symptoms? Well, I know you can, of course, but *that* serious? And completely out of the blue like that? And so advanced? It makes you shudder to think of it, doesn't it?"

"Yes, it can happen and it happened to Miguel. But don't worry, that particular form of melanoma is, fortunately, very infrequent and very rare. Nothing like that will happen to you. Or to Luisa or to me or to Professor Rico, that would be too much of a coincidence."— He had noticed my instantaneous fear of illness. He waited for his baseless prediction to take effect and reassure me as if I were a child, he waited a few seconds before going on.—"Miguel didn't say a word to me about this until he had all the facts, and he didn't even tell Luisa about the early stages, when there was as yet nothing to fear: not even that he had an appointment with an ophthalmologist, nor that his vision was slightly blurred, because the last thing he wanted was to worry her unnecessarily, and she's very easily worried. And he certainly didn't tell her about what followed. In fact, he didn't tell anyone anything, with one exception. After the consultant's diagnosis, he knew his illness was terminal, but the consultant didn't give him all the information, not in detail, or perhaps he tried to play it down, or perhaps Miguel didn't even ask, I don't know, he preferred to ask a doctor friend who he knew would hide nothing from him: an old school friend, a cardiologist, who gave him the occasional check-up and whom he trusted completely. He went to see him with his final diagnosis and said: 'Tell me what I can expect, tell me straight. Talk me through the various stages. Tell me how it's going to be.' And his friend described to him a prospect that he found quite simply unbearable."

"Right," I said again, like someone determined to doubt, to disbelieve. But I couldn't keep up that tone. I tried, I did my best, and finally managed to come out with these completely neutral words: "And what were those terrible stages?"—Although that neutrality was a lie; the description of the whole process, of the discovery, terrified me.

"It wasn't just that there was no cure, given how widely the disease had spread throughout his organism. There was barely any palliative care they could give him, or the treatment that was available was almost worse than the illness itself. Without any treatment, his friend gave him four to five months, and not much more with treatment. A course of extraordinarily aggressive chemotherapy with devastating side effects would gain him a little time, but whether that time would be worth gaining was another matter. There was worse, though: the intraocular melanoma distorts the eye and is hideously painful, the pain is apparently unbearable, according to his cardiologist friend, who, true to his word, kept nothing back. The only way to avoid this would be to remove the eye, that is, take it out, what doctors call 'enucleation,' according to Miguel, because of the size of the tumour. Do you understand, María? An enormous tumour inside his eye, which pushes outwards and inwards, I suppose; a protuberant eye, an increasingly bulbous forehead and cheekbone; and then a hollow, an empty socket, and that wouldn't be the final metamorphosis either, even in the best-case scenario, and it wouldn't even really help."—This brief, graphic description increased my feelings of distrust, it was the first time he had resorted to gruesome, imagined details; up until then, he had spoken very soberly.—"The patient's appearance becomes increasingly horrific, and the progressive deterioration is pitiful to see, and it doesn't just affect the face, of course, everything begins to collapse with alarming rapidity, and all you achieve with the removal of the eye and that brutal chemotherapy are a few more months of life. If you can call it life, that dead or pre-dead life of suffering and deformity, of no longer being yourself, but an anguished ghost who does nothing but enter and leave hospital. One positive thing was that this transformation in appearance wouldn't happen immediately: he had a month and a half or two months before the facial symptoms would appear or become visible, before other people would notice anything, so he had that amount of time in which to conceal the truth from the world and to pretend."—Díaz-Varela's voice sounded genuinely affected, but he might have merely been affecting that affect. I have to say that he didn't seem to be when he added in a bitter, doom-laden voice: "A month and a half or two months, that was the deadline he gave me."

I MORE OR LESS KNEW what the answer would be, but I asked anyway, because some stories need the encouragement of a few rhetorical questions in order to continue. This particular story would have continued anyway, I simply chivvied it along a little, eager for it to be over as soon as possible, despite my personal interest in it. I wanted to hear the whole thing and then go home and stop hearing it.

"Why did he give *you* a deadline?" However, I couldn't resist telling him what I could guess he was about to tell me.—"Now you're going to say that he asked you to do what you did to him as a favour: getting him stabbed to death by some nutcase in the middle of the street, is that right? A somewhat disagreeable, roundabout way of committing suicide, given that there are pills you can take and so many other ways too. And it meant putting you and your friends to an awful lot of trouble."

Díaz-Varela shot me an angry, reproving look; my comments clearly struck him as inappropriate.

"Let's just make one thing clear, María, and listen well. I'm not telling you this because I want you to believe me, I really don't care if you believe me or not, Luisa's another matter, of course, and I hope never to have such a conversation with her, and that, in part, will depend on you. The only reason I am telling you is because of what happened earlier, that's all. I don't like having to do it, as you can imagine. Ruibérriz and I didn't like doing what we did, which was tantamount to murder really. Well, technically, that's what it was, and a judge and jury wouldn't care two hoots about the real reason we did it, and we couldn't prove that anyway. They base their judgment on the facts and they are what they are, that's why we were so alarmed when Canella started to talk about mobile phone calls and the rest. It was bad luck, too, that you overheard us that evening, or, rather, that I was stupid enough to allow it to happen. And on the basis of what you heard, you've come up with a false or inexact idea of what happened. Naturally, I don't like that, why would I, and I want you to know the real facts. That's why I'm telling you, in a personal capacity, because you're not a judge, and so that you'll have a better understanding of what lay behind what we did. Then it's up to you. You can decide what you do with the information. But if you don't want me to go on, I won't, I'm not going to force you to listen. It isn't up to me whether you believe me or not, so if you want, we can stop this conversation right now. If you think you know it all already and don't want to hear what else I have to say, there's the door."

But I did want to hear more. As I said, I wanted to know the end, wanted him to finish his story.

"No, no, go on. I'm sorry," I said. "Go on, please, everyone has the right to be heard, of course."—And I tried to lend a touch of irony to that last "of course."—"So why *did* he give you that deadline?"

In the light of Díaz-Varela's pained, offended tone, I noticed the faintest of doubts creeping into my mind, even though that is one of the easiest tones to put on or imitate, and the one that almost any-one guilty of anything immediately resorts to. As do the innocent. I realized that the more he told me, the more doubts I would have, and that I certainly wouldn't leave there with no doubts at all, that's the problem with letting people talk and explain, which is why we so often try to stop them, in order to preserve our certainties and leave no room for doubts, that is, for lies. Or, needless to say, for the truth. He took a while to answer or to resume speaking, and when he did, he returned to his previous tone of voice, one of sorrow and retrospective despair, which he hadn't, in fact, completely abandoned, merely adding to it, for a moment, the tone of someone deeply wounded.

"Miguel had few qualms about dying, if one can say such a thing of a man whose life was going well, who had small children and a wife he loved, or, rather, with whom he was in love. Of course it was a tragedy, as it would be for anyone. But he was always very aware that the fact we are here at all is entirely thanks to an improbable coming-together of various chance events, and when that coming-together ceases, we cannot really complain. People think they have a right to life. Indeed, religions and most countries' legal systems, even their constitutions, say the same thing, and yet he didn't see it like that. How can you have a right to something that you neither built nor earned, he used to say. No one can complain about not having been born or not having been in the world before or not having always been in the world, so why should anyone complain about dying or not being in the world hereafter or not remaining in it for ever? He found both points of view equally absurd. We don't object to our date of birth, so why object to our date of death, which is just as much a matter of chance. Even violent deaths, even suicides, depend on chance. And since we were all once denizens of the void or enjoying a state of non-existence, what is so strange or terrible about returning to that state, even though we now have something to compare it with and the capacity to miss what went before? When he found out what was wrong with him, when he knew he was about to die, he was devastated and cursed his ill luck as roundly as the next man, but he also remembered how many others had disappeared at a much younger age than him; how they had been eliminated by that second chance event of their lives, with barely enough time or opportunity to experience anything: young men and women, children, newborns who were never even given a name . . . In that respect, he showed great integrity and didn't fall to pieces. What he couldn't bear, though, what demoralized him and drove him mad, was the manner of his death, the whole dreadful process, the slowness contained within the swift encroachment of the disease, the deterioration, the pain and the deformity, everything, in short, that his doctor friend had warned him about. He wasn't prepared to go through all that, still less allow his children and Luisa to witness it. Or anyone else, for that matter. He accepted the idea that he would cease to be, but not the senseless torment, the months of suffering for no reason and no reward, the thought of leaving behind him the image of a defenceless, disfigured, one-eyed man. He didn't see the point, and he did rebel against that, he did protest and rail at fate. It wasn't in his power to remain in the world, but he could leave it in a more elegant manner than the one in prospect, he would simply have to depart a little early."—"A case," I thought, "in which it would be inappropriate to say: 'He should have died hereafter,' because that 'hereafter' would mean something far worse, involving more suffering and humiliation, less dignity and more horror for his nearest and dearest, so it's not always desirable for everything to last a little longer, a year, a few months, a few weeks, a few hours, it isn't always true that we will think it too soon to put an end to things or people, nor is it true that there is never an opportune moment, for there may come a time when we ourselves say: 'That's fine. That's enough. What comes next will be worse, an abasement, a denigration, a stain,' when we will be brave enough to acknowledge: 'This time is over, even though it's our time.' And even if the ending of things did lie in our hands, everything would go on indefinitely, becoming grubby and contaminated, with no living creature ever dying. We must not only allow the dead to leave when they try to linger or when we hold on to them, we must also let go of the living sometimes." And I realized that in thinking this, I was, momentarily and against my will, believing the story that Díaz-Varela was telling me now. We do tend to believe things while we're hearing or reading them. Afterwards, it's another matter, when the book is closed and the voice stops speaking.

"Why didn't he just commit suicide?"

Díaz-Varela again looked at me as if I were a child, that is, as if I were an innocent.

"What kind of question is that!" he said. "Like most people, he was incapable of committing suicide. He didn't dare, he couldn't bring himself to decide the 'when': why today and not tomorrow, if today I see no further changes in myself and feel quite well? If that decision were left up to each individual, hardly anyone would ever find the right moment. He wanted to die before the effects of the illness took hold, but there was no way he could put a date on that 'before': as I said, he had a month and a half or two months, possibly a little longer, no one could tell. And, again like most people, he didn't want to know for certain beforehand when that would happen, he didn't want to wake up one morning and say to himself: 'This is my last day. I won't see another night.' Even if he got others to help him, he would still know what was going to happen, what they were up to, he would still know the date in advance. His friend mentioned a serious-minded organization in Switzerland called Dignitas, which is run by doctors and is, of course, totally legal (well, legal there), and people from any country can apply to them for an assisted suicide, always assuming there's sufficient reason, a decision taken by the doctors, not by the person involved. The applicant has to submit an up-to-date medical record, and its accuracy and authenticity are then checked; apparently, except in cases of extreme urgency, they put you through a meticulous preparatory process and, initially, try to persuade you to remain alive with the help of palliative care, if that's available but for some reason hasn't already been offered; they make sure you're in full possession of your mental faculties and aren't merely suffering a temporary depression, it's a really excellent place, Miguel told me. Despite all these requirements, his friend didn't think there would be any objections in his case. He spoke to him about this place as a possible solution, as a lesser evil, but Miguel still felt unable to contemplate it, he just didn't dare. He wanted to die, but without knowing how or when it was going to happen, not at least with any exactitude."

"Who is this doctor friend?" it occurred to me to ask, forcing myself to suspend the belief that tends gradually to invade us when we listen to someone else's story.

Díaz-Varela didn't seem overly surprised, well, perhaps just a little.

"Do you mean his name? Dr. Vidal."

"Vidal? But which Vidal? That's not exactly telling me much. There are loads of Vidals."

"What's wrong? Do you want to check up on him? Do you want to go to him and have him confirm my version of events? Go ahead, he's a really friendly, helpful guy. I've met him a couple of times. His name is Dr. Vidal Secanell. José Manuel Vidal Secanell. He'll be easy enough to find, you just have to look him up on the register of the Medical Association or whatever it's called, it's bound to be on the Internet."

"And what about the ophthalmologist and the consultant?"

"That I don't know. Miguel never mentioned them by name, or if he did I've forgotten. I know Vidal because, as I say, he was a childhood friend of Miguel's. But I don't know the others. Nevertheless, I shouldn't imagine it would be that difficult to find out who his ophthalmologist was, if you really want to. Are you going to turn detective? Best not ask Luisa directly, though, unless you're prepared to tell her the whole story, to tell her the rest. She knew nothing about the melanoma or anything else, that was how Miguel wanted it."

"That's a bit odd, isn't it? You'd think it would be less traumatic for her to find out about his illness than see him stabbed to death and bleeding on the ground. You'd think it would be harder to recover from such a violent, vicious death. Or to move on, as people say nowadays."

"Possibly," said Díaz-Varela. "But although that was an important consideration, it was a secondary one at the time. What horrified Miguel was having to go through the phases Vidal had described to him, and having Luisa see him in that state, although, admittedly, that thought wasn't uppermost in his mind, it was a minor consideration by comparison. When you know your time has come, you tend to be very sunk in yourself and have little thought for other people, even those closest to you, even those you most love, however much you try not to ignore them and not to lose sight of them in the midst of your own tribulations. The knowledge that you're the only one who'll be leaving and that they'll be staying can give rise to a certain degree of annoyance, almost resentment, as if they were somehow removed from and indifferent to it all. So, yes, while he wanted to save Luisa from being a witness to his death, more than that, he wanted to save himself from it. Bear in mind, too, that he didn't know what form his sudden death would take. He left that to me. He didn't even know for sure that he would meet a sudden death or would, instead, have no option but to endure the evolution of his illness until the end, or hope that he might get up the courage to throw himself out of a window when he got worse and began to notice his face becoming deformed and to experience terrible pain. I never guaranteed him anything, I never said Yes."

"Said Yes to what? Never said Yes to what?"

Díaz-Varela gave me his usual hard look, which somehow never felt hard, but, rather, drew one in. I thought I caught a glimmer of irritation in his eyes, but, like all glimmers, it didn't last, because he answered me at once and, as he did so, that hard look vanished.

"What do you think? To his request. 'Get rid of me,' he said. 'Don't tell me how or when or where, let it be a surprise, we have a month and a half or two months, find a way and do it. I don't care what method you use. The quicker the better. The less suffering and pain the better. The sooner the better. Do what you like, hire someone to shoot me, or to run me down as I'm crossing the street, or have a wall collapse on top of me or make my brakes fail or my lights, I don't know, I don't want to know or think about it, you do the thinking, whatever you like, whatever you can, whatever occurs to you. You must do me this favour, you must save me from what awaits me otherwise. I know it's a lot to ask, but I'm incapable of killing myself or flying to some place in Switzerland knowing that I'm going there in order to die among strangers, I mean, who could possibly agree to such a grim journey, travelling towards your own execution, it would be like dying over and over while you were on the plane and while you were there. I prefer to wake up here each morning with at least a semblance of normality and to carry on with my life while I can, but always with the fear and the hope that this day will be my last. With the uncertainty too, that above all, because uncertainty is the only thing that can help me; and I know I can bear that. What I can't bear is knowing that it all depends on me. It has to depend on you. Get rid of me before it's too late, you must grant me this favour.' That, more or less, was what he said to me. He was desperate and terribly afraid too. But he wasn't out of control. He had thought about it a lot. Almost, you might say, coldly. And he could see no other solution. He really couldn't."

"And what was your answer?" I asked, and as soon as I had, I

realized again that I was thus giving his story some measure of cre-
dence, however hypothetical and transient, however much I told
myself that my question had really been: "And always supposing
that what you say is true, and let's imagine for a moment that it is,
what was your answer?" The truth is, of course, that I didn't put it
that way.

"At first, I refused point-blank, and wouldn't even let him continue. I told him it was impossible, that it was simply too much to
ask, that you couldn't expect someone else to perform a task that
only you could do. That he should either get up the necessary courage to end his own life or else hire a hit man, it wouldn't be the first
time someone had commissioned and paid for his own execution.
He said he was perfectly aware that he lacked the necessary courage, but also that he couldn't bring himself to hire his own killer and
then, inevitably, be aware of the how and, almost, the when: once
contact had been established, the hit man would set to work, they're
efficient people and don't hang about, they do what they have to do,
then move on to the next job. That wouldn't be so very different to
making the trip to Switzerland, he said, it would still be his decision,
it would mean fixing a specific date for his death and renouncing the
minor consolation of uncertainty, and the one thing he was incapable
of deciding was whether it should be today or tomorrow or the day
after tomorrow. He would keep putting it off from one day to the
next, the days would pass and he still wouldn't have screwed up the
necessary courage, the right moment would never come and then
the full force of the disease would fall on him, which was what he
wanted to avoid at all costs . . . And I did understand what he meant;
in those circumstances, it's very easy to say to yourself: 'Not yet,
not yet. Perhaps tomorrow. Yes, definitely tomorrow. But tonight
I'm going to sleep at home, in my bed, with Luisa by my side. Just
one more day.' "—"I should die hereafter, and meanwhile linger on

a little," I thought. "After all, there'll be no coming back. And even if I could come back: the dead should never return."—"Miguel had many virtues, but he was weak and indecisive. Perhaps we all would be in those circumstances. I imagine I would be too."

Díaz-Varela stopped talking and looked away as if he were putting himself in his friend's shoes or remembering the time when he had done so. I had to shake him out of his stupor, regardless of whether he was faking it or not.

"That was how you reacted at first, you said. And afterwards? What made you change your mind?"

For a few moments, he remained thoughtful, stroking his chin, like someone checking that he was still clean-shaven or that his beard hadn't started growing again. When he spoke, he sounded very tired, perhaps worn out by his explanations and by that conversation in which he was doing most of the talking. His gaze remained abstracted, and he murmured as if to himself:

"I didn't change my mind. I never did. From the first moment, I knew that I had no alternative, that, however hard it was for me, I would have to grant his request. What I said to him was one thing, but what I had to do was quite another. I had to get rid of him, as he put it, because he would never dare to do so, either actively or passively, and what awaited him was truly cruel. He insisted, he begged, he offered to sign a piece of paper accepting full responsibility, he even proposed going to a lawyer. I refused. If I agreed, he would have the feeling that he had signed a kind of contract or pact, he would have taken it as a Yes and I wanted to avoid that, I preferred him to believe that I had said No. In the end, though, I didn't entirely close the door. I told him that I would think it over, even though I was sure I wouldn't change my mind. I said he shouldn't count on it, should never broach the subject with me again or ask about it, that it would be best if, for the moment, we didn't see or phone each other. It would be impossible for him to resist bringing the subject up again, if not in words, then with a glance, a tone of voice, an expectant look, and I couldn't bear that: I didn't want to hear that macabre commission, to have that morbid conversation again. I told him that I would get in touch with him from time to time to find out how he was, that I wouldn't leave him all alone, and that, meanwhile, he should get on with his life—that is, with his death—but without relying on my participation. He couldn't involve a friend in such a project, it was up to him to solve the problem. But I allowed him a tiny doubt. I didn't give him hope, but at the same time I did: enough for him to be able to enjoy the saving grace of uncertainty, so that he would neither entirely rule out my help nor feel that there was any real and imminent threat or that his elimination was in train. That was the only way in which he would be able to continue living what remained of his 'healthy' life with a semblance of normality, as he had put it and as was his vain intention. But who knows, perhaps, insofar as it was possible, he did do that, at least to some extent. So much so that he perhaps didn't even connect the *gorrilla*'s attack on Pablo or his insults and accusations with his request to me, I can't possibly know, I don't know. I did end up calling him sometimes, to ask how he was and if he had experienced any pain or any other symptoms or not yet. We even met on a couple of occasions and he kept strictly to his word, he didn't raise the topic again or pester me, we acted as though that other conversation had never taken place. But it was as if he were relying on me, I could tell; as if he were waiting for me to dig him out of that hole and deliver the *coup de grâce* when he was least expecting it, before it was too late, and still saw me as his salvation, if such a word can be used to describe his violent elimination. I hadn't for one moment agreed to help him, but basically he was right: from the very first instant, as soon as he explained his situation to me, my brain had begun to work. I asked Ruibérriz to help me out and he took charge of setting things in motion, and, well, you know the rest. My mind had to start working and plotting like the mind of a criminal. I had to consider how to go about killing a friend promptly and within a specified time limit without it looking like a murder and without anyone suspecting me. And so, yes, I delegated, used intermediaries, avoided soiling my hands, other people's wills intervened, I left plenty of loose ends for chance to do with as it wished and detached the deed from myself and my influence so effectively that I came to imagine I had nothing to do with it or only as its instigator. But I was also always aware that, as the instigator, I had to think and act like a murderer. So it's not really so very strange that you should see me as one. But frankly, María, what you believe really isn't as important as you might perhaps think."

Then he got up as if he had finished or didn't feel like going on, as if he felt that the session was over. I had never seen his lips so pale, despite the many times I had looked at them. The fatigue and dejection, the retrospective despair that had appeared in him a while before, had grown suddenly very marked. He really did seem exhausted, as though he had made not just a verbal effort, but a huge physical effort too, as he had announced, almost at the very start, by rolling up his sleeves. Perhaps someone who had just stabbed a man nine or perhaps ten or sixteen times would look equally exhausted.

"Yes," I thought, "a murder, nothing more."

IV

THAT, AS I IMAGINED it would be, was the last occasion on which I saw Díaz-Varela alone, and quite some time passed before I met him again, and then in company and by chance. But for most of that time he haunted my days and my nights, at first intensely, then only palely loitering, as Keats put it. I suppose he thought we had nothing more to say, he must have been left with the feeling that he had more than fulfilled the unexpected task of giving me an explanation he had doubtless assumed he would never have to give to anyone. He had acted imprudently with the Prudent Young Woman (I'm no longer so very young, nor was I then), and he'd had no choice but to tell me his story, sinister or sombre depending on which version he gave. After that, there was no need for him to stay in touch with me, to expose himself to my suspicions, my looks, my evasive comments, my silent judgements, nor would I have wanted to submit him to them, we would have become enveloped in an atmosphere of grim unease. He did not seek me out nor did I seek him out. We had said an implicit goodbye, had reached a conclusion that no amount of mutual physical attraction or non-mutual love could delay.

The following day, despite his weariness, he must have felt that a weight had been lifted off his shoulders or been replaced by another far lighter one—I now knew more, having been present at a confession—because it was even less likely than ever that I would go to anyone with my still unprovable knowledge. He, though, has passed a weight on to me, because far worse than my grave suspicions and my possibly hasty and unfair conjectures was the burden of having two versions of events and not knowing which to believe, or, rather, knowing that I would have to believe both and that both would cohabit in my memory until it grew weary of the duplication and turfed them out. Anything anyone tells you becomes absorbed into you, becomes part of your consciousness, even if you don't believe it or know that it never happened and that it's pure invention, like novels and films, like the remote story of Colonel Chabert. And although Díaz-Varela had followed the old precept of keeping the "true" story until last and telling me the "false" story first, that rule is never enough to erase the initial or previous version. You still heard it and, although it might be momentarily refuted by what comes afterwards, which contradicts and gives the lie to it, its memory endures, as does our own credulity while we were listening, when, not knowing that it would be followed by a denial, we mistook it for the truth. Everything that has been said to us resonates and lingers, if not when we're awake, then as we drift off to sleep or in our dreams, where the order of things doesn't matter, and it remains there tossing and turning and pulsating as if it were someone who had been buried alive or perhaps a dead man who reappears because he didn't actually die, either in Eylau or on the road back or having been hanged from a tree or something else. What has been said continues to watch us and occasionally revisits us, as ghosts do, and then it never seems enough, we recall even the longest conversation as having been all too brief and the most thorough explanation as being full of holes; we wish we had asked more questions and listened more closely and paid more attention to non-verbal signs, which are slightly less deceiving than verbal ones.

Needless to say, I considered the possibility of tracking down Dr. Vidal Secanell, with a surname like that there would be no problem finding him. Indeed, I learned from the Internet that he worked for an odd-sounding organization called the Anglo-American Medical Unit, based in Calle Conde de Aranda, in the Salamanca district of Madrid; I could easily make an appointment and ask him to check me over and give me an electrocardiogram, well, we all worry about our heart. Unfortunately, I lack the detective instinct, it's just not me, and, besides, I felt it was a move that was as risky as it was futile: if Díaz-Varela had been happy to tell me his name, the doctor was sure to corroborate his version, whether it was true or not. Perhaps Dr. Vidal was an old school friend of his, not of Desvern, perhaps he had been told what he should tell me if I came to see him and questioned him; he could always deny me access to a medical record that may never even have existed, confidentiality rules in such cases, and what right did I have, after all: I should really go there with Luisa and have her demand to see it, but she knew nothing about her husband's illness and had not the slightest suspicion, and how could I so abruptly open her eyes, something that would involve multiple decisions and taking on an enormous responsibility, that of revealing the truth to someone who possibly didn't want to know it, because you can never tell what someone wants to know until the revelation has been made, and then the evil has been done and it's too late to withdraw, to put it behind you. Vidal might be yet another collaborator, he might owe Díaz-Varela enormous favours, he might be part of the conspiracy. Or perhaps it wasn't even necessary. Two weeks had passed since I eavesdropped on that conversation with Ruibérriz; Díaz-Varela had had plenty of time in which to come up with a story that would neutralize or appease me, if I can put it like that; he could have gone to that cardiologist on some pretext or other (the novelists we publish, with that vain man Garay Fontina at their head, were always pestering all kinds of professionals with all kinds of questions), and asked him what painful, unpleasant, terminal illness could credibly justify a man preferring to kill himself or, if he couldn't bring himself to do that, asking a friend to get rid of him instead. Dr. Vidal might well be an honest, ingenuous sort and have given Díaz-Varela that information in good faith; and Díaz-Varela would have counted on my never going to visit the doctor, however tempted I was, as turned out to be the case (that I was tempted, I mean, but did not go). It occurred to me that he knew me better than I thought, that during our time together, he had been less distracted than he seemed and had studied me carefully, and, foolishly, I found that thought vaguely flattering, or maybe that was just a remnant of my infatuation; such feelings never end suddenly, nor are they transformed instantly into loathing, scorn, shame or mere stupor, there is a long road to be travelled before one arrives at those possible replacement feelings, there is a troubled period of infiltrations and mixtures, of hybridization and contamination, and the state of being infatuated or in love never entirely ends until it becomes indifference or, rather, tedium, until one can think: "What's the point of living in the past, why bother even thinking about seeing Javier again. I can't even be bothered to remember him. I want to drive that whole inexplicable time from my mind, like a bad dream. And that's not so very difficult, given that I'm no longer the person I was. The only snag is that, even though I'm not that person, there are often moments when I can't forget who I was and then, quite simply, my very name is loathsome to me and I wish I wasn't me. At least a memory is less troublesome than a living creature, although a memory can, at times, be somewhat devouring. But this memory no longer is, no, it no longer is."

As is only to be expected and as is only natural, such thoughts took time to arrive. And I could not help considering from a hundred different angles (or perhaps it was only ten angles repeated over and over) what Díaz-Varela had told me, his two versions, if they were two versions, and pondering details that had remained unclear in both, for there is no story, whether real or invented, without blind spots or contradictions or obscurities or mistakes, and in that respect—that of the darkness that surrounds and encircles any narrative—it didn't really matter which was which.

I revisited the articles I had read on the Internet about Desvern's death, and in one of them I found the sentences that kept going round and round in my head: "The autopsy revealed that the victim had been stabbed sixteen times by his murderer. Every blow struck a vital organ, and according to the pathologist who carried out the autopsy, five of the wounds proved fatal." I didn't quite understand the difference between a fatal wound and one that struck a vital organ. At first sight, to a layman, they seemed to be the same thing. But that was only a secondary cause of my unease: if a pathologist had been involved and had drawn up that report, if there had been an autopsy, as was inevitable after any violent death and certainly after a homicide, how was it possible that no one noticed a "generalized metastasis throughout the body," which Díaz-Varela had told me was the diagnosis given by Desvern's consultant? On that afternoon, it hadn't occurred to me to ask Díaz-Varela, the penny hadn't dropped, and now I didn't want to or couldn't phone him, still less about that, he would have felt suspicious, wary or simply weary, he might have come up with other ways of neutralizing me, when he saw that his explanations or the act he had put on had failed to appease me. I could understand that the newspapers might not have made much of it or that the information wasn't even given to them, because it bore no relation to what had happened, but it seemed very strange that no one had informed Luisa. When I spoke to her, it was clear that she knew nothing about Deverne's illness, which was precisely as he had wanted, according, that is, to his friend and indirect executioner, the "instigator" of his death. I could also imagine what Díaz-Varela's response would be, if I had been able to ask him: "Do you really think that a pathologist examining a guy who's received sixteen stab wounds is going to take the trouble to look any further and inquire into the victim's previous state of health? He may not even have opened him up and so wouldn't know; maybe he didn't even carry out a proper autopsy and merely filled in the form with his eyes shut: it was obvious what Miguel had died from." And he may well have been right: that had been the attitude of the two negligent surgeons two centuries before, despite being under orders from Napoleon himself: knowing what they knew, they didn't even bother to take the pulse of fallen, trampled Chabert. Besides, in Spain, most people do only the bare minimum and have little desire to probe beneath the surface and waste time doing something they deem to be unnecessary.

And then there were those overly technical terms used by Díaz-Varela. It was highly unlikely that he would have remembered them after having heard them once from Desvern some time before, nor even that Desvern would have used them when telling him about his misfortune, however often they were used by his doctors, the ophthalmologist, the consultant and the cardiologist. A desperate, terrified man wouldn't resort to such dry-as-dust terminology when telling a friend he was under sentence of death, that just wouldn't be normal. "Intraocular melanoma," "a very advanced metastatic melanoma," the adjective "asymptomatic" or the noun "enucleation," all those expressions struck me as having been recently learned, or recently heard from Dr. Vidal. But perhaps my distrust was unfounded: after all, I haven't forgotten them and much more time has passed since I heard him say them, and only on that one occasion too. And perhaps they would be repeated and used by someone suffering from an illness, as if that way he or she could somehow explain it better.

On the other hand, in favour of the veracity of his story, of his final version, was the fact that Díaz-Varela had been very restrained when speaking of his own sacrifice and suffering, of the heart-rendingly contradictory nature of his situation, of his immense grief at finding himself forced to do away with his best friend, the one he would most miss, and in such a precipitate and violent way—any precipitate death is, alas, bound to be violent. With time against him and with a deadline set, knowing that in this case, more than ever, "there would have been a time for such a word," as Macbeth had added when he found out about his wife's unexpected death. That is, there would have been time, another time, for such a phrase or fact: and to let in that other time, which he would neither have brought about or accelerated or disturbed, all Díaz-Varela would have had to do was refuse the commission and turn down the request, and allow things to take their natural and, inevitably, grim and pitiless course. Yes, he could have spun me some line about his accursèd fate, he could have used that very phrase to describe his task, he could have emphasized his loyalty, stressed his selflessness, even tried to arouse my compassion. If he had beaten his breast and described his anguish to me, how he'd had to keep his feelings to himself and dredge up the necessary courage to save Deverne and Luisa from a far worse fate, slower and more cruel, from deterioration and deformity and from having to contemplate both, I would have felt more suspicious of him and would have had few doubts about the falsity of his feelings. He had spared me that and given a very sober account; he had merely set out the facts and confessed his part in it. Which he had said, from the outset, was what he knew he had to do.

IN THE END, everything tends towards attenuation, sometimes little by little and thanks to great effort and willpower on our part; sometimes with unexpected speed and contrary to our will, while we struggle in vain to keep faces from fading and paling into nothing, and deeds and words from becoming blurred objects that drift about in our memory with the same scant value as those we've read about in novels or seen and heard in films: we don't really care what happens in books and films and forget about them once they're over, although, as Díaz-Varela had said when he spoke to me about *Colonel Chabert*, they do have the ability to show us what we don't know and what doesn't happen. When someone tells us something, it always seems like a fiction, because we don't know the story at first hand and can't be sure it happened, however much we are assured that the story is a true one, not an invention, but real. At any rate, it forms part of the hazy universe of narratives, with their blind spots and contradictions and obscurities and mistakes, all surrounded and encircled by shadows or darkness, however hard they strive to be exhaustive and diaphanous, because they are incapable of achieving either of those qualities.

Yes, everything becomes attenuated, but it's also true to say that nothing entirely disappears, there remain faint echoes and elusive memories that can surface at any moment like the fragments of gravestones in the room in a museum that no one visits, as cadaverous as ruined tympana with their fractured inscriptions, past matter, dumb matter, almost indecipherable, nearly meaningless, absurd remnants preserved for no reason, because they can never be put together again, and they give out less light than darkness, are not so much memory as forgetting. And yet there they are, and no one destroys them or pieces together their sundry fragments scattered or lost centuries ago: they are kept there like small treasures or out of superstition, as valuable witnesses to the fact that someone once existed and died and had a name, even though we cannot see the whole person and reconstructing him is impossible, even though no one cares at all about that someone who is now no one. The name of Miguel Desvern will not vanish entirely, even though I never actually knew him and merely enjoyed watching him from a distance, every morning, as he breakfasted with his wife. The same is true of the fictitious names of Colonel Chabert and Madame Ferraud, of the Count de la Fère and Milady de Winter or, as she was in her youth, Anne de Breuil, who, with her hands tied behind her back, was hanged from a tree only mysteriously not to die and to return, "*belle comme les amours.*" Yes, the dead are quite wrong to come back, and yet almost all of them do, they won't give up, and they strive to become a burden to the living until the living shake them off in order to move on. We never eliminate all vestiges, though, we never manage, truly, once and for all, to silence that past matter, and sometimes we hear an almost imperceptible breathing, like that of a dying soldier thrown naked into a grave along with his dead companions, or perhaps like the imaginary groans of those companions, like the muffled sighs which, on some nights, he still thought he could hear, perhaps because he lay cheek by jowl with them for so long and because he so nearly shared their fate, was on the point of becoming one of them and perhaps was one of them, which means that his subsequent adventures, his wanderings in Paris, his re-infatuation and his hardships and his longing to be restored, were like those of fragments of gravestones in a room in a museum, of a few ruined tympana with illegible, fractured inscriptions, of the shadow of a trace, an echo of an echo, a tiny curve, a piece of ash, a scrap of past, dumb matter that refused to pass or to remain dumb. I could have played that role for Deverne, but I couldn't do that either. Or perhaps I didn't want even his most tenuous lament to filter into the world, through me.

THAT PROCESS OF attenuation must have begun, as all such processes do as soon as something ends, the day after my last visit to Díaz-Varela and my farewell to him, just as the attenuation of Luisa's grief doubtless began on the day after her husband's death, even though she could only see that day as the first day of her eternal sorrow.

It was dark by the time I left, and on that occasion, I left without the slightest hint of a doubt. I had never felt sure that there would be a next time, that I would return, that I would ever again touch his lips or, of course, go to bed with him, everything was always very vague between us, as if each time we met, we had to start all over, as if nothing ever accumulated, as if no sediment built up, as if we had never covered that territory before, and as if what happened one evening was no guarantee—not even a sign or a probability—that the same thing would happen on another evening, in the near or distant future; only a posteriori would I discover that it would, but that was never any help when it came to the next opportunity; it was always an unknown, there was always the lurking possibility that there would be no next time, although there was also, of course, the possibility that there would, otherwise what ended up happening would not have happened.

On that occasion, however, I was sure that his front door would never open to me again, that once it had shut behind me and I had walked towards the lift, that apartment would remain closed to me, as if its owner had moved or gone into exile or died, one of those doors that you try not to walk past once you have been excluded, and if you do pass by it, by chance or because a detour would take too long and there is no way of avoiding it, you glance at it out of the corner of your eye with an anguished shudder—or perhaps simply the ghost of an old emotion—and quicken your step, in order not to become submerged in the memory of what was and is no longer. At night in my room, looking out at my dark, agitated trees, before closing my eyes to go to sleep, or not, I saw this quite clearly and said to myself: "Now I know I won't see Javier again, and that's just as well, even though I'm already missing the good times and the things I so enjoyed when I used to go there. That was over even before today. Tomorrow, I will begin the task of making all that happened cease to be a living creature and become instead a memory, even if, for some time, it remains a devouring one. Be patient, a day will come when that will cease too."

However, after a week, or possibly less, something interrupted that process, when I was still struggling to get it started. I was leaving work with my boss, Eugeni, and my colleague Beatriz, slightly late because, as we all do when we apply ourselves to that slow task of forgetting and to not thinking about what we inevitably tend to think about, I was trying to spend as many hours as possible there, in company and with my mind occupied by things I didn't much care about. As I was saying goodbye to them, near the café towards the top of Príncipe de Vergara, where I still had breakfast every morning and where I always, at some point, thought of my Perfect Couple, I immediately spotted, pacing up and down on the pavement opposite, a tall figure with his hands in his overcoat pockets, as if he had been hanging about there for some time and had got cold, as if he had arranged to meet someone who had not yet turned up. And although he wasn't wearing a leather overcoat, but a rather old-fashioned camel-coloured and even, possibly, camel-skin coat, I recognized him at once. It couldn't have been a coincidence, he was clearly waiting for me. "What's he doing here?" I wondered. "Javier must have sent him," and mixed up in that thought—as with everything connected to the latest version of Javier, the two-faced or unmasked version, if you like—were both irrational fear and foolish hope. "He's sent him to find out if I'm still neutralized and appeased, or purely out of interest, to ask after me, to find out how I'm coping after all his revelations and his stories, but whatever the reason, he still hasn't managed to dislodge me from his mind. Or perhaps it's intended as a threat, a warning, and Ruibérriz is going to tell me what will happen if I don't keep my peace until the end of time or if I start snooping around or going to see Dr. Vidal; Javier is the kind of man who broods on things, that's what he did after I eavesdropped on their conversation." And while I was thinking this, I was also wondering whether to avoid him and head off with Beatriz and accompany her wherever she happened to be going, or to follow my first instinct and stay there alone and allow him to approach. Succumbing once more to curiosity, I chose the latter path: I said my goodbyes and took seven or eight steps towards the bus stop, without looking at him. Only seven or eight, because he immediately crossed the road, dodging the cars, and stopped me, touching me lightly on the elbow, so as not to startle me, and when I turned round, I was confronted by his flashing teeth, a smile so broad that, as I had noticed on that first occasion, his top lip folded back to reveal its moist interior, it was quite striking really, as if his lips were on the wrong way round. He had the same appraising, male gaze, even though, on this occasion, I was fully clothed rather than wearing only my bra and a skirt that was either rumpled or had ridden up. It made no difference, he was obviously a man with a synthetic or global vision: before a woman knew it, he would have examined her in her totality. I didn't feel greatly flattered by this, because he seemed to me to be one of those men who lower their standards as they grow older and need little incentive to go chasing after any woman who still has a slight spring in her step.

"Why, María, what a delightful coincidence," he said and raised one hand to his right eyebrow, mimicking the gesture of taking off his hat, as he had when he said goodbye to me on that other occasion, as he was about to get into the lift.—"You remember me, I hope. We met at Javier's apartment, Javier Díaz-Varela. To my great good fortune, you didn't know I was there, do you remember? You got a shock and I a dazzling and all-too-fleeting surprise."

I wondered what he was playing at. There he was, pretending that this was an entirely chance encounter, when I had seen him waiting there and he must have seen me see him, he hadn't taken his eyes off the door of our office while he was walking up and down, who knows for how long, perhaps since the theoretical end of our working day, which he could have ascertained over the phone, but which had nothing to do with the real end. I decided to humour him, at least to begin with.

"Oh, yes," I said, and I smiled back, out of politeness. "Yes, that was a bit embarrassing. It's Ruibérriz, isn't it? An unusual surname."

"Ruibérriz de Torres, actually. Yes, it is unusual. We're a family of soldiers, prelates, doctors, lawyers and notaries. Oh, I could tell you a tale or two. I'm on the family's black list, of course, I'm the black sheep, you know, although you wouldn't know it today."— And he stroked the lapel of his coat with the back of his hand, a disdainful gesture, as if he were not yet used to wearing that particular item of clothing and felt awkward without his usual black Gestapo leather. He laughed for no reason at his own mini-joke. Or perhaps he found himself funny or was trying to infect me with his humour. He looked every inch the rogue, but one's first impression was that he was a cheerful, rather inoffensive rogue, and it was hard to believe that he had been involved in fabricating an assassination. Like Díaz-Varela, although each in his own way, of course, he seemed a perfectly normal guy. If he had taken part in that murder (and he had taken a very active part, that much was certain, whatever his motives were, whether vaguely loyal or unquestionably vile), he seemed unlikely to reoffend. "But perhaps," I thought, "that's how most criminals are, pleasant and amiable, when they're not committing crimes."—"Let me buy you a drink to celebrate our meeting. If you have time, that is. How about here?"—And he pointed to the café where I usually had breakfast.—"Although I know hundreds of infinitely more amusing places and with far more atmosphere too, places you wouldn't even imagine could exist in Madrid. Later on, if you fancy it, we could go to one of them. Or what about supper in a nice restaurant? Are you hungry? Or we could go dancing, if you'd rather."

I was tickled by this last suggestion, that we go dancing, which seemed to belong to another age. And how did he expect me to go dancing straight from work, at an absurdly early hour and with an almost complete stranger, as if I were sixteen again? And because the idea tickled me, I laughed out loud.

"What are you talking about? How can I possibly go dancing now, dressed like this? I've been at work since nine o'clock this morning." And I gestured with my head towards the door of the office building.

"I did say later on, after supper. It's up to you. If you like, we can drop by your apartment, you can shower and change and then we'll go out on the town. You obviously don't realize that there are places where you can dance at any hour of the day. Even at noon." And he let out a guffaw. Even his laughter was dissolute. "I don't mind waiting or I can pick you up somewhere."

He was invasive and mischievous. The way he was behaving, he didn't give the impression of having been sent by Díaz-Varela, although he must have been. How else would he know where I worked? And yet he was behaving as if he were acting on his own initiative, as if he had clung on to that scantily-clad image of me from a few weeks before and decided, quite simply, to take a chance, to dive in, on a kind of urgent whim, it's a tactic some men use and it usually works too, if they're the jolly, convivial sort. I remembered feeling then that, not only was he immediately registering my existence, he also deemed our summary introduction to each other to be some sort of step forward or even an investment for the near future; that he had noted me down in his mental diary as if hoping to meet me again very soon, alone and in another place, or was even blithely considering asking Díaz-Varela for my phone number later on. Perhaps Díaz-Varela had referred to me as a "bird" because that was the only term Ruibérriz de Torres was capable of understanding: because that's all I was to him, "a bird." I didn't mind, I myself think of some men simply as "guys." He was the kind of man who possesses limitless self-confidence and cheek, so much so that it's almost disarming sometimes. I had put that attitude down to the two men's mutual lack of respect, to their being accomplices and knowing each other's weakest points, to being partners in crime. Ruibérriz didn't seem to care what my relationship to Díaz-Varela was. It also occurred to me that perhaps the latter had told him there was no relationship now. And that idea bothered me, the possibility that he might have given Ruibérriz the green light without so much as a flicker of regret, without the slightest trace of jealousy, with no sense that, in some diffuse way, I belonged to him—that, if you like, he had discovered me—and that idea made me more determined to take that shameless individual down a peg or two, albeit gently, wordlessly, because I was still intrigued to know what he was doing there. I agreed to have a drink with him, a very quick one, I told him, nothing more. We sat at the table next to the window, the one where the Perfect Couple used to sit, when they existed, and I thought: "What a falling off was there." He removed his overcoat with the dramatic, resolute gesture of a trapeze artist, and immediately puffed out his chest, he was doubtless proud of his pectorals and considered them an asset. He kept his scarf on, he must have thought it suited him and went well with his close-fitting trousers, both items being light stone in colour, a distinguished colour, but one more appropriate for spring, he clearly didn't pay much attention to the seasons.

HE CONTINUED FIRING flirtatious remarks at me and spoke of trivialities. His remarks were direct and unashamedly adulatory, but not in bad taste; he was trying to get off with me *and* appear witty—he was, in fact, wittier when he wasn't trying so hard, his jokes were predictable, mediocre, slightly gauche—that was all. I grew impatient, my initial friendliness was wearing thin, I found it hard to laugh, I was beginning to feel the effects of a long day at work, and I hadn't been sleeping very well since I said goodbye to Díaz-Varela, being tormented by nightmares and by troubled awakenings. I didn't dislike Ruibérriz despite what I knew about him—well, perhaps he really had been repaying a favour or helping out a friend who had the terrible task of providing a swift death for another friend who should have died yesterday, far too early or at least before his natural or appointed time (before the second chance event in his life, which comes to the same thing)—but he didn't interest me in the least, he was too smooth, I couldn't even appreciate his gallant compliments. He was quite unaware that he was getting on a bit, closer to sixty than fifty, but he behaved like a thirty-year-old. Perhaps this was partly because he kept himself very fit, that much was undeniable, and at first sight, he looked about forty or so.

"Why has Javier sent you?" I asked suddenly, taking advantage of a moment of silence or a lull in the conversation: he either didn't realize that his courtship was fast running out of steam, along with any chance of success, or else he was invincibly tenacious, once he put himself to the task.

"Javier?" He seemed genuinely surprised. "Javier didn't send me, I'm here on my own account, I had some business on this side of town. And even if that wasn't the case, don't underestimate your-self, I certainly wouldn't need any encouragement to come and see you." He never missed a chance to flatter me, but got straight to the point. As I said before, he was acting on an urgent whim and had an equally urgent need to see if he could or couldn't satisfy that whim. If he could, great. If not, on to the next thing; he certainly didn't seem like a man who would bother trying twice or would linger over a hoped-for conquest. If something didn't work out after his first and probably only attack, he wouldn't waste time trying again, for, since he wasn't particularly choosy, there was no shortage of candidates.

"Really? But how did you know where I work? Don't give me that stuff about how you just happened to be passing. I could see you'd been waiting a while. How long had you been there? It's a cold day to be hanging about in the street, you're going to an awful lot of trouble on your own account, and I'm not that special. When Javier introduced us, he didn't even give you my surname. So how were you able to locate me with such precision if he didn't send you? What does he want to know? If I believed his tale of friend-ship and sacrifice?"

Ruibérriz slowly interrupted one of his smiles, or, rather, his smile, because the truth is he never entirely stopped smiling, he doubtless considered his dazzling Vittorio Gassman–like teeth to be another of his assets, indeed his striking resemblance to that actor did contribute to making him more sympathetic. Or, rather, the interruption was not slow exactly, it was more as if his backward-folded upper lip became caught or stuck on his gums—which can happen when your mouth is dry—and he took longer than usual to liberate it. That must have been what happened, because he made some rather strange rodent-like movements with his lips.

"No, he didn't give me your surname then," he answered, as if perplexed by my reaction, "but we talked about you later on, over the phone, and he let slip enough information for me to be able to track you down in two ticks. Make no mistake, I'm a pretty good detective, and I've got contacts aplenty too, and nowadays, what with the Internet and Facebook and all that, almost no one can slip through the net once you know the odd detail about them. Is it so very hard for you to believe that I fancied you like mad the first time I saw you? Come on. I think you're a knockout, María, that much must be obvious. I feel the same today, despite meeting you in very different circumstances and attire from that first occasion, but then one doesn't always strike so lucky. That really was a mind-blower, though. God's own truth, María, I haven't been able to get that image out of my head for weeks."—And he nonchalantly regained his smile. He was quite happy to refer again and again to my half-naked state, it didn't bother him that he might appear rude, for he clearly assumed that his arrival had interrupted Díaz-Varela and me in mid-shag, more or less. That hadn't been the case, but almost. He said "knockout" and "mind-blower," words that already sounded old-fashioned, and the expression "slip through the net" is on its way out as well: his vocabulary betrayed his age, more than his appearance did, for he did preserve a certain elegance.

"You talked about *me*? But why? Our relationship wasn't exactly public knowledge. On the contrary. He was most put out that you should see me, that we should meet, or didn't you notice, that it really bugged him, I mean? I find it very odd that he should mention me to you later, I'd have thought he would want to forget all about that particular encounter . . ."—I stopped talking, because then I remembered what I had thought afterwards, that Díaz-Varela would have tried to reconstruct with Ruibérriz the dialogue they'd had while I was listening from behind the door, to calculate precisely how much and what I might have heard, how much I would have pieced together; and that, after sifting through their words, Díaz-Varela would have reached the conclusion that it was best to meet me face to face and offer me an explanation, to invent a story or confess to what had happened, and, at the least, provide me with a better story than the one I had imagined, which was why he had phoned to summon me after those two weeks had elapsed. And so, yes, it was highly likely that they had talked about me, and that Javier would have told him enough for Ruibérriz to have come looking for me on his own account and, if I can put it like this, without permission. Although, he was clearly not the kind of guy to ask anyone for their permission before approaching "a bird." He was the sort who neither respected his friends' wives or girlfriends nor considered them off-limits; there are far more such men than you might think and they trample over everyone. Perhaps Díaz-Varela really didn't know about this approach, this incursion. "Wait a minute," I added quickly. "He did speak to you about me, didn't he? As being a problem, I mean. He was worried and told you that I'd overheard your conversation, that I could get you both into a lot of trouble if I decided to tell my story to someone, to Luisa or to the police. That's why he spoke to you about me, isn't it? And I presume the two of you then came up with that story about the melanoma or perhaps Vidal helped you out. Or maybe it was your idea, you're a resourceful man. Or was it him? No, now that I think about it, it probably wasn't you, but him; being a reader of novels, he's sure to have a few stories up his sleeve."

Ruibérriz lost his smile again, with no transitional phase this time, as if someone had wiped it from his face with a cloth. He grew serious, I caught a glint of alarm in his eyes, he immediately stopped playing the frivolous gallant and even moved his chair away from mine, having, earlier on, tried to move a little closer.

"So you know about the illness? What else do you know?"

"He told me the whole melodrama. About what you did to poor Canella, about the mobile phone and the knife. I hope he's grateful, after all, you did the dirty work, while he stayed at home. Directing operations, like Rommel."—I couldn't resist sliding into sarcasm, I had a grievance against Díaz-Varela.

"You know what we did?"—This was more a statement than a question. He hesitated before continuing, as if he had to digest this discovery, or so it seemed. He used his fingers to draw down his upper lip, a swift, furtive gesture: it hadn't got stuck again, but it was a little high up. Maybe he wanted to make sure that he was no longer smiling. What he had just heard worried him, he didn't like it at all, unless, of course, he was pretending. Finally, he added in a disappointed tone of voice: "I thought he wasn't going to tell you anything, that's what he said. The prudent thing would be to leave things as they were and hope that you hadn't heard too much or that you wouldn't put two and two together, or that you would simply keep quiet about it. Oh, and he mentioned that he was going to break off his relationship with you. It wasn't anything serious, he said, he could easily just let it die. It would simply be a matter of not getting in touch with you again or not returning any calls you made or else fobbing you off with some excuse. Not that he thought you would insist. 'She's very discreet,' he said, 'she never expects anything.' Nor was he under any obligation to you. He would just hope that you would gradually forget what you might have heard of our conversation. Best not to give you any facts, he said, and in time you would start to doubt what you had heard. 'It will end up seeming quite unreal to her, as if it had all been in her imagination, her auditory imagination.' Not a bad plan really. That's why I assumed the way was open for me, with you, I mean. And that you'd know nothing about me, as regards that business."—He fell silent again. He seemed sunk in thought, so much so that what he said next sounded as if he were talking to himself, not to me: "I don't like it, I don't like the fact that he doesn't keep me informed, that he thinks it's perfectly acceptable not to tell me about something that directly affects me. He shouldn't have told anyone that story, because it isn't his alone, it's more mine, in fact, than his. I've run more risks, and I'm more exposed. No one saw him. I don't like it one bit that he should have changed his mind and told you, especially without telling me. You must have thought me a right fool, now, I mean, with you."

He looked thoroughly fed up, his gaze abstracted or absorbed. His ardour for me had cooled. I waited a while before saying anything.

"Yes, well, if you're going to confess to a murder committed by various people," I said, "you really should consult the others first. That's the least you can do."—I couldn't resist getting a little dig in.

He sprang to his feet, outraged.

"Now you watch what you say. It wasn't a murder. It was a case of giving a friend a better, less painful death. All right, all right, there's no such thing as a good death, and the *gorrilla* did get rather carried away with the stabbing, but that wasn't something we could have foreseen, we didn't even know for sure he would use the knife. But what awaited him otherwise was just awful, dreadful. Javier described the whole process to me. At least he died quickly, once and for all, and without having to go through various stages, involving terrible pain and deterioration, with his wife and kids watching him slowly turning into a monster. You can't call what we did murder, come off it. It was something else entirely. An act of mercy is how Javier put it. A merciful homicide."

He sounded convinced, he sounded sincere. And so I thought: "It could be one of three things: the melodrama is true and not an invention; Javier has lied to this guy about the illness as well; the guy is playing a part under orders from the man paying him. And if the latter is true, then I have to say he's a very good actor." I remembered the photograph of Desvern that had appeared in the press and of which I had seen only a poor reproduction on the Internet: without a jacket or tie or even, almost, a shirt—where could his cufflinks have got to—full of tubes and surrounded by ambulance staff manipulating him, with his wounds on display, lying in the middle of the street in a pool of blood and on view to passers-by and drivers alike, unconscious and dishevelled and dying. He would have been horrified to see himself or to know that he had been so exposed. It's true that the *gorrilla* did get carried away, but who could have foreseen that? It was a merciful homicide, and perhaps it was, maybe it was all true, and Ruibérriz and Díaz-Varela had acted in good faith, up to a point and bearing in mind the convoluted nature of their plan. And its recklessness. And as soon as I had admitted those three possibilities and recalled that image, I was overcome by a kind of dismay or perhaps surfeit. When you don't know what to believe, when you're not prepared to play the amateur detective, then you get tired and dismiss the entire business, you let it go, you stop thinking and wash your hands of the truth or of the whole tangled mess—which comes to the same thing. The truth is never clear, it's always a tangled mess. Even when you get to the bottom of it. But in real life almost no one needs to find the truth or devote himself to investigating anything, that only happens in puerile novels. I made one last attempt, albeit a very reluctant one, because I could already imagine the answer.

"I see. And what about Luisa, Deverne's wife? Is it also an act of mercy for Javier to console her?"

Ruibérriz de Torres again looked surprised or did a brilliant impression of looking surprised.

"His wife? What do you mean? What kind of consolation are you talking about? Naturally, he'll help her and console her as best he can, as he will the kids. She's his friend's widow, they're his friend's orphaned children."

"Javier has been in love with her for years. Or has insisted on being in love, which comes to the same thing. Getting rid of the husband has proved highly providential to him. They really loved each other, that couple. He wouldn't have stood a chance with Deverne alive. Now he does stand a chance. Patiently, little by little. By staying close."

Ruibérriz immediately, effortlessly, recovered his smile. It was a smile of commiseration, as if he felt sorry to see me so hopelessly barking up the wrong tree, to see how innocent I was and how little I understood the man who had been my lover.

"What are you talking about?" he answered scornfully. "He's never said a single word to me about that, and I've certainly never noticed anything. Don't delude yourself, don't console yourself thinking that he's finished with you because he loves someone else. That's just ridiculous, Javier isn't the kind to fall in love with anyone, no way. I've known him for years. Why do you think he's never married?"—He gave a short laugh intended to be sarcastic.—"'Patiently,' you say. He doesn't know what patience is, not at least when it comes to women. That, among other reasons, is why he's still a bachelor."—He made a dismissive gesture with his hand.—"What rubbish. You have absolutely no idea."—Nevertheless he again remained silent for a while, thinking or searching his memory. How easy it is to introduce doubts into someone else's mind.

It was likely that Díaz-Varela had never told him anything about that, especially if he had deceived him as to his motive. I remembered that when he mentioned Luisa in the conversation I overheard, he didn't refer to her by name. In Ruibérriz's presence, I had been "a bird," but she, in turn, had been "the wife," *"la mujer"* in the sense not of "woman" but of "wife," someone else's wife. As if she wasn't someone who was dear to him. As if she were condemned to being just that, his friend's wife. Ruibérriz had obviously never seen the two of them together, otherwise, he would have been as struck by this as I was the very first moment I met him, that evening at Luisa's house. I imagined Professor Rico must have noticed too, although who knows, he seemed too absorbed in his own thoughts, too abstracted, to be aware of the outside world. I chose to say nothing more on the subject. Ruibérriz's gaze was, once again, pensive, absorbed. There was nothing more to say. He had abandoned his courtship of me, which had, it seems, been genuine; he must have been very disappointed. I clearly wasn't going to make any more sense of it all, and, besides, I really didn't care. I had just washed my hands of the matter, at least until another day, or another century.

"What happened to you in Mexico?" I asked suddenly, intending to shake him out of his relative stupor, to cheer him up. I sensed that it would be fairly easy to grow to like him. Not that there would be an opportunity, I had no intention of ever seeing him again, and the same went for Díaz-Varela and for Luisa Alday and for the whole lot of them. I just hoped that the publishing house didn't commission Professor Rico to write a book.

"In Mexico? How do you know about that?"—This question did take him very much by surprise, he had obviously forgotten.—"Not even Javier knows the whole story."

"I heard you mention it at Javier's place, when I was listening from behind the door. You said you'd got into a bit of trouble there, that you were wanted by the police or had a record or something."

"Bloody hell, so you heard that too?"—And he immediately added, as if he needed to explain something of which I was still unaware: "That wasn't a murder either, not at all. It was pure self-defence, it was either him or me. And besides, I was only twenty-two . . ." He stopped, realizing that he had said too much, that he was still remembering something or talking to himself, but doing so out loud and before a witness. The fact that I had referred to Desvern's death as a murder had clearly touched a nerve.

I was startled. It had never occurred to me that he might have another corpse lurking in his past, whatever the circumstances of that first killing. He seemed to me an ordinary, straightforward crook, not really capable of violent crimes. I had seen the killing of Deverne as an exception, as something he felt obliged to do, and, when all was said and done, he hadn't been the one to wield the weapon, he, too, had delegated, although to a lesser extent than Díaz-Varela.

"I didn't say anything about that," I responded rapidly. "I've no idea what you're talking about. I was just asking a question. But I'd almost prefer not to know, not if there was another death involved. Let's drop the subject. The lesson is: never ask questions."—I glanced at my watch. I suddenly felt very uncomfortable to be sitting where Desvern used to sit, talking to his indirect executioner.—"Anyway, I have to go, it's getting late."

He ignored my last words, still pondering. I had sown doubt in his mind, I just hoped he didn't go to Díaz-Varela now and ask him about Luisa, demand an explanation, and that Díaz-Varela did not then summon me again, I don't know, to give me a telling-off or something. Or perhaps Ruibérriz was reliving what had happened in Mexico all those years ago, which clearly still weighed on him.

"It was all Elvis Presley's fault, you know," he said after a few seconds, in a quite different tone of voice, as if he had suddenly alighted upon a new way to impress me and not leave entirely empty-handed, so to speak.

I giggled slightly, I couldn't help it.

"You mean *the* Elvis Presley?"

"Yes, I worked for him for about ten days, when he was shooting a film in Mexico."

This time I laughed out loud, despite the sombre nature of the conversation.

"Oh, yeah," I said, still laughing.—"And I suppose you know which island he's living on. That's what his fans believe, isn't it? Who is he currently hiding out with: Marilyn Monroe or Michael Jackson?"

He looked annoyed and shot me a cutting glance. He really was annoyed because he said to me:

"Don't be such a dickhead, woman. Don't you believe me? I did work for him, and he got me into deep trouble."

He sounded far more serious than he had at any other point in the conversation. Genuinely miffed and angry. But that couldn't possibly be true, it sounded like pure bluster, or else a delusion; but he had taken my scepticism very much to heart. I swiftly backpedalled.

"Sorry, sorry, I didn't mean to offend you. But you must admit it does sound a touch unbelievable."—And I added, in order to change the subject without completely abandoning it, without beating a retreat that would lead him to believe that I thought him either a complete fraud or a nutter: "How old are you, then, if you worked with the King no less? He died years ago, didn't he? It must be nearly fifty years." I was still struggling not to laugh, but fortunately, managed to contain myself.

I noticed at once that he was recovering some of his old flirtatiousness. But he began by ticking me off.

"Don't exaggerate. It will be thirty-four years ago next 16th of August, I think. That's all."—He knew the exact date, he must be a real fan.—"All right then, so how old do you think I am?"

I wanted to be kind, to make amends. But I couldn't go too far, I mustn't flatter him too much.

"Oh, I don't know, about fifty-five?"

He smiled smugly, as if he had already forgotten the offence I had caused him. He smiled so broadly that his top lip once again shot upwards, revealing his healthy, white, rectangular teeth, and his gums.

"Add another ten, at least," he replied, pleased. "What do you think?"

So he really was very well preserved. There was a childish quality about him, which was what made him so likeable. He was doubtless another victim of Díaz-Varela, whom I was now growing accustomed to calling not by his first name, Javier, that name I had so often spoken and whispered in his ear, but by his surname. That's pretty childish too, but it helps to distance us from those we have loved.

IT WAS THEN that the process of attenuation began in earnest, after that first act of washing my hands, after thinking for the first time—or not even thinking it, perhaps it has less to do with one's mind than one's spirit, or with one's mere breath: "Why should I care, what's it got to do with me anyway?" That thought is always within the grasp of anyone regarding any situation, however close to home or serious it might be, and if someone can't shake a situation off, it's because they don't want to, because they feed on it and find it gives meaning to their lives; it's the same with those who happily carry the tenacious burden of the dead, who are always ready to continue to loiter at the first indication that someone wants to hold on to them, because they are all would-be Chaberts, despite the rebuffs and the denials and the grimaces with which they are received if they actually dare to return.

The process is a slow one, of course, and it's hard work and you have to apply willpower and effort and not be tempted by memory, which returns now and then and often disguises itself as a refuge, when you walk past a particular street or catch a whiff of cologne or hear a tune, or notice that they're showing a film on TV that you once watched together. I never watched any films with Díaz-Varela.

As for literature, of which we did have some shared experiences, I immediately warded off that danger by facing it full on: although our publishing house usually only publishes contemporary writers—to the frequent misfortune of readers and myself—I persuaded Eugeni to bring out an edition of *Colonel Chabert*, in a new and very good translation (the most recent one was, indeed, abominable), and we added three more stories by Balzac to bulk it out, because the story itself is quite short, what the French call a *nouvelle*. It was in the bookshops within a matter of months, and I thus shuffled off its shadow by producing a fine edition of it in my own language. I thought of it while I had to, while we were editing and preparing it for publication, and then I could forget about it. Or I at least ensured that it was never going to catch me out or take me by surprise.

I was on the point of leaving the publishing house after that final manoeuvre, so as not to have to continue going to the same café, so as not even to have to continue seeing it from my office, although the trees did partially block my view; so that nothing would remind me of anything. I was also tired of having to cope with living writers—what a delight to deal with dead authors, like Balzac, who don't pester you or try to manipulate their future—with Cortezo the Bore's clingy phone calls, with the demands of mean, repellent Garay Fontina, with the pretentious cybernetic nonsense of the fake young men, each of whom managed to be, at one and the same time, more ignorant, stupid and pedantic than the last. However, the other offers I received, from our competitors, did not convince me, despite a promised increase in salary: I would still have to continue dealing with writers of overweening ambition and who breathed the same air as me. Eugeni, moreover, having grown a little lazy and absent-minded, urged me to take more of the decisions, and I did: I trusted that the day would come when I could get rid of the odd fatuous author without even asking Eugeni's permission, my sights being set particularly on that ever-imminent scourge of King Carl Gustaf, who was still tirelessly polishing his speech in garbled Swedish (those who had heard him practising assured me that his accent was execrable). Above all, though, I realized that I mustn't flee that landscape, but master it as best I could, just as Luisa must have done with her house, forcing herself to continue living in it rather than suddenly moving out; stripping it of its saddest and most sentimental connotations and conferring on it a new day-to-day routine, in short, remaking it. I knew that the publishing house was, for me, a place tinged with sentiment, which is impossible to conceal or avoid, even if the sentiment is only half-imagined. You simply have to get on good terms with it and appease it.

Almost two years passed. I met another man whom I found sufficiently interesting and amusing, Jacobo (who is not, thank heavens, a writer), I got engaged to him at his insistence, we made tentative plans to get married, plans that I kept postponing without actually cancelling them, well, I've never been that keen on matrimony, but in the end, what convinced me was my age—late-thirty-something—more, at least, than a desire to wake up in company every day, I don't really see the advantage of that, although it's probably not that bad, I suppose, if you love the person you go to bed with and sleep next to, as is true in my case—needless to say. There are things about Díaz-Varela I still miss, but that's another matter. It doesn't make me feel guilty, for nothing is incompatible in the land of memory.

I was having supper with a group of people in the Chinese restaurant at the Hotel Palace when I saw them, about three or four tables away, shall we say. I had a good view of them both, in profile, as if I were in the stalls and they were on stage, except that we were on the same level. The fact is, I didn't take my eyes off them—they were like a magnet—apart from when one of the other guests spoke to me, which wasn't very often: we had come from a book launch, and most of the guests were the proud author's friends, whom I didn't know from Adam; they chatted among themselves and hardly bothered me at all, I was there as the publisher's representative—and to pay the bill, of course; most of the guests looked strangely like flamenco artistes, and my main fear was that they might whip out their guitars from some strange hiding place and start singing loudly, between courses. Quite apart from the sheer embarrassment that would cause me, it would have been sure to make Luisa and Díaz-Varela look over at our table, for they were otherwise too immersed in each other's company to notice my presence in the midst of that assembly of dark, curly heads. It did occur to me, though, that she might not even remember me. There came a moment when the novelist's girlfriend noticed my gaze permanently trained on that one point. She turned round rather ostentatiously and sat looking at them, at Javier and Luisa. I was afraid that her uninhibited stare might alert them to my presence, and so I felt obliged to explain.

"I'm sorry, they're a couple I know, but whom I haven't seen in ages. And, at the time, they weren't a couple. Don't think me rude, please. I'm just very curious to see them like that, if you know what I mean."

"Don't worry," she replied warmly, after shooting them another impertinent glance. She had understood the situation at once; I must be very transparent at times. "I'm not surprised. He's gorgeous, isn't he? Anyway, don't you worry, it's your business. Nothing to do with me."

Yes, they really were a couple, that's something that usually even complete strangers can tell, and I knew him very well, but not her, whom I knew very little, or only from talking to her at length on one occasion—or, rather, from her talking to me, she could have been speaking to anyone that day, I was just a useful pair of ears. But I had observed her in a similar situation over several years, that is, with her then partner, who had been dead for long enough now for Luisa not to describe herself first and foremost, as if it were a definitive state, with the words: "I've been widowed" or "I'm a widow," because she wouldn't be that at all, and that fact or piece of information, while remaining the same as before, would have changed. She would say instead: "I lost my first husband, and he's moving further away from me all the time. It's such a long time since I saw him, whereas this other man is here by my side and is always by my side. I call him 'husband' too, which is odd. But he has taken the other husband's place in my bed and by virtue of that juxtaposition is gradually blurring and erasing him. A little more each day, a little more each night." And I had seen them together before, again only once, but enough to sense his love and solicitude for her and her obliviousness and blindness to him. Now it was all changed. They were both talking vivaciously, hanging on each other's every word, occasionally gazing into each other's eyes without speaking, or holding hands across the table. He was wearing a wedding ring, they must have got married in a civil ceremony at some point, perhaps very recently, perhaps the day before yesterday or even yesterday. She looked much better, and his looks had certainly not deteriorated, there was Díaz-Varela with those same lips, whose movements I followed at a distance—some habits we never lose or else recover immediately, as if they were automatic. Unwittingly, I made a gesture with my hand, as if to touch those lips from afar. The novelist's girlfriend, the only one of the guests who occasionally glanced in my direction, noticed this and asked kindly:

"Sorry, did you want something?" She perhaps thought I had been signalling to her.

"No, no, don't worry." And I waved my hand, adding: "Just personal stuff."

I must have looked if not upset, then troubled. Fortunately, the other guests were offering endless toasts and talking very loudly. Worryingly, one of them was beginning to sing to himself (I heard the words "*Ay de mi niña, mi niña, Virgen del Puerto*"), but I've no idea why they should all resemble performers in a flamenco show, because the novelist wasn't like that at all, he was wearing an argyle sweater, the kind of glasses a rapist or maniac might wear, and had the look of a neurotic, who, for some incomprehensible reason, had a very pleasant, attractive girlfriend and sold a lot of books—a pretentious con trick, each and every one of them—which is why we had taken him to that rather expensive restaurant. I offered up a prayer—a short prayer to the Virgen del Puerto, even though I had no idea who she was—that the song would go no further. I didn't want to be disturbed. I couldn't take my eyes off that stage-like table, and suddenly a sentence from those now old newspapers started going round and round in my head, the same newspapers that had carried the news for just two wretched days, then fallen silent about it for ever: "He hovered on the brink of life and death for five hours, during which time he never recovered consciousness; the victim finally succumbed late that evening, with the doctors unable to do anything more to save him."

"Five hours in an operating theatre," I thought. "It's just not possible that, after five whole hours, the doctors wouldn't have noticed that 'generalized metastasis throughout the body,' which is what Javier told me they had told Desvern." And then it seemed to me that I saw clearly—or at least more clearly—that the illness had never existed, unless the fact of those five hours was false or errone-ous; after all, the newspaper reports didn't even agree about which hospital the dying man had been taken to. Nothing was conclusive, of course, and Ruibérriz's version hadn't actually contradicted Díaz-Varela's. That didn't mean a great deal, though, because it all depended on how much of the truth Díaz-Varela had revealed to Ruibérriz when he first gave him that cold-blooded commission. I suppose it was irritation that led me to that momentary belief—well, it lasted longer than a moment, that is, for at least some of the time I was in the Chinese restaurant—the belief that I could see things more clearly (later, it all seemed far more obscure, when I went home, and the couple were no longer there and Jacobo was waiting for me). It irritated me, I think, to see that Javier had got what he wanted, to discover that things had worked out exactly as he had foreseen. I did feel some resentment towards him, even though I had never had any real hopes and certainly couldn't accuse him of having given me false hopes. It wasn't moral indignation that I felt, nor a desire for justice, but something much more basic and perhaps more mean-spirited. I really didn't care about justice or injustice. I was doubtless suffering from retrospective jealousy or spite, from which, I imagine, none of us is immune. "Look at them," I thought, "there they are, at the end of all that patient waiting, of all that time: she is more or less recovered and happy, he is exultant, there they are married, and with not a thought for Deverne or for me, I barely left so much as a trace. It's in my power to ruin that marriage right now, and to ruin the life he has built as a usurper, yes, that's the word, 'usurper.' I would simply have to get up, go over to their table and say: 'Well, well, so you finally got what you wanted, you removed the obstacle without her ever suspecting a thing.' I wouldn't have to say anything more or give any further explanations or tell the whole story, I would turn on my heel and leave. Those hints would be all it would take to sow the seeds of uncertainty in Luisa's mind and for her to demand to know what it meant. Yes, it's so easy to introduce doubt into someone's mind."

And no sooner had I thought this—although I spent many minutes thinking it, repeating it over and over as if it were a tune I couldn't get out of my head, and silently getting myself all fired up, with my eyes fixed on them, I don't know how they didn't notice, how they didn't feel burned or pierced by them, my eyes were like hot coals or like needles—no sooner had I thought this than I stood up, again unwittingly and unthinkingly, just as I had when I reached out my hand to touch his lips, and still clutching my napkin, I said to the much-fêted-conman's girlfriend, who was the only one still aware of my existence and who might, therefore, miss me if I was gone for long:

"Excuse me a moment, I'll be right back."

I REALLY HAD no idea what my intentions were or else those intentions changed several times at great speed while I took the steps—one, two, three—that separated my table from theirs. I know that into my head came this fleeting idea, which would take much longer to put into words, while I walked without realizing—four, five—that I was still clutching my soiled and crumpled napkin: "She hardly knows me and, after all this time, there's no reason why she should recognize me until I introduce myself and tell her my name; as far as she's concerned, I'll be a complete stranger coming over to their table. He, on the other hand, knows me well and will recognize me instantly, yet, in theory, in Luisa's eyes, he has even less reason to remember me. In theory, he and I have only ever seen each other on one occasion, when we happened to meet at her house, one evening, over two years ago, and when we barely exchanged a word. He'll have to pretend he doesn't know who I am, if he didn't, it would look very strange. And so it's also in my power to unmask him in that respect too, we women can usually tell at once if the woman who comes over to say hello to the man we're with has had a relationship with him in the past. Unless the two ex-lovers can pretend to perfection and not give themselves away. And unless we're mistaken, for it's also true that some of us tend to attribute to our partners a whole host of past lovers, often quite wrongly."

As I advanced—six, seven, eight, skirting round the odd table and avoiding the pell-mell Chinese waiters, it wasn't a straightforward trajectory—I could see them better, and they looked very calm and happy, immersed in their conversation, pretty much oblivious to anyone else but them. At one point, I felt for Luisa something resembling happiness or perhaps acceptance or was it relief? The last time I had seen her, all those months ago, I had felt real pity for her. She had spoken to me about the hatred she could not feel for the *gorrilla*: "No, hating him serves no purpose, it doesn't console or give me strength," she had said. And about the hatred she couldn't have felt either for some newly arrived, abstract hit man, had he been the one hired to kill Deverne. "But I could hate the instigators," she had added, and then read me part of the definition of "*envidia*" or "envy" in Covarrubias, dated 1611, regretting that she couldn't even blame the death of her husband on that: "Unfortunately, this poison is often engendered in the breasts of those who are and who we believe to be our closest friends, in whom we trust; they are far more dangerous than our declared enemies." And just after that, she had said: "I miss him all the time, you see. I miss him when I wake up and when I go to bed and when I dream and throughout the whole of the intervening day, it's as if I carried him with me all the time, as if he were part of my body." And then I thought, as I approached—nine, ten: "She won't feel like that now, she will have freed herself from his corpse, from her dead husband, his ghost, who has been kind enough not to come back. She has someone there before her now, and they can use each other to hide their own fate, as lovers do, according to a line I vaguely remember, a line of poetry I read in my adolescence. Her bed will no longer be sad or woeful, a living body will enter it each night, a body whose weight I know well and once greatly enjoyed."

I saw them turn to look at me as I approached and they sensed my shape or my shadow—eleven, twelve and thirteen—he with horror, as if asking himself: "What's she doing here? Where did she spring

from? And why is she coming over? To unmask me?" But I didn't
see that expression on her face, she was already looking at me with
great sympathy, with an open smile, wide and warm, as if she had
recognized me instantly. And she had, for she exclaimed:

"The Prudent Young Woman!" She had doubtless forgotten my
name.

She stood up at once to kiss me on both cheeks and almost
embrace me, and her friendliness stopped in its tracks any intention I might have had of saying anything to Díaz-Varela that might
turn Luisa against him or cause her to view him with mistrust or
stupefaction or disgust or, as she had said, to hate the instigator;
nothing that would ruin his life and therefore ruin hers as well—
again—and thus ruin their marriage, as it had occurred to me to do
only shortly before. "Who am I to disturb the universe," I thought.
"Even though others might do it, like this man here, pretending
not to know me even though I loved him well and have never done
him any harm. The fact that others disrupt and buffet and generally maltreat the universe doesn't mean that I should follow their
example, not even on the pretext that, unlike them, I would be
righting a wrong and punishing a possibly guilty man and impos-
ing justice." As I said, I cared nothing for justice or injustice. What
business were they of mine, for if Díaz-Varela had been right about
one thing, as had the lawyer Derville in his fictional world and in
his time that does not pass and stays quite still, it was this: "Far
more crimes go unpunished than punished, not to speak of those
we know nothing about or that remain hidden, for there must inevitably be more hidden crimes than crimes that are known about and
recorded." And perhaps also when he said: "The worst thing is that
so many disparate individuals in every age and every country, each
on his own account and at his own risk, and not, in principle, subject
to mutual contagion, separated from each other by kilometres or

years or centuries, each with his own thoughts and particular aims, should all choose the same methods of robbery, deception, murder or betrayal against the friends, colleagues, brothers, sisters, parents, children, husbands, wives or lovers whom they once loved the most. Crimes committed in ordinary life are more scattered, more spaced out, one here, another there; and because they only trickle into our consciousness, they cause less outrage and tend not to provoke waves of protest, however incessantly they occur: how could it be any other way, given that society lives alongside them and has been impregnated with their very nature since time immemorial." Why should I intervene, or perhaps I should say contravene? If I did, what difference would that make to the order of the universe? Why should I denounce a single crime, which I'm not even sure was a crime, nothing was quite certain, the truth is always a tangled mess. And if it was a premeditated, cold-blooded murder, whose sole aim was to occupy a place already occupied by another, at least the person who caused that death took it upon himself to console the widow, namely the surviving victim, the widow of Miguel Desvern, businessman, whom she will no longer miss quite so much: not when she wakes up or goes to bed or when she dreams or throughout the whole of the intervening day. Fortunately or unfortunately, the dead are as fixed as paintings, they don't move, they don't add anything, they don't speak and never respond. And they are wrong to come back, those who can. Deverne could not, and that was just as well.

My visit to their table was brief, we exchanged a few words, Luisa invited me to join them for a moment, I declined, saying that my guests needed me, which was a pure lie, of course, except when it came to paying the bill. She introduced me to her new husband, forgetting that, in theory, he and I had met at her house, because, then, he still only existed in the shadows. Neither of us refreshed her memory, what did it matter, what would be the point? Díaz-Varela had stood up almost at the same time as her, we kissed each other on both cheeks as is the custom in Spain when a man and a woman are first introduced. He had lost the look of horror when he saw that I was being discreet and was prepared to play my part in the pantomime. And then he, too, regarded me with sympathy, in silence, with his almond eyes, so hazy and enveloping and indecipherable. They regarded me with sympathy, but they did not miss me in the least. I won't deny that I was tempted to linger, despite all, so as not to lose sight of him just yet, but to palely loiter. It wasn't right, though, the longer I spent in their company, the more likely it was that Luisa would detect some trace, some remnant, some still-warm ember in my gaze: my eyes were drawn as always to his lips, it was inevitable and, of course, involuntary, and I didn't want to harm either him or Luisa.

"We must get together some time, give me a call, I'm still living at the same address," she said with genuine warmth and not a hint of suspicion. It's one of those things people come out with when they say goodbye and which they forget once the goodbyes have been said. I would not reappear in her memory, I was just a prudent young woman whom she knew largely by sight and who belonged now to another life. I wasn't even that young any more.

I preferred not to go over to his side of the table again. So after exchanging the obligatory farewell kisses with her, I took two steps towards my own table, still looking back at her as I gave her my answer ("Yes, I'll call you. I'm so pleased that everything's worked out for you"), so as to gain a little distance, and then I waved goodbye. In Luisa's eyes, I was saying goodbye to both of them, but I was really saying goodbye to Javier, properly this time, definitively and for real, because now he had his wife beside him. And as I walked back to the idiotic world of publishing I had left only a few minutes before—minutes that seemed suddenly very long—I thought, in order to justify myself: "No, I don't want to be an accursèd fleur-de-lys on his shoulder, which betrays him and points the finger and prevents even the most ancient of crimes from disappearing; let the past be purely dumb matter and let things simply fade and hide themselves away, let them keep silence and neither recount nor bring with them new misfortunes. Nor do I want to be like the wretched books among which I spend my life, whose time stands still and waits inside, trapped and watching, begging to be opened so that it can flow freely again and retell its old and oft-repeated story. I don't want to be like those written voices that so often sound like muffled sighs, groans uttered in a world of corpses in the middle of which we all lie, if we drop our guard for a moment. It doesn't matter that some, if not most, civilian acts go unrecorded, ignored, as is the norm. Men, however, tend to strive to achieve quite the opposite effect, although they often fail: to leave branded on the skin a fleur-de-lys that perpetuates and accuses and condemns, and possibly unleashes more crimes. That would probably have been my intention with anyone else, or with him too, had I not fallen stupidly and silently in love, and if I did not still love him a little, I suppose, despite all, and that 'all' is no small thing. It will pass, it already is passing, that's why I don't mind acknowledging it. In my defence, I have just seen him when I did not expect to, looking well and happy." And I continued to think as I turned my back on him, and my steps and my shape and my shadow were moving away from him for ever: "Yes, there's nothing wrong with acknowledging that. No one is going to judge me, there are no witnesses to my thoughts. It's true that when we get caught in the spider's web—between the first chance event and the second—we fantasize endlessly and are, at the same time, willing to make do with the tiniest crumb, with hearing him—as if he were the time itself that exists between those two chance events—smelling him, glimpsing him, sensing his presence, knowing that he is still on our horizon, from which he has not entirely vanished, and that we cannot yet see, in the distance, the dust from his fleeing feet."

A HEART SO WHITE

Juan knows almost nothing of his father, Ranz's, interior life. But when Juan marries, he's compelled to consider the past anew, and begins to ponder what he doesn't really want to know. As family secrets—their possible convenience, their ultimate price, and even their possible civility—hover, *A Heart So White* becomes a sort of anti-detective story of human nature. Intrigue; the sins of the father; the fraudulent and the genuine; marriage and strange repetitions of violence: Marías elegantly sends shafts of inquisitory light into shadows and onto the costs of ambivalence as it chronicles the relentless power of the past.

Fiction

ALL SOULS

A visiting Spanish lecturer, viewing Oxford through a prismatic detachment, is alternately amused, puzzled, delighted, and disgusted by its vagaries of human vanity. A bit lonely, not always able to see his charming but very married mistress, he casts about for activity; he barely has to teach. Yet so much goes into simply "being" at Oxford: friendship, opinion-mongering, one-upmanship, finicky exchanges of favors, gossip, adultery, book-collecting, back-patting . . . back-stabbing. In this sly campus novel and love story, Marías demonstrates a sweet tooth for eccentricity.

Fiction

While her husband is away on business, Marta invites Victor, whom she has only just met, to dinner at her Madrid apartment. Her two-year-old son finally asleep, Marta and Victor retreat to the bedroom. Undressing, Marta feels suddenly ill; inexplicably, she dies in his arms. What should Victor do? Remove the compromising tape from the answering machine? Leave food for the child's breakfast? These are just his first steps, but he soon takes matters further; unable to bear the shadows and the unknowing, Victor plunges into dark waters. Javier Marías, Europe's master of secrets, of what lies reveal and truth may conceal, is on sure ground in this profound, quirky, and marvelous novel.

Fiction

ALSO AVAILABLE

When I Was Mortal
Dark Back of Time